Man In The Fire

Jon Hill

Banzai Press

Note From the Author

Thank you for picking up the third book in the Jack and Stacey Green series. Before you're dropped into the action, I just wanted to say that I was feeling rather nostalgic when I began plotting this story, recalling the steady diet of adventure movies I grew up on in the '80s—with their big, over-the-top villains out to destroy the world, and the crazy, perhaps hard-to-believe action that it took to stop them. So, with these diabolical bad guys and their secret bases in mind, I wanted to make this final installment more reminiscent of a James Bond/Ethan Hunt Hollywood production rather than a more technical Jack Ryan novel. I hope you'll forgive me for that (actually, I hope you'll thank me, but I'll settle for you simply not hating me).

To ensure the focus remained on the characters, I avoided things that I normally would have included. Like fifty years' worth of NATO-US-Russia history that could support Jack's views on the Ukraine situation. Or perhaps more detail behind flying a Black Hawk, or how to operate certain weapons and what kind of bullets they used. But I'm assuming that, by now, you have a general idea of what Jack and Stacey are capable of, and to try to reinforce it at this stage of the game just seemed like an unnecessary addition of words to an already longer than expected story. Besides, I figure you're not really picking up book three in the hopes of learning the ins and outs of Russian politics but rather to find out what simply happens to the Green family! (I read quite a few books on the Romanovs but decided not to include that research since every time I went to add it, it felt

like I was trying to fit a square into a round hole—the flow of
the story just didn't allow it).

Because I knew that I would be ending the series as a trilogy
(though maybe someday we'll see *Man In The Air*?), I wanted to
ensure an actual resolution to the Green's drama. I hope that I've
done so in an exciting, page-turning fashion. Thank you so much
for sticking with these characters! This book is for you (whether
you like it or not).

Yours,
Jon Hill

1

SHE SLAMMED ON THE brakes and yanked the wheel to the right, locking the F-150's large wheels and leaving two wide stripes of rubber arcing through the intersection. The truck bed fishtailed, but she compensated by steering into the spin, straightening out in time to avoid an oncoming minivan. Ignoring the sudden chorus of blaring horns and screeching tires, she transferred her foot from the brake pedal back to the gas and pressed it all the way to the floorboard. The engine roared, the tires caught, and her head slammed backward against the headrest. She glanced into the rearview just in time to see two cars kissing beneath the traffic light, their hoods now dented into teepees.

A speed-limit sign flew past. Its blurred number read: 45. She looked down at the speedometer. 67 and rising. "C'mon," she whispered. She pushed harder against the pedal, even though it was already down as far as it could go. She could feel her calf muscle stretching the denim fabric of her jeans.

75 mph.

Up ahead was another red light. It hung suspended in the air, glowing bright against the backdrop of an overcast and dreary October sky.

She leaned on the horn and swerved around a Honda Civic that was itself traveling ten miles an hour over the speed limit. It veered onto the shoulder as she moved the big black truck past it and straight into the intersection. An old Nissan Pathfinder was coming at her from the right, its traffic light green.

It was 9:45, and rush hour was over, everybody sentenced to a nine-to-five work day already settled into their cubicled prison cells and working on their second or third cup of coffee. Kids were in school, and the busses were either off the roads or on their way back to the depot. Traffic had eased, and cars were able to pass through standing green lights without the need to slow down—as was the case for the Pathfinder.

And the cement truck coming from her left at fifty miles per hour.

She swore.

The driver of the cement truck must have caught the speeding F-150 from the corner of his eye, because at the last second, already over the thick white lines of the intersection, he cut hard left and passed through the red light himself. Either the guy worked as a stunt driver on the weekends or he was just incredibly lucky, because he somehow managed to make the turn without flipping the truck.

Stacey Green maneuvered the F-150 to the right, missing the Pathfinder's rear fender by inches as it traveled from right to left in a blur across her windshield. The cement truck, making the unexpected turn at such speed, had continued its turn left through the red light and across the oncoming lanes before going up on a sidewalk and through a row of well-manicured bushes lining the front of a bank. Stacey steered around the Pathfinder and left the entire scene in the rearview. She gave one fleeting glance to the mirror, briefly concerned for those left in her wake, but they were not her primary concern right now.

As she navigated the two-lane blacktop, maneuvering around the vehicles in her way, she reached down and grabbed her cell phone from the cup holder. She held in a button, activating the voice command, and said, "Call Brian's school."

She heard a dial tone. Then, "Good morning, this is—"

"Hi, Samantha, it's Shannon Blackway—" She came up on two cars traveling side by side at the same speed. She gritted her teeth, waited for a bus coming in the opposite lane to pass, and then crossed over the double yellow lines, passing what turned out to be an older couple traveling five miles below the speed limit but firmly planted in the fast lane. She swerved in front of them and back into her lane just in time to avoid an oncoming SUV.

Samantha was in the middle of saying something that Stacey hadn't heard. She cut her off. "Samantha, listen, we're having a little family emergency here, but there's no time to explain it right now."

Someone honked at her.

"I need you to take Brian out of class and keep him with you until my sister can pick him up, okay?"

Hesitation on the other line. "Is everything alright?"

"Yeah, it'll be fine, but we're in a hurry. Look, I don't want Brian to be freaked out, so can you just tell him that his aunt Monica is coming to get him?"

"Shannon, you're scaring me."

"It's okay, Samantha. I'll explain later. My sister is five feet four and has shoulder-length black hair. Her eyes are brown, and she's forty-two."

Now Samantha's voice sounded really panicked. "Okay, Shannon. I'll go get him. Is there anything else we should know?"

Stacey couldn't imagine what the girl was thinking, all the different scenarios that could be playing through her head. A death in the family? The boy's biological father coming to take him away? Fleeing the FBI as they closed in on them for some heist they'd pulled off years ago? "Samantha, listen to me very carefully," she said in a voice as controlled as she could manage. "Don't let him go with anyone but Monica. You understand?"

She didn't, clearly.

Stacey gripped the steering wheel until her knuckles were white. She didn't have time for this. "She'll be there soon. It'll be okay." She hung up.

Maybe she should have prepped Samantha for this day, warned her that it might come. It was why she'd gotten to know her, why she'd gone out for drinks with her those few times. Why she'd invited her over to their new house, why she'd brought her coffee some days, and why she'd always sat next to her at the PTA meetings. All so that she could make the call she'd just made and be certain that Samantha would do what was asked of her. But maybe she should have spent more time creating a back story that would have better prepared her. Or not. Maybe it would've just given Samantha more time to think about this new family who had suddenly showed up from out of state. And the last thing Stacey wanted was for people to become curious about her and her family.

She turned onto a side street, knowing a short cut that would get her home a minute sooner.

She tried dialing Jack.

2

JACK RAN THROUGH THE Fergusons' backyard. He sprint-ed straight through their flower garden and hopped over the chain-link fence, landing in the Donnelys' yard. He quickly made his way to the corner of the red-brick house and peered around its side, looking up the concrete path between the two houses and to the street out front. A man appeared, walking along the sidewalk and passing between the houses. He was holding a leash in his hand, but whatever was attached to it hadn't come into view yet. Then a little white dog appeared, its short legs trying to keep up with the man's gray running sneakers.

The guy was built like a linebacker, dressed in blue jeans and a black hooded sweatshirt. The hood was pulled up over his head, and he seemed to be staring down at the ground ahead of him, utterly disinterested in the dog. Jack thought of Arnold Schwarzenegger walking a little canine in the James Cameron movie *True Lies*, and wondered where this dog could have come from. Was there some rent-a-dog outfit for spies, or had this guy just snatched the first dog he'd come across? Because whoever this guy was, he was definitely in the game. If only Jack knew whose team he was on.

Jack moved onto the patio and went to the kitchen window that stood overlooking the backyard. He peered through the glass and could see all the way out the living room's bay windows in the front of the house. The head and shoulders of the hooded man appeared and then quickly moved past.

Jack's heart hammered in his chest. He pulled out his cell and fired off a text message to Stacey.

911-3.

It was time.

He thrust the cell back into his pocket and pulled out the pistol he'd taken from the glove compartment before leaving his 4Runner at the top of the street. He'd been on his way back from the local coffee shop, turning onto their road, when he'd spotted an unfamiliar panel van parked a few doors down and opposite their house. He'd slowed right away, pulling instead into Fred and Bonnie Canan's empty driveway. He knew they'd both be at work by now and that they always left their garage door unlocked.

He'd sat there for thirty seconds studying the van, which he could clearly see due to the way the road bent to the right in front of his house. He figured it could be any number of things. A plumber fixing the neighbor's toilet. Or a carpenter or an electrician or a dog catcher. But the van had no letters on its sides identifying it as one business or another. Just a blank white van.

He'd quickly surveyed the rest of the street before getting out of the car and casually making his way into the unlocked garage. Once inside, he'd gone straight out the rear door and into the back yard. Whoever these people were, they either hadn't noticed him pulling onto the street, or they weren't familiar enough with him to know what his car looked like. Jack figured they must be amateurs, which suggested hired hands.

He spun back away from the window, hoping none of the other neighbors were home bird-watching from their back windows. If Mrs. Cottonwood stepped out onto her patio in her pink slippers and saw him with his back against the Donnelys' house with a gun in his hand... Well, she'd either have a heart attack, go back in to call the police on her old rotary phone, or march right over to him and demand to know what he was doing. The latter would be the worst-case scenario for him, and obviously a heart attack would be no good for her. But there was no sign of activity from the house between the Donnelys' and his own.

He hopped into the widow's yard, landing in a pile of crap left by her yappy poodle, Burt (named after Burt Lancaster, whom, she'd told him on more than one occasion, she'd had quite a thing for).

He ducked low and crossed the patio, passing the back door and putting his back up against the house's blue siding. He peered around the corner and now up the space that separated Mrs. Cottonwood's home from his own. Beyond the trashcans they kept near the front of the house, he could see the road and the houses on the other side of it. The van, however, was out of view, still a few doors down. He saw no one else on the sidewalk.

He began to second-guess himself. What if he'd overreacted to the van and the guy walking the dog? What if the two were completely unrelated and the guy was someone from the next street over, or just doing a neighbor a favor? What if his 911 text to Stacey had set in motion a series of events they wouldn't be able to take back? How would they explain it to the school?

There was no time to think about it now. His instincts had told him that something was wrong, and Stacey had taught him to trust those instincts. Besides, it was better to be safe than sorry—to have to start all over again than to be dead. Suddenly, he looked back across the yard and to the acres of woods that stood towering across the edge of the back yards some fifty yards away. A cool breeze swept from right to left and sent the trees dancing, some leaves coming off branches and fluttering through the sky.

Damn.

He'd been so concerned with the activity out front that he hadn't even stopped to consider that maybe they'd be coming from behind too. And wouldn't they? It would be a good place for a sharpshooter. And here he was, making himself into a perfect target, standing up against the side of Mrs. Cottonwood's house like some cardboard cutout.

He thought back to his school yard days, of the game he used to play at recess. "Suey," they'd called it. Short for suicide, he believed. You had to run up and touch the wall while shouting, "Suey!" before someone could peg you with the ball. If you got hit three times, you then had to stand spread-eagle against the wall while someone got a free shot at you with whatever ball they were using that day—either a tennis ball or racquetball usually. That was how he felt in this moment, spread out against the wall and about to get pegged. All the hairs on the back of his neck stood tall, and his testicles shriveled up inside him as he braced for the blast.

Move, he told himself. His body obeyed, darting away from the side of the house just as something smacked into the siding where his head had been. He looked back and saw a hole.

All doubt as to what was happening vanished in that instant, and he reached out for the fence, hopping into his own yard as a metallic *clink* rang out. He could tell that the ricochet came from nearer the back of the yard where the swing set was. Which meant that the shooter was either positioned to his right behind Mrs. Cottonwood's house or directly behind his own.

He went for cover behind the shed that stood off the corner of the patio, ten feet from the back of the house. It stood eight feet tall and six feet wide with a single metal door facing the house. He ducked behind it. No more shots came, but he realized that he was now in plain sight of all the house's back windows. If anyone was inside... He looked at the bay windows and could see into their living room. No movement caught his eye. He looked up to the second-floor windows. Still no—

A curtain moved in his and Stacey's bedroom.

He spun toward the shed door while digging his keys from his pocket with his free hand. Quickly selecting the red, color-coded key from the ring of others, he slid it into the keyhole and unlocked the deadbolt, pushing his way through the door and into sudden darkness. He turned back to shut and lock the door behind him, and as he did so, he realized that he hadn't heard anything from Sam, their German shepherd. Since they'd gotten the dog mostly for that purpose (as well as to help Joseph make the transition into this new chapter of their lives) and had never discouraged the K9 from barking, it was odd that the watchdog hadn't already alerted the entire neighborhood to the presence of an intruder. Jack knew there could only be one reason why.

As he moved about in the darkness, he wondered if the sniper covering the back of the house was there to prevent him from escaping into the woods or if they were calling the shots like Michael Biehn's GOD character in *Navy SEALS.* Either way, when the scope's data lines had intersected his body against the back of Mrs. Cottonwood's house, the shooter hadn't hesitated.

Which meant they were here to kill him and weren't too concerned about how they went about doing it. How they planned to spin it or cover it up depended on which team they were part of, but Jack didn't have time to think about that now.

He reached for the LED lantern that he kept on a shelf near the door and turned it on. The shed lit up, revealing shelves full of paint cans, buckets of nails, grass seed, and other maintenance items—though it was all mostly for show. He pushed the lawn mower off a large piece of plywood while sticking the pistol into the back of his waistband. Then he bent over and used his fingertips to grip the edge of the wood. He lifted it onto its side and leaned it against the wall. Then he knelt and began brushing away at the dirt floor until he found a rope. He pulled on it, his biceps bulging, and a metal door swung open, spilling dirt off its face and filling the dimly lit room with clouds of swirling dust.

Jack grabbed the lantern and held it over the black hole that now sat in the shadow of the open door. A ladder descended to a concrete floor below. He climbed down the ladder, pulling the metal door closed on top of him as he went. Never had he thought that he'd be using the hidden passageway to get *into* the house. Its primary function had been to provide a way of escaping the house, the tunnel stretching from a safe house in the basement all the way to the woods behind the house.

One of the main reasons they'd moved here in the first place was because of the woods. Access to two hundred acres that were bisected by railroad tracks used by freight trains two to three times a week and pulling up to seventy-two cars (according to Joseph's highest count). If you walked straight south through the woods, you'd come to a highway. If you walked southeast, you'd come to another small town, which led to another and another after that until you eventually found yourself looking out over the Atlantic and toward Bermuda. There was a cave and what Joseph had named "the mudslide"—which was just a steep hundred-foot drop from high ground down to the creek bed below (Joseph had tried using his "MacGyver board"—a two-by-twelve he'd taken some of Jack's tools to—and tried to snowboard down it this past January, nearly killing himself in the process). The creek flowed past a little bamboo forest and at some point connected to a river across the state line—or so Jack was told. They had never gotten around to verifying that fact. But they could get lost in these backwoods if they needed to, or find their way someplace else altogether if more extreme measures were needed.

But now here he was, and all that planning was now out the window because they'd never entertained a scenario like this—coming home and finding the house surrounded and people already inside. He'd received no notifications on his phone from any alarms being tripped, which was curious in and of itself. His only weapon was a pistol, and even if he got to the woods, without knowing how many people were there waiting for him, what would he do once he got there?

He stepped off the ladder and dropped to the floor, heading for the basement as the lantern in his hand cast chaotic shadows all around him. He'd get into the panic room and decide what to do from there.

As he ran down the corridor, the sound of banging echoed after him.

Someone was trying to get into the shed.

3

WHEN MRS. HATFIELD POKED her head through the classroom door and her eyes began sweeping over the students, obviously looking for someone in particular, Joseph thought that some tragedy must've befallen one of his fellow classmates. Maybe someone's parents had been killed in a car accident on the way to work, or a grandparent had suffered a heart attack. A knot began to form in his stomach as he wondered who it could be, and he put himself in their shoes. But then it hit him.

Those shoes were his own.

The teacher, Ms. Elicker, was still going on about the Emancipation Proclamation and hadn't yet noticed the secretary snooping on her class. Joseph followed Mrs. Hatfield's eyes with his own until their eyes met in what felt like a cosmic explosion that confirmed his premonition. The knot in his stomach tightened, and his heart thumped in his chest.

Finally, Mrs. Hatfield rapped her knuckles against the door, opening it wide enough so that Ms. Elicker could see her. "Sorry to disturb your class, Ms. Elicker," she said. "But I need Mr. Blackway to come with me."

"That's quite alright, Samantha," Ms. Elicker said. She looked at Joseph. "Go ahead, Brian." She nodded toward the door.

To her credit, Mrs. Hatfield was doing a superb job at keeping her worry and confusion from showing. She even managed a polite smile, which Joseph found to be very pretty. He knew that some of the other boys had a crush on her, and he'd seen the way some of their fathers looked her way on Back To School Night. Even overheard Bobby's dad refer to her as "Sexy Sam" when talking to Taylor's dad by the water fountain.

He slid his legs out from beneath the desk and stood. He could feel all the eyes in the classroom turn to him, his friends thinking the same worried thoughts he'd just been thinking about them.

When he reached the door, Mrs. Hatfield opened it wider, allowing him to walk past her and out into the hall. She closed the classroom door behind them. "Why don't you get your stuff from your locker, Brian."

While her face hid the tension and anxiety she was feeling, her eyes certainly did not. Joseph had just watched *Kindergarten Cop* with his dad last summer, and he couldn't help but wonder if scenes of a bad guy on his way to abduct a student weren't playing through Mrs. Hatfield's brain. He wanted to smile at her, to flash a reassuring look and say, "'Boys have penises; girls have vaginas.'" Something totally off the wall and maybe a little bit inappropriate that might break the tension between them. He imagined her response being, "That's *exactly* what I was think-ing." Not about penises and vaginas, but about the movie's plot. However, if she'd never seen Arnold Schwarzenegger scream, "It's not a tuuuma!" then maybe his quote wouldn't go over so well. Maybe, in some perverse way he didn't quite understand, she would take it as some kind of innuendo. A sexual suggestion or something. Maybe get himself kicked out of school, or at the very least make things incredibly awkward for the rest of his time here. He decided against using the movie line on her.

As he worked the combination on his locker, he could see in his periphery Mrs. Hatfield standing with her arms crossed. She was lifting her shoulders like she was cold, but he knew it was because she was scared or nervous. But her arms po-sitioned beneath her chest like that had elevated her breasts and stacked a substantial amount of cleavage up over the cut of her blouse. At least it seemed substantial to fourteen-year-old Joseph. Joseph thought of those medieval contraptions that made women's boobs pop out. What had Elizabeth Swann called them? Corsets?

He opened the metal door and grabbed his book bag while chiding himself for even noticing Mrs. Hatfield's boobs. He'd thought Bobby's and Taylor's dads were gross and inappropriate for talking about her like that (they were all married, for goodness' sake). And then he was thinking about that song he'd heard his parents listening to on the radio. Something about Stacey's mom. At the time, he hadn't understood the lyric, but now he did. But it was weird because Stacey was his mom's name, and her mom was his grandmom. He shook the thought from his head before things could get any weirder, and the Governator, pirates, and boobs left him alone. Taking their place, however, was the sudden realization that his entire life had just turned upside down.

His beating heart seemed to freeze in his chest, and the floor felt like it had opened up beneath him. He had the sense of falling, his stomach lurching upward into his chest, but he was still at eye level with the textbooks stacked on the lone shelf of his locker. He gripped the door like he was going to close it but was really just using it to steady himself. All the preparations over the last two years were about to be put to the test. And though he was glad they had prepared, he would have preferred it if the day had never come.

He felt sick.

"Brian," Mrs. Hatfield said.

He blinked and caught a glimpse of his reflection in the mirror hanging in the back of his locker. He saw the scar tracing his neck. And remembered. Remembered being in the woods. Hiding beneath the cabin. Stabbing that guy with a makeshift spear. He remembered surviving.

And he stopped falling, the seasickening flip into the Upside Down suddenly complete. It was a different world now than it had been two minutes before, but the roller-coaster ride between the two realities was over.

He reached out and grabbed the metal hanger from the hook beneath the shelf and knelt beside his backpack, the open door blocking Mrs. Hatfield's view. On the same Back To School Night he'd heard Sexy Sam being talked about, he'd sneaked into the janitor's closet and grabbed another locker bottom from an open box of spare locker parts that the maintenance workers kept in there. He'd then placed the extra bottom on top of the actual bottom. On another day, he'd lifted the false bottom and placed Hugh—the knife his dad had given him and that he'd named after Hugh Jackman via Wolverine—between them. He used the hanger to lift the false bottom, and he grabbed the knife. He quickly slipped it into his book bag.

"Brian, c'mon," Mrs. Hatfield insisted.

He stood, threw the backpack over his shoulder, and shut the locker door. He spun the dial on the lock and followed Sexy Samantha to the front office. It was time to meet this lady he knew she would be calling "Aunt Monica."

4

STACEY SAW A LINE of cars stopped at a red light up ahead and turned the big Ford off the road, up over the sidewalk, and into the front yard of a green bungalow, passing the waiting cars on her left. She drove straight through the picket fence that separated the green house from its baby-blue neighbor, the wooden slats splintering and bouncing off the windshield. She flew down the grassy slope of the yard and into the driveway of the next, passing behind and barely missing a restored 1955 Chevrolet Bel Air Nomad. She cut across the front lawn of the last house, turning right and churning up grass and fall leaves as she circumnavigated the intersection by roaring through the side yard of the property. She was now parallel to the street she wanted and cut over the sidewalk, the big tires coming off the curb and finding blacktop again. The car behind her honked, but she just pushed the accelerator back to the floor. It was now a straight shot into the rural area of town. And to Jack.

The text that Jack had sent her was one of many codes she'd had him memorize, each one signifying a specific situation. The one he'd used told her that the enemy was at their house but that he was not inside the house himself. He hadn't sent an update or called though, which meant he was too preoccupied to do so. That wasn't good. Had Jack headed for the woods like they'd discussed? If so, why hadn't he sent the expected follow-up text? Were they there for all of them, or were they content to take one Green out at a time? Would she find Jack dead and the assailants gone? Or would they still be there waiting for her?

She glanced at her cell. Nothing from "Monica" yet either.

Though Monica was not the main reason they'd moved to this small North Carolina town, her nearby presence was an added bonus. A retired FBI agent who lived about fifteen miles from the school, she was someone Agent Johnson had vouched for and suggested be brought into their trust. They'd been glad to have the little extra sense of security, even if they had never actually met her and hoped they would never need to.

It was actually the old house that had brought them to the Tar Heel state. It had been built in the middle of a forest a long time ago, the nearest neighbors an hour away by wagon. But as the decades came and went, civilization had pressed closer and closer until, finally, the old colonial house found itself standing in the center of a neighborhood and surrounded by houses almost two hundred years younger.

None of the newer homeowners had any clue about the old house's history though. That in the 1800s it had been used by the Underground Railroad or by the mafia during Prohibition. And they certainly didn't know that it had been used by WITSEC as a safe house in its more recent years. With each of these peculiar uses came new renovations, and it was these renovations that had caught Agent Johnson's attention. There were underground tunnels that ran from the basement to the remaining two hundred acres of woods out back. And there was a panic room.

But those reasons for settling down here would turn out to be moot if their enemies had somehow managed to get into the house while they were all outside of it. Where would that leave them?

She'd find out in about two minutes.

5

AFTER ACCESSING THE PANIC room via a keypad, Jack closed the big metal door behind him and turned on the lights. As the fluorescent bulbs flickered to life, he crossed the room and made sure the door leading to the house was locked too. He was in the basement, locked in the panic room, and confident he was safe—at least for the moment. He set the pistol down on a desk that housed two glowing computer monitors. A live feed into every room of their house was displayed in tiny squares across them. He studied them, his long black hair falling in strands over his eyes.

There.

And there.

Two men inside. One upstairs looking in a closet, the other downstairs, heading for the back door. They were dressed in plain clothes—jeans and flannel shirts—with semiautomatic rifles. Ski masks covered their faces. They had vests over the flannel, and when one of them turned away from the hidden camera that was mounted in the light fixture, he got a glimpse of the rectangular patch on the person's back and the three big letters stenciled across it.

FBI.

What the hell?

He moved the mouse and clicked on a button, bringing up the outside cameras. There were two more men with assault rifles trying to get into the shed, and he could make out a figure sitting behind the wheel in the van across the street. He didn't see anyone else.

Two inside, two outside, at least one in the van, and at least one sniper in the woods.

He looked at his watch. Stacey would be here in a few minutes, and he had to let her know what she would be walking into. He didn't have cell service in the safe room, so he used the computer to fire off a quick email, hoping she'd get it in time.

He turned away from the monitors and went over to the far wall. Rows of weapons ran across it. Jack called the room the "Reba Room" because it reminded him of Michael Gross and Reba McEntire's house in *Tremors*. Only he didn't have an elephant gun.

He pulled a tactical vest off a hook and slipped it over his head. Then he selected an MP5SD off the wall and grabbed two thirty-round mags that had been taped together with gaff tape. He inserted the magazine and slung the silenced submachine gun over his gray Panthers sweatshirt. Then he took a Heckler & Koch MP7A2 with an attached silencer and rammed a 40-round mag of 4.6x30mms into the handle. He stuck another thirty-round magazine into his back pocket.

He checked the video feeds one more time, slid a hand through his hair, and turned to leave. He had to take care of this before Stacey got here.

He punched the code into the door lock and slipped past the big steel door and into the rest of the open basement. He took the steps that led up to the dining room hallway two at a time. Once at the top, he opened the door. Because he knew where the men were, all moving toward the back of the house, he didn't bother taking his time. The basement door actually doubled as a false back to a large wardrobe that had been built up against the hallway wall adjacent to the dining room. Jack knew that if anyone were to study the house, they would eventually find missing spaces. But if you were to just come right in and look around, there was no way you'd suspect that the wardrobe in the hallway would actually take you to the basement.

Reaching through the hanging coats, he pushed open the double doors and stepped into the hallway, extending the gun's retractable buttstock and bringing it tight to his shoulder. He grasped the foregrip he'd previously attached to the underside rail and swept the small, pistol-like submachine gun back and forth.

He bent into a tactical crouch and began moving down the hallway, the kitchen ahead of him, and flicked his eyes left and right through the open doorways as he passed them. He wanted to make sure he hadn't missed anyone on the cameras. But he saw and heard no one else, just movement from the kitchen.

He stopped ten feet from the entranceway, the kitchen window that overlooked the backyard directly in front of him. He wondered if the sniper could see him standing there through his or her scope. If so, there would be a call over the radio, and things would get very interesting very fast.

He didn't hear a radio, though, just the man walking around on the tiled floor. He could tell the man was walking toward him, that he was going to pass across the face of the entranceway, moving from his right to his left. He'd have to put him down before the intruder got a glimpse of him in his periphery and spun around to shoot. But the window would be behind the guy, and if his shot missed and shattered the glass, he'd be alerting everyone outside to his presence inside. He crouched lower and raised the MP7, staring down the iron sights. He'd take out the guy's legs, shooting beneath the window frame, and then finish him off with a head tap as he fell.

The toe of the man's boot appeared first, stepping into the doorway. As it flattened against the floor, the barrel of a semi-automatic rifle appeared next. Then the rest of the gun and the man's masked face. His hands and elbows. His left shoulder. And then he was standing there, silhouetted by the light coming through the window, framed by the doorway.

Jack fired a short burst at the pair of denim knees. The trio of armor-piercing rounds tore through the jeans and the kneecaps, splintering bone and ligaments and spraying blood onto the kitchen chairs nearby. The man went to the ground, and Jack shot him through the mask, into the cheekbone beneath his left eye. The intruder's head hit the ground, and for the briefest of moments his eyes met Jack's. And then they fell out of focus, and he was dead.

Jack quickly went over and knelt beside him. He searched the pockets, but of course they were empty. He pulled the earpiece from the guy's ear and held it to his own. A man was speaking into it, giving orders. Was it the sniper? Had they seen the guy drop beneath the window? He slid across the tile floor, careful to stay beneath the windowsill, and came to a stop beside a wooden hutch that held glassware in the cabinets, silverware in the drawers. It was about five feet wide and only a few inches from the ceiling. He leaned his shoulder into it and pushed it in front of the window, blocking the sniper's view into the ground floor of the house and reducing the amount of natural light that was coming into the kitchen.

Jack stood and listened as a report of what he'd just done came over the earpiece. So the sniper was watching through his scope.

He heard someone coming down the stairs from the upper floor, and ran to the doorway, putting his back to the wall, the dead man lying on the floor at his ten o'clock. He made sure he wasn't casting a shadow across the floor and stared ahead at the hutch. One of the cabinet's glass doors was reflecting the kitchen and the hallway behind him. He could see the wardrobe doors left open by the front door. He flexed his hand on the foregrip and took a deep breath. Waited.

The man came down the stairs and swung his rifle into the hallway, moving it back and forth, searching for signs of activity. Jack watched in the reflection as the man noticed the open wardrobe. He began walking toward it, his attention momentarily diverted from the kitchen. It was all Jack needed. He spun into the hallway and fired from his shoulder, striking the man in the chest, neck, and head. The intruder collapsed and lay sprawled in the middle of the hallway. Blood splatter spotted the front door and the white walls beside it.

Two down.

There were at least four more, maybe five if the dog walker wasn't one of the men he'd seen at the shed. And could there be more in the back of the van, or even another vehicle parked somewhere farther down the road? Was the sniper alone in the woods, or was there a whole paramilitary unit out there ready to take over the entire town *Red Dawn*-style?

He went to the hutch and stole a glance around it, through the space between its back and the window, and saw that the two men who had been trying to get into the shed were gone, the shed door still closed.

And then the front door banged opened, and a canister came flying down the hallway, spraying smoke. Another went into the dining room.

As the house began to fill with gas, he wondered if they were trying to smoke him out or if they were about to come at him with thermal-imaging cameras. He couldn't see anything outside the kitchen, the hallway filled floor to ceiling with dark gray smoke. He moved away from the doorway and back toward the stove.

The earpiece in his ear had gone silent.

6

STACEY'S PHONE HAD DINGED two minutes ago, and she'd glanced down to the cup holder to see an email alert from Jack. She could think of only one reason why he'd be emailing her instead of calling or texting—he was in the panic room. She didn't dare try to read the message while driving, and as she turned onto their street, she immediately saw Jack's 4Runner parked in the neighbor's driveway. Then she noticed the van parked across from their house. She glanced in the rearview and saw a black Audi turn onto the road behind her. She'd never seen an Audi in this area before and thought it so stereotypical that she almost laughed. She knew they hadn't been tailing her all morning. She would've noticed them a lot sooner if they were. Which meant they must've been waiting for her.

She reached under the seat and pulled out an auto-seared Glock 17 with an extended mag. She set it on the seat beside her and rolled down her window. She scanned both sides of the street for any activity as she rolled by. As she came up on their house, she looked through the open front door and saw the smoke. She also saw a beam of red light jerking back and forth, up and down in the hallway. Someone was in there with a laser sight.

The truck's rear window shattered, and three holes appeared in a neat line across the center of the windshield in front of her. Instinctively, she ducked and glanced at the sideview. Saw a person aiming a gun out the window of the Audi. She hit the gas and flew past her house, taking the bend in the road at 40 mph, passing the parked panel van on her left. The Audi followed.

The street ended in a T, and when she reached it, she slammed on the brakes while pulling the wheel hard to the left. She slid into the T, the tires smoking as the truck spun around. She used her palm to work the wheel and brought the F-150 out of the turn at 180 degrees so that she was now facing the oncoming Audi. She shifted the truck into neutral and flung the door open. She grabbed the converted machine pistol off the passenger seat and stepped down onto the road in one fluid motion. As the truck began to roll backward down the sloped road and toward the field behind it, Stacey backpedaled to keep pace with it, firing through the open window and using the door as a shield.

The driver of the Audi slammed on the brakes, but it was too late. Stacey had spun the truck, opened the door, and stepped out so fast that they barely had time to register what was even happening before muzzle flashes filled the big Ford's open window. Instinctively, the driver pulled the wheel to the left, swerving off the road and up onto the sidewalk. Stacey emptied the rest of the mag by holding down the trigger and tracing the car from the windshield all the way to the rear passenger door. Empty shells bounced like raindrops all around her. The car went into the grass and smashed into a tree.

Stacey stepped back up into the truck and hit the brake, stopping its roll just as the rear tires left the asphalt. She shifted the truck back into drive and closed the door. As she sped past the Audi, she was able to see through its lowered passenger window two slumped bodies leaning against the steering wheel and dashboard. "Assholes," she muttered.

The panel van was coming up on her right now, still parked, no sign of—

A man ran out from behind the van, a long gun pressed against his shoulder and already coming up. He stopped to aim just beside the van's rear tire. Stacey pressed the accelerator and turned the wheel into the van.

The guy managed to squeeze off two rounds before the truck's front right fender struck his thighs and smashed his body into the van, pulverizing his legs. Stacey straightened the wheel and scraped the truck along the entire side of the van, smearing the guy across it until he fell beneath the truck, and the rear wheels bounced over him.

She turned the truck toward their house, driving it straight up the lawn and stopping just two feet from the open front door. She quickly stole a glance at the carnage she'd left in the street behind her as she replaced the empty mag with another from the glove compartment and stuck her phone in her pocket. Then she jumped out of the truck.

Behind her, directly across the street, Mrs. Grow was standing like a pillar of salt at the end of her driveway, bunny slippers on her feet, curlers in her hair, a cup of steaming tea in one hand and a folded umbrella in the other. Stacey had always been kind to Mrs. Grow, who had lost her husband to a heart attack a month before they'd moved in. They often waved whenever they saw each other. Joseph had taken her cookies on a few occasions, had raked her leaves last fall.

And even though Mrs. Grow's face was a picture of shocked disbelief, it didn't stop her hand from slowly rising into the air in an unsure wave. Then, leaving the rolled-up newspaper at her feet (her husband had gotten the paper every day for all of their fifty-one years of marriage, and even though she didn't read it herself, she couldn't bring herself to stop them from coming), she slowly turned and began making her way back up the driveway.

But Stacey didn't see any of that because she was already jumping from the hood of the truck and up onto the awning, working her way to a second-floor window.

7

JOSEPH SAT IN A chair in the back of the office, his palms flat and pressed onto his knees to keep them from shaking. He watched Mrs. Hatfield working at her desk. She answered some calls and typed some emails. Every once in a while she'd turn and look over her shoulder and flash a gorgeous smile at him. Yet he could see the dying questions sitting there on her tongue, just behind her gleaming white teeth. She wanted to ask him if he knew what was going on. And of course, he did. Or at least to some extent. He was sure his mom and dad had left out half of it, but he knew its flavor, and offering her a bite would only make Mrs. Hatfield more anxious than she already was.

He looked up at the clock. Mom and Dad had said it would take "Aunt Monica" about half an hour to get there and to just sit tight until she did. They'd given him a picture of her so that he knew what she'd look like when she arrived. She would be taking him to a safe place where he would simply ride out the unfolding events watching movies or playing video games (though under no circumstance was he to log into any gaming accounts).

"Are you okay, Brian?" Mrs. Hatfield asked.

He nodded, and she stared at him a moment longer, looking into his eyes, hoping that he would give her something more. But he averted his gaze, instead glancing out the window across the room and into the parking lot beyond.

"Okay, then," she said. "But I can get you something if you want. Something from the vending machine, or—"

He looked back at her. "Actually, could I use the bathroom?"

"Sure," she said. "Just back there." She pointed to a hall across from him.

He knew where it was, even if he'd never used it before. His friend Zane had used it though. And he'd said that he'd left the toilet clogged without telling anyone. He'd laughed when telling the story at lunch one day. "I mean, I planted a friggin' *tree* in that porcelain pot!" he'd said. "They probably had to call a lumberjack to get that crap straightened out!" They'd all laughed.

"Thanks," Joseph said. He got up with his backpack and walked down the short hall, passing the doors to a few offices, and finally reached one that had a pair of stick figures on it. He knocked, and when no one answered, he pushed the door open and went in. It was just a single bathroom. One sink, one toilet. He locked the door and took out his cell phone. No missed calls. Which meant that Mom and Dad were preoccupied. He could only imagine with what.

8

JACK BURIED HIS FACE in the crook of his elbow, shielding his eyes from the smoke while backpedaling toward the garage door. He listened for someone entering the kitchen in front of him, ready to shoot in that direction.

His back struck the garage door, and he reached behind him, feeling for the doorknob. He turned it and pulled it open, intending to slip out of the smoke-filled kitchen and down to the concrete floor of the garage. But just as he released the door from its frame, something struck him in the back, pushing him forward.

Even as he tried to maintain his balance, his mind processed in a flash what had happened—he'd pulled open the garage door at the same moment someone else had tried to push it open from the other side, and now the two of them were stumbling through the kitchen and trying to keep from landing on their faces.

Jack could feel the person right on his back, and he turned on the ball of his foot, reaching out and swiping a clawed hand at where he imagined the person's face must be. But instead of striking flesh, he ended up hooking his fingers into the straps of a headset. When he pulled, he felt infrared goggles come off the person's face and go flying across the room. He heard them skitter across the tile floor.

Jack brought up the silenced MP7A2 and fired into the man's side (he could tell it was a man from his gruff breathing), but the man had grabbed the barrel and pushed it away at the last second, sending the burst into the refrigerator instead.

Jack heard the distinct sound of a knife being unsheathed. Not like in the movies where some sort of metallic friction rang out whenever a blade was extracted—whether from a cutting block or a sock. No, it wasn't anything so dramatic as that. Rather, it was a subtle sound, barely recognizable at all, but Jack's brain had rendered an appropriate interpretation, and now he was keyed on the noise, reaching for it. He needed to find the guy's wrist before the six-inch blade found its way between his ribs.

His first attempt missed, his fingers just brushing the sleeve of the man's flannel shirt. There was no time for a second attempt. His first try had left his entire left side open to attack, and if not for the smoke, he'd have been stabbed three or four times already. So he lifted his knee into the guy's groin. The man huffed in response, but as he bent over, he slammed his head down into Jack's face.

Jack stumbled backward, both of them disengaging from one another and further disappearing into the smoke. Jack swung the MP7 around, firing a line of bullets from left to right across the kitchen. He was about to come back toward the right again at a lower angle in case the guy had ducked, when the guy came barreling into him, appearing out of the smoke like a rocket and striking him in the stomach with his shoulder. They both went down, and Jack felt the guy's knife stab into his tactical vest when they hit the floor. The blade glanced off, tearing at his Panthers sweatshirt but missing flesh. Jack heard the blade bounce off the floor a couple of feet away.

They grappled, and somewhere in the process, Jack lost his grip on the MP7. Now he was on his back, the MP5SD still slung over his shoulder and between the floor and his vest. He reached up and grasped the intruder's face with his palm, trying to keep from sliding backward on the MP5 and the mag still in his back pocket while doing so. He poked his fingers into the guy's eyes, and the man let go of him.

The smoke started to clear, and Jack could finally make out the form of the person straddling him. He reached behind the guy's head with his left hand and found a fistful of hair. This guy wasn't wearing a mask. Jack yanked his head back, exposing his neck, his Adam's apple showing like an arrowhead pushing against stretched skin. Jack punched it.

The guy gagged and rolled off him, holding his throat.

Jack jumped to his feet and reached for the counter where he knew he'd left his *Last Starfighter* mug earlier that morning. His fingers brushed the porcelain, and he picked it up, holding the handle in his fist, the mug itself curved against his knuckles. He stepped toward the man, ignoring the yellow letters across his vest. FBI or not, they'd just tried to execute him.

The man was on his knees, still holding his neck with both hands, when Jack punched him with the mug right between the eyes and against the bridge of his nose. The sound of the mug breaking the bone was sickening, and the guy swayed backward on his knees. When he came swaying forward, dazed, Jack punched him with the mug again, and this time the cup with the picture of Alex Rogan staring up into the stars shattered, half the mug crumbling to the floor, the other half still connected to the handle and in Jack's hand. Jack punched him again and again, the jagged edges of the broken porcelain digging into his face and tearing away flesh. Jack kept striking him until he realized that it was his grip on the man's vest that was keeping him upright. Whether unconscious or dead, Jack didn't know, but the man's head was flopped back and to the side like a limp noodle. Jack struck him one more time out of rage, and fear, and triumph. Then he let go of the vest, and the man careened sideways and collapsed to the floor.

As the smoke continued to dissipate, his work materialized. The man on the floor had no face left. Just two sightless eyes staring out through red pulp and splintered bone.

Jack dropped the mug to the floor, and the handle snapped off. His whole body shook with adrenaline, and he had to fight the urge to vomit. There was blood everywhere. He took a step back and ran a hand over his face, trying to escape the moment and collect his senses.

He spotted his MP7A2 over by the refrigerator and saw what must've been the guy's own MP5 in the doorway to the garage. He must've dropped it when they collided. Thank God for that.

A noise from behind.

He swung the MP5SD off his shoulder and spun back to the hallway, his finger already squeezing the trigger.

There was someone there in his periphery, coming into the kitchen through the last whispers of smoke. A voice broke through the blood that was pounding in his ears.

"Jack, it's me!"

He released the trigger just in time and saw Stacey standing there with a Glock in her hand and blood splattered across her face.

9

JACK WENT TO STACEY and threw his arms around her, holding her tight. But his eyes were down the hallway. "There were at least—"

"I got them all," she said, cutting him off. She looked around the room, saw the hutch in front of the windows, saw the faceless man lying there in blood and teeth. "I trained you well, grasshopper."

He pulled away, knowing that the reference was meant to reduce the seriousness of their situation. To keep him from losing it. "There's a sniper in the woods."

She shook her head. "They'll be leaving now. After this."

"Should we go after them?"

She shook her head again. "They'll have an ATV or a dirt bike. We'd never catch them."

Stacey walked across the room and picked up Jack's MP7. Then she came back and took his hand. "You used your *Last Starfighter* mug."

"Yeah."

"Now who's gonna help fight Xur and defeat the Ko-Dan Armada?" She led him out of the kitchen, taking note of the slash in his sweatshirt.

He wrapped his arm around her waist and stepped over the bodies in the hallway, the two he'd shot and two more that Stacey must've handled. He stopped suddenly. "Sam."

As they passed the dining room, Stacey pointed into it.

Jack turned his head and saw a mound of black and brown fur in the corner of the room. He bent down and looked beneath the table and could see the shepherd's legs.

Joseph had named the dog after Will Smith's dog in *I Am Legend*. And this Sam had been just as protective of Joseph as Smith's Sam had been of him. Every day, the dog sat by the front door, waiting for Joseph to walk in from school. And he either slept in Joseph's bed with him, on the floor beside him, or in the hallway outside his door. The two were practically inseparable. This was going to wreck Joseph.

"C'mon," Stacey said, and pulled him toward the basement door. "We don't have much time."

"Is he okay?"

"Joe? I talked to Samantha just like we planned. Monica should be getting there soon."

"But you haven't heard anything since?"

"Been a little busy. Picked up a tail on my way back."

"FBI?"

"Not unless they started driving black Audis."

Jack frowned and stole a glance back at one of the bodies sprawled in the hallway, the three yellow letters across the vest staring up at the ceiling. He pulled out his cell and dialed Joseph. They'd given him the phone on the condition that he carry it at all times. Stacey led him down the stairs while he listened to the dial tone. "Voicemail," he said.

Stacey went to the panic room and opened the door. "He's probably in transition. We'll be getting a call from Monica any second." She went to the monitors and spent a second studying each feed. Satisfied, she pulled out a large black duffel bag from beneath the desk and tossed it against the Reba wall. "Come on, Jack Wick, time to bug out."

Jack watched his wife. He knew she'd been trained as an operative, cold and ruthless in the heat of battle and all that. Hell, he'd watched her take on Seth Baker in the woods of West Virginia—the one who had rendered her barren and had put that scar across her throat. But seeing her this way, this calm and calculated after what she'd just been through, still unnerved him. And now, with her hair dyed black and pulled into a ponytail, the blood of other men streaked down her face, it was like he was looking at someone else. "You might want to wash your face," he said.

"Later," she said.

He clenched his hand into a fist to keep it from shaking and went to help her load the bag.

10

JOSEPH BEGAN TO OPEN the bathroom door but stopped when he heard voices coming from the front counter. He closed the door to a crack and listened. Mrs. Hatfield was talking to someone, but the tone in her voice indicated that it wasn't just a friendly conversation with a co-worker or even a familiar parent. "You're Monica?" he heard her ask. And he took a deep breath. This was it. He'd go with this lady, and she'd keep him safe until his mom and dad came back to get him. He lifted his cell and saw that he'd just missed a call from his dad. He fired off a quick text back.

SHES HERE

He slipped the phone back into his pocket and opened the door. As he stepped into the hallway, he could see Mrs. Hatfield standing at the reception desk, though the desk itself was outside his view. As was Monica. He adjusted his backpack and—

Mrs. Hatfield's hand.

He stopped while simultaneously reaching back to stop the bathroom door from slamming shut behind him. Mrs. Hatfield was talking to Monica face-to-face, but her left hand, which was beneath the counter and out of Monica's line of sight, was flapping urgently in his direction. He squinted. Was she trying to tell him to...

"He's marked absent today," he heard her tell the unseen woman.

Joseph frowned, beginning to sense that something was wrong.

And then Mrs. Hatfield's eyes went wide, and her mouth started to open in surprise. But before she could raise her hands or cry out or even take another breath, her head whipped backward.

The movement was so fast that her hair stayed frozen in place for a second, hanging in midair as her face looked up to the ceiling and then all the way back to the wall behind her. A red mist hung in the air like a halo around her head while red paint splashed the wall ten feet behind her. She rocked back on her heels, her toes coming off the carpet, her body falling straight as a board.

Time seemed to slow, and Joseph noticed the way her arms swung away from her sides, her hands staying where they'd been, her hair pulling forward and covering the sides of her face. It was as if he were witnessing her fall in a post-edited version of the scene. Her hair, her hands, her toes, the blood, even the necklace he hadn't noticed before swinging up and away from her neck... He registered all these things. Until the sound of her skull cracking against the floor snapped him back into real time. He'd seen similar versions of what had just happened acted out in a hundred movies, and his brain had no trouble whatsoever filling in the blanks and interpreting what had just happened.

Mrs. Hatfield was just shot in the head.

Yet there had been no bang. Which meant a suppressor, right? And only people in suits or tactical gear used those.

Joseph spent one more second staring at her body lying there, the top of her head gone, her eyes open and looking lifelessly in his direction. Even in that far-off death stare, her gaze seemed to be screaming for him to run. His stomach somersaulted with sudden revulsion...and revelation, understanding that she would not be going home to her husband today...or ever again. And that at the next Back To School Night, all the dads would be talking about how unbelievable it was, what had happened to Sexy Sam.

He backed into the bathroom and closed the door as quietly as he could. He locked it and then climbed up onto the back of the toilet and began feeling for the latches on top of the window that was positioned above it. He found them and turned them toward each other. He raised the window as high as it would go. The space wasn't big, but he thought he'd be able to get his shoulders through. He hoped so. He didn't want his butt sticking out of the wall and his legs dangling in the air when the killer finally got in. He took Hugh out of his backpack and sliced through the screen. Then he pushed his backpack out the window.

The doorknob rattled.

He tossed the knife out the window. Then he gripped the windowsill and pulled himself up, squirming through the mesh and falling head-first after it. He tucked his head and rolled, using his forearms to break the fall. His right shoulder took the brunt of the impact, but he was back on his feet in a flash. He grabbed his pack and the knife and took off for the tree line that stood on the other side of the soccer field, the soccer field itself adjacent to the school.

He had a wild thought that a few students might look out the window and see him booking across the grass in the middle of the period. Maybe one of his friends would slowly stand and walk to the window. "What is Brian doing?" they'd ask. Then the teacher, lesson interrupted, would walk over to the window and see for themselves the boy hightailing it to the woods with a knife in his hand. But then another, not so wild thought came. One that imagined a bullet tearing through the back of his head before he could reach the centerline.

But no such shot came, and he managed to make it into the woods unharmed. When he finally stopped to catch his breath, he noticed that tears were streaking down his face.

11

JACK WATCHED STACEY START up the ladder that had been placed at the end of the tunnel who knows when. He didn't like her going up first, but he knew that if a sniper was still out there, she was far more qualified to deal with it than he.

Her ass was in his face, and despite everything going on, he couldn't resist giving it a little pinch. She looked down at him with an expression of unbelief.

He shrugged. "Sorry. Couldn't help it."

She shook her head and climbed up out of the hole, quickly moving to a nearby tree and taking up a kneeling position next to it. She swept a Smith & Wesson M&P15T semiautomatic rifle that she'd taken from the Reba wall back and forth through the woods, searching for any sign of movement. Then she told him to throw the gear up.

Jack tossed the bag up out of the hole before climbing up himself. He turned and lowered the wooden door back down to the ground but didn't bother covering it. There was no use trying to hide it now. They'd never be coming back to this place again.

He joined his wife beside the tree, his own MP5SD raised and ready, the MP7A2 on his shoulder. They sat still for a while, trying to detect whether or not there was anything still out here that didn't belong. Jack listened for sirens, wondering how long it'd take the cops to get there. He thought it impossible that the neighbors hadn't called 911 yet. Unless someone had told the police to stand down.

Finally, Stacey stood and heaved the heavy army bag up onto her shoulder. Her knees wobbled ever so slightly under its weight. "C'mon," she said. She started to jog, heading deeper into the woods.

Jack went after her.

They ran over the multicolored ground, leaves crunching underfoot, ducking under branches and circumnavigating thorny thickets. Finally, out of breath and sweating, they reached their destination. Stacey dropped the bag and approached what looked like a five-foot-tall mound wedged between two trees. She reached out, appearing to grab a fistful of dirt, and then with quick force, tore it away. And just like that, the mound disappeared, leaves and dirt flying loose as the camouflaged cover whipped past her and landed on the ground. Now sitting in its place was a black 1991 Honda Accord.

Jack's phone vibrated, and he pulled it out of his jeans. "A text from Joseph," he said. "Said Monica's there."

Stacey paused, her hand on the door handle of the old car, and nodded.

"Should I call him?" Jack asked.

She looked around. "Wait until we're on the road." She nodded toward the bag. "Toss it in the trunk, and I'll let you pinch my ass again."

He smiled, though it was forced. The adrenaline was beginning to wear off, and he could feel himself crashing.

Stacey noticed. "You didn't eat breakfast, did you?"

He shook his head. "It's still in my car."

"We'll stop soon." She slid into the driver's seat and reached for the key they'd hidden beneath it. She turned the ignition, and the car started right up. She felt the back of the car dip when Jack dropped the bag in. As she waited, she pulled out her own cell and saw the same text Joseph had sent Jack. She fired off a text to the number she'd memorized for Monica.

ALL GOOD?

She set the phone on the center console as Jack closed the trunk. Then he was coming around and sliding into the passenger seat beside her. She noticed that he'd taken the tactical vest off. He looked around the car. "Wasn't sure this day would actually come." He shut the door, and she put the car into drive. She began slowly coasting their way through the trees, the tires rolling up and over the gentle swells of the terrain. There was a subtle path through the woods that would lead them to a nearby park.

"You think it's him?" Jack asked.

Stacey frowned. "Who else would it be?"

He shrugged, though the same old possibilities came to mind. "They would've been watching us, right? Before making their move?"

She turned the wheel and drove between two bushes that scraped the sides of the car. "I'd assume so."

"So then they knew you'd be on your way to work. That I would've been home if Joe hadn't missed the bus this morning."

She was silent.

"Doesn't make sense," he said. "Not if he was after you."

"It's personal now," she said.

"*Now?*"

"Okay, more so now."

"You're saying he's saving you for last?"

"Something like that."

Jack wasn't so sure. "No sirens yet."

She looked over at him, but didn't say anything.

"If it's him, then that wasn't really the FBI," Jack said.

Again she didn't respond.

There was open space through the trees now, and Stacey slowed. "See anything?" she asked, peering through the windshield and looking for signs of a trap.

"No, looks clear," Jack answered.

She moved the car forward again, letting it coast in neutral. A swing set appeared. And a sliding board. A few women standing near strollers as four-year-olds ran across the woodchips that covered the playground. When the car caught their eyes, they stopped talking and looked over. They watched in a sort of stunned silence, with wide eyes and travel mugs suspended halfway to their mouths, as the car rolled out of the woods, across the grass, and onto the gravel jogging path.

Jack waved as they drove past them. "Morning, ladies," he muttered.

Stacey drove out of the park and turned onto the road.

Sirens sounded in the distance.

"There's your sirens," she said.

He nodded, but he wasn't reassured as much as he should have been.

She drove past their street and through the intersection she'd engaged the Audi in with her modified Glock. They could see the Audi now, its front end still pressed up against a tree.

"You do that?" Jack asked.

She nodded.

Jack also caught a glimpse of the white van farther down the street. He could see that its side was now dented, and there were black and red streaks across it. The black he knew must have come from Stacey's truck, and the red from the crumpled form lying in the street beside it. "That too?"

This time she didn't respond, just drove straight past it.

Jack turned in his seat and looked back at their house. He could just make out the F-150 parked up against the front door. *Damn.* He stared at their house as long as he could, thinking about the last two years. Stacey and even Johnson had told him from the beginning not to get attached to the place, that the day might come when they'd have to leave it on a moment's notice. But how could he not? They'd spent nearly twenty-four months within its walls, laughing, crying, *living*. There were memories woven into those walls. Nerf-gun wars, hide-and-seek, the squeaky step that told him Joseph was awake every morning while he sat with his coffee, staring out the window and into the back woods... So many things, he suddenly realized, that he had never really paid any attention to before. Having to leave their last house had been hard, but they'd had time to adjust to the idea and plan for the next step. Now, they were leaving everything behind with only a completely uncertain future ahead of them.

Suddenly, the street was gone and with it that part of their lives. Jack turned forward and stared ahead.

"Good job, by the way," Stacey said.

"Huh?" Jack asked, in a daze.

"You took out, what? Four of them?"

"I think so." He looked over at her, blinked, and found that he only wanted to sleep.

Stacey's phone sounded. A text. She brought the cell up and read. Then frowned and handed the phone to Jack.

It was from Monica.

ETA 10 MIN

Jack shook his head, confused. "To where?"

"Ask."

It was way too soon for her to be arriving at the undisclosed location with Joseph. It was a three-hour drive from the school. He texted back: WHERE?

Thirty seconds passed. Then:

THE SCHOOL

Jack's heart stopped in his chest, and he took a big breath, his hands going to his sides and gripping the seat.

Stacey didn't even have to ask. She turned the wheel hard to the left, and the old car swung around and into the opposite lane. She slammed on the gas, now heading for Joseph's school.

12

JACK'S HEART RACED AS he dialed Joseph's cell phone. He glanced over at Stacey, who had yet to say a word, but her jaw was set, and the skin around her eyes was tight. She had that look in them—fierce determination rimmed with silent fury. It was the same look he'd seen in her eyes when she went after Seth Baker. With the blood still smeared on her face, she reminded him of William Wallace walking his horse into the bedchambers of Mornay, smashing his head in with a ball and chain for betraying him at the Battle of Falkirk.

Mel Gibson, he thought. And he remembered his conversation with Joseph out in the woods before he was kidnapped, about the theme that seemed so prevalent in most of his movies. *Revenge.* He wondered if their own lives would ever be free of it. Of Stacey's past. Of this SVR or KGB asshole who was out to destroy them for what Stacey had done to him all those years ago. But the answer was right there in his wife's eyes. *Yes*, they said. *One way or another, this ends now.* It was the very look he'd imagined her having while he was hanging over the fire and begging Cullin to go to their house and try to lay his hands on her. This was it for Stacey. Nothing would stop her now.

After getting the *Anastasia* poster in the hospital, they had spent the next six months searching for the bastard. Even with Agent Johnson's help and resources, they'd come up with nothing, and they began to wonder if perhaps he'd decided to return to Russia and live out the remainder of his days in obscurity, having failed in his mission. Or perhaps the Kremlin had taken care of him, tying off a loose end that wasn't worth the headache. But no. In the sixth month of their search, a book had appeared in

Joseph's school locker—Jules Verne's *Michael Strogoff*. It looked to be a brand-new copy. And given Stacey's past with exchanging books with him, there was no second-guessing where it had come from.

What the particular title was meant to convey, they had no idea. But it meant that while they had been running around looking for him, he had actually been watching them. And so they ran, starting over somewhere else—new identities, new possessions, new jobs, new schools, new friends, new everything. They never stopped looking for the Russian, but deep down they knew that he would find them first. What they didn't know was what he would do when he did.

Now they had that answer.

But there would be no more hiding, no more dead ends, no more living in the shadow of this threat. No, it would be Stacey's face that Fedyenka would see coming through the flames, fire dancing in her eyes, blood dripping from her hair, and he would crap himself even before she reached him, knowing that his end had come...and then she would slowly open him up and end all this madness once and for all.

He blinked, the premonition so strong that he had to turn his head and look out the window to the passing traffic to reorient himself.

The phone was on the third or fourth ring, still pressed to his ear, when a voice finally answered.

"Dad?"

It was Joseph, and Jack breathed a heavy sigh of relief. "Where are you? Are you okay?"

"Dad..." He seemed to stammer, not sure how to say the next thing or if he even could. "Mrs. Hatfield..."

Stacey's eyes shot over to Jack, obviously able to hear Joseph's voice through the cell.

Jack put the phone on speaker.

"What about her?" Stacey asked.

The answer came back trembling in a young man's scared voice. "They shot her."

Of course, the natural response wanted to be, "*Who* shot her?" But they already knew the answer to that question, didn't they?

And what difference did it make? So neither of them asked it. There was no time for it. Instead, Jack asked again, "Where are you?"

Joseph sniffed at the other end of the line, and for the first time they could tell that he'd been crying. But he seemed to refortify himself, the question bringing into focus what needed to be done now, of the plan that needed to be made. "I went out the bathroom window and ran into the woods."

"You're in the woods now?" Stacey asked.

"Yeah. I'm facing the school. I can see it through the trees."

There was only one side of the school that bordered a tree line, and it was the side with the soccer field. Stacey knew that on the other side of those trees was a firehouse. "Is there any commotion around the school that you can see?"

"No, not yet."

"Okay," Stacey said. "This is what I want you to do." She changed direction, turning instead toward the firehouse. "Make your way through the woods, away from the school. You'll come to—"

"The firehouse," he interrupted.

"Yeah. We'll pick you up there."

"Okay."

"It's gonna be okay, Joe," Jack said. "We'll be there in three minutes."

"Okay. See you then."

The call ended.

Jack and Stacey exchanged a glance that carried with it an epic novel of unsaid fears. How many people had been sent to the school for their son? Had anyone spotted him running across the soccer field?

Stacey turned the car onto another street, the woods to their left and the fire house coming into view up ahead. "How could they know?"

Jack understood the "they" to mean Fedyenka. Or at least he thought he did.

13

JOSEPH WATCHED THE SCHOOL for a moment longer, realizing that this would be the last time he'd ever see it. And even though the specific urgency of the moment was foremost on his mind, he did manage to allow himself a single commercial break—an idea about his friends, whom he would also never see again. Zane and Charlie, whom he played soccer with. Tommy, Jackson, and Moses, whom he spent every lunch period talking about movies and video games with. Then there was Scott, who was the first to take him under his wing when he'd first arrived halfway through the last school year. And Bryan the Tall with heterochromia, (that was how he liked to introduce himself to people). He was the funniest kid in school, and the nicest. Known for his epic weekend shopping trips (no one knew what his parents did, but the three most popular opinions were that of money launderer, lawyer, and real estate tycoon), everyone in the class looked forward to seeing what new stuff he'd show up with on Monday mornings. And sometimes, he'd even show up with gifts for the whole class. In fact, the pack of trading cards Joseph had in his backpack right now were from such a Monday. Then there was Jessica and Fiona, who sat with him at art; Priscilla, whom he'd had a crush on since day one—

He blinked, the commercial cut short as his thoughts suddenly veered onto an offramp, looping around and heading in another direction.

All his friends were in that building right now. And so was a person with a gun who was looking for him. Mrs. Hatfield had told them he hadn't come in today, but would they buy that, or would they decide to look for themselves? Joseph realized that *everyone* he'd come to care about over the last year and a half might be in danger. What would the killer do now? Would they go classroom to classroom? Would they—

A loud noise erupted from the school. Even with a soccer field positioned between him and the building, the alarm was ear-shattering and insanely aggravating. He'd participated in a few fire drills during his time here, and he knew firsthand that those flashing lights and sirens were enough to scramble a kid's brains for the rest of the day. He'd needed to go to the nurse for some ibuprofen after the last one.

The sound swept over the field, through the trees, and re-bounded off the brick buildings that accompanied the firehouse. And then people began to appear, streaming out of the school and heading toward their assigned spots for roll call. *Well, that's one way to see who's here*, Joseph thought, knowing instinctively that the killer had pulled the fire alarm in order to have the students leave the building.

Suddenly, Joseph began looking around, wondering if the person who had shot Mrs. Hatfield might have an accomplice. Could there be someone else out here in the woods with him? Someone with a rifle and zooming in on his friends' faces at that exact moment? But he dismissed the idea. If that were the case, he wouldn't have made it across the soccer field.

Then he remembered something Tommy had said once as they all stood out on the grass during the last fire drill. "You know what I'd do if I wanted to kill a bunch of people?" He'd asked the question while sweeping his eyes to the woods. And Zane had shaken his head, saying: "It's a gun-free zone, dude. You wouldn't be able to." To which Tommy responded, "Oh, yeah, because if I wanted to kill people, I'd give two turds about breaking *that* law." And then Zane's brow had furrowed as if for the first time realizing how absurd it was that someone would be sure to plan a killing spree in a place where they were permitted to carry a gun. "You want to work your way toward the middle of the crowd," Tommy said. "You know, to protect yourself."

At the time, Joseph hadn't really thought anything of it. After all, given his past experiences and the things he'd seen, he was already accustomed to picking out possible threats and playing out certain daydream scenarios in his head. But now, watching his classmates spill onto the soccer field, all he could think about were Tommy's words, and it was all he could do to keep them from pulling him to his feet and then racing out of the woods to warn them. But that would only serve to give the possible shooter the target they were looking for. *No,* he thought. He'd obey Mom and D ad and get to the firehouse. They'd know what to do.

He jumped to his feet, turned, and sprinted through the woods, the sound of the alarm masking the crunching leaves and snapping twigs beneath his feet.

14

STACEY PULLED INTO THE firehouse parking lot, and they could tell immediately that something was happening. Firefighters in big black pants held up by suspenders were climbing onto trucks, which were starting up and beginning to roll out of the garage.

"What the hell?" Jack said.

Stacey drove to the woods that met the back of the parking lot and parked. She scanned the woods for any sign of Joseph. "Do you see him?"

Jack had turned to watch three red engines pull onto the street, sirens going, their deafening horns blaring. He turned back around and looked into the woods himself. "No." Then he added, "But you might want to do something about your face before he sees you."

She quickly looked into the rearview and started using the sleeve of her shirt to rub the blood off. It was sticky, and she needed to spit into her hands to help wash it away.

"Gross," Jack said. And then, "There." He pointed out the windshield.

He could see Joseph flashing in and out of view as he navigated the trees, making his way toward the parking lot. He was sweeping branches out of his way with his hands, the backpack shifting on his shoulders as he cut left and then right, navigating the terrain like a kick returner reading his blocks.

Jack knew that the events in the mountains almost two and a half years ago had changed the trajectory of what would have been a normal maturation process for his son, turning him into a young man almost overnight. But watching him now, the way he moved, it was almost uncanny. There were no clumsy quirks to his movements. As tall as he'd gotten recently, there was no hint of that lanky "growing into your body" awkwardness that most of the kids his age exhibited. Watching from afar, there was nothing that Jack could discern that would identify Joseph as a boy in puberty. The grace, fluidity, strength, and intention of his movements resembled a twenty-year-old combat soldier more than a fourteen-year-old running scared toward his parents. It both impressed Jack and saddened him.

The sound of the driver's door made him turn his head. Stacey was stepping out of the car. Jack quickly pushed in the MP7's stock and stuck it up under his sweatshirt as he jumped out of the car himself, searching the woods behind Joseph and looking for anyone who might be chasing him.

Stacey hopped over the concrete parking block and went into the trees. Jack walked after them, still cautious and moving awkwardly while trying to conceal the submachine gun. He turned, backpedaling, and looked up and down the street. The blaring siren and the departing trucks attracted the attention of a few passing drivers, but other than that, he spotted nothing that resembled a threat.

Stacey threw her arms around Joseph and squeezed him tight, but Joseph wouldn't let her hold him for more than a couple of seconds. He pushed her off and pointed back toward the school.

"They pulled the fire alarm," he said. "The whole school is being evacuated onto the soccer field." The urgent, almost crazed look in his eyes communicated what he thought that could mean. Of what might happen.

"The fire trucks," Jack said, coming up on them and overhearing. "They're going to the school."

Stacey laid a hand on Joseph's shoulder and looked into his eyes. She no longer needed to bend over to do so. In fact, she had to look up a bit. "Joseph, they're just doing that to find you. They're not interested in—"

The loudest sound Jack had ever heard drowned the rest of her words as a wave of heat blasted through the woods, sending autumn leaves whirling through the air all around them and giving the appearance that the woods themselves were on fire.

The force of the blast knocked them to their knees. When they looked back to the school, they saw only flames.

Jack stood, his ears ringing, and stared out across the soccer field. All the students and teachers who had been standing in rows were now scattered across the grass. Flaming debris was everywhere around them.

Anticipating Joseph's reaction, Jack threw out his arm and grabbed his son as he tried sprinting for his friends. "No!" he yelled, but he wasn't sure if Joseph could hear him. He couldn't hear himself. Stacey came over and helped pull Joseph back toward the car. Finally, Joseph gave in and went with them, looking back over his shoulder, eyes wide with a thousand emotions.

Jack wanted to run onto the field and help too, but just what was it that they'd be running into? The person who killed Samantha could be out there looking for Joseph. Besides, it looked like the explosion had happened on the opposite side of the building and away from the soccer field. And the firetrucks were already pulling up to the school.

By the time he and Joseph reached the car, the ringing in his ears had subsided, and he could hear the screams echoing over the sirens.

15

STACEY STOPPED HALFWAY BACK to the car and looked back to the school. Her heart slammed into her ribs as she herself fought the urge to sprint toward the flames. There were at least a hundred people, mostly kids, scattered between the netted goals on the soccer field. The blast had sent them all to the ground, but now most of them were beginning to rise on unsteady legs.

One teacher was running for the parking lot, waving an arm and urging the group of kids chasing after him to hurry. Other kids were looking for friends and forming into little groups once finding them. She saw a teacher kneeling beside another teacher who wasn't moving. A person she recognized as the gym teacher was running around and kicking away pieces of burning debris.

The firefighters, to their credit, drove straight up over the concrete walkway. The first truck pulled alongside the front of the building, while the second drove right onto the soccer field, all but the driver hopping out before the truck even stopped. They were shouting into their radios while ushering everyone toward the parking lot and away from the building. Stacey watched one of them bend down and scoop up a crying girl. Two more fire trucks pulled onto the scene.

She wasn't needed. And the police would be here soon. She looked to the burning building, ignoring Jack calling out for her from the car, and tried to figure it out. But it didn't make sense. Why would Fedyenka blow up the school? Unless the explosion was meant to explain Joseph's sudden disappearance. Mimic a gas leak, evacuate the building, and just let everyone assume that Joseph didn't make it out?

Only Joseph was right here, so why continue to blow up the building? Maybe there hadn't been a way to stop it? But Fedyenka was too careful and calculating to set a trap that couldn't be unset if circumstances were to change on him.

She took one last look at the burning building and the triage taking place on the soccer field before turning back toward her family.

16

JOSEPH HAD NO IDEA where this car had come from, and would've asked if his parents had stolen it if he even cared. Which, right now, he didn't. The only thing he cared about was his friends.

He pulled out his cell phone and started punching in Priscilla's number. He'd never called it before. Had never even sent a text to her. Never added it to his contacts. And if someone ever asked him why not, he sure wouldn't be able to explain it. He only knew that the number seemed magical, like some secret formula that could decipher all the secrets of the universe. It was a codex, the combination to her heart, every digit a universal truth. It was like *pi*. 3.14. Or maybe it was more like the movie. The black-and-white one he'd watched with Moses for extra math credit. Something to do with Cabala or numerology—*Pi* being the name of God, which all existence was tethered to. Yeah, that was sort of what Priscilla's phone number was to him.

He stared at the numbers. They were just glowing there on the screen. His thumb hovered over the call button. But then, in the last second, he chose not to hit it. Instead, he replaced her number with Tommy's. Why would Priscilla want a text from him right now, anyway? And what would she be able to tell him even if she did answer? He really just wanted to know that she was okay, that they were all okay, and though it would be nice to hear her voice confirming it, it was Tommy who would be most likely to provide the information he was looking for. Tommy who would've found his way to the safest place and from there assess the situation.

He was typing out a text to him when his dad turned in the front passenger seat and grabbed the phone out of his hand.

"What?" Joseph asked.

His dad looked at the screen and then shook his head. "I'm sorry, Joe, you can't. Not yet."

"Why?" He saw his mom's eyes glance up in the rearview.

"It might not be safe," she said.

Joseph didn't know what to say to that. Why wouldn't it be safe to text his friends? Why were they in this strange car? Where were they going? Where was Sam? What happened to the real Monica? Why was his dad hiding a gun under his sweatshirt?

He looked out the window, his mind too overwhelmed to argue or to even ask questions. He saw that his hands were still trembling. He gripped his knees to try to steady them. It didn't work. The time in the mountains, being kidnapped by those men, had steeled him in many ways, and he'd learned a lot about himself over that period of time and the days and months that had followed. But this was different. This was, in some way he didn't yet understand, bigger. And it wasn't just him that he was worrying about, but all his friends, his teachers...

Mrs. Hatfield.

The way her head had whipped back. How she had waved to him, warning him away just an instant before. The sound her skull made when it hit the floor...

"Mrs. Hatfield saved me," he said, watching the trees go by the window. "I was in the bathroom, and when I came out, she was talking to someone. She told them I wasn't in school today and waved me back into the bathroom."

He didn't turn his gaze from the window, but could see in his periphery his parents' heads turn toward each other over the center console. "Then they shot her in the head."

"Joseph," his father started to say, turning in his seat and looking back at him.

Joseph glanced at him and saw real sorrow in his dad's eyes. "Where's Sam?" Joseph asked before his dad could get out whatever it was he was trying to find the words for.

Then the pain already so present in his dad's eyes took on yet another layer of unmistakable sorrow. Whatever resolve Joseph had left shattered. Tears flowed down his face. This couldn't be happening, right? He wanted to hit himself in the head, to force himself to wake up from this awful dream. But he knew it would only give him a headache.

The nightmare was real.

17

JACK'S HEART CRACKED AT the sight of his son crying in the back seat of the car. Because he knew that these tears were more substantial than maybe any he'd ever cried before. After all Joseph had been through, this was different. Different from pretending that a strange man was his father (which he'd been too young to fully appreciate). Different from even the physical pain of steel slicing through his neck (twice). Different than the trauma that came with being kidnapped in the mountains, believing that his dad was dead, and needing to drive a makeshift spear into a man's stomach. No, this pain was a more mature pain, alive in a person who now knew enough to know that he didn't know anything at all. Who had been doing his best to trust his parents and not to ask too many questions. Who, when told his life needed to be uprooted and that he'd have to start all over again in a strange new place with a strange new name, hadn't even complained. But now, this young man, who just wanted to grow up to be a park ranger and whose favorite movie was still *River Wild*, had been hit with an entirely different sort of blow. A blow he hadn't even known existed, let alone could see coming.

His friends—*all* of them.

He needed to know that they were okay. More than anything else in the world, Joe needed to know that his friends had survived. Jack understood that. Hell, if it had been Jack's friends back in tenth grade who had nearly been blown up, he would've done whatever it took to find a way back to them. And Jack allowed himself to see things from that point of view, to remember what it was like back then when friendships were brotherhoods, and such sacred pacts were more intimate than one's relationship with his or her own family. Though in this old flashback scenario, tenth-grade Jack would never have been the target of such an attack. Which was what Joseph needed to understand if he was ever going to forgive his parents for what they were making him do now—to be absent from the very people that every fiber of his being screamed he needed to be with.

Jack looked away from Joseph and turned his attention to Stacey. She was a different story altogether. He could read the determination and the fury in her eyes, all the calculations that were running at high   speed through her brain, but he also saw the softness around the edges of those eyes, the caulk there beginning to crack and come loose a little. It was guilt, he knew. Beneath all the tough CIA training that had her focused on what their next move should be, there was the agonizing thought that this had all happened because of her. Because of her past.

All of it.

Those kids and teachers back at the school, Jack and Joseph in the mountains two years ago, the cruise ship and her mother and Joseph's scar...

Jack reached over and placed a hand on her thigh.

"This needs to end," she said.

He nodded. "Do we call Johnson?"

She shook her head. "Call Monica first. See what the hell happened."

He dialed. Looked up. "No answer."

"Try again."

He tried three more times. "Nothing." He stared ahead at the big green signs that were hanging over the road. "Johnson?"

She thought about it. "Not yet." She turned onto the highway and headed north as raindrops began splashing against the windshield.

18

U2'S *ACHTUNG BABY* ALBUM was playing over the Honda's speakers. The old tape must have been left in the cassette player years ago, back when AA-battery-operated Walkmans and black fuzzy headphones were commonplace. "Mysterious Ways" was on its second run, and once again, Jack couldn't help applying the lyrics to his wife.

She'd obviously fully recovered from the knife wounds Seth Baker had inflicted on her. At least if the dead bodies scattered around their house was any indication. CIA assassin, sure. He got it. Yet, after all these years, he still had trouble letting the fact of it sink in. And though she'd come clean on her ongoing employment with the CIA over the last eight years, he knew she still hadn't told him everything. There were still mysteries there, though he did believe her when she told him that whatever secrets remained weren't worth mentioning and had no bearing on their present or future. Besides, it was all classified. So he had let it go. Again.

Yet, in four songs, he knew that Bono would be singing "Love is Blindness." And of course there was that. Because how could he really trust her after all the lies she'd spun ten years ago? After she kept changing her story to compensate for the things that he was finding out? Like when she acted surprised when he told her in the hospital that Viktoriya had been KGB? Or who wrote the letters and sent the books? Or the fact that she told him she'd killed Fedyenka with a fire extinguisher in Trenton when in fact she'd shot him? He'd never even brought up what Johnson had said over the radio, about the gun used to kill Fedyenka being the same gun that was used to kill her doctor. He didn't even want to know. But Johnson hadn't been correct in his report, anyway, had he? Because Fedyenka certainly wasn't dead, so how could his body have been recovered?

Jack hadn't thought about all this in a long time, but he knew if he were to start now, he would have plenty of holes he no longer could fill with facts—whether he had forgotten them over time or never had them to begin with. And then there was the lie that she'd held on to the longest, one she'd held on to for years—that she, in fact, had always worked for the Central Intelligence Agency. That she'd been recruited and then went to Russia. Jack's brain had nearly exploded at that revelation.

He turned his thoughts away from the rabbit hole of his wife's past as a secret-agent woman and looked back at Joseph. He was still asleep. He'd passed out at some point during the first round of "One."

Jack reached over and slipped his hand underneath Stacey's black hair (she'd begun dying it after the move), gripping the back of her neck. He squeezed his fingers and kneaded his way down to her shoulders. She was tight, stress keeping her shoulders raised while she drove. "You sure about this place?" he asked.

"Yeah. It's off the books. Only me and one other person knew about it, and he's dead."

He wanted to ask what the secret location had been used for, but did he really want to know? Probably not.

The rabbit hole stared at him.

"How much farther?" he asked.

"A few hours."

"You sure you don't want me to try calling Johnson?"

She shook her head. "Not until we can piece together what happened."

"You don't trust him?"

Stacey tilted her head. "I don't know why we can't get in touch with Monica. Why she hasn't called us back. And why hasn't he called *us* yet? He must've heard about the explosion by now."

"I guess it depends on how it's being treated. If they're calling it a gas leak, then national coverage will be light."

"Or maybe he considers himself free from us," Stacey said. "His favor to Donny ten years ago finally having run its course. Or maybe he's in the middle of an operation. Hell, maybe he isn't even in the country."

"Which would mean we're on our own," Jack said. He listened to the Edge work the guitar for a moment, then asked her, "What do you think this is?"

She glanced over at him. "It has to be him. He sent someone to the school to get Joseph, just like before."

"But how would he know about Monica?"

She had no answer to that.

19

THE TAPE ENDED, AND Jack looked at the clock on the dash. They'd been driving north for three hours and were just now coming up on Virginia. Stacey had turned the windshield wipers off about an hour ago, though the sky was still a dreary gray. She took an exit ramp and turned down the first side street they came to. She followed it while keeping an eye out for a secluded space. She found one a few turns later and pulled over onto the side of an empty road surrounded by grass and tall trees.

"Hurry," she said, and she popped the trunk.

Jack jumped out and ran to the back of the car. In it, he found a screwdriver and a stack of license plates. He picked one with a peach on it and quickly got to work unscrewing the old North Carolina plate. It came off easily, since they'd used new screws when hiding the car in the woods last year. He tossed the plate into the trunk and stole a quick look down the road behind them. Still empty.

He screwed the other plate on, not bothering with the bottom two holes, and stood up just as a car appeared on the horizon. It was coming toward them in the opposite lane, and Jack quickly shut the trunk. Then he stepped onto the grass and turned his back to the approaching vehicle, folding both his hands in front of him to make it look like he was taking a piss.

The car passed without slowing down.

Once it disappeared from view, Jack rapped his knuckles on the trunk. He watched through the back window as Stacey leaned forward and hit the trunk release again. Once more, the trunk popped open, and once more he handled the stack of license plates. If they were to get stopped and searched by police, he didn't want to have to explain why they would need a deck of license plates with them. He lifted the spare tire and slid the metal numbers beneath it. Then he pulled off his Panthers sweatshirt and tossed it into the woods. He didn't want anything that could associate him with the Carolinas. He closed the trunk and slid back into the passenger seat.

"Good?" Stacey asked.

"Good." He looked behind them and saw that Joseph was still asleep. He was glad. He wanted to avoid having to explain as much as possible to him—like why they would be switching license plates before crossing state lines. And when he looked back to Stacey, he could tell she was in the same headspace. "You thinking what I'm thinking?" he whispered.

"*The Americans*?" she answered. She was, of course, referencing the daughter of the KGB agents and specifically the series finale.

He nodded.

She put the car in drive and did a U-turn, heading back to the highway. "We'll think of something."

We'd better, Jack thought. They couldn't exactly sit Joseph down and explain that his mother was an ex-CIA assassin who was being hunted by a former SVR acquaintance she'd betrayed. *Oh, and your* other *father was the one who almost cut your head off.* But they had to give him something, and it would have to be compatible with the story they'd given him about maybe one day having to pick up and go—a story about Colt and James and whoever had hired them. And while it was possible that Joe had overheard some of their conversations with Johnson and knew more than he'd ever let on to, there were still things that had never been talked about. Things that he could never find out about. Things like Trenton. *But Stacey is good at fabricating progressive revelations, isn't she?* Jack was able to push that thought away again, but it was starting to get heavier.

Stacey turned back onto the highway and headed into Virginia.

Jack propped an elbow against the door, running his fingers through the short beard he'd sported along with his new identity, and stared out the window. He thought back to the school.

Wondered if anyone had been hurt in the explosion. He thought of Samantha, of her husband living the rest of his life without her. All because they had chosen to move into that district and had enrolled Joe in that school. It *was* their fault.

He swallowed the lump in his throat and turned his attention past Mrs. Hatfield and onto the more mathematical concepts of the morning. Like why Fedyenka would want to blow up the building. If it was simply to cover his tracks, like with the whole "camping accident" he'd planned before, weren't there easier ways to accomplish it? Why not blow up their house? Why try to kill them at home and then kidnap Joe from school? Fedyenka had proved himself resourceful, so why not kill them in their sleep, replace Joe's body with someone else's, and burn the house down? At least that was how Arnold Schwarzenegger had "erased" people when giving new identities to people going into WITSEC.

He closed his eyes and pressed his thumb and forefinger against them, playing the morning out again and again.

Stacey said something.

He opened his eyes and blinked, the pressure leaving white spots floating around his periphery. "What?"

"Just wondering what his plan could've been. For me and Joseph."

He shrugged and closed his eyes again, listening to the rhythmic sound of the engine. He thought of their dog. Of his *Last Starfighter* mug. Of their house.

Again of the kids and teachers.

The next time he looked over at Stacey, he caught the faint reflection off a tear as it slid down her face.

20

STACEY SAW A SIGN ahead for gas and restrooms. She glanced down at the fuel gauge and saw the needle resting on the quarter mark. Not knowing when the next gas station would be, she decided it was best to take advantage of the opportunity now. She could really use a coffee anyway. She signaled and took the offramp, finding the gas station just half a mile later.

She looked over at Jack and saw that he was sleeping. She thought about what he'd done this morning, and had to admit that she was impressed. She had trained him well. Or at least well enough. She had started calling him Jack Wick after the hospital, and damn if he didn't sort of resemble Keanu Reeves with his long black hair and black beard.

She tried to imagine what he might be going through after that mess in the kitchen. She knew he'd killed the man in their garage ten years ago. And he'd told her a little about the guy in the woods he'd tortured the day Joseph was taken. But this morning, he had quite literally shredded a guy's face off with a broken mug. She could only hope that his dreams wouldn't be forever preoccupied with a pair of bulging white eyes staring up at him through a hamburger mask.

She glanced back at Joseph. He was still sleeping too. Jack and Joseph had stayed up late last night, watching the end of a baseball game that went into extra innings. *Probably a good thing,* she thought as she reached beneath the seat and retrieved a wig and a hat. Though she was sure Fedyenka was behind this whole thing, until they heard from Johnson, she wasn't going to take any chances.

She adjusted the wig with one hand while using her other to steer into the station and pull up beside a pump. She chose a pump that put the car out of view from whoever was in the store. They'd be able to see the color of the car and possibly make out the model, but they wouldn't see the license plate or her sleeping family.

She pulled the hat down over the wig and took a look in the rearview. A couple of quick adjustments to the red hair, and she opened the door, stepped out, and walked across the empty lot to the small service station. A bell rang when she opened the door, and an older guy sitting behind the counter looked up ever so briefly before returning his attention to his phone.

She went to the wall of snacks and grabbed a bag of pretzels. Then she got a couple of waters from the refrigerator. She took them to the counter and set them down in front of the attendant. He looked up in time to see her walk away, leaving the items on the counter as she went to the coffee station.

As Stacey filled two paper cups with steaming coffee from a glass pot, she stole a look out into the parking lot. No movement around the car. She put plastic lids on the cups and walked them back to the counter, setting them beside the pretzels and water. "Can I get forty regular on pump two," she said, taking cash out of her pocket.

The man stood, set his phone aside, and started hitting the keys on the register. He didn't say a word, expecting her to see the glowing green digits displayed on the register for herself. She handed over some bills, and he got her change from the drawer.

"Thanks," she said, accepting the coins and dropping them in her pocket. The guy didn't offer her a bag, so she stuffed the two water bottles into her pockets too. She positioned the pretzels under an arm and had both hands wrapped around the coffee cups, about to turn and leave, when she noticed that a small television set was resting on a counter up behind the man's head.

It was one of those old black-and-whites that people used to keep in their kitchens in the late '80s or early '90s. She spotted a digital converter sitting next to it. Not too many people used antennas anymore, let alone on a television set that required a converter, so she figured the program playing must be a local broadcast.

She started to turn, taking one step back and rotating her shoulders toward the door, when suddenly she stopped. Though it was black-and-white and only in standard definition on a small screen, there was no mistaking the picture that just appeared on the TV.

She dropped her head and hurried out of the station. And though she wanted to run, she forced herself to remain calm. She didn't want to leave a lasting impression on the attendant (which was also why she hadn't objected to him not offering her a bag). Even still, she would drive out of the station in one direction before turning around and heading back in another, just in case the guy decided to look up from his phone or someone later had a reason to pull up the surveillance video.

She rested the coffee on the roof of the car while she worked the door. She set the water and pretzels on the dashboard behind the steering wheel, and then got the coffees, leaning in and setting them in the cup holders. As she walked around to the back of the car and unscrewed the gas cap, her mind spun.

It didn't make sense.

She stuck the nozzle in the gas tank and pulled the lever, the digital numbers beginning to climb on the pump. The sound of the front passenger-side window going down made her turn her head. She saw Jack staring at her.

"You okay?" he asked.

"Yeah," she answered. "Got you coffee." She nodded toward the cup holders.

He turned his head to look. "Thanks," he said. Then he looked back and squinted. "Nice hair."

She didn't answer. Instead she just watched the numbers on the pump, allowing them to draw her into a sort of trance.

What the hell is going on? she thought.

21

JACK LOOKED OUT THE window and to the autumn palette above them. Stacey had them traveling over canopy-covered back roads, navigating the Pennsylvania mountains with the precision of someone all too familiar with the area. Jack wondered just how many times she'd visited this place that was "off the books." Again, something he probably didn't want to know, and again he hammered down the nails coming loose on the boards he'd secured over the rabbit hole.

The red, orange, and yellow fall colors were highlighted in high definition by the early evening sun. Under normal circumstances, he'd find himself moved by the glory of it, but the images of all those scared kids running for the parking lot this morning had inoculated him against its usual magic. "Back in the Poconos," he mumbled.

Stacey glanced at him, but didn't say anything. She'd been doing a lot of that, it seemed, keeping quiet. It was starting to bother him, but he figured she was just trying to process all the day's shit herself. She slowed the Accord and turned down a gravel path.

"This is it," she whispered.

"What is it?" Joseph asked, leaning forward in the back seat. He was growing more and more agitated with each passing hour. He desperately wanted to know that his friends were okay, and why they were driving to some secret place in the mountains. He wanted to know who had killed his dog and who had killed Mrs. Hatfield. The vague promise that things would be explained to him in greater detail once they got to where they were going had supported the weight of his curiosity for a little while, but now it was like melting ice cracking beneath him.

"Somewhere safe," she said.

Joseph didn't ask any more questions. He didn't have to. He'd asked them over and over in the hour after the gas station, and the unanswered questions were still printed on his eyeballs like big neon signs, flashing and flickering in the car's interior. At first, his questions came with desperation, tears, and pleadings, wanting to understand what was happening, where they were going, what any of this had to do with his classmates, what had happened to Sam and their house, and a frenzy of the like. But over the last five hours, his silence had become even more deafening, those neon lights almost unbearable. Jack knew his son was about to explode. He had to get out of the car soon.

Stacey pointed ahead.

A cabin appeared at the end of the road. Jack frowned, his brow furrowing into Ws as he looked around.

"What?" Stacey asked, noticing.

"Nothing," he mumbled, though he thought there was something strangely familiar about the place.

Stacey turned off the path and rolled up onto the grass in front of the house. She put the car in park and turned the key. After listening to the hum of the motor for hours on end, the sudden silence was unnerving. Still in their seats, they looked around, taking in the cabin and the surrounding area until, finally, Stacey opened the door and stepped outside.

Jack looked back at Joseph. "You okay?"

"Guess." He flung the back door open and stepped out, too.

Jack took a deep breath and joined them.

Standing there with the evening breeze blowing through his hair and watching the leafy branches rock back and forth, he again had the strangest sense of déjà vu. He turned his head and watched as Stacey walked off toward the tree line, to an old woodshed that looked to be rotted and ready to collapse in the next big storm. When she reached it, she bent over beside it and lifted a rock.

Jack blinked.

No...

He looked around again. Could see a lake through the trees. *No way.* Stacey was walking to the cabin now, a key in her hand. She used it to unlock the door.

Jack swallowed, and his head seemed to spin for a second. He felt dizzy.

Joseph was about to enter the cabin after Stacey when he looked back at him. "What?" There was still an edge to his voice, but Jack could tell by the look on his face that his son was genuinely concerned.

He blinked. He couldn't speak. Couldn't say a word.

Stacey came back to the doorway. "Jack? What's wrong?"

He slowly moved his gaze from one end of the cabin to the other. Then, without answering either of them, he walked up the stairs and pushed past Stacey, entering the house himself. He stood in the middle of the room and looked around. To the fireplace. To the window. To the rocking chair. He looked at Stacey.

"What?" she asked.

"This is the place that no one knew about but you and one other dead person?"

Her eyes narrowed, and she stepped close to him. "Yeah. Why?"

He looked past her and into the small kitchen. He ran a hand through his hair, slightly aware that maybe Joseph shouldn't be hearing this, but not really caring at the moment. "Because this is the place Johnson took me to when he wanted me to lie low."

She laughed.

His eyes snapped back to her.

"No," she said. "It might be similar. Another small house in the Poconos, but—"

"No. This is the *same* house."

"That's not possible."

"What are you talking about?" Joseph asked, still standing by the door.

They both turned toward him, hesitated, and then in unison answered, "Nothing."

"Yeah. Nothing," Joseph repeated, and he wagged his head in disgust. "Is there a bathroom in this place?"

"Joseph—" Stacey started, but Jack put a hand on her shoulder and drew her attention back to him.

"How could Johnson have known about this place?"

"He couldn't," she said. "No one did."

"Who owns it?"

"Now?"

"Now, then, how did you find out about it? Johnson said it belonged to a friend of a cousin or something."

"Jack," she said softly, eying Joseph. "I think you're mistaken." She touched his arm.

But he shook it off and pointed at the rocking chair in the corner. "I moved that rocking chair into the kitchen"—he pointed into the kitchen with his other hand—"and sat in it, watching a bear out back."

Joseph looked up through a lock of hair that was hanging over his left eye. "The bear that you told me about was *here*?"

But Jack didn't know how to answer his son right now. What to say and what not to say. He stared at Stacey until he saw belief start to creep into her eyes. She blinked and stepped away, looking out the window and into the woods.

"Joseph," Jack said, "can you give Mom and me a minute? Go see if the beds have sheets or whatever."

Jack knew that he'd just offended his son's sense of fourteen-year-old prominence by treating him like he belonged at the little kids' table, and Joseph confirmed as much by shooting him a look of utter contempt. Though beyond the contempt, Jack could also make out a twist of blame. On some level, their son understood that his friends had been put in harm's way because of his parents. All the secrets and lies over the years were swimming in his eyes—eyes that had not so long ago looked on his father with admiration and unquestioning trust. Now they projected anger, skepticism, and accusation.

"Look, we'll talk to you about all this. It's something that we should have talked about before, but..." He didn't know how to say it. "Just give us a couple of minutes, okay? Then we'll fill you in on what we think might be going on. Because, honestly, Joseph, whether you believe it or not, we really don't know what's happening."

Joseph's eyes narrowed. He pulled the collar of his T-shirt down, exposing the twin scars cutting across his neck. "Are we finally going to talk about this too?" And he turned and walked out of the room, leaving Jack and Stacey standing there utterly speechless.

Stacey covered her mouth with an unsteady hand.

"Shoot," Jack said, staring down the hall.

Stacey's eyes turned to glass.

"We need to tell him now. It's not fair," Jack said.

"And what are we going to tell him?"

"I don't know. Didn't you come up with a story? You knew this day would come." But he could tell from her face that she hadn't. "Shoot," he whispered again. "Fine. We'll figure that out later." He walked to the fireplace, rubbing his temples. "What could it mean that Johnson knows about this place?"

"There's something else," she said.

The way she was looking at him told him that it was something he should probably brace himself for. "What?"

"When I went into the gas station..." She looked down the hall and lowered her voice. "The TV was on. The news was reporting on the explosion."

"What were they saying?" He thought she was going to whisper the number of casualties, and that the number would be far worse than they'd feared. But what she said instead, he could never have prepared himself for.

"They're saying it was a bomb. And that you're the bomber."

22

JACK STOOD STARING OUT over the lake. He was attempting to work through the day once more, this time with the new added ingredient Stacey had just dropped into the mix. But he didn't even have the questions to the answers he was looking for. How could he? Without the values of x, y, and z—at least some of that being Stacey's past—how could he even begin to guess at what was happening? All he knew for sure was that someone wanted him dead—again. And that someone of ill will had gone to the school looking for Joseph.

He blinked and remembered seeing an eagle swoop down and snatch a fish out of the lake the last time he'd been here. It seemed like forever ago. Another life even. So much had happened since then, and when he looked back on his old self, pulling him up and standing him in front of a mirror, he saw an old acquaintance, someone he knew well enough, sure, but it was no longer him that was staring back. The things his younger version thought and felt were so different than the way he saw things now. He'd been a scared, frail man back then, plagued by feelings of inadequacy and doubt. Now he was strong, well trained, and had all the confidence of a man set on fire with purpose. These two versions of himself, forced nose-to-nose with each other by this place that seemed to be a hole in time, presented a very strange juxtaposition, and it left him feeling a little unhinged.

The setting sun caught the surface of the water and ignited a line of orange fire racing across it. He squinted, holding the display in his gaze as long as he could before looking back to the cabin. He could see Joseph sitting in the rocking chair, watching him through the window. Jack forced a smile. Joseph looked away.

Jack sighed and ran a hand through his beard. He didn't know how they were going to get out of this one. The plan had been to hunt down Fedyenka and take him out once and for all, but in the time since the Appalachian incident, they hadn't even managed to locate him, let alone put an operation together to eradicate him. Apparently, not even the FBI or CIA could find him. He was a ghost. At least until the book appeared in Joseph's locker. And then, instead of going after him, they'd ended up being the ones having to run.

Johnson was still looking into things, of course. Trying to nail down Fedyenka's whereabouts and promising to let them know if ever he found something, but there hadn't been anything. At least nothing that had been passed along to them. Nothing at all.

But how could he have found them without any of Johnson's people knowing? There had been checkpoints and other precautions in place that were supposed to have alerted them to anyone caught sniffing around, right? And since they hadn't heard from Johnson, they'd assumed that none of those safeguards had been tripped. Which meant what?

And the bombing... Again, he couldn't make sense of it. Emptying the building in order to find Joseph, fine. But then to blow up the building? Just to set him up? But that would make him a giant piece of whatever puzzle this was, and he couldn't fathom why anyone would find him that important. Unless it was about Stacey, and he was just collateral. He had no doubt that had things gone the way they were supposed to this morning, the authorities would've found all kinds of "evidence" in their house after the so-called "FBI raid" left him dead. But he wasn't dead, so how would that change their narrative?

Narrative.

If local news stations were already broadcasting his picture, then this had to have been something created and packaged well in advance, able to be leaked to the media in the immediate aftermath. And who would have the ability to make that happen? Did he actually believe that Fedyenka could be the one responsible for getting his face all over CNN just hours after the explosion?

It didn't feel right.

He thought about everyone he'd ever known now seeing his face on the news, the suspect in a school bombing. What would the people he'd met at Joseph's school be thinking? He couldn't even imagine. He was tempted to get in touch with them, to tell them it wasn't true. He wanted to scream out that he was innocent. That he didn't kill any kids. But getting in touch with anyone right now and from here would not be a good idea. How long before the media reported their real names? Did the script the media was being fed go that deep?

He turned and started walking back to the cabin.

23

JOSEPH LOOKED AWAY FROM his father and leaned forward in the rocking chair. He got to his feet and walked across the old wooden floor, back to the bedroom where he'd left his backpack. Thank God he'd brought his MP3 player to school with him this morning. He didn't listen to it nearly as much as he used to now that he was able to listen to most music on his cell, but there was a playlist on the MP3 player that he'd wanted to listen to today, and a song he'd hoped to be able to share with Priscilla.

He heard his mother in the bathroom as he passed it, and wondered just what his parents were involved in and how deep. He'd picked up enough over the last two years to know that there was something his parents had been involved in years ago, back when he was a boy. Or maybe even earlier. He wasn't sure. All he had were pieces of past conversations that when put together seemed to allude to some greater long-reaching story arc. But though they seemed to be pieces from the same box, he couldn't get any of them to connect to each other.

There were the conversations his kidnappers had had around him—someone hiring them to take him and to kill his dad. And then there was that FBI guy who had helped them, and the stuff he'd said about Russians and the KGB and Cold War agents still hiding out in the mountains. But what could that possibly have to do with his parents? With him?

And then came the flashbacks, those faint memories of when he was four. Of that guy who talked like Grandmom and who he had to pretend was his dad. Looking back on it now, it seemed so ridiculous that he wondered if he was even remembering it right, or if it had all gotten muddled with weird dreams somewhere along the way. After all, he barely even remembered his grandmom. He remembered asking his dad about her while they were camping the night before he was kidnapped. He'd asked why they didn't have any pictures of her around the house. He hadn't realized at the time that most family photos had been destroyed when their house burnt down.

But then there was that too, wasn't there? His mom and dad had told him that their old house burning down was an accident, but was it? None of this stuff seemed like anything his parents wanted to talk about, so he never brought it up.

If Grandmom was Russian, and the guy talked like her, then he was probably Russian too. And if Grandmom was Russian, then that would mean that his mom was Russian. And so was he. All Joseph knew about Russia was that they'd invaded Ukraine. It was always part of the current-events stuff they watched in class (his dad said not to believe 99% of what he saw on the news, but he was usually drowning out the anchor's voice with daydreams of Priscilla anyway). The movies he'd seen always made the Russians look like America's archenemy. But again, what would any of that have to do with his family and with everything that had happened in the mountains?

And then there was the whole Monica business, the strange car they'd just spent most of the day in, this weird cabin that seemed to have his dad really confused, Mrs. Hatfield being shot with a silencer just like in the movies, and the guns that he knew were in the bag his parents had carried into the house from the trunk.

He remembered seeing his mother fight with Seth and later thinking, "Whose mom can fight like that?" His parents were acting like they were characters in *Patriot Games* or *Homefront* with Jason Statham, both of which he'd seen on TBS. Were his parents ex-secret agents? Was that why his dad always acted so shady whenever they were in public? Because he was looking for spies? They'd told him that the people who had been behind his kidnapping might someday try again—which was the reason they'd moved to that new house in North Carolina, why he had to go by Brian. But whenever he'd ask why these people would want him, or why they wanted to kill his dad, they'd always found a way to change the subject.

But that was going to change now. He wasn't a little boy anymore. He was old enough to know the truth. No more lies.

He sat on the bed. The sheets smelled like dust, but he didn't care. He pulled his MP3 player out of the bag and stuck the headphones into his ears. He didn't like using the earbuds because they never stayed in his ears, but he had them with him today because he'd planned on letting Priscilla use one while he used the other, his cheek brushing against hers. At least that had been the dream. Now he wasn't even sure if she was alive. And the not knowing, this waiting, was absolutely killing him. His mom and dad had said they'd have a plan worked out by morning, so he'd listen to his music and try to sleep through the wait time.

Tomorrow, his parents had better have answers for him. He was done being left out of the loop. This was his life, and he had a right to know why it kept trending back toward shit.

He lay back and closed his eyes, a bass line thrumming in his head as the setting sun fell behind a cloud and plunged the room into shadow. He wished his dog were here with him.

24

IT WAS DARK OUT, and the clouds that had come sliding over the late afternoon sky from the west had brought with them more cold rain. It was still raining five hours later, lightning flashing in the distance, thunder sounding ten Mississippis later.

Jack sat rocking in the rocking chair and staring out the window, watching the flashes of light illuminate the forest as his brain tried to escape the hamster wheel it was trapped in. All the dots he tried connecting just formed ideas that ended up chasing their own tails. He needed to find a piece of information that could break the loop.

Stacey was leaning against the stone fireplace. They had a little fire going, and it was casting shifting light across the room. She had a glass of wine in her hand and was staring deep into the dancing flames. The wine had been in the back of an otherwise empty cabinet, and once again Jack had to deflect thoughts of what its presence implied. He wondered if the bottle had been there ten years ago. If she'd been here since. He knew someone had, because there were a few differences from the last time he was here. But that was all part of the past, and he had already accepted the fact that Stacey's past was a minefield best left alone. Even when that past was his past too. The rabbit that lived in this rabbit hole was that killer rabbit from *Monty Python and the Holy Grail.* "Run away! Run away!" his survival instincts kept telling him whenever the bloody-nosed rabbit tried to lure him down into its labyrinth.

Joseph was asleep in the back bedroom, or at least had his eyes closed with his earbuds in. The boy wasn't happy with them, and

Jack knew it was because he'd grown tired of all the deflections and half-truths. He needed answers.

"He must be starving," Stacey muttered after taking another sip of the red liquid.

Jack looked away from the rain streaking down the windowpane. "There's a place not far from here. Or at least there used to be." Though she probably knew that, didn't she? Maybe that was where she'd take her late-night—

He punched the rabbit in the face.

"Your long hair and beard won't be enough to disguise you," she said.

He remembered his run-in with the guy behind the counter at Ma's. If the guy was still there and believed what CNN was reporting, then he'd probably take it upon himself to put an end to him right then and there. Though him believing anything CNN had to say seemed rather unlikely given their conversation ten years ago. "We'll figure something out," he said.

Her eyes escaped the fire and met his. "We need to tell him."

He looked at her with sympathy. "Tell him what?"

She shrugged. "Everything."

"Everything?"

"Redactions, of course, but we can tell him about my parents, about me working with Vadim and Fedyenka, about the CIA."

"About how you had me thrown off a cruise ship to save him?"

She paused. "No, we'll have to edit that part."

"The knife?"

She nodded, and the fire caught the water forming in her eyes. "Okay."

Another flash of lightning was followed by thunder. It was louder, closer.

Stacey set the glass of wine on the mantel and stepped into the middle of the room. She motioned for Jack to come to her, and he did. They held hands and stared into each other's eyes, realizing that their relationship with their son was about to change, that his world would be forever altered with the information they would be giving him. Would it change his course? Send him down a completely different path than the path he was on now? Instead of becoming a park ranger, would he become a journalist? A spy himself? Would he find some kind of inspiration in it, or might it tear his sense of reality apart and set him on a much darker path?

They read all this in each other's eyes.

"It's his choice to make," Jack said. "I guess we should err on the side of truth."

Stacey blinked, and a tear fell down her cheek. Jack brushed it away with his thumb.

"I was starting to think the day might never come," she said. "Guess we're getting old."

"Our son is fourteen."

"How'd that happen?"

"I have no idea."

But there was an even bigger problem than introducing Joseph to the vault of family secrets, and that was what they had to spend the remainder of the night trying to figure out.

"How the hell are we going to get out of this?" he asked, shifting over to a lane that was concerned with living long enough to even have that conversation with their son.

She shook her head, not saying anything, and all they could hear was the crackling wood in the fireplace and the rain striking the roof and the windows.

He sighed. "How long do you think we can stay here?"

"I don't know."

"You said nobody knows about it, right?"

"Well, apparently Johnson does, if you've got the right cabin. And if Johnson knows, then we have to assume that the FBI knows too."

It still didn't make sense that Johnson could have known about this place. It meant that he'd known about Stacey long before he showed up at his house as a favor for Donny. And it meant he'd been lying to them all this time. Yet, he had certainly helped save them in the mountains.

"Do you have somewhere else in mind?" Jack asked.

She thought about it. "We could always head to Alaska. Live off the grid."

He frowned. "How would we do that?"

She stepped away from him and walked back to the fireplace. She began running her hands over the masonry, feeling the rocks, slipping her fingers between the cracks. And then she stopped on one, gripped it, and pulled. It came free, leaving a gap in the stonework. She looked back at him and winked.

He stepped forward.

Reaching her hand into the empty space, she came away with a Ziploc bag. She tossed it to him.

Jack caught the plastic and walked it over to the fire, kneeling before it and holding the bag up to its light.

Passports. Social Security cards. Cash. Credit cards.

He looked up at her as he opened the bag, shock on his face. "Who are you, Jason Bourne?"

He pulled out the passports and flipped them open. Pictures of the three of them. And not from that long ago either. Which answered the question as to when the last time she'd been here was. He looked at the issuance dates. They were only two years old. She must have done it soon after getting out of the hospital. He looked up at her, thankful she'd had the foresight to plan for this, but hating that the secrets hadn't ended after all.

He glanced back at his picture. "Miles Viola," he read aloud. He flipped to hers. "And Katherine Viola." He shuffled the blue books and opened the third. "And their son, Mark Viola." His first inclination was to doubt the believability of the names. But names were names. Nobody ever responded to an introduction by saying, "Are you sure you didn't just make that up?"

He pushed the passports back into the bag and slid out the credit cards. They had even earlier issue dates, going back three years. The names on them belonged to the Violas. He put them back, glanced at the Social Security cards, and then thumbed through the stack of cash.

"Seven hundred," she said.

He frowned. The stack of hundreds was only about five inches. Seven hundred *thousand* would be seven thousand bills.

"There's more," she said, reading his confusion.

Jack stood and handed her the bag back. She took it in one hand while reaching her other back into the hole and up into the masonry. She pulled out another plastic bag filled with cash.

"You are Jason Bourne," he said.

She put it all back and replaced the stone, then stared at him in front of the fire. The heat of the flames warmed their jeans. They embraced.

"Making Joseph start over with another identity..." He brushed the back of her head.

"I know. But what other option do we have? The whole country is after us. What can we do?"

"I suppose we can't turn ourselves in and explain everything."

"Not without knowing who's behind it."

Jack watched the fire flicker in her eyes, but didn't bite on that thought. Evidently, she was second-guessing the degree of Fedyenka's involvement too. Instead, he asked, "When do we leave?"

"First thing," she said.

"Anyone at the Agency know about this little contingency plan of yours?"

"No. If I ever needed it, I figured it would be to get away from the Agency."

He raised an eyebrow and cocked his head to the left a little.

"It's possible," she said, reading his mind. "Though I don't know what reason they'd have."

Thunder rattled the windows.

She stepped back out of his arms. "Jack, I'm—"

She stopped, and her eyes shot sideways toward the kitchen. "What?"

But she didn't answer. She was listening.

Rain lashed the side of the cabin, the wind picking up and driving it in sheets. How she could hear anything over that, Jack had no idea, but he found himself going for the MP7 he'd left leaning against the rocking chair.

Stacey reached for the Glock in her waistband.

She stepped across the room and put her back against the wall, beside the kitchen doorway. She looked down the hall to the bedrooms. Everything was quiet. She motioned for Jack to check the front door.

Jack's heart began pounding in his chest, and he quickly crossed the room and took a position next to the door. He tried the handle, making sure it was locked. Then he turned away from the door and faced the window beside it. He put the suppressed barrel of the Heckler & Koch between the pane and the curtain and slowly moved the curtain away so that he could get a glimpse outside. But he couldn't see anything. Though his mind had no problem creating a scene in which a strike team—CIA, SVR, contract killers, FBI, the local residents led by Ma's finest patrons, it didn't matter—was moving into position.

The cabin scene from *Public Enemies* flashed through his mind, and he wondered how long they would last in a shootout. Probably not as long as the Dillinger gang had. The people coming after them had a lot more than Tommy guns at their disposal.

He looked back toward Stacey. "Anything?" he whispered.

She shook her head and motioned for him to come back to her.

"Stand over there in the hallway," she said, nodding to the wall opposite her. "Stay away from the windows and cover me."

He stepped across her and put his back against the hallway wall, positioned at her eleven o'clock. He was no longer in view of any of the windows, but with just a single sidestep to his left, he'd have an unobstructed view of the small kitchen.

Stacey crouched and began making her way to the back door. There was a lit candle on the stove reflecting off the windows, making it impossible to see out of them. When she got to the door, she gripped the handle and prepared to open it.

"What are you doing?" Jack mouthed to her, craning his neck so that he could see through the doorway. And then they froze.

A noise from outside.

Someone, or something, was walking up the steps. They could hear it over the weather.

Stacey raised two fingers to her own eyes and then pointed to the back of the house.

Jack nodded and quickly went down the hall and stepped into the room Joseph was sleeping in, gun raised and sweeping over the two windows. Nothing. Just Joseph lying on his stomach, his head turned toward the wall. One of the earbuds had fallen out of his ear, and Jack could hear faint music coming from it. He hurried back to Stacey and gave her a thumbs-up. He raised the

HK and crouched low, aiming at the door, hand flexing on the foregrip.

She took a deep breath and swung the door open just as a bolt of lightning ripped open the sky and lit up the yard all the way back to the tree line and the shed.

The silhouette of a person flashed in the doorway, both hands open and raised.

"Don't shoot," the figure said.

Jack nearly crapped himself and thought it was a miracle Stacey hadn't shot the figure out of pure reflex. Instead, she stood and stepped back, allowing the figure to step into the kitchen but ready to put a bullet in his forehead if needed. Jack saw her glance behind the stranger, looking for shadows running around in the rain, before telling the person to close the door.

The person obeyed, twisting at the waist and closing the door with one hand while still keeping the other raised.

"Step forward," Stacey said.

Again, the figure obeyed and took a step farther into the kitchen. Dripping wet, the person slowly pulled the hood off his head. The candlelight wasn't enough to make sense of the scene, so Jack clicked on the flashlight he'd attached to the gun's side rail. He pointed the beam right at the person's face.

The man squinted and turned away from the light, but there was no mistaking who it was.

"Holy shit," Jack said.

It was Johnson.

25

"HEY, JACK," JOHNSON SAID. Then he looked at Stacey, who still had her Glock trained on him. "What the hell? I thought you'd be happy to see me."

Jack stepped into the kitchen, and while his gun wasn't aimed directly at Johnson, it was close enough to be of concern. "We were just talking about you," he said.

"Ask and you shall receive." He held out his hands and smiled. Water was dripping off his face, off his clothes. A puddle was forming on the floor around his feet.

"That wasn't what we were asking," Stacey said. She motioned with the gun. "Go take a seat by the fire."

He nodded and walked out of the kitchen, past Jack. As he did so, he stole a glance down the hallway. "Where's Joseph? Is he okay?"

"No," Stacey said, following behind him. "You don't get to ask questions yet."

But Jack could tell that in the split second between Stacey's answer and the explanation for it, Johnson had caught the impression that something bad had happened to Joseph, and genuine concern filled his eyes.

Johnson went to the fireplace and held his hands to it, palms out, absorbing its heat. He looked around the room and then looked at Jack.

More thunder.

"Friend of a cousin, huh?" Jack asked, referring to the obvious lie Johnson had fed him about the cabin ten years ago.

Johnson looked at Stacey. The gun was still pointed at him. He sighed. Then he looked around. "Not exactly."

"So what is this place? How did you know about it ten years ago?" Jack asked.

Johnson stared into the flames as he answered, "I was monitoring Stacey. That's how I came to know about this place. You needed a place to lie low, and because of Stacey's situation at the time, I knew no one would be here."

Stacey stepped forward. "What do you mean you were monitoring me?"

Jack frowned. "You didn't even know she existed until Donny contacted you on my behalf..."

Johnson ran a hand through his wet hair and then shook the water off his hand. He pulled off his jacket. "That's not entirely accurate."

"What do you mean?" Jack felt the floor begin to move beneath his feet.

Johnson looked at him and nodded toward the rocking chair. "Why don't you sit down before you fall down, Jack."

"Just keep talking," he answered.

"You remember what Agent Lowry says in *Conspiracy Theory*?"

Jack's eyes narrowed. "Don't tell me that I'm your Jerry Fletcher, that—"

He waved him off. "Don't worry, you're no MK-Ultra CIA assassin." Then he turned his head and looked at Stacey. "Stacey, on the other hand..."

Stacey returned his stare. "You watch other agencies. You said that before. You're part of some Overwatch program."

"Let's just say it's a pretty safe bet that you've never heard of the agency I work for," Johnson said.

"You were watching the CIA?" Jack asked.

"We had our eyes on Stacey from the beginning. Thought there was a good possibility that she might end up in some asshole's black op."

"From the beginning?" Jack asked, wondering just when he thought the beginning had started for her.

He nodded.

Stacey lowered the gun.

"If you were watching them, then why didn't you stop them?" Jack asked. "In Trenton."

"We knew they had planned something, but we didn't know when. We were late."

Stacey smirked at that. "No, you weren't."

Johnson blinked.

"You let it happen. It was the only way you could nail them. You couldn't step in to prevent it without revealing your identity, and stopping a crime from taking place would be a hell of a lot messier for you than proving who was behind one."

Johnson didn't say anything.

"Is that true?" Jack asked. "Did you know about it and let it happen?"

"We couldn't reveal ourselves until we had enough to give the other agencies. We were never going to be the ones in front of the cameras, bringing them down. We would make sure that damning evidence found its way to certain government officials, and they'd lead the charge. That's how our little group works. It's harder to catch people when they know they're being watched."

They all stood in silence, listening to the rain.

Jack went and sat. Then he asked, "What about Donny? He said you owed him."

Johnson shrugged. "We selected him because he was close to you. Just in case anything happened and we needed a viable way in. He wasn't the only one, just the only one we needed."

Jack leaned forward and put his head in his hands. Then he stood and pointed at him. "No, I saw your face when Donny was killed. You cared about him."

"I did. I liked Donny a lot. But our friendship wasn't organic. Or at least not our meeting."

"What about your call into that radio station?" Jack asked.

"Like I said, our agency doesn't exist."

"So you needed to get the information out in some other way that would make people look closer."

"The White House and the intelligence agencies monitor that particular station very closely."

"I bet," Jack muttered. "So you didn't get reassigned to Arizona?"

"No. At that point, I had to put distance between us. I couldn't have you thinking I was right around the corner to answer your every question. Not when other eyes had taken an interest in you."

"And two years ago?" Stacey asked.

"You called me, and I came to help. Nothing more than that."

"For someone who doesn't exist, you sure got a lot of people to help you out on a moment's notice."

"Oh, I exist." He reached into his pocket and pulled out his ID. Flipped it open.

FBI.

"So you're a double agent?" she asked.

"Let's just say that a select few from various initials are invited into the babysitter's club."

Jack began rocking back and forth in the chair. "An undercover internal affairs?"

"Sort of."

"You lied to us," Jack said.

"First of all," Johnson answered, "if you want to make this about who's been lying to whom over the last ten years…" He nodded his head toward Stacey.

"Okay," Stacey said, "can you please just tell us what the hell is going on?"

But Jack stopped rocking and held up a hand, signaling for them to wait a second. "How did you know we were here?"

Johnson nodded toward Stacey again.

"What does that mean?" she asked.

"I tagged you."

"What?" She reached for the back of her neck.

Johnson shook his head. "Your back. Beneath the mole by your left shoulder."

"Holy shit," she said. "When the hell did you do that?"

"The first time?"

She blinked.

"Well, the last time was while you were sleeping on the plane."

"The plane?"

"The night we flew to the mountains."

"Why did—" But she fell silent. If Johnson's little team of counterintelligence spies had been chipping her two years ago, then they must've known she was still running ops. And she didn't want to have that conversation in front of Jack. Didn't want to get into that whole thing with Senator Newell either. She'd told Jack all she thought he needed to know, choosing to edit out certain details, and as far as she knew, Johnson had kept what he'd seen at the senator's house to himself as well. There was no need to jeopardize that discretion here and now.

"Does anyone else know we're here?" Jack asked, getting things back to the present.

"Anyone else who knew about Stacey and this cabin, or that we were tracking her, is dead."

"What do you mean?" Stacey asked.

"I mean that my team is being systematically taken out."

Jack stood. "Monica?"

"She wasn't part of my team in any official capacity. She actually was retired and just glad to return a favor. But it didn't matter. She got stuck in traffic on her way to pick up Joseph. Shot in the back of the head. Tap behind the left ear. Whoever shot her walked right up to the car."

Jack immediately thought of someone dressed as a police officer or a road crew worker. Hell, a crossing guard. In any event, it meant that not only did whoever was behind this know the intimate details of their plan, they'd managed to make quite a large operation out of it. Jack's earlier doubts concerning Fedyenka's involvement began to resurface, the men at their house with "FBI" on their vests pulling the sticks out of the Fedyenka theory like a Kerplunk game. "So what do you know?" he asked.

Johnson eyed the glass of wine sitting on the mantel. "Have any more of that?"

26

JACK WONDERED JUST HOW many people in his life he was going to find listed on the scrolling credits of this alternate version of the *Conspiracy Theory* movie he was in, where he was Jerry, Agent Johnson was Agent Lowry, and Stacey was...Alice? Or maybe Jonas. No, she might have been a spook under the direction of a Jonas, but no Jonas herself (regardless of what the rabbit's muffled voice might be trying to suggest from beneath the boarded-up hole).

They were in the kitchen, sitting on some metal folding chairs that Stacey had pulled out of a closet.

"Tell me again what happened at your house this morning," Johnson said.

The story had come out fast and in pieces the first time. Now they both took their time, reconstructing a play-by-play narrative. Jack started with his pulling onto their street and noticing a suspicious-looking van across from their house after dropping Joseph off at school and stopping for breakfast. He said he'd texted Stacey, at which point Stacey interjected her own timeline, telling of the Audi that had picked her up on her way back.

"They were definitely trying to kill me," Jack said. "But the only reason Stacey was there was because I called her back. They couldn't have planned on her being there."

"Which means they either had other plans for me," she said, "or they were going to take me out another way."

"Or they didn't know one way or another who, if anyone, would be home. You're assuming whoever this was had been watching you for some time," Johnson said.

Stacey nodded. "That's our assumption."

"Anyway," Jack said, "they sent someone to the school, pretending to be Monica."

"Which means you have a leak," Stacey said.

"So it seems."

"So who's behind it? Fedyenka?"

"Maybe," said Johnson.

Jack asked, "Who else, then?"

Johnson glanced down at the tip of his shoe as he wiggled his foot. "We have an idea what Fedyenka's been up to."

Stacey leaned forward. "What?"

"Since when?" Jack asked, suddenly indignant. After all, Johnson had promised to relay any such developments.

"We never found him, but the raid on that compound did lead to some interesting discoveries."

Jack knew he was referring to the leftovers of the Illegals Program who had apparently formed some sort of KGB base of operations in Appalachia. Stacey had told him about the raid she'd witnessed from the helicopter on their way to find him and Joseph. Johnson said that the calls made to her, passing along instructions, had come from within it. "Such as?" Jack asked, putting his anger aside.

Johnson paused.

"What?"

He sighed. "Over the last five years, and maybe even longer, he's been recruiting former agents."

"Former agents?" Stacey asked, skeptical. "KGB agents? From the Illegals Program? What agents?"

"Appalachia was one of his recruiting grounds."

"Recruiting for what?" Jack asked.

Johnson leaned back and rubbed his jaw with the tip of his fingers. Whatever he was about to say, he realized it was going to sound unbelievable.

Stacey pressed. "What?"

"He seems to be selling a resurrected imperial Russia. Or at least some version of it."

Stacey laughed. If she'd had wine in her mouth, she would have spit it all over Johnson's face. She doubled over in her chair, clutching her stomach.

Jack looked at Johnson, and Johnson shrugged.

Stacey wiped tears from her eyes. It wasn't a totally outlandish concept, there were always political proponents of such an idea, but to associate Fedyenka with such a movement was like trying to imagine the chairman of the Federal Reserve spearheading the "Audit the Fed" movement. "You're trying to tell me that Fedyenka wants to replace the Federation with a monarchy? Put a tsar back in St. Petersburg?"

"That's what he's selling, though we don't believe he's serious about it."

Jack looked at Stacey. "Is that what the *Anastasia* poster was about in the hospital?"

Stacey laughed again and then caught herself, looking instead to Johnson. "Is it?"

"Maybe."

"So if he's not serious about it, then he's what?—using it as a political platform to..."

"Disrupt the next election. At least that was our theory. Levy enough power away from the current administration to allow for the entrance of a new one."

"One that he will be part of," Jack interjected.

"Or has control over," Johnson agreed.

"Doesn't he need a Romanov heir?"

"Maybe, maybe not. I don't know. But from what we can tell, he's claiming to have a candidate who will generally be accepted. He knows not to disclose the identity now, because the current people in power would eliminate them if he did."

"The FSB knows about this?" Stacey asked.

"Yes. And as far as we can tell, they want it put to an end. Besides the disruption to the current power structure and possibly the election, they don't like that one of their own has gone rogue and is out raising their own personal army."

Jack scratched the back of his head. "What does this personal army look like? What are we up against?"

"We believe he's the head of a company called Osprey."

"Never heard of it," Jack said.

"Mercenary outfit," Johnson explained.

"You're shitting me," Stacey said. "He's got his very own Blackwater?"

Johnson nodded. "And it's all legit. Through Osprey, he'd have connections all the way to the White House. We're pretty sure he's been using the company as a recruitment tool for years. Osprey's members are people from all over and from every organization you can think of."

"How is that possible?" Stacey asked. "How did the Agency or NSA not pick this up?"

Johnson looked her in the eye, both of them knowing the answer to that question.

Jack picked up on the exchange himself. "You're saying that we did know about it but let it happen? That a faction of the US government might actually be backing him?"

Stacey leaned back in her chair and folded her arms across her chest. "They're using him to destabilize Russia."

"We're pretty confident that the Agency is making generous contributions to Osprey through various NGOs."

Jack put both his hands on his head and grabbed his hair. "You said on the radio that his body had been recovered in Trenton. That he had been shot with the same gun that had killed Stacey's doctor." He glanced quickly at his wife. "Obviously they didn't recover his body because he wasn't dead. They released the statement to make the Kremlin believe he was dead. So they could continue to use him without interference from the FSB."

Johnson nodded.

But Stacey was still trying to wrap her head around this empire fiction. "The Agency is supporting this tsar idea?"

Johnson shrugged. "Why not? Would they prefer a tsar in control of Russia again? Maybe. Absolutely if they had a say in who it is. Are they thinking that it's actually a possibility? Hell no. But if Fedyenka can make enough waves to give Moscow a headache, then why not help him do it? The bigger the party, the bigger the hangover."

"So he's using this so-called movement as his very own Bull Moose party."

Johnson squinted, not getting his meaning.

Jack quickly explained, "J.P. Morgan and the rest of the Monopoly Men tried to establish a private bank to control the nation's currency. The Aldrich Bill. But Taft shot it down. The banksters supported Teddy Roosevelt in the Republican primaries, but when he didn't win, Woodrow Wilson asked for their support, promising to sign their bill in exchange. Roosevelt formed a third party, called the Bull Moose Party, which took enough votes away from Taft to ensure a Wilson victory. The Aldrich Bill, renamed the Federal Reserve Act, was passed by Wilson, and the nation's economy was transferred over to unelected oligarchs."

Johnson shrugged. "Makes sense."

"But what does it have to do with us?" Jack asked.

Johnson brought the glass to his lips and tipped his head back, draining the remainder of the wine. He set the empty glass on the table in front of him and wiped his mouth with the back of his hand. "I have no freaking idea."

Jack stood and walked over to the sink. "What if it's not Fedyenka? What if it's someone making it *look* like him?"

"Him who?" a voice asked from the hallway.

They all turned to see Joseph stepping into the candlelight.

"What are you talking about?" Joseph looked back and forth between his parents and then finally to the man who had come to help save him in the mountains.

"Hello, Joseph," Johnson said. "It's nice to see you again."

Joseph blinked. "What's he doing here?"

Jack exchanged a glance with Stacey, and both their shoulders sagged in defeat. There was no avoiding it now.

"Sit down, Joseph," Stacey said. "We need to tell you some things."

27

JOSEPH BLINKED, UNABLE TO fully grasp all that his mother had just told him. About her being a double agent. About his grandmother and grandfather being KGB. About the men who had abducted him, and the man who had been behind it. Someone his mother used to know. Someone who had been trying to start a war. All of it was enough to keep his mind occupied for the rest of his life, but it was his friends and what had happened at the school this morning that took precedence over all this bizarre family history.

"Why did they shoot Mrs. Hatfield?" His hands were clenched into fists on the tabletop. "Why did they do that?"

"I don't know," Johnson answered softly.

Joseph looked up at him, into his eyes. Wind rattled the windows. "Are you able to find out if anyone else was hurt?"

"I'll try," he said. "In the meantime, we need to get you somewhere safe."

"This place isn't safe?"

Johnson looked at Stacey and then at Jack before answering, "I'm not sure. If I could find you here, others might too."

Joseph looked at his dad. "That's why you act the way you do. Always looking around for threats, like you're expecting someone to pull a gun or something."

Jack nodded. "Probably."

"That's why we had to move."

"You knew that already," Stacey said. "We told you that the person who had you kidnapped might try again, and when he left the book in your locker—"

He closed his eyes and replayed the last year in his head, trying to recall those conversations he'd heard his mom and dad having in the kitchen when they thought he was asleep or playing video games or listening to music with headphones on. "You were trying to find him."

"We were all trying to find him," Johnson said.

"And you couldn't?"

Johnson shook his head. "No. Not yet."

"But we will," his dad said. He walked over to him and took a standing position behind his chair. Put his hands on his shoulders and squeezed. "We will find him, and we'll stop all of this."

"But we need to get you somewhere safe, like Mr. Johnson said," his mom explained.

"Where?"

"I have a place," Mr. Johnson said.

Joseph could see the hesitation on his parents' faces. They weren't so sure about going with this guy despite his having already saved their lives in the mountains. Or maybe his parents were afraid that he'd been compromised? Like in that movie with Johnny Depp when he was younger, the one where the bad guys kidnap his daughter and are going to kill her if he doesn't shoot the governor in the next ninety minutes. But Mr. Johnson didn't seem like the kind of person who would do that. He was too strong and in control to let that happen to him. He was like Agent Mulder in the *X-Files* show his dad was always watching whenever it came on TV. Agent Mulder would never kill an innocent person to save someone he loved, right? Fox would figure a way out of it. And so would Mr. Johnson.

"What kind of place?" his dad asked.

"A place we can all go to in the morning and plan our next move."

"Where?" Mom asked.

"Somewhere off grid."

"And no one else knows about it?" Dad asked. What he didn't add, but that everyone could hear, was *like the house you put us in that was raided this morning?*

Agent Johnson shook his head. "By the time anyone can figure out where it is, we'll be long gone."

"Then we'll leave first thing in the morning," Mom responded.

Another blast of thunder shook the cabin.

Joseph yawned, and his eyes watered. He wondered if this could all still be a dream.

28

THE PLACE JOHNSON HAD in mind sounded perfect. He'd come across a case that had involved a doomsday prepper knocking off the people he'd hired to build his secret bunker once the job had been completed. The guy was in prison, serving a life sentence. He'd killed the entire contract team, poisoning them with celebratory drinks on the last day. Now his bunker lay dormant and unused, unknown to the public, and completely out of the mind of the government. The guy had managed to stock a couple of years' worth of food and supplies while the builders were wrapping up, so Johnson said they'd be able to stay there for as long as it took to figure this whole thing out.

Jack stared up at the ceiling as flashes of lightning lit up the windows. The explosion at the school was replaying in his head again. All the kids lying on the ground... His first thought had been that everyone was dead, and even though it seemed that most were okay as they began to get to their feet and run for the parking lot, it was that first initial dread that sat in his gut now. He knew it was really guilt. Because whether everyone in the building had been killed or not didn't matter. They *could* have been. Maybe even *should* have been. And definitely *would* have been if someone hadn't pulled the fire alarm first. And it was his fault. Stacey's fault. Their presence here had put all those kids and their teachers at risk. His neighbors. The Greens were a magnet of destruction that attracted danger to all those around them.

And if his face truly was on the news as Stacey said it was, then he couldn't imagine what all those parents were thinking about him and Stacey right now. But that wasn't actually true, was it? He knew exactly what they were thinking, because it was what he would be thinking if he were in their shoes. Ed, William, Carl, Savanna, Chrissy, Jason, Robin... People they'd met at school board meetings and had cocktails with on cool spring evenings. And then he wondered if he actually could be in their shoes. Maybe this had nothing to do with him and his family at all and it was just a coincidence that—

But he couldn't let himself grab onto such a fantasy. Not if it was his picture on the television. Whoever had done all this had set him up for it. No one else. Him. So it had everything to do with him and his family.

If only he knew what.

Well, he thought, some time spent in a secret bunker might just buy them the time they needed to figure that part out. And then, perhaps, just what to do about it.

He craned his neck, feeling the tension in his shoulders protest the movement. He let his eyes drift over the cabin again, taking in the details. He couldn't believe this was the same place he'd been ten years ago. That Stacey had been using it for "special" meetings.

The walls were beginning to talk to him, pictures appearing on them like scenes from a movie. Stacey's bare back arched, her muscles taut as her hips writhed atop some unseen figure that she was straddling, her hair hanging down between her shoulder blades before falling over her face as she leaned forward, looking down into the stranger's face. But who was she screwing? A foreign agent? A politician? Someone the Agency just wanted to get some dirt on?

The rabbit hole had turned into a black hole, and he couldn't lie there the rest of the night trying to keep from being sucked in. He needed to leave, to do something. And there was only one other place that he knew of that was within walking distance. Or at least had been. Who knew if it was still there.

He quietly got out of the bed, turned, and noted Stacey's form beneath the blankets. He thought of *The Americans* again. Of Keri Russell and the kinky stuff she'd done for Mother Russia. He wondered what kind of stuff Stacey might have done for Uncle Sam in this very bed. Stuff he didn't even know existed?

Red Sparrow stuff? Was being here triggering memories of the things she'd done under this roof? Did they all disgust her, or had she enjoyed some it—some of *them*? Had the guys all been fat slobs, or had she been with athletes and movie stars?

He walked out of the room, pushing all that from his mind. He checked on Joseph and saw that he was asleep. Then he went down the short hall and into the living room. Johnson was asleep in the rocking chair by the window, his feet propped up on a piece of firewood, ankles crossed.

Jack waited for another blast of thunder before opening the door. Then he stepped out into the rain and tried to retrace the steps he'd taken a decade ago.

JACK STOOD IN THE street and stared through the rain at a glowing red light that hovered and shimmered like a UFO in the night. He looked at his watch. 2:30 a.m. He ran a hand through his soaked hair and left the street, walking onto the grass and eventually to the front door of the old restaurant. He wasn't sure what surprised him more, that he was able to find it or that it was still there to be found. He tilted his head and tried to see through the windows, but all he could make out was the same glowing EXIT sign that he'd seen from the street. If not for that, he would've never spotted the building in the dark and pouring rain.

He tried the handle on the door, but of course it was locked. He went around to the back, near where the EXIT sign hung inside, and found another door. It was locked too.

The woods behind the building stood just ten feet away, and with his arms extended in front of him, he walked to them. He needed a stick. If he left one poking through the window, then hopefully people would mistake his breaking and entering as a mere product of the storm. No need to call the police and get fingerprints or anything.

He found a large branch lying on the ground and carried it back to the door. He poked it through the big windowpane, hardly noticing the sound of the breaking glass over the weather. He reached his arm through and unlocked the door. Swinging it open, he stepped out of the rain and into a place he'd visited only once before. He could see in the flashes of lightning that not much had changed. At least the seats were still in the same places he remembered them.

He walked across the wooden floor, dripping all over it, and made his way to the cash register in front. He recalled the face of the man who had stood there before, talking to him about raw milk and government raids. But what he couldn't remember was if there had been a television hanging from the ceiling behind him. He didn't think there had been. He recalled looking for signs of civilization, and he was pretty certain that a television in this place would've stood out to him. If there hadn't been one, he could only hope that Ma had done some updating in the last ten years. He went behind the register and the counter it rested on and waited for another flash.

Bingo.

There was a fifty-inch LED TV mounted to the wall and angled toward the rest of the small restaurant. He reached up and ran his hand across the bottom of it until finding the power button. When he pressed it, an old black-and-white rerun of *The Rifleman* immediately appeared, casting its light throughout the dark room.

Jack turned away from it, using the illumination to search for a remote. He found it on the counter next to the register. He took it to the first booth and sat at the table. His legs were tired from the walk, and he was freezing cold. He shivered as he tried working the buttons. He flipped through the channels, looking for the news.

CNN.

He stopped. Blinked. The water that was dripping from his hair and puddling on the tabletop was suddenly deafening, his heart frozen in his chest. He fumbled with the remote, trying to turn up the volume.

There he was. Right there on the TV, framed by a box in the upper right-hand corner of the screen behind the talking anchor. He looked terrible in the picture and had no idea where it had come from. It looked like a mug shot, only he'd never been arrested or had his picture taken by law enforcement. At least not that he knew of.

He increased the volume as the picture changed to that of a crime scene. Yellow police tape stretching all around a school. Scattered officers bent over and examining things the camera was too far away to capture. Beneath the images, the scrolling text offered the "facts" of the developing story. He read them, ignoring the female voiceover that was saying something about the first responders and how quickly they had arrived on scene.

Three dead. Two missing. A dozen injured.

He figured the two missing were Joseph and Samantha.

Three dead.

He seemed to come out of his body a little, like he was instantly drunk, another dimension suddenly added to his realm of experience, the effect of it dizzying. His face went numb, and he couldn't move his hands, but his brain tingled with shock. He stared at the TV, hoping to see the three victims, yet not wanting to see them at all. Were they Joseph's friends?

Who cares? They'd be someone's *friends.* Someone's *kids.* Someone's *mom or dad, brother or sister, aunt or uncle.*

And *he* was being blamed for it.

His hands trembled, his eyes glued to the screen, not able to hear the narrative. The restaurant seemed to spin away from him. How could this be happening?

He thought of Trenton. Another bomb. One Stacey had had something to do with. Could she have had something to do with this too? Could this have been another false-flag black op? No, her involvement in something like this didn't make any sense. No way would she have put Joseph at risk like that. Maybe if she'd made Joseph stay home today, those thoughts would have a starting point, but as it was, there was no foundation for such thoughts to build upon.

He stared up at the television, his vision blurred, completely forgetting how cold and wet he was. The lies being spoken started to make their way into his head again. He stood and stumbled over to a refrigerator against the wall by the front counter. He opened the big glass door and pulled out a beer. He drank half the bottle in one shot, then finished it in the second. He grabbed another bottle and walked to the counter.

The talking head was saying something about the identities of the bombers. How they'd been living in the area under false names. How their son had been enrolled in the school. How the woman was a Russian spy. That their house had been raided by the FBI. And that they'd managed to escape.

"Fuck me," Jack said, and drank.

29

STACEY WOKE UP TO find Jack missing. At first she thought maybe something had happened to him. Maybe they were surrounded, men in the woods coming in and taking them out one at a time. Or maybe Johnson had done something to him—though he was sound asleep in the rocking chair. She looked out the window as a bolt of lightning tore open the sky, and saw that both cars were still sitting in front of the house. He hadn't driven anywhere. She searched the house again. Could he be in the shed?

Her heart started pumping harder, and she was about to wake Johnson up when she heard someone climbing up the steps to the front door. She whipped the Glock out of her pants and brought it up just as the doorknob turned and the door swung in toward her.

Jack stepped in out of the rain. He was soaking wet and shaking. He closed the door behind him.

"What the hell," she said, crossing the room and throwing her arms around him. "Where'd you go?" She could smell beer on his breath.

He put his hands on her shoulders and moved her back a step. He looked into her eyes. Blinked.

She couldn't tell if the water dripping from his eyes was rainwater or tears, but she knew he was upset about something. His gaze was distant, shocked.

"We're all over CNN," he mumbled.

"I know," she said.

His gaze narrowed. "They're saying we were living there under false names. They're saying you're a Russian spy."

Her hands fell to her sides, and she took another step back. "What?"

He looked into the kitchen and then walked past her. His shoulder nudged hers as he went, leaving a wet mark on her shirt. He pulled another beer out of his pocket and set it on the kitchen table as he sat.

Stacey sat down beside him.

"They're saying we blew up the school. That when they went to arrest us at the house, we escaped."

Stacey leaned forward on her elbows and folded her hands. Her brow furrowed as she let his words sink in. "If they're saying we were raided—"

"Then they could've been real agents," Jack finished for her.

She blinked, trying to process the possibility.

Jack then looked up and locked eyes with her. "Stacey..." He swallowed.

"What?" She could see his eyes filling, the redness from the alcohol making it look as if he was about to start sobbing.

"They said three people were killed."

She didn't know what to say to that, so she just reached out and grabbed his hands. She squeezed them and lowered her head to the table. On the one hand, it could have been a lot worse. Yet three people... She looked up. "Did they say who?"

He shook his head.

"Joseph and Samantha?" she asked.

"Two missing, three dead, a dozen injured is all they said."

She bowed her head again, and they both sat in silence for a while, the rain the only noise.

Finally, Jack asked, "If Fedyenka is behind all of it, why would he want everyone to believe you're a Russian agent?"

She let go of his hands and sat up straighter, wiping her eyes with the back of her hand. "Trying to start a war again..."

"So how would he go about convincing the FBI of it?"

"Anonymous tip."

"Sure. I could buy that as a reason for the raid and the nationwide manhunt for us. But—"

"But not how the media got its script."

He nodded. "This has CIA written all over it, doesn't it? I mean, you know that most news agencies are getting money from the CIA, funneled through various departments—"

"Like USAID," she said.

Jack nodded, acknowledging the old conspiracy theory that the 1961 JFK-created department had been hijacked by the CIA and used as a front for regime change across the globe. Jack was sure it was how hundreds of different news outlets could simultaneously come up with the exact same talking points, using the same catch-phrases all at once. "The MSM got this nice and packaged and all ready to run."

She turned her head and stared out the kitchen window.

Jack lifted the bottle to his lips. "Like the reporter telling the world that Building Seven had already collapsed, even though it was standing right there behind her in the background..."

She rubbed her forehead and then reached for his bottle. He let her take it from him, and she took a long sip.

He continued, "If this is Fedyenka and the CIA, could it be a distraction? Get the whole country looking at this"—he indicated the space to his left with his left hand—"while they set something else up over here?" He waved his right hand.

Johnson appeared in the doorway and leaned against its frame. "Maybe. Doesn't explain trying to grab Joseph, or setting you up as the fall guy though."

"Whoever it is," Stacey said, "knows about your agency. Knows your people."

He nodded.

"The only options are the CIA, the FSB, and Fedyenka, right?" Jack asked.

"Eliminating outrageous coincidences, I would agree," Johnson said.

Stacey took another gulp of beer and stood, handing what remained in the bottle back to Jack. She stared straight into Johnson's tired eyes. She could tell that he'd been through a lot himself. "Anyone try taking you out yet?"

"No." He scratched an itch under his right eye.

"Why not?" she asked. "If they're trying to terminate your unit, why not start with the head?"

He didn't answer.

"You think they might know you'd come to us? Think they could be tracking you?"

"You mean as a contingency plan? If they didn't succeed in killing you?"

"Killing Jack. Not sure what they were planning for me, remember?"

Johnson nodded. "Could also be that there's more than one player in this game." He shrugged. "But do I think someone could be tracking me since this morning? I don't think so."

"Before then?"

"I doubt it."

"Still," Jack said, standing himself, "we should probably make sure."

Johnson blinked slowly and raised his arms, stepping into the kitchen and turning to face the wall. Stacey went over and searched his person. Checked inside his collar, his pockets, his sleeves.

"Shoes," she said.

Johnson took them off so she could check them.

"Clean. As far as I can tell," she said.

Jack leaned against the wall with his right elbow and pinched the bridge of his nose. "What about his car?" he asked, gesturing toward the front lot with his other hand. He was holding the beer bottle by the neck.

"I'm pretty sure—" Johnson started to say.

"But you can't be one hundred percent certain," Jack interrupted.

"No," he said.

Jack finished off the bottle and, through glassy eyes, said, "Then we should leave now. Just in case."

No one said anything. They just moved to collect their things. And to wake Joseph.

30

THEY LEFT JOHNSON'S CAR parked behind the cabin and out of view from the driveway. It was a rental car that he'd acquired under a false identity, so no one would be able to trace the car back to him even if they did somehow find it (assuming it wasn't already being tracked).

The sun was coming up behind them, the red-orange crown breaking the tree line and shining off the Accord's sideview mirrors. They were heading west. Had been for a couple of hours now. Ohio was their destination, and they still had another four hours to go.

Johnson was driving, and Jack was sitting in the back with Joseph. They weren't sure if Stacey's face had made the news or not, but she was wearing the wig and hat in the front passenger seat just to be safe.

Jack looked over at his son. Since being woken up and hurried out of the house to yet another secret location, Joseph hadn't said more than two words to them. Jack couldn't tell if he was shutting down completely, or if he was just giving them the silent treatment because he was pissed at them. He thought he'd prefer the latter. The poor kid had enough scars already, both literally and figuratively. He didn't need any more trauma-induced baggage to carry around for the rest of his life. Relational issues with his parents could be overcome, but the shock of friends having been blown up at his school? Which was why Jack hadn't told him about the casualties yet. Didn't want to until they had names to match them. No sense in driving him crazy with the need to find out who they were. Not at this point.

A grumbling sound came from the seat beside him. He looked over at Joseph. "Hungry?"

Joseph didn't take his eyes off the passing scenery, but he did give a subtle head nod. Jack considered it progress. "Can we stop somewhere soon?" he asked, leaning up between the two front seats.

"Sure," Johnson said. "As soon as we find somewhere fitting."

Johnson wanted to avoid drive-thru fast-food spots full of surveillance cameras, so "fitting" ended up being an old diner half an hour later.

After parking under a tree in the furthest spot away from the building, Johnson said, "Stay in the car."

"Could we use the bathroom?" Jack asked. He knew Stacey wouldn't ask in a million years but figured she probably had to go.

"We can stop farther on down the road for that. None of us need to be seen together." He got out of the car and walked across the parking lot and up the front steps to the diner.

Stacey looked back at Jack and Joe. "You two okay?" She reached back and put a hand on Joseph's knee.

He looked up at her. "When you woke me up..." He trailed off, then tried again. "At first, I forgot what happened. Then when it started coming back, I thought I was remembering a dream. Thought I'd fallen asleep during the baseball game and was going to be late for school."

She frowned and looked away.

"We were going to watch *Good Night, and Good Luck* in history today." He said it in a whisper.

"Good movie," Jack said.

Joseph turned his face so that they couldn't see his eyes watering. "Tommy couldn't wait."

Jack put his arm around Joseph and pulled him close, away from the window. He knew he was taking a risk, but he needed Joseph to know that he was still the same dad he'd talked to about poop trenches just a couple of years ago. The same dad who had literally climbed mountains to save him. But it was also true that Joseph was not the same kid anymore. Again, Jack wondered what this teenage body he was holding in his arms had done with his son. But that was how things went. It was life. Babies grow into men, and those men, while having babies of their own, then bury their fathers, who had somehow managed to become even older men themselves.

"We'll find out what happened, okay?" Jack said, resting his chin on the boy's head and thinking of their future. He could only hope that one day they'd be able to live a normal life, though he wasn't sure if that was even a possibility so long as Stacey was in the picture.

"I can't believe you're a spy," Joseph said to Stacey. "But I don't understand what that has to do with me." He touched the scars on his neck.

Jack glanced at Stacey. There it was. The one place they'd hoped this wouldn't go. But they'd opened the door, and now, after hearing the question put to them, it was obvious that the information they'd given him last night could only have ever led to this place. But it was also a question that Jack himself had been harboring for years. And as far as he was concerned, he still hadn't received a satisfactory answer to it. Vadim had been married to Stacey and believed Joseph was his son, so that made sense that he'd want them back. But why would Fedyenka want him? Just to get back at Stacey in a way that would hurt her the most? He didn't buy that. Never had.

"Well, they held you in the mountains to try to get me to do something," Stacey said.

"What?"

"They wanted me to kill a senator. They said they'd kill you if I didn't."

"Like the Johnny Depp movie," Joseph said.

"Yup," Jack said, knowing that Stacey probably didn't know the reference and saving her from having to tell yet more lies. Because that was what she was doing. She was lying. That was not why they had tried to kill him and kidnapped Joseph. At least not because they wanted Newell dead. Or maybe they did want him dead but wanted to toy with Stacey a while first, making her think she was going to die as a suicide bomber when in fact the plan had always been for her to be implicated in the murder of the senator. Jack wasn't really sure. The details of that whole thing were fuzzy, and he'd never really pressed Johnson for the exact details.

"Agent Johnson helped us out of that," she explained. "And he's going to help us out of this too." She transferred her hand from Joseph's knee to Jack's. She squeezed it. It was meant to be a reassuring gesture. One of intimate trust.

But Jack didn't buy it. There was something that Stacey wasn't telling him, and it was close to what Joseph had just touched on. He wondered if Joseph had picked up on the fact that his mom's answer didn't explain why anyone would *still* be after him, since the senator had since withdrawn his bid for the presidency and no longer seemed to be a threat to anyone.

He looked out the window and saw Johnson step out of the diner. He had two plastic bags in his hand. When he opened the driver's side door, he handed them across the seat to Stacey and slid in behind the wheel.

"Pancakes, eggs, sausage, bacon, and hash browns," he said. "That's okay, I hope?"

"Perfect," Stacey said, digging the Styrofoam containers out of the bags.

Johnson turned the key, put the car in drive, and headed out of the parking lot.

31

THEY'D STOPPED A FEW more times to use a bathroom, get gas, grab lunch, and to switch the license plates. All along the way, Stacey had observed the traffic around them. People were singing to music, chatting to the person next to them, talking on their cells... It could have been any other day. Which made the events of yesterday seem like a dream all the more.

Stacey adjusted the wig as she continued to work through what Johnson had said about Fedyenka working to re-establish an imperial Russia. It sounded so absurd. But she knew that there would be enough imperialists to maybe make a difference in the next elections—which, Johnson had suggested, was the point. And if the US was part of it, then no doubt the Agency had already been pouring funds into the movement.

Anastasia Romanov. The imperial family. The movie poster sent to her. That he'd called her "my little Anastasia." *Michael Strogoff* in Joseph's locker... Could this have been his agenda from the start? Working to mold public opinion for a tsar back in St. Petersburg all the way back when she first met him? If so, had the Agency latched onto his mission, or was it possible that they had matched him to theirs? He himself was not part of the royal family, so he could never float the idea of himself as tsar. But as a Rasputin? Even if, like Jack had said, this was a whole third-party plot to pull enough votes away from the current power base, he would still need a candidate who would pass as a descendant of the last imperial family, which was the Romanovs.

Where the hell is he going to find a Romanov? she thought.

She forced herself to take a step back, to look at the whole thing from a different perspective. If she went too much further with this theory, she might end up boxing herself into it, unable to see it from any other angle. So like an Etch-A-Sketch, she shook it up and began working anew on a blank screen. But it stayed blank because the only other theory was that someone else was behind it and making it *look* like Fedyenka was behind it. But that didn't add up. Who else would even know about him?

She shifted her train of thought from the Romanov tracks onto the Fedyenka Yevstigneyev mainline. The man had been obsessed with her. Jealous that she had ended up with Vadim instead of him, he'd exposed Vadim to the CIA, knowing that he wouldn't have a choice but to turn. Then he'd leaked the betrayal to the Kremlin, hoping they'd send someone to assassinate him.

In the meantime, he'd begun once more working on wooing Stacey. With Vadim out of the picture, he must've thought his chances were pretty fair. But Stacey knew that Fedyenka was a demented piece of shit. And even if Jack hadn't been in the picture then, there was no way she would ever get involved with the psycho. She'd seen him with other girls way back when she was in Russia. Saw girls leaving his place in the morning with scarves wrapped around their faces, trying to hide swollen lips and black eyes. She'd seen some of the pictures he liked to paint. Grotesque things that resembled the exploitation films of the '70s and '80s. Naked women on their knees, their hands tied behind their backs and gagged. Even Vadim had mentioned how, on occasion, he'd taken things too far with the prostitutes.

She'd never mentioned any of this to Jack. She didn't need him thinking about what the guy might be planning to do to her once he finally got his hands on her. It was one of the reasons she believed Fedyenka was behind what had gone down at their house. He was trying to get Jack out of the way for a third time, and with Joseph in his care, she would be at his mercy. And this time, she didn't think he would be asking her to blow up a building. No, recalling some of the paintings she'd seen, she had no trouble imagining what he'd be asking her to do this time.

She looked at Johnson as he drove them down a road between two cornfields. He had a right-handed, twelve-o'clock grip on the steering wheel, leaning against the driver's side door with his elbow, his head propped up against his left hand. He looked tired. Had barely said a word since breakfast. She wondered if he thought they had any chance at all of coming out of this alive.

"Almost there," he said, as if feeling her gaze boring into the side of his face. "Just a couple more minutes, I think."

"You think?" Jack asked.

And then a car appeared up ahead. It was parked on the shoulder.

Johnson slowed and flashed the headlights at it.

The car, a Toyota Camry, pulled onto the road, and Johnson followed it.

"What's going on?" Jack asked.

"That's Agent Brown," he answered. "He's going to lead us the rest of the way."

Stacey looked over at him. "You said no one else knew about this place."

"No one did. Until I called last night and told someone."

"What?" She stole a glance at the sideview mirror, but saw only empty road behind them.

"There's only a few people left I trust. He's one of them," Johnson said.

"But what if they're watching him?" Stacey asked.

He looked over at her, taking his eyes off the road for just a second. "We need all the help we can get. We need to figure out what the hell is going on and find out how to stop it. The three of us alone aren't enough."

"Hey," Joseph objected, leaning up from the back seat.

Johnson's eyes shot up to the rearview, and—*God bless him*, Stacey thought—he smiled. "Sorry. *Four* of us."

Joseph leaned back into the seat and crossed his arms, the faint trace of a smile tugging at the corner of his mouth.

The Camry braked and then turned right.

They followed.

Johnson's index finger extended from the hand clutching the wheel, pointing at the car ahead. "I asked him to look into the property. Make sure it's still vacant and to meet us here."

"I'm assuming he has a secure line?" Stacey asked.

"We're operating according to a contingency plan. It involves backup phones nobody else knows about."

"Where's yours?" she asked.

"Didn't have time to grab it. But I memorized his number and called it from a pay phone."

They turned onto an overgrown dirt road that was hardly visible and definitely passable if you weren't looking for it. It split the weeds and high grass of an overgrown field and led through a tree line two hundred yards away. The trees stood tall and were spread across the field. Agent Brown's car kicked up dust as it bounced over the uneven road, and they drove through it, passing trees on their left and right.

Once through the woods, they came to another field, this one overgrown as well. But in the midst of all the weeds stood a white farmhouse.

They continued down the long driveway. Broken fences followed alongside them. A stagnant pond reflected sunlight off its green surface to their right. They saw an ax head buried in a piece of wood, its handle sticking into the air beside a pile of wood already split. Barbed wire had been run out over the tops of wooden posts before the spool had been left abandoned with a hundred feet of posts still to go. A barn sat next to the house, its doors open, one of them hanging at an angle.

Agent Brown parked in front of the house, and Johnson pulled up beside him. He put the Honda in park and leaned forward over the steering wheel, peering up through the windshield and studying the house. Then he unbuckled himself and turned to face Jack and Joseph. "Stay here a minute," he said. He hit the trunk release and then looked at Stacey. She nodded, and they both flung their doors open and stepped out. They walked around to the back of the car and extracted weapons from the trunk, all the while their eyes sweeping the surrounding area.

Agent Brown walked over to them. He was a big black man, and she instantly associated his build with that of a defensive safety. Maybe a little leaner than a linebacker, but thicker than a wide receiver. A taller Brian Dawkins, she thought. He had a combat shotgun resting on his shoulder and wore a side holster that looked to be holding an M9 Beretta.

"Any problems?" Johnson asked, stepping forward and shaking the man's hand.

"No," he said as his eyes went past Johnson to Stacey and then to the two figures still in the back seat of the old Accord. "But there's been a development."

"Later," Johnson said, then, "Jim, this is Stacey Green." He turned toward Stacey. "Stacey, Jim Brown."

She raised an eyebrow as she removed her wig. "Jim Brown?"

He didn't respond, just swung the shotgun off his shoulder. "Let's go," he said, and he turned toward the house.

Stacey and Johnson fell in behind him, and they went up the porch steps in a single line. Then Stacey and Brown split, each taking positions on opposite sides of the door.

Stacey glanced at the car and caught Joseph staring at her through the back window. The look on his face was a mixture of fear and awe, and in that moment Stacey thought she could read his mind—*Holy crap, my mom is Rambo.* She smiled inwardly before turning her attention back to the door. There was no screen door that they had to worry about. Brown reached his left hand out and grabbed the handle.

"Wait," Johnson said, stopping him from turning the handle.

Brown's hand fell away from the knob as his eyes met Johnson's. Stacey read the message passed between them, and she backed away from the door, looking back over her shoulder and toward a window positioned five feet behind her. The wooden porch creaked beneath her feet.

Brown and Johnson took a step back as well, their weapons trained on the other windows. Johnson made a hand gesture, and Brown disappeared around the left side of the house.

"WHAT ARE THEY DOING?" Joseph asked.

"They're making sure the house isn't booby-trapped," Jack said. "Could be that the people who lived here set traps in case they were ever raided."

"Raided?"

"By the government maybe. Or zombies."

"To protect their bomb shelter?"

"I guess." Though Jack had no idea who this guy had been. Was he just a doomsday prepper, or had he been part of a militia? Johnson had said the guy was serving a life sentence, so the authorities should know all about him by now, whether he was militia or not. Jack could sympathize with some militias. Hell, in another life maybe he'd even be a member of one himself. He also sympathized with preppers, and if he had the money, he'd most certainly have his own bunker somewhere.

But this guy had murdered the people he'd hired to build his bunker, and that put him on the crazy list. He couldn't sympathize with that, and if the guy was capable of killing innocent people to keep his secret safe, then he was certainly capable of rigging the property with traps. Jack just hoped that all the signs of unfinished work around the property meant that whoever was last here hadn't gotten around to planting land mines and running trip wires throughout the house.

"But I thought the guy was in jail," Joseph said.

Jack nodded. "That's what Agent Johnson said."

"But then wouldn't the police have searched the house and everything?"

Jack looked over at Joseph. "You bet."

"So then they would've found any traps back then."

Jack nodded again. "I think Mom's more worried about any cousins who may have visited since. They're just being careful."

Joseph seemed to accept that and turned his attention back to the house. A minute later, they watched the big black guy kick the front door in. The door tore off the top two hinges and careened awkwardly into the house, still attached to the bottom hinge. The agent stepped past it with the shotgun held firmly against his shoulder, sweeping it back and forth.

Jack saw movement through the windows and picked out Stacey's clothes. She and Johnson must've found another way in. Jack turned his attention away from the house and scanned the property, looking for signs of activity. For anyone who might be making a run for it. Or coming in for an attack.

Nothing.

The land was large and quiet, lit up under the afternoon sun as a gentle fall breeze moved through the high grass and the distant trees. It was eerie. Like a ghost town. He wondered where the contractors had died and what other secrets this land might hold. His imagination began to spin all kinds of scenarios, giving this place a history that dated all the way back to the Civil War—one that was perhaps spawned by the very history of the Harriet Tubman house he'd been staying in, though perhaps one a bit more nefarious.

His daydream was shattered by Stacey stepping out the front door and back onto the porch. Johnson and Brown came out after her, all of them bounding down the steps and approaching the car.

Jack opened the rear door and stepped out.

"All clear," Stacey said.

"Find the bunker?" Jack asked.

"Not yet."

"Jim, take Jack and Joseph into the house. Stacey and I will hide the cars." Then Johnson opened the back door of the Accord and bent over. "You can come out, Joe."

Joseph climbed out of the back seat and stepped into the grass, stretching.

"Joe, this is Mr. Jim. He's a real good friend of mine, and he means to take really good care of you, okay?"

Joseph stepped forward and took the hand Brown had extended.

"Nice to meet you, son," Brown said, giving the boy's hand two firm pumps.

Jack smiled, knowing exactly what his son was thinking and just waiting for him to say it aloud.

"Wow," Joseph said, letting go of the massive hand.

Here it comes, Jack thought.

"You look just like Wesley Snipes."

Brown straightened and smiled with what Jack took to be genuine amusement.

"How old are you?" Brown asked.

"Fourteen."

"And you know who Wesley Snipes is, huh?"

"Of course. *Passenger 57* is, like, one of my favorite movies."

Brown looked at Jack. "Your doing, I suppose?"

Jack shrugged. "I may be guilty of certain indoctrinations."

Brown smiled and looked back at Joseph. "*Passenger 57* was a good one. I liked *U.S. Marshals* myself."

"Yeah, that was good, too," Joseph said. Then he cocked his head and looked up at the towering man, squinting at the sun shining over his shoulder. "Is your name really Jim Brown, Mr. Jim?"

"You know, little man, your mom just asked me the same question. I didn't answer her, either." And he winked at him before turning and walking back to his car.

"The cornfield over there," Johnson said to Stacey, pointing behind the house and to the right.

Jack put a hand up to his eyes, shielding the sun, and saw that there was indeed a cornfield in the distance.

Stacey nodded and got behind the wheel of the Accord while Johnson made his way to Brown's Camry.

Brown had retrieved a bag from the front passenger seat of his car before joining Jack at the trunk of the Accord. They moved the gear onto the grass at their feet and closed the trunk.

"Good to go," Jack said to Johnson and Stacey.

Johnson started the Camry and drove away, navigating a fence and disappearing around the house. Stacey followed him in the Accord.

Jack looked over to Wesley Snipes and saw that he was staring intently toward the cornfield. "What?" Jack asked.

Brown blinked. "Just praying we don't hear any bangs."

"Yeah," Jack muttered, again thinking of land mines. "Amen."

"C'mon, let's get inside," Brown said. He turned toward Joseph. "Little man, grab one of these bags, will you?"

Joseph ran over and grabbed the bigger bag, the one from the Honda that Jack and Stacey had packed. He got it up onto his shoulder, but Jack could tell he was struggling to get it up the porch steps. He was obviously trying to impress the secret-agent man who looked a lot like one of his favorite action heroes. Joseph didn't see an Agent Brown when looking at their new friend, but rather ex-cop John Cutter who fought terrorists on hijacked airplanes.

Jack grabbed some of the supplies while Brown grabbed his own stuff.

Somewhere in the woods, a hawk cried out.

32

JOSEPH LOOKED AROUND THE house. It was cool and sort of creepy at the same time. It was full of cobwebs, and a lot of stuff was overturned and scattered across the floor. He thought it was probably the aftermath from the cops or FBI or whoever searching the house for evidence. He didn't think the guy's cousins had come here. Nobody had. And that belief seemed to take some of the weight off his shoulders. For the first time since Mrs. Hatfield had called him out of class yesterday morning, he felt safe. Or at least saf*er*. He still couldn't imagine how all of this was going to play out, but at least he felt like he could sleep soundly tonight. Especially with Mr. Johnson and Mr. Jim here.

He reached to his side and felt the reassuring touch of Hugh. He might feel safe from people who wanted to kill them, but that didn't mean there weren't snakes or badgers or whatever Ohio's version of ROUS was that had made themselves at home here. He thought of the three little bears as he walked to a light switch and flipped it. Nothing. "Where do you think it is?" he asked his dad.

"The bunker?"

"Yeah."

"I have no idea." His dad looked at Mr. Jim. "Any idea?"

"Yeah, but let's wait for them to get back before we try tackling that," Mr. Jim said.

"Not sure we'll even need it," Jack said. "Could just stay here."

Joseph looked to Mr. Jim for a response, but Mr. Jim just looked away, opening the army bag his mom and dad had brought along in the car.

"Holy shit," Mr. Jim said. Then he quickly glanced over at Joseph. "Pardon my French, kid."

"I don't give a shit if you say shit," he said. Which got him a glaring look from his dad. He apologized with his eyes and then went to a staircase that led to the second floor. "Can I go up?"

"Yeah," his dad said. "Just be careful."

Joseph went up the creaky old stairs, grasping the banister as he went and getting a splinter when he slid his hand over the old wood. He held his hand to his face and pulled the wooden shard from between his thumb and forefinger. He shook it off and kept moving.

At the top of the stairs there was a little bathroom with an old tub in it. The kind of tub that had been in the Bakers' cabin. The sight of it took him back to that place, the smells and sounds…how he'd felt. And then he saw himself thrusting his sharpened branch into that man's stomach. It was a replay that he was familiar with and not one that he particularly enjoyed. Despite the guy kidnapping him and trying to kill his dad, he'd kind of liked him. He liked to think of the guy as your stereotypical redemption character portrayed in most movies, the bad guy who finally decides to listen to his conscience and turn on the real bad guys. Like Darth Vader in *ROTJ*.

He slammed the door shut on the bathroom and all those memories.

"You okay?" his dad called up. The bang had echoed through the whole house.

"Yeah. Sorry."

He entered a bedroom that had a bed, a rocking chair, and an old dresser. The mattress was half on the bed frame and half on the floor, and the drawers were spilling out of the dresser. There was a mirror on top of the dresser, but there was so much dust coating the glass that all Joseph could see was a faint mirage of himself standing in the sunlight coming through the window.

He turned to the window and moved a curtain aside. He wiped his hand across the glass and made a transparent rainbow in the dirt and grime. He was facing the cornfield that Mom and Mr. Johnson had taken the cars to and could see that they were walking back now. His mom had his schoolbag over her shoulder. *Thank you, Mom*, he thought. He'd forgotten to grab it when getting out of the car. They were about a hundred yards away, walking through the high grass. He scanned the area around them from his bird's-eye view, able to see all the way to the tree line in one direction and to the cornfields in the other. All was clear.

"Mr. Brown," he called down the stairs, still watching his mom.

"Yeah?" His deep booming voice echoed back.

"Why *Jim* Brown? Why not James or Antonio or Tim?"

"Or Bobby, Clancy, or Dan?" Mr. Brown shot back.

"Or Charlie," Joe responded, laughing.

"Maybe Jim is just my name."

"Yeah, right," Joe muttered under his breath. Then, "Mom's back." He knocked on the glass, and when they looked up from the porch, he waved. "Can we find the bunker now?"

33

"SO WHERE IS IT?" Jack asked. "This bunker?"

Johnson looked at Brown. "Were you able to find out?"

Brown walked through the dining room and into the kitchen. He called back over his shoulder as they followed, "No blueprints or anything. But some of the reports I was able to find seemed to mention the kitchen in relation to the bunker."

There was a closet door off to the side of the room, what one might assume led to a mudroom if the door had led into the yard. But the door wasn't on an exterior wall.

Brown opened it.

Darkness.

"A cellar?" Stacey asked. Joseph was trying to get a glimpse himself, pushing his way between them.

"Light," Brown said, holding back his hand.

Johnson took a small flashlight from his pocket and placed it in Brown's hand.

Brown aimed it down the steps and clicked it on. The tight beam painted a bright circle on a dirt floor. Brown moved the light back and forth, illuminating small wooden stairs. He began sidestepping his way down.

"Look out for traps," Johnson said. Then he put his hand against Joseph's chest. "Maybe you'd better stay here for a minute."

Jack saw Joseph frown, but he took a step back anyway. Jack stepped close to him and put a hand on his shoulder, and the two of them watched the government agents descend into the darkness without them. Stacey gave them a quick look, smiled, and then followed Johnson.

Jack could hear their muffled voices coming from below and caught only the sporadic movement of the flashlight as it swung about like a white laser.

"Think they'll find it?" Jack asked Joseph, not knowing what else to say but feeling he should say something.

"I hope so," Joseph said.

A few minutes later, Stacey's face appeared at the bottom of the steps. "Found it," she announced. "C'mon."

Jack led Joseph down after her, one hand on the wall to balance himself, and the other on Joseph to balance him. "Careful," he said. "These steps are neck-breakers." Indeed, each step was only about eight inches wide with a two-foot drop separating them.

"This place must be pretty old," Joseph said. "Built back when people were tinier."

"Tiny people?"

"Yeah, learned about it in history class."

"Like gnomes?"

Joseph chuckled as he navigated the last couple of steps. "Yeah, Dad, gnomes built America."

"Ah," Jack said. "*The Gnome Gangs of New York.* Didn't that win an Oscar?"

Joseph shook his head.

"Over here," Stacey called.

Jack placed his hand against Joe's back and nudged him toward her. It wasn't really a push, just the weight of his hand. He'd done it out of parental instinct, but also as a test to see if Joseph would tolerate it—a sort of litmus test to gauge the current status of their relationship. And to his delight, Joseph did not pull away or try to shrug him off.

Without the flashlight that Jack had put in the bag before leaving the cabin, Stacey appeared before him as a gray outline standing against a deeper black. He reached for her hand, and she took it. Then Jack took Joseph's hand, forming a three-person chain.

Stacey led them through some kind of opening that Jack couldn't decipher in the dim light.

"It's a hallway," Stacey said. "Carved into the ground and concealed by a false wall we moved aside. It goes on for about a hundred to two hundred feet before hitting a large steel door."

Up ahead, Jack could see a sliver of moving light. He guessed it was Johnson checking out the inside of the bunker, the door Stacey had just referenced now standing partially open.

Jack couldn't help but feel a sense of excitement. It was in the air like static electricity. He appreciated it for the distraction it was, but also knew it would be short-lived. Once they figured out the bunker and got all their oohs and aahs out, it'd be back to the business at hand—which basically amounted to a madman sending out professional killers to hunt them down. Or worse, an entire government wanting them for a school bombing that the ratings-driven media would no doubt be trying to compare with the Bath school massacre that killed thirty-eight children in 1927.

They reached the end of the hall and stepped up and through what he thought resembled a submarine door. "Watch your head and your shins," he said to Joseph.

"Ready?" he heard Johnson ask.

"For what?" he answered.

And then Brown's light fell onto Johnson, and they all saw that he had his hand on a large lever extending from a power box.

He threw the switch, and the lights flickered to life.

FROM WHERE THEY WERE standing near its entrance, the bunker's floor plan ran away from them for maybe thirty feet before stopping at a T. In that stretch of curved and corrugated metal walls was what appeared to be a small apartment. An area rug spanned half the room. A three-cushion couch sat against the right wall and faced an old forty-five-inch plasma television that was on a TV stand against the opposite wall. The stand had an open space beneath the top surface that housed a DVD/VHS combo player. Beside it and beneath it were a couple of shelves filled with DVDs and VHS tapes.

Bookshelves lined the wall, reaching six feet up to where the ceiling began to arch. They stretched from the TV all the way to the end of the room. They were full of magazines, paperbacks, hardbacks, and stacks of CDs.

A small table with a lamp was positioned next to the couch, an American flag, hung upside down, floated above it—the top pinned to the ceiling, the bottom to the wall.

The five of them walked around slowly, scrutinizing every detail of the room as if moving through a museum.

In the far right corner of the room was the kitchen. A sink was positioned beneath a window that had been fitted with curtains, a faux view fitted within the frame glimpsing a distant mountainside. A refrigerator sat near it, and a small table with two chairs occupied the rest of the space. There were cabinets built into the low wall that separated the kitchen from the living room, and they were filled with plates, bowls, containers, and utensils.

Stacey moved past the kitchen area and to the top of the T. To the left was a twenty-by-ten-foot area fitted with industrial shelving stocked with bottled water, canned drinks, k-rations, and all types of canned foods. To the right of the T was a small stand-up shower and a toilet, a row of big blue drums of what she assumed was water lining the wall beside them. There was also a black drum that had a biohazard symbol painted on its side, which she assumed was for human waste.

Johnson stuck his head around the corner and glanced around her. Then he pointed up at the painted ceiling and at a vent. "Air-filtration system."

"Running water," she answered, pointing to the hoses coming out of the blue barrels.

"Guy was ready to spend at least a year down here," he said.

"Where's the power coming from?" Jack asked from the kitchen area.

"Must be a generator somewhere," Johnson said.

"Hey, what do you think this is?" Brown called out from all the way back near the entrance.

They made their way back to him and saw that he was looking at a big red button on the wall next to the steel door. There was an orange diamond-shaped flip placard beneath it. The kind you'd see on trucks transporting hazardous material. It read 1.5 BLASTING AGENTS 1.

They stood there staring at it for a minute before Stacey took Johnson's flashlight out of his hand and moved in front of the doorway. She shined the light down the dirt corridor. "There," she said, concentrating the beam on the ceiling of the passage-way. Wires ran across the wooden slats.

Brown frowned. "Det cord?"

"This guy wasn't playing around," Jack said.

"Just ask the people who built it," Johnson mumbled back.

"There has to be another way out, then, right?" Joseph asked, understanding what det cord was and what it meant.

Stacey looked at her son. "There's gotta be a hatch some-where." She saw Joseph trying to think through something. "What?" she asked.

He closed his eyes and moved his hands. "The field you parked the car in is that way." He pointed. "So this would be under the ground between the house and the field. Maybe a little to the left of it."

"Yeah?"

"So I was looking over the area from a bedroom window and didn't see any hatch in the ground."

"All right," Johnson interjected. "Just no one hit that button." He motioned for Stacey to return his flashlight. "So we know where the bunker is. Now let's go figure out what our next move is going to be."

He reached over and pulled on the lever, plunging the bunker back into darkness. In the distance, the light from the kitchen shined down the wooden stairs and beckoned them back to the world above and all of its current problems.

34

JACK UNSCREWED THE CAP from his water bottle and took a sip. Then he handed it to Joseph. "You need to stay hydrated."

Joseph took the water bottle and gulped.

They were sitting around the dining room table, the chairs having been picked up and returned to their proper places. The afternoon was stretching on, the sun shining through the windows and cutting through floating dust in broad bands of light.

"Any news on the rest of the unit?" Johnson asked Brown. "Brady, Thompson, McConell?"

Brown shook his head. "No response."

"Doesn't mean anything," Johnson mumbled, staring down at his hands. "They could've gotten out." He met Brown's eyes. "What else? You mentioned a development."

Jack stole a glance at Stacey. Developments were exactly what they needed.

Brown folded his hands on the table in front of him and leaned forward onto his elbows. "Sokolov was killed last night."

Johnson blinked, and now Stacey leaned forward.

"How?" Stacey asked.

"Assassinated."

"Who's Sokolov?" Jack asked.

"The director of the SVR's Line S," Johnson said.

Jack frowned, his face asking, *And?*

Stacey looked at Johnson. "That's half a dozen of the president's inner circle taken out in the last three weeks."

Jack looked at his wife and wondered how she could know that, and suddenly, there was that damn rabbit peeking out of its hole again. It was like some arcade whack-a-mole that was laughing at him, taunting him, knowing it was too fast for him.

"Fedyenka?" Johnson asked.

"Without a doubt," Brown said. "CIA captured the whole thing. They had surveillance on Sokolov at the time. Live feed straight back to Langley. The other hits seem to have been mafia jobs, which Fedyenka has influence with. But this one..." He paused for dramatic effect. "The assassin is on Osprey's payroll."

"What's Moscow saying?" Johnson asked.

Brown leaned back and crossed his arms. "They're blaming Ukraine. It's a story that serves them better than admitting a rogue faction of the FSB is taking out top Kremlin brass. But the Agency is picking up a lot of chatter, too. The FSB wants Fedyenka dealt with yesterday. They've completely run out of patience, and they're all wondering who's next. They've beefed up their private security and started limiting their exposure. The Agency believes that the SVR has begun activating their agents in the US to go after Osprey."

"The Osprey they're funding and supporting," Jack said as he wrung his hands beneath the table.

"Maybe," Johnson warned. "We don't have proof."

Jack rolled his eyes.

"Anything else?" Johnson asked Brown.

"That's all I was able to get before you called." He tapped his forefinger on the tabletop. "They gunned down Monica in traffic, and she wasn't even part of our team."

"Nope. Just doing us a favor," Johnson said.

"Which means someone had intimate knowledge of our contingency plans."

"Our entire operation," Johnson said.

Brown started, "You think Brady or Thompson—"

"No," Johnson said, cutting him off. Then he sighed. "But it makes the most sense."

"You think Fedyenka got to them? Paid them off?" Jack asked.

"This isn't Fedyenka," Stacey said. She looked up at Johnson. "Is it?"

Johnson held her gaze, not saying anything.

"This is the Agency not even bothering to use Osprey. They're cleaning up after themselves," she said. "Erasing me from their books. Vadim, Jack, Trenton, Newell, your Overwatch...all of it."

Now Jack leaned forward, inserting himself between them. "If that's true, if they're scrubbing everything but Fedyenka, then they must have some pretty big plans for him, right? Plans that, once executed, there's no way that 'Project Vadim'—or whatever they called it—could ever end up in front of a senate judiciary committee."

"Something bigger than just influencing a Russian election," Brown mumbled.

They sat in silence for a moment, and then Johnson asked Brown, "You have your personal cell?"

Brown dug the unsecured cell phone out of his pocket and held it up.

Johnson looked at Stacey for approval, and Stacey seemed to grant it, though not without a moment of hesitation.

"What?" Jack asked, not understanding.

"It's an unsecured line," Stacey explained. "One they'd probably be monitoring."

"No probably about it," Brown said.

Jack blinked. "You're telling them where we are?"

"With the bunker, it's our safest and quickest way to see who is behind this," Johnson said. "We can't run forever."

"But won't they know it's intentional?"

"Maybe. But they'll still have to come," Johnson said.

Jack slid the chair back and stood. He walked over to the window and stared out at the tree line. He didn't like it. Mainly because they had no idea who would be coming. It could be the whole freaking FBI that showed up, intent on eliminating domestic terrorists wanted for bombing a school. Or a CIA death squad. Or members of Fedyenka's private army. But he knew Johnson was right. This was the fastest, easiest way to find out what they were dealing with. They had nothing otherwise. Whoever it was who had started taking out Johnson's team had first primed the playing field by eliminating all channels of information. They were shut out and closed off, unable to turn to anyone for help.

And Jack thought that the bombing must have been both the plan and backup plan rolled into one. If Jack had been killed at the house, and Joseph and Stacey had been taken, then there would be no need for all this drama. In fact, maybe the explosion would have been reported as a gas leak. Nothing to see here. But in the event that something didn't go according to plan, the explosion option had presented an adaptable story that could be used to turn the entire world against them. To trap them. Jack could only hope that, this being their plan B, they hadn't made every allowance for their still being alive. Perhaps there was a loophole somewhere, a weak point Stacey and Johnson could find and take advantage of.

Jack turned back toward the table, took a long look at Joseph, and then nodded. "Okay."

"SO YOUR BOY KNOWS who Wesley Snipes is," Brown said. He was holding a pair of binoculars.

Jack looked at him and smiled. "Like I said, I've kind of forced him to relive parts of my own childhood."

Brown shook his head. "Nothing wrong with that. He seems to really enjoy it. Bet he wins all the movie trivia games."

"Some of his friends are movie buffs too, I think. They actually pick out some of this stuff for themselves. A lot easier with Netflix and everything. I tried explaining Blockbuster to him, and he couldn't believe it."

"Be kind and rewind and all that?" He chuckled. "Spoiled kids."

"I know, right? I remember having to set my alarm for 6 a.m. on Saturday mornings to watch my favorite cartoon."

"You didn't have the VCR set to record it?"

"Didn't trust it."

Brown laughed. "And commercials!"

"I don't even think they know what commercials are outside the adds they see on YouTube. And they sure as hell ain't the same as what we grew up on. I mean, those jingles..."

Brown nodded. "You mean like the LEGO Maniac tune. Or the Rice Krispies song?"

"Or Folgers in your cup," Jack said.

"Tony the Tiger."

"My Buddy."

Brown shook his head. "Damn. You're right. We could probably go on all day with this."

"I think just about every cereal had its own song or its own catchphrase. Sometimes I'll pull one out when handing a box to Joseph. Like if he asks for Trix, I'll repeat the silly rabbit line. Of course, he looks at me like I'm an idiot."

Brown laughed.

The two of them were standing on opposite sides of a window on the upper floor. They were looking out over the property, watching for signs of activity while Stacey and Johnson prepared for their little operation below.

"Seems like a good kid," Brown said, his tone more serious.

Jack met his eye. "He is."

Brown seemed to consider it for a moment before breaking eye contact and looking back out the window. But something in that split-second moment struck Jack as odd, as if there was some emotional weight hanging from the back of the man's eyes. Jack probed. "You have a family?"

Without turning back to face him, Brown simply nodded.

"Kids?" Jack asked.

"Two."

"Gotta be hard in this line of work," Jack said.

Another nod, and Jack swore he saw a sparkle appear in Brown's eyes. He didn't know what to do with that, and he rethought their conversation. *Crap*, he thought. Had he projected his own childhood experience onto Brown's? He didn't know where Brown grew up, but being an African-American kid in the '80s, there was a pretty good chance that he didn't view those days the same as he did. He was about to ask about it when the sound of footsteps came up the stairs behind them and broke whatever tension had started priming the walls of the room.

Jack turned and saw Joseph.

"Mom wants to know if you're ready," Joseph asked him.

"Sure."

Joseph turned and took the answer back down the stairs with him.

Jack looked at Brown again. The secret-agent man stood, took one more sweeping look over the fields with his binoculars, and then headed for the stairs.

Jack followed him down.

Stacey had all the gear they'd grabbed from the house out of the bag and laid out across the dining room table. She and Johnson were checking magazines and loading the weapons. When he stepped close, she handed him the MP7A2 he'd used yesterday morning. He checked it and then slung it over his shoulder.

"Joe," he called.

Joseph walked over, pulling an earbud from his ear. "Yeah?"

He took a vest off the table and handed it to him. "Put this on."

Joseph took the tactical vest and pulled it over his head. Jack tightened it. Then he slipped into a vest of his own, the same one that had been slashed by a knife the day before. He handed Stacey hers.

Brown stepped to the table and surveyed the remaining arsenal. "Shotgun's going to be a little loud. Mind if I grab this UMP?"

"Please," Stacey said, nodding at the suppressed semiautomatic.

Brown picked it up.

"You have the radios?" Johnson asked Brown.

"Right here," he answered. He unzipped a pocket in the side of an army bag and began pulling them out and laying them on the table. "Only have three though." They each had a wired earpiece with a mic.

Stacey finished looking over the MP15T that she'd taken from the Reba wall and grabbed her seared Glock and a radio off the table. She clipped the radio to her vest and fitted the earpiece over her ear. Then she grabbed a smoke grenade off the table. She looked at Jack. "Take Joe to the bunker."

Jack stepped close to her, and despite the recent stirring of distrustful feelings, he wrapped his arm around her waist. "You be careful."

"Always."

He looked up at Johnson, who was handling a couple of grenades. "You watch her."

He snickered as he clipped one of the radios to his belt. "More like she'll be watching me," he said.

Again Jack got the impression that Johnson knew more about his wife's capabilities than he did. He tried not to let it bother him. Instead, he turned his attention to Brown and nodded. "Good luck."

Brown reached out and shook his hand. "Name is Marcus Bryant. Our unit took the names of famous athletes. Jim Brown was my favorite." He moved his gaze to Joe and winked.

Jack looked at Johnson, realizing that he'd never heard the agent's first name, or if he had, he'd long forgotten it. "Brad?" he asked with a smile.

Johnson frowned as he examined a bolt-action M24 sniper rifle from Jack and Stacey's bag. He slung it over his shoulder. "The quarterback for the Vikings? No." He smiled as he picked up an MP5SD. "Magic."

Joseph brought a hand to his mouth and laughed.

"Wow," Stacey said. She looked at Jack and nodded toward Johnson. "Magic."

"I heard. But I'm thinking of a different kind of Magic."

"That's what I was thinking too," Stacey said.

Brown smiled. "His real name actually *is* Mike."

Johnson hung his head as Jack sounded off a little techno beat, and they all laughed.

The laughter relieved the tension, but only for a moment.

Stacey reached out and grabbed Joseph's shoulders, pulling him into herself. She wrapped her arms around him and held him tight. Jack could tell she was trying not to cry. He could see the conflict in her face, the mother who might never see her son again tugging against the cold stoicism of a trained professional.

When she let him go, it was Joseph who had tears running down his face.

"It's going to be okay," she told him. She leaned forward and kissed his forehead. "I love you. And I'm sorry for all of this."

Joseph couldn't speak. He was trying too hard to keep from crying in front of Wesley Snipes.

"Okay, Magic Mike," Stacey said to Johnson while disengaging from her family, "let's get this show on the road."

She, Johnson, and Brown cleared off the rest of the table, stuffing their pockets and strapping on the remaining equipment.

Jack took Joseph's hand and led him into the kitchen. He looked back at Stacey before descending into the cellar and mouthed the words, "I love you." Even though, at the moment, that fact was a bit blurred, like he was seeing it through the rain. It was a feeling he was familiar with ever since learning that she wasn't really Stacey but Anna. Though the feeling had always been temporary, the rain eventually stopping and the reemerging sun evaporating his doubt. But for some reason this time seemed different. As if finally just realizing that there would never actually come a day that she would trust him with the entire story.

And while it was true that he could see through her eyes that she would want to protect him from certain unpleasant facts, he knew that she was deceiving him. After all, she'd led him to believe that she'd left the Agency after Trenton, only for him to find out in the aftermath of Joseph's kidnapping that she'd still been very much in its employ, sneaking off on special assignments and lying to him about it. He'd gotten over it though, and once again, she'd promised to tell him everything going forward.

Yet, it was obvious from her conversation with Johnson just now that she was still in the loop when it came to certain matters of intelligence. Did that mean that she was still working for them? Either way, she'd left Jack out of it. And whether it was to protect him or not, he was finally getting a glimpse of the final picture—old with great-grandkids playing at their feet and still not knowing how much of what he believed about her was true. Not knowing what she thought about, what memories tormented her. Whom she'd killed, had sex with.

He blinked and waved, wondering if he'd ever see her again. He took the narrow steps one at a time, his vision blurred by stinging emotion. *What a life,* he thought. And out of nowhere, and for some strange reason he couldn't possibly understand in the moment, he thought of Bethany, his little daughter who had never lived to see her first birthday.

"Dad?"

Jack looked around and saw that he was already at the bottom of the steps, and that Joseph was waiting for him over by the booby-trapped corridor. Jack joined him and then pulled the false wall closed behind them.

35

STACEY STOOD BY BROWN'S car, looking out over the tall grass that surrounded them. She held the Smith & Wesson tactical rifle in her hands, flexing her fingers around the handgrip attached to the quadrail. "How long do you think?" she asked over her shoulder. She watched as Brown activated his personal phone and dialed Monica's number.

Brown held up a finger, telling her to wait a second. "Monica, it's me, Brown. Where are you? What happened? We're holed up in Ohio. Call me back, and I'll give you the coordinates. God, I hope you're okay." He paused. "Sorry for getting you into this." And he hung up. Then he tossed the phone into the car.

"I think that'll do it," Stacey said, staring through the car window and to the phone sitting on the passenger seat. She tried to imagine its signal broadcasting into the sky, whoever was looking for it suddenly jumping to their feet, shouting orders and preparing people to move out. They would come, alright. "You sure you don't want to move the car somewhere else?"

Johnson shook his head. "I know what you're thinking. You want the battle as far away from that bunker as possible. But strategically, this is the best location we're gonna find in the small amount of time we have. If we get them to converge on the car, we have overlook from the house, the hill, and cover from the woods. We have a kill zone right here."

She knew he was right.

Johnson raised his hand over his eyes to shield them from the setting sun. He pointed to the west, to the hill. "Jim, why don't you take the hill." Then he turned his head, looking east. "Stacey, the tree line. I'll take the roof of the house."

"Once they pinpoint your location, you'll be trapped," Stacey said.

"Then I guess I'll just have to count on you two to cover me. Radio check."

They checked the radios that Brown had brought to make sure they were on the same frequency and in working order.

"Okay, let's go get in position." He made eye contact with both of them. "Good luck."

Without another word, Brown turned and started jogging to the hill, the submachine gun in his hands.

Stacey smiled at Johnson. "Bet you never thought it would all end up here."

He shrugged, the sniper rifle on his back poking upward as he did so. "I always thought it'd be *against* someone like you, not *beside* you. But one way or another, you were always in my finale."

Stacey dropped her gaze. "If it is the Company that's coming, then our government betrayed us both."

He laughed. "Our government has been betraying a lot of people for a long time. Thus the reason for my special unit."

"So you always knew they'd come for you?"

"There were always two possibilities. Either we rooted out the corruption we found, or we would discover that the corruption went so fundamentally deep that it would be impossible to fix without killing the whole tree."

"Making yourself a liability in the process."

He nodded. "Unfortunately, it looks like it's the latter, and now it's my team that's being eradicated."

"So the whole system is terminal, then?"

"I think that those who rise to power within a corrupt system must be corrupt themselves. Or if not, the system will do everything it can to destroy them."

"The system," Stacey repeated under her breath.

"The people who make up the system," Johnson clarified.

"I hope you're wrong about that," Stacey said.

"So do I. And yet, here we are."

Brown's voice cut through the space between them, sounding out in each of their left ears. *"You two just gonna stand there all night?"*

Stacey looked up at the sky and to the dark blue-gray hues that outlined the clouds. Was there a satellite positioning on the cell signal right now? She resisted the urge to raise a middle finger to the sky and instead stepped back away from the car. She nodded to Johnson, nothing more needing to be said between them. They ran off in opposite directions.

But Stacey didn't make it halfway to her designated position before she spotted movement in the trees ahead of her.

36

JACK SAT ON THE couch and watched Joseph as he stood in front of the shelves that lined the wall beside the television and called out the movie titles he found there. Jack was trying not to think about what was happening on the surface and was happy for the distraction.

"*End of Days*," Joseph called out, holding a VHS tape in his hands.

"With Arnold," Jack acknowledged. He considered it. "Two, two and a half stars."

Joseph slid the movie back onto the shelf and pulled out the next. "*Innerspace.*"

"What?" Jack exclaimed. "This guy has *Innerspace*?" He could hardly believe it. It just didn't seem to gel with the image of the redneck prepper his mind had conjured up. "It's a classic! Dennis Quaid, Meg Ryan, and Martin Short. Five stars, hands down."

"Really?" Joseph asked, flipping the box around so he could read the description on the back.

"Absolutely. Still holds up. We should watch it."

"Now?"

"Why not?" He watched Joe slide the cassette out of the sleeve and examine the black box like it was something from another planet. Jack laughed and stood, reaching for it. "I'll show you." He bent over and pushed the power button on the VCR. Then he hit the eject button in case there was already a movie in it. There was. A cassette popped out, but there was no label on it. Jack pulled it out and looked it over.

"Fuji?" Joseph asked, seeing a white label on the face of the cassette.

"It's a blank tape. Or was. For recording on. Fuji is just the brand." He held it up. "I'm a little curious to know what's on it."

"Me too," Joe said.

Jack showed Joseph how to push the cassette into the VCR, and they both stood there, listening to the old machine accept the tape as it clicked and whirred. Jack turned on the TV and saw that the correct channel was already cued. The tape was playing.

The picture was not good, and white static moved back and forth in long bands across the bottom as the word TRACK-ING appeared on the screen along with a white status bar that couldn't seem to make up its mind.

"What's happening?" Joseph asked.

Jack was a little worried that once the snow cleared, they'd be staring at some hardcore post-apocalyptic porn or something. "The VCR is auto-tracking, trying to correct the picture."

"How does it do that?"

Jack thought about it. "I have no idea." He started to look for a remote to see if he could adjust it manually, but then the lines disappeared. "There we go," Jack said.

Joseph squinted. "The picture is horrible."

"Yeah, well, you're looking at magnetic tape. Quality depends on how well the tape holds up, the speed the guy recorded it, and what the actual picture looked like on the TV while he recorded it. At best, I think you're looking at 240 lines. The Blu-ray player and TV at home—" He paused, a little shocked at his own mental slip. "When we had a home, I mean," he added, trying to make a joke out of it. "Blu-ray, or HD, is 1080 lines. Almost five times clearer."

"And 4K UHD is 2180," Joe said.

Jack nodded. "Yeah."

Joseph pointed at the blurry image. "So what are we even looking at?"

"Looks like old news footage of..." He stopped, recognizing the date that was displayed on the screen. April 19, 1995. He knelt back down and hit the fast-forward button, sending the female news anchor on the screen into high-speed, jerking spasms. Then men in blue coats appeared, walking back and forth in a static time-lapse. Then the building.

Jack let go of the FF button and stood back. "Oklahoma City." He looked back over to the shelving, paying closer attention to the books and their titles, and was surprised that he actually recognized quite a few of them. "Interesting," he muttered. And suddenly this redneck prepper he had imagined waving a Confederate flag in one hand and a Don't Tread On Me flag in the other began transforming into something a little more familiar. Instead of the Confederate flag, he was maybe now holding the old Colonial flag with its thirteen stars and stripes. And instead of the Gadsden flag was perhaps a copy of the US Constitution. Jack wondered if there might be more to the story behind this guy's imprisonment. After all, it wouldn't be the first time a patriot had been set up and wrongfully imprisoned, would it? *Calm down, Jack,* he told himself. *He could just be a Tim McVeigh fan.*

"What happened in Oklahoma City?" Joe asked.

"A bombing. Official story is that a domestic terrorist blew up the building with a truck bomb."

"Why?"

"Supposedly to get back at the federal government for Waco and Ruby Ridge. To start a revolution."

"What do you mean, 'official story'?"

Jack looked at him and smiled, wondering if now was the right time to introduce his son to the red pill. He didn't think it was. "Let's just say that the police reports from that morning kind of paint a different scenario." He looked back at the TV. "And I'm guessing that's what this is. Recordings of the news, live as it was happening. Reports of multiple bombs found within the building. But we'll talk about all that later. Just, in the meantime, don't believe everything you hear on TV. Or learn in school." He hit the STOP button and ejected the tape.

"I know. You've told me that a hundred times."

"In the words of *Braveheart*, 'History is often written by those who hang heroes.'"

"You think the bomber was a hero?"

Jack blinked. "Hell no. I'm just saying that the people in charge usually get to put their version of events in the history books."

"Like JFK?"

"Yeah, like JFK. What do you know about it?"

"Mr. Cella showed us some of it a few weeks ago. We were supposed to watch more of it later."

"The Kevin Costner one?"

"Yeah. But Tommy showed me some other documentary that had something to do with George H. W. Bush and the CIA."

"Really?" Jack had seen that documentary. Used to have it until it melted in the fire that destroyed their first house. "Why didn't you tell me?"

Joseph shrugged.

"Dude, that stuff is my jam. Or at least it used to be."

"Dad, I don't think anyone says that anymore."

Jack frowned. "Oh, sorry. I won't say it again."

"Tommy and Moses said that E. Howard Hunt, the guy Ed Harris played in *All The President's Men*, and—"

"Wait," Jack said, holding up a hand and shaking his head. "Your friends know who Ed Harris is?"

Joseph shot him an impatient look.

Jack smiled. "You know who E. Howard Hunt is from Mr. Cella?"

"I don't think so. Moses is really into all that conspiracy stuff. He reads books about it."

"Really?" Jack couldn't believe that his own son had been introduced to this stuff by someone other than him. He'd thought it was still too early to start feeding him red pills, and now it looked like someone else had capitalized on his hesitation. Figured. He wondered what other topics he might have waited too long to broach.

"Yeah, but some of the other teachers get mad at him when they see him with them, so he hides them."

"The books?" Now Jack was beginning to understand. "Is that why you didn't tell me? Because you thought I'd be mad like the other teachers?" Jack certainly understood that, having lived through it himself. Granted, it seemed more acceptable to question official stories now, even despite all the "fact-checking" that the "invisible government," as Edward Bernays called them, used to try redirecting people back to the "official" narratives.

But back when Jack was doing his Jerry Fletcher thing, just questioning the official timeline of an event had been enough to get one branded as an unpatriotic commie tinfoiled-hat nutjob who hated freedom and should be shot for treason. He'd lost more than a handful of friends over heated debates on what the laws of physics allowed versus certain accepted narratives.

Joseph shrugged, thinking about it for perhaps the first time. "I don't know. Maybe."

"Well, you can talk to me about anything anytime. I'll never make you feel stupid about it. Whatever it is. Got it? My motto is to question everything, and I'd be honored to help you do that."

"Okay," Joseph said. Though they both pretended that the ceiling didn't just open and that an elephant wearing ten years of secrets hadn't just descend into the room, twirling in aerial ribbons like a zoo rendition of some Cirque du Soleil act.

Talk to me about anything except our family, Jack thought. He just didn't have the mental stamina to get back into that ring right now, so he changed gears. "Go ahead. Put *Innerspace* in." He set the Fuji tape on the top of the TV and went back to the couch, letting Joseph take a shot at working the old machine.

Suddenly, Dennis Quaid appeared, standing in the middle of the road, with a towel around his waist.

"You're going to have to rewind it," Jack said.

"How do I do that?"

"Well, you can hold down the rewind button and watch the whole thing go backwards, or you can hit STOP and then hit REWIND. It'll go a lot faster that way."

"Okay." He hit stop, and the screen went blue. Then he hit the REWIND button, and left-facing arrows appeared in the bottom corner of the screen as the machine whined. "Do you have to do this at the end of every movie?"

"Yeah. If the tape runs all the way to the end, then it would usually rewind automatically. If you returned a rental and it wasn't rewound, they could hit you with a fine."

"So weird."

"Ancient technology, I know." He chuckled. "I was just talking about this with Agent Brown."

The VCR clicked, the arrows replaced by the word STOP.

Jack leaned back and interlaced his fingers behind his head. "Okay, let's do it. Hit PLAY."

Joseph did and then sat down on the couch next to him. They watched the movie, both of them trying not to think about what might be going on above them.

37

STACEY HAD DROPPED TO her stomach immediately and was now lying still in the tall grass, looking through the scope of the MP15T. There was definitely movement in the trees ahead of her, about a hundred yards out. The sun had dipped beneath the horizon behind her, and the sky was afire in a myriad of pink hues and purple clouds. The autumn tree line seemed to glow gold, the leafy branches swaying in a gentle evening breeze as the grass rustled around her.

She couldn't tell how many there were, but they were definitely there. At first she thought it had just been an optical illusion—that she'd imagined it or that maybe it had been a deer. But she'd seen through the scope, bisected by the data lines, a flash of the unmistakable black steel of an assault rifle and a gloved hand gripping the barrel. It had only been a fraction of a second as the figure passed quickly between two trees, but it had been enough. They were about to be attacked. The questions were: by who, how many, would they wait until dark, and how the hell had they gotten here so fast?

The who and how didn't matter. Not right now. If they survived the how many and when, then those questions would become of utmost importance, but not until they outlived the other two.

She hit the mic on the wire and whispered, "We have company east. At least one in the trees."

Johnson's voice whispered back, *"Copy that."*

"Won't make it to the roof, then," she said.

"Negative. Will have to use window."

She could tell from the strain in his voice that he was in the house and running up the steps, hurrying to get into position. She tilted her head toward her left until the house was in her periphery. The sunset behind it made it hard to look at, and she hoped the brightness had covered Johnson's dash back into it.

"*Brown, anything west?*" Johnson asked.

No response.

"*Brown, do you copy?*" he said into the mic again.

Still nothing.

"*Stacey, can you see him?*"

She waited for another breeze and then slowly rolled onto her back, sitting up just enough to catch sight of the hill they'd last seen Brown heading for. She brought the rifle up and looked through the scope. She expected to see the bottom of his feet as he lay on his stomach, watching their western flank, but all she saw was grass. "Negative. Hill is empty. Maybe he went down the other side."

"*Scanning eastern tree line. Not seeing any signs of movement.*"

She could hear the next question in Johnson's voice, even if he didn't say it out loud. "Yeah, I'm sure. Assault rifle, gloved hands. It was only a flash, but I saw it."

"*What time?*"

"My twelve o'clock."

"*I got you.*" A pause. "*Not seeing anything. Cover the tree line. I'm moving to the west window.*"

"Copy." She rolled back onto her stomach and aimed the rifle back into the shadowed woods. She figured that whoever was out there hadn't seen her, or else she'd already be dead, either from a sniper's bullet or from an all-out assault. She figured they were probably settling down and waiting until dark to make their move. She looked at her watch and figured they had about forty-five minutes. So that answered the when. "Any sign of Brown?" she asked.

"*Negative. West looks clear. Checking north and south.*"

She blinked and felt her heart rate begin to accelerate. It had been a long time since she'd been in this position, lying still behind a scope. She tried to distract herself from thinking about Jack and Joseph hiding in the bunker by reciting everything her father used to tell her about Lady Death, the Russian sniper Lyudmila Mikhailovna Pavlichenko, the woman whom she grew up wanting to become. And now here she was, acting out the role. Only she wasn't fighting for the Red Army. She wasn't fighting for *any* army. Or any flag. She was simply fighting to save her family. And she would go to war with any flag she needed to if that's what it would take. She believed that her father would have done the same. In fact, had done the same by arranging for her to have a life in the United States.

And again, as she often did, she wondered what kind of things her father had done while with the KGB, the things he had been willing to compromise, the things he regretted, where loyalty to the Motherland ended or if it even had. She wondered what he would think of the things she'd done for her own flag, if he would've been the one person she could've talked to who would've understood.

She blinked. This was not where she'd intended her thoughts to go, and she thew them out of her head. Sentimentalism would not aid her in what was about to go down. *Lady Death*, she told herself, *credited with 309 kills. Born 1916 in present-day Ukraine. 54th Stenka Razin Rifle Regiment in 25th Rifle Division. Siege of Odessa. Siege of Sevastopol.* She searched for the inspiration that usually came from thinking of such a person, a woman in the Red Army who had fought the Nazis. *Volunteered for the infantry when Germany invaded. Was accepted as a sniper. Due to weapon shortages, she'd only been issued a frag grenade. Taking a rifle from a fallen comrade, she'd proven her skill by hitting her first targets. Promoted to senior sergeant after one hundred confirmed kills.*

Stacey took a deep breath, imagining herself beside the famed sniper. *As the sniper. She married another sniper, but he was killed shortly after.*

But Stacey would not lose her husband. Not today, and not to these assholes.

"What are we thinking?" she asked, speaking into the mic.

"If you're right, then I'm thinking we have about half an hour before they move in."

"What else are we thinking?"

He didn't answer. But he didn't need to. They both knew the answer to her real question, the one that guessed as to how they could have already been found.

They waited in silence as a growing darkness spread from the east, chasing the fiery hues across the sky and over the horizon.

<h1 style="text-align:center">38</h1>

THEY WERE FORTY-FIVE MINUTES through the movie. It was silly and entertaining, and if not for the circumstances, Joseph would have really enjoyed this time spent with his dad. But he couldn't stop thinking about what might be going on above them. Was his mom okay? Was their plan working? The not knowing was driving him insane, and as much as he tried to let the fuzzy images of Martin Short and Meg Ryan transport him somewhere else, it just wasn't happening.

He knew his dad felt the same way, because he kept looking at his watch. Finally, his dad got up and walked over to the VCR and hit pause. The screen froze. Sort of. A string of white lines appeared, running horizontally across Meg Ryan's face and distorting it like a carnival mirror.

"Not working, is it?" his dad asked.

Joseph shook his head.

His dad sat back down beside him and turned so that he was facing him, his right leg crossed over his left and his right arm extended over the back of the couch.

"Joe," he said.

Joseph met his eyes and knew that he didn't want to hear whatever it was his dad was about to say.

"At the school..."

Joe swallowed the lump that had just climbed into his throat. He could feel his heart begin racing in his chest. *No.* He didn't want to hear this.

His dad looked away for a moment, unable to bear looking into his glassy eyes, which was confirmation enough that the information he had was going to be painful. Was it Priscilla?

Zane? Bryan? Was it *all* of them? Were his friends dead? "Who?" he heard himself whisper.

His dad looked back at him. "I don't know who, Joe. I just know that they're reporting three deaths."

Joseph felt as if the entire universe had just punched him in the gut. His world teetered and spun. His vision grew fuzzy, like the paused VHS tape, and he leaned back against the couch. He turned his face into it, wanting to hide the stinging tears from his father, but before he knew it, his father was holding him tight, his strong arms wrapped around him and squeezing. Joe could feel his dad's chest against his own and could tell that he was crying. Joe clutched at his dad's shirt and let his own tears fall.

"Was Mrs. Hatfield one of the three?" Joseph asked. He could feel his dad shake his head.

"I don't know. It's possible that you and she are both included in the three. Which would leave only one other."

And then they separated, wiping their eyes and noses. They sat quietly for a few minutes, just staring at the paused screen, drawn into the white static lines as if they were the mesmerizing flames of a campfire.

"Hey," his dad said, finally breaking the silence. "Your mom and I used to play this game back in the day. You ever hear of Six Degrees of Kevin Bacon?"

Joe wiped his nose on his shirt. "No."

"Okay, so it's based on the theory that any actor can be linked to a movie with Kevin Bacon within six movies."

Joe raised an eyebrow.

"'Six degrees of separation' is a theory that says that any two people are just six or fewer acquaintances apart from each other. So Six Degrees of Kevin Bacon is a modified movie version of that premise."

"Okay, so, like, I have to link Chris Hemsworth to Kevin Bacon in six movies or less?"

"Yeah, and the fewer connections, the higher the score. For example, Chris Hemsworth was in *Bad Times at the El Royale* with Jeff Bridges, who was in *Blown Away* with Tommy Lee Jones, who was in *Batman Forever* with Val Kilmer, who was in *The Saint* with Elisabeth Shue, who was in *Hollow Man* with Kevin Bacon."

Joseph blinked.

"And that was just off the top of my head," his dad said. Then he wiped a lingering tear off his cheek and said, "But your mom and I just played actor to actor. We didn't use Kevin Bacon as the common denominator. So we'd just come up with two random actors and see who could link them in the fewest movies. But the goal is to completely stump the other person."

"What was the hardest one you ever came up with?"

"I think it might have been Van Damme to Steven Seagal. Mind you, that was before the *Expendables* movies."

"Okay, then." Joseph rubbed his chin, pondering a pair. "Danny DeVito—"

"Danny DeVito?" Jack cried, leaning forward and shaking his head. "Wow. I really did brainwash you with my own childhood."

"As I was saying. Danny DeVito to...Charles Bronson."

"What?"

Joseph shrugged.

"Wow, okay." He thought about it. "Okay. Charles Bronson was in *The Magnificent Seven* with Yul Brynner, who was in *The Ten Commandments* with Charlton Heston, who was in *Tombstone* with Michael Biehn, who was in *Terminator* with Arnold, who was in *Twins* with DeVito." He slapped his knee. "Blam!"

Joseph laughed. "I'm gonna have to fact-check *Tombstone*, but okay."

"You do that. Now I have an easy one for you. Brie Larson to Sylvester Stallone. And by the way, I have it in two."

Joseph leaned back against the couch, and as his tears dried, he allowed himself to get lost in the game.

39

"SHOULD I MAKE MY way back to Brown?" Stacey asked through the radio.

"*Negative,*" Johnson's answer came back in her earpiece. "*If they're there, they'll see you. Besides, I don't see him anywhere.*"

Stacey didn't know where he could've gone. Maybe he was hiding in his car? Maybe in the cornfield? Or maybe he had run right into the enemy and was already dead.

She glanced up at the sky. It was a deep purple now, and the clouds were nearly invisible. They'd be coming any moment. She shifted her weight ever so slightly, trying to keep her shoulders from locking up. She'd been leaning on her elbows for half an hour, and her body was starting to protest.

"*Drone launched from the north.*"

She thumbed the mic. "Can you take it? If they have infrared, I'm dead."

"*Copy that.*"

Silence.

She turned her head and tried looking up to her left, to see if she could spot the drone. She knew it would still be on the other side of the house and too far away for her to make out, but she couldn't help trying. If it was able to pick up her heat signature and they saw her just lying there in the middle of the field...

"*Drone down.*"

She sighed with relief.

"*Here they come. From the north. I count six...seven...ten... I got twelve approaching from the north. Anything east?*"

She swore under her breath and looked through the scope, sweeping it over the tree line. She hit the night vision, and the dark trees turned green and white. "Neg—" But then she saw them. "Yes. I count…" She moved the scope to the left and picked up more bodies. They were stepping out of the tree line, crouched with weapons raised. They had night-vision gear strapped to their heads. And though they were sweeping their weapons back and forth, she could tell that they were mostly focused on the house. "I got ten fanning out from the woods."

"Checking south."

While she waited for the report, she set her crosshairs over the face of the person furthest away. With any luck, her silenced round would drop him or her without the others noticing. If so, maybe she could pick off half of them before they even noticed.

"One other wave coming from the southwest. I count another ten."

That made thirty-two. "Maybe this wasn't such a good idea. Why aren't they going for the car?"

"Just take your time. Choose your targets from the back. I've got one down. Two."

She still had the person's face in her crosshairs and squeezed the trigger. The person's head whipped back and out of the scope. She moved the rifle to the right an inch just in time to catch one of the others looking back at the sound of their teammate going down. She put a bullet through their head too. "Two down."

That left twenty-eight.

"Two more."

Twenty-six.

She knew that their window of opportunity was closing fast. That at any moment one of the attackers would notice—

Machine-gun fire erupted from the north, the sound of it traveling over the fields and rebounding off the tree line.

"Shit. I'm made," Johnson's voice reported.

Stacey turned to see muzzle flashes near the house. When she looked back through the scope, she saw that the people in front of her, now about fifty yards away, had taken off for the house. She let them run past her, pivoting on a knee and swinging the rifle around at their backs. She squeezed the trigger. One green body went down. She adjusted and fired again. Missed. Adjusted and squeezed. Another down. She shot one more person, but the bullet failed to kill them instantly, and the target started screaming out to the others.

She dropped back to the ground and lay still. She said into the mic, "Three more down, but I could use some cover."

"Hold on."

There were five left in front of her, and now they were all turned away from the house and facing back toward the tree line, searching for whoever had just shot at their backs. If she shot them now, they'd get a fix on her location, and she wouldn't stand a chance with mere grass as her cover. She could only hope that Johnson could get off a shot or two and draw their attention back to him.

Then one of them pitched forward, their head gone, and the rest of them did turn back to the house. She sighed in relief as Johnson shot another one. The three who remained didn't stand around trying to determine where the shots were coming from. They knew there was at least one behind them and at least one up ahead, and they took off, spreading away from each other and each running in a zigzag pattern for the house.

"Grenade," Johnson said.

An explosion cut through the machine-gun fire, momentarily drowning it out as a flash of light filled the front yard of the house. She knew what that meant. They were getting close to breaching the house, and Johnson had tossed a grenade out the window in an attempt to keep them back.

Stacey stood and aimed the rifle in the direction of the hidden cars positioned southwest of the house. She could see little green shadows sprinting across the grass and converging on Johnson's position. No way he could survive that.

Suddenly, another explosion erupted, though not one from any grenade, and the night turned into midday. She dropped the scope from her eyes, blinded from glimpsing the spectacle through the night vision. A line of fire ripped from north to south across the back end of the property along where they'd seen a fence standing earlier.

"What the hell was that?" Johnson asked.

"Explosives across the western gate," she said, rubbing her eyes and seeing nothing but bright spots and floating stars. She stumbled back to her feet and trudged toward the house.

And that was when everything turned to chaos.

40

"WHAT WAS THAT?" JOSEPH asked as soon as the lights stopped flickering.

Jack looked over at the door, wondering the same thing. It sounded like an explosion. A huge explosion. Like the house had just blown up. Did someone trip an old booby trap left by the prepper, or had a drone fired missiles into the old barn house? "Sounded like an explosion." He saw no reason to lie to him. They were in this together now.

"You think Mom's okay?"

How the hell would I know? "I'm sure she's fine."

They sat in silence for a while, waiting for the sound of another explosion, or the door to open, or...anything. But nothing happened.

Finally, Joseph looked up at him. "Dad?"

Jack met his gaze. "Yeah?" He watched his son bring his fingers to his throat and trace the scars. His little fingers seemed to stir memories out from within those thin white lines. Jack swallowed hard.

"Will you tell me what happened?"

They had told him most things back at the cabin, but they hadn't gotten to this, and they had obviously sidestepped the whole cruise-ship ordeal. But he deserved to know. Maybe not the cruise ship, but everything else. "Do you remember anything?"

"I remember the hospital. I remember after. I remember something about a big house. And Grandma."

Jack took a deep breath.

And this time, he told him everything he knew. Even the cruise ship and the Trenton Thunder game, though he downplayed Stacey's role in both of them.

41

STACEY LOOKED THROUGH THE scope, trying to find any sign of their attackers in the aftermath of the explosion that had ripped open the western field. She didn't see them anywhere and wondered if they could've given up on the house, believing that they'd walked into a trap and retreating into the woods. Or maybe they were crawling through the grass, still on their way to Johnson.

"*See anything?*" Johnson asked.

"No."

"*Dammit. They're ghosts now.*"

"Are they still coming?"

"*Oh yeah.*"

"I'm moving toward you to cover the house."

"*Negative. There could be more traps. Cover from the woods if you can.*"

She sighed. "Copy that." She began backpedaling out of the field in a low crouch. She kept her eye in the scope as she went, hoping that she'd spot a shooter before they spotted her. In the distance, pieces of the wooden fence lay scattered and burning alongside a stretch of scorched earth. She could only hope that the explosion had taken out most of the ten operators Johnson had seen coming from that direction.

Operators.

That was what they had to be, right? Whether members of Fedyenka's private army or a CIA kill team, they were definitely some sort of special ops. If she hadn't happened to spot their movement earlier, then she'd already be dead or captured. She'd gotten lucky.

"They're in the house," Johnson said.

Stacey turned and looked back over her shoulder. It was dark now, and she could barely make out the trees. "Screw it," she muttered. And as flashes began lighting up the windows in the house, she ran for cover.

"Do you —py?"

She raised a hand to her ear, pressing the earbud further into her ear and cupping her hand over it. She was sprinting and couldn't be sure, but she thought that it was Brown's voice that had just come broken through the radio. She cut to her right, mimicking the maneuvers she'd just witnessed the attackers use, hoping they'd be as effective for her as they had been for them. She cut left, then right, and then was in the trees.

She went a few rows deep into the woods before stopping and turning back to face the house. Muzzle flashes continued like strobes lighting up the windows. Johnson was holding his ground, but she didn't know how much longer he'd last. She spoke into the mike. "Brown, is that you?"

"Affirmative. They overran from the west, and I had to go silent. They just moved past me for the house."

"Are you hurt?"

"Not too bad."

She looked through the scope, sweeping it over the field. She didn't see any signs of activity between her and the house. She looked past the field and to the western hill. "Where are you now?"

But before he could answer, Johnson's voice broke over the line. *"I could use some help in here."*

Stacey aimed the rifle at the house but couldn't make out anything other than muzzle flashes. "I have no shot," she said.

"Me neither," Brown added.

"Then get your asses over here and find one!" Johnson screamed back.

"Copy that," Brown responded. *"On my way."*

But Stacey waited, using the scope to see if Brown's approach to the house would draw anyone else out.

There he was. She picked out his green shape moving through the field to her left. But he wasn't coming over the hill from the west like she'd expected. He was coming from the south. *How the hell did he get over there?*

Movement in the grass to her right caught her attention. She swung the rifle over. "Brown, get down—"

A head, shoulders, and then a semiautomatic rifle materialized out of the grass, the intruder sending a burst of shots in Brown's direction before he could respond.

Stacey fired, and the masked target fell to the ground.

"Brown, you okay?" she asked into the radio, moving out from behind the trees. She looked for more activity, to see if anyone else was hiding in the field. Nothing. She focused on where Brown had been when the shooter opened fire. She saw only grass.

Dammit. She took off running and entered the field, the needled grass whipping at her waist. "Brown!" she called out again.

Still no response.

"Johnson, I think Brown's been hit," she said.

No response from Johnson, just an explosion on the ground floor of the house. She figured he'd resorted to tossing grenades down the staircase.

She slowed as she approached the spot she'd last seen Brown in. Started calling out his name. She brought the scope to her eyes and swept the area around her. In the night vision, the grass was painted with white-speckled streaks about ten yards ahead. "Brown," she whispered.

A groan.

She jogged to the sound and came upon a body sprawled in the dirt.

"I'm hit," Brown muttered.

Stacey knelt beside him. "Where?"

"Gut."

"How bad?"

"Bad."

He lifted his head and looked at himself. "Shit." Then he dropped his head back to the ground.

She put her hands over his stomach and felt hot blood ooze through her fingers.

"I'm sorry," he said.

She looked at his face but could only see the whites of his eyes. "For what? You risked your life to help us. I owe you everything."

He squeezed his eyes shut, and a tear trickled down his cheek. It reflected the firelight still burning in the western field. He shook his head. "No."

Stacey looked back at the house. It had grown a lot quieter, only sporadic pistol shots sounding off now. Johnson's grenade must've taken out most of them. She looked back down to Brown and saw that he had his cell phone in his hand. He was trying to give it to her.

She'd seen him toss his personal phone into the car, so this must be the secured line Johnson had called him on earlier. She accepted it. Looked at the screen.

A string of text messages.

Her eyes shot back to him.

"I'm so sorry," he whispered. "They have my family."

For a split second, Stacey fought the urge to put the Smith & Wesson to his head and pull the trigger. But before she could, Brown lifted his hand and pointed at the phone.

"Scroll to the top," he said.

"This is your personal cell?" She thumbed past texts reporting on their actions throughout the day. The very first message in the thread was a picture of a woman with a high-school-aged boy and a middle-school-aged girl. Their wrists were bound, and they were gagged. Tears were streaking down their faces, their eyes wide with terror.

"They said they'd cut them up one piece at a time, one in front of the other, if I didn't do exactly what they said. And then they'd leave me to the Agency."

Stacey blinked and was surprised when she felt a tear of her own drop onto her cheek. She grabbed his hand.

"They've been tracking my phone," he said. "I never called anyone. They were already on their way. It was the secured phone I tossed in the car."

That explained how they'd gotten here so fast. "C'mon. I'm gonna get you back to the house. We have a med kit."

But he shook his head. "No use. And I can't face Johnson with this."

She knew it was no use arguing with him. "Who is it?" she asked. "Who took your family?"

"Fedyenka's men. Osprey."

"We'll do what we can to get them back," she said. And then she watched as his face reflected the agonizing awareness that there was nothing anyone could do to help his precious wife and children. They were totally at the mercy of that psychopath, a hundred fates more likely than them simply being let go. It was his parting revelation—how his family would most likely be tortured to death, crying out for him to rescue them. His grip tightened on her hand as a flood of tears washed over his face, and he began to cough up blood.

She should hate him. And not long ago she would have. But how could she blame him? Hadn't she, not too long ago, been in the exact same position as him? Just a breath away from pushing a button she'd been convinced was the only way to save her son, ready to not only kill herself but an entire room full of innocent people? "Hey." She squeezed his hand. "We're gonna get this piece of shit, and we're going to save your family. I swear it." And she let him see it in her eyes. She might be wrong about it, but at least he'd be able to pass with the hope of her sincerity...and forgiveness.

"They said they could keep us safe..." He was growing tired and losing focus.

"Safe?"

"From the Agency. But...they can't..."

She was confused. "Why would you need to be protected from the Agency?"

He shook his head and pointed past her, to the house.

"That's CIA?" Stacey asked.

His eyes began to close. "They know about the bunker."

She froze. "Who does?"

"Not...them." He was fading.

She knew she only had seconds left before he was gone forever. "*Who* knows about the bunker?" she repeated.

And at that moment, she heard a helicopter come whipping out from behind the trees. She looked up and could barely make it out against the starlit sky. It rotated counterclockwise and settled into a hover, the rotors beating the air. She didn't need the night-vision scope to know that operatives were fast-roping out of it.

She looked back to Brown. "Is that—"

But she would get no more answers from him. He was dead.

She slipped his cell phone into her pocket, hoping there would be more information on it, and turned to face the black locust hovering seventy yards off the eastern side of the house.

"*What the hell is that?*" Johnson's voice finally came back over the radio.

"Helicopter." She raised the rifle and looked through the scope in time to see the last four figures disappear down the ropes. "More targets on the ground." She set the data lines over the cockpit, waiting for a clear shot on the pilot. Were they going to land nearby, or would they come back? And if they came back, would they come back with reinforcements?

"Johnson," she said into the radio, "if they land nearby—"

He finished her thought for her. "*We can get their flight plan. Risky, but your call.*"

She hesitated as the pilot's helmeted head drifted into her crosshairs. Destroy the bird or hope it hangs around so they can try to steal it?

She lowered the rifle, grabbed Brown's radio and UMP, and ran toward the helicopter as it banked and accelerated back over the trees. She'd come at the new arrivals from behind.

She ran hard, Brown's words like a wrecking ball in her brain. *They know about the bunker.* But who? The CIA or Osprey?

Halfway to the house, the people from the chopper began exchanging fire with the first set of operatives. She could see the muzzle flashes in the dark, a row of them going off in the night, another row responding.

"What's happening?" she asked into the mic.

"*They're shooting at each other.*"

"You need to get out of there," she said. She lifted the scope to the top floor just in time to see a figure jump out a window. They landed like a paratrooper, rolling their knees and pitching forward into a tuck and roll. They got to their feet, and it was Johnson's face in her crosshairs. She saw him touch his ear.

"*Where are you?*" he asked, looking around.

"Your three o'clock. About fifty yards." He looked right at her, but she could tell he didn't see her. "You're looking right at me. Just run."

He took off in a dead sprint, heading for the tall weeds as the gun battle raged behind him.

When he got close, she whistled, and he adjusted his course. He almost ran right past her, but she reached out and grabbed him, pulling him down beside her.

They both lay there on their stomachs, watching the light show erupt around the house.

"Who the hell are they?" Johnson asked, and then, "Where's Brown? Wasn't he just on the radio?"

"He's dead."

"What?" He snapped his head toward her.

She wanted to tell him what Brown had told her, but she didn't know how he'd take it, and now wasn't the time to find out. "I'm sorry," was all she could think of to say.

He looked away, the muscles in his jaw working hard beneath his skin. Finally, he looked back at her. "What do you want to do?"

She thought about it. There were a few options. They could try to get Jack and Joseph out using the gunfight as cover. They could wait until one side won the gunfight and take out whoever was left standing. Or they could lock themselves into the bunker with Jack and Joseph and shoot whoever managed to come through the door. The problem with the latter was that if Fedyenka's operatives could verify their presence in the bunker, then he'd have his whole private army here in a matter of hours, waiting them out.

She didn't know what to do.

They watched as the number of flashes slowly decreased, those that remained moving closer to the house until the gunfight found itself completely contained within its remaining walls.

42

THERE WAS A FAINT boom, and some dust fell from the bunker's ceiling. *That was in the house*, Jack thought. They were fighting right above them. He stood up from the couch and grabbed the MP7, staring at the big steel door. There was no way anyone could get in without him unlocking it from the inside. Unless they had military-grade explosives or cordite or one of those diamond-tipped drills he'd seen used in heist movies. Actually, he had no idea what this door was able to withstand.

And what of the explosives lining the hall? Could he set them off if he needed to, or would he be trapping himself and Joseph down here until someone could dig them out? And what if whoever was coming for them had Stacey with them? No, he couldn't risk blowing the tunnel.

"What's wrong?" Joseph asked.

Jack looked at him and could see that his son was still reeling from all he'd just been told. "You said earlier that you thought there had to be another way out of here."

Joseph blinked, trying to push aside the pallet of new information—boxes and boxes of things he'd spend the rest of his life unpacking—in order to allow space for the here and now. "If the prepper guy blew up the tunnel"—his eyes flashed to the button and the yellow triangle by the door—"then he wouldn't be able to get out."

"Right." He glanced over Joseph's head to the back of the bunker. "C'mon," he said. He moved past him, placing a hand on his shoulder and pushing him along. "If there is another way out of here, we're going to find it right now." He set the MP7 down on the couch.

"Why?"

"Just in case."

When they got to the top of the T, Jack pointed to the left. "You check that way." He went to the right, his eyes on the ceiling, following the hoses and ductwork, looking for anything that might signal a way out. But there was nothing. No creases that might be the edges of a hatch, no other doorways, no—

"Found something," Joseph's voice echoed from behind him.

Jack turned toward his son and could just make out his shoulder sticking past the shelving on the other side of the hall. He quickly made his way over to him and found that he was holding a square piece of wood that was painted the same color as the wall but with a deadbolt screwed to it. Joe had moved one of the shelves over and must've found an access panel in the wall.

Jack knelt down in front of the open hole. "Good job, Joe."

"You think it leads out?"

Jack shrugged. "Only one way to find out."

And then a sound began to echo throughout the bunker.

"What is that?" Joseph asked, looking up at the ceiling.

It was a fizzing sound. Like someone had popped open a can of soda, only the release of carbonated air just kept on going. He knew what it was. He took out his flashlight, which he'd recovered from the duffel bag before coming down, and aimed it into the black hole.

Another tunnel.

He had no idea how far it went because it outdistanced the beam of light. But they were out of options.

"Stay here," he said, and he ran back to the couch and grabbed the tactical vests, the MP7, and Joe's backpack. The sound was louder there, and he paused to look at the door. A small red dot materialized in the center of it before starting to expand, slowly changing in color. So much for torch-resistant stainless steel.

Jack was tempted to hit the button, to blow the det cord and bury whoever was out there. Except he didn't know who was out there. And he didn't know where the tunnel in the back would lead them.

He went back to Joseph and handed him the vest. "Put this back on." As his son obeyed, Jack slipped into his own again.

Then, when Joe was ready, he handed him the flashlight and his backpack. "Go," he said. "I'm right behind you."

Joseph looked back at him as he slung his pack over his shoulders, panic in his eyes. "What's wrong?"

"They're coming." Then he pulled the backpack off Joe's shoulders. "No, wear it in front so you can bend over while you walk and it won't hit the ceiling."

After Joe slipped his arms through the loops and was holding the bag in front of him like he was carrying a baby, Jack pushed him forward into the dark. He went in after him, stopping to turn and drag the shelves back in front of the opening and to set the door back in its place. Only the latch was on the other side, and the door wouldn't stay flush against the wall. But there was nothing he could do about it, so he just turned in the cramped space and followed Joseph's bouncing light.

"DAMN, STACEY, YOU LEAVE any of these guys' faces intact?" Johnson asked after turning over the third body they'd come across. The bullets from Stacey's MP15T had punched through their heads and mangled their faces beyond recognition. Johnson was trying to snap a picture with his phone so that he could send it to a friend who might be willing to run it through the NSA's recognition database for him.

"I think over there," she said, pointing to a patch of grass to the left. "Body shot."

She followed him over. The three corpses they'd looked at had all been men. All dressed in black fatigues with masks and night-vision optics. They had pictures of her and Joseph tucked into a wristband, so there was no doubting the primary object of their mission—or at least whom it concerned.

"Here we go," Johnson said, turning a body over and ripping the mask off its face. Another male. He held his phone up and took a picture, hoping the flash didn't attract the attention of whoever was still alive and still shooting in the house.

Of course, none of them had any identification on them. Which meant they weren't FBI or SWAT or any other legitimate law enforcement agency out trying to apprehend the person believed to be responsible for blowing up a school.

Johnson tucked the cell back into his pocket, swung the MP5 off his shoulder, and turned his attention back to the house. "Okay, let's go."

"Right behind you," Stacey said.

The two of them moved quickly for the house.

THE TUNNEL FINALLY CAME to an end after about a hundred yards. No shots had been fired from where they'd started, which told Jack the little door behind the shelves hadn't yet been discovered. Hopefully, they hadn't even breached the door yet. But he felt the spiders on his neck spinning webs over his nerves. At any moment they could be discovered, someone sticking their head into the tunnel and seeing their flashlight at the end of it.

There was a ladder. Jack took the flashlight from Joseph and pointed it up. The beam settled on what appeared to be an old storm-cellar door about twelve feet away. He turned back to Joseph. "I'm gonna go up first in case the door is hard to open and to make sure it's safe to go out. Stay right on my heels, but don't let me kick you in the face."

Joe nodded, his shadow mimicking him on the encroaching dirt walls. He flipped the backpack around to his back so that he could climb freely.

Jack handed the flashlight back to him. "Keep it facing up at that hatchway as best you can." Then he repositioned the MP7 and started climbing.

The ladder was firm and held his weight just fine. He could sense Joseph at his feet. When he reached the door, he didn't find a handle or a latch. He pushed against it, but it didn't budge. He pushed harder. It still didn't move. He lifted his right foot to the next step so that he could use the added leverage to drive his shoulder up into the wood. He pushed against it, driving upward with his legs. The wood moved, but it felt like there was something heavy sitting on top of it. Like a car. Dirt shook loose and fell on them.

"Watch your eyes," Jack said.

"How am I supposed to do that?" Joe asked.

Jack smiled. His son was making jokes. That was good. He drove with his shoulder again, and more dirt fell. The door moved another inch.

"Hand me the light again," he said, reaching a hand back. He felt the metal strike his palm, and he swung the light up to examine the edges of the door. The wood looked to be pressure-treated two-by-fours held together by a two-by-six frame and a diagonal cross-piece. He stuck his finger beneath the edges of the wood and found more wood. The hatch was resting on a wooden frame. He traced the perimeter of the door with the light, looking for hinges or any indication of which way the door was made to open. He found nothing.

He handed the light back to Joseph and kept driving at the wood with his shoulder. Each time he struck it, the gap between the door and the frame grew another half inch.

Jack was starting to sweat, and he had to wipe it from his eyes. It was also getting stuffy in the small space, and he knew they had to be running out of air. Between that and their impending discovery, he knew he had to get the door open now.

What if there is something on top of it? A boulder. Or a tank? What if it's nailed into the frame?

He hit it again. And this time he thought he heard something rip and tear.

Roots.

The hatch had been buried with topsoil and grass.

He went back to work with new determination, knowing that their escape was not impossible. Finally, he bullied his way through the shallow root system and worked the door free. It swung open and fell to the side, landing upside down on the grass beside him. He scrambled up the last two steps of the ladder and stepped up into open air. Then he got down on the ground and turned on his stomach, reaching back into the tunnel for the flashlight. He took it from Joseph and clicked it off. He slipped it into his pocket and grabbed his son's hands. Pulled him up and out of the earth.

44

THEY APPROACHED THE BACK of the house, and Johnson climbed up through a broken window, sweeping the MP5SD back and forth through the house, the M24 slung across his back. He turned to offer Stacey a hand up through the window, but she was already coming through it and hopping down next to him. Without bothering to check her corners or clear the room, and ignoring Johnson's pleas for her to slow down, she went straight for the cellar.

She passed through the dining room area before entering the kitchen, briefly noting the unmoving bodies and the blood sprayed on the walls. In the kitchen was a single corpse lying facedown in a puddle of blood. She stepped over the body, but there was no getting around the blood. She left red footprints across the floor on her way to the cellar doorway, and they chased her all the way down the tiny stairs.

When she reached the bottom of the stairs, almost twisting her ankle in the process, she saw that the tunnel leading to the bunker sat exposed, the hidden wall removed. As she quietly made her way to the entrance, she could make out three black-clad figures all the way at its end and standing at the bunker's door. Only the door wasn't closed anymore. The smell, the sight of the equipment lying on the ground at their feet... She knew they'd made quick work of the old steel door with cordite, cutting around the locks that had held the door in place. They had come prepared and had known right where to go. *Damn you, Brown*, she thought. Even though she still couldn't blame him.

She entered the passageway and squeezed the trigger on the MP15T, hitting the three operators in the back and dropping them where they stood.

A shot sounded from within the bunker.

"Stacey, get down," Johnson cried from behind her.

Crap. She was halfway down the tunnel, the proverbial fish in a barrel.

Another shot, and a spray of dirt exploded out of the wall next to her, stinging the side of her face.

"Down!" Johnson yelled again.

She hit the deck, and immediately gunfire erupted from behind her. Johnson was shooting over her and lighting up the bunker.

"No!" Stacey cried, certain that Jack and Joseph must still be inside. She unclipped a smoke grenade from her vest, pulled the pin, and tossed it down the hall and through the open door.

Johnson stopped firing and nearly stomped on her as he ran past, jumping over her while she stumbled back to her feet. They were gambling, hoping the operator didn't have infrared capability that would allow him to see through the smoke and target them like lit Christmas trees.

But Johnson made it through the smoke without taking any more fire. Inside the bunker, they took up crouching positions on opposite sides of the doorway. As they waited for the smoke to clear, they wondered why the operative wasn't at least shooting blindly into the tunnel at them.

A minute later, they got their answer. They moved into the bunker, the smoke slowly being sucked out of the small space by the humming air-filtration system, and found the body of the operative. He was bent forward over the counter that separated the kitchen area from the living area, his arms hanging down, the back of his gloved hands resting on the floor, fingers curled into claws. There was a hole in the back of his head and blood splatter on the ceiling. Both the location of the wound and the direction of the red spray told them that one of the rounds from Johnson's long burst had ricocheted off something in the kitchen—probably one of the three cast-iron skillets hanging on the wall by the stove—and had struck the guy in the back of the head.

"Lucky," Johnson muttered.

She knew he was right. Because the guy did have thermal goggles strapped to what was left of his head. If not for the bullet's lucky bounce, she and Johnson would most likely be corpses themselves right now.

She kept moving, looking for Jack and Joseph. They had to be here somewhere.

But they weren't.

"They're not here," she said after checking the rest of the bunker.

"Maybe that's a good thing," Johnson said.

She knew what he meant, that their bodies not being here indicated that they had either been taken alive or had somehow gotten away, but at the moment, she was having trouble appreciating such a silver lining.

Johnson moved past her to check for himself.

"They could be on the way back to the chopper with them," Stacey said. She started moving for the door. She ducked through the space and stepped over the three bodies.

She sprinted down the corridor and came out into the cellar just as a shadowy figure was coming down the steps from the kitchen. They both saw each other at the same time, and it was a race to see who could get the first shot off. She had to raise her rifle almost forty degrees, whereas the person coming down the stairs already had her in their sights. Maybe they had to adjust a couple of degrees to their right, but it was no contest. If this person was a professional, then there was no way she was going to get her shot off. She could only hope that they would miss as she dropped to a knee and raised her weapon. Maybe such a quick maneuver, coupled with a possible split-second hesitation at the sudden surprise of seeing her running toward them, would buy her the moment she needed to return fire.

It didn't happen.

She did manage to get off a shot, but the gun on the stairs flashed before hers. Both shots seemed simultaneous, but when the rounds were traveling at over two thousand feet per second, the first shot would be buried in its target while the other bullet was still spinning down the barrel.

But she felt no impact.

Instead, the operative was pitching forward, flying awkwardly through the air and down the stairs.

Her initial shot had missed too, but she adjusted, tracking them as they soared down the small stairs. Her bullets traced after them, punching a line of holes in the wall, though she thought she tagged them in the lower body before they finally hit the ground.

The figure landed with an audible *crack* and a shout of pain. Stacey raced forward, sights on the person's head, and kicked the rifle away from them. They were on their stomach, a leg folded at an unnatural angle beneath them.

"On your back, now!" she hollered.

The person complied, though it was obviously painful as hell to do so.

She wanted to lean forward and rip the mask off, but she wasn't going to give them any open windows in which to make a move. "Take your mask off."

Johnson came up beside her.

"Lucky again," Stacey muttered as the person pulled the mask off their head. If not for the suicide steps and the exact moment of her coming into the operator's view to distract him, she'd be dead again.

When the mask came off, a man's face appeared. He seemed to be in his late thirties, early forties. "Fuckin' stairs," he spat. "Unbelievable."

He was American.

"You Osprey?" Johnson asked.

"Two tours in Iraq, two more in Afghanistan... And it's a girl and an old set of stairs in Ohio that ends up punching my ticket. Unreal."

"Where is my husband and son?" Stacey asked, not caring about anything else.

"Don't know, lady. They weren't in there."

She frowned and remembered Joseph thinking there had to be another way out of the bunker. Could they have found one? Had they made it out before these assholes breached the bunker?

Stacey kicked the man's foot, and he gritted his teeth, trying but failing to keep from showing the pain he was in. His face turned white, and she thought he might pass out. A piece of bone was sticking out of his leg. Blood was dripping from the other. One of her bullets *had* found him. "Looks like you're gonna have to find a new line of work."

He looked at his leg, examining the white sticking out of it. "Bitch."

She kicked him again.

He leaned forward and pitched to his side, reaching for his shin.

Johnson squatted before him. "You're a liability now, and you know more than anyone that he doesn't allow loose ends."

No response.

"Which means," Johnson continued, "that your best bet at surviving this is for us to get to him and kill the Russian bastard."

"I don't know anything about who's behind Osprey. Don't give a shit. Most of us are just private military contractors going wherever the money is. If you're saying that some Russian dickhead is behind it and you want to take him out, then good luck. You got my vote."

"Most of Osprey feel this way?" Johnson asked.

"I don't ask, but no, not all of us."

"Why do you say that?"

"A lot of foreigners seem to be in it for some cause or another."

"Hmm. Foreigners with Russian accents, maybe? And you never thought to question just what that cause might be?"

"And why would I want to know that?"

Stacey glanced at her watch. She was feeling the pressure of time, but this right here was the entire point of why they'd set this trap, and it could be the only chance they got at some real answers. "What was your mission?"

"To grab the boy," the man said. "You if possible. No other survivors."

"Traitor trash. Just a real genuine piece of human shit, aren't you?" Johnson seethed.

The mercenary just flipped him the middle finger with a your-moralism-bores-the-hell-out-of-me indifference. "Says the man helping the people who blew up a school."

Ignoring the desire to stomp on the guy's shattered leg, Stacey asked him what they wanted with Joseph even though she already knew what his answer would be.

"Hell if I know."

"What was your exit strategy?" Johnson asked.

"Helicopter's settled in a field a couple of klicks north."

Stacey readjusted the rifle and flexed her fingers. "Where is Fedyenka?" Again, a question she knew he didn't know the answer to but that had to be asked.

"Is that the guy's name?" The former soldier shook his head. "No idea."

"In-country?"

"I got the impression that whoever runs the company is abroad, whether that's this Fedyenka person, I have no clue."

"What kind of chopper?"

"Black Hawk."

"What do you know about the pilots?"

"Only one pilot."

Stacey glared at him, knowing it took two pilots to fly a Black Hawk.

"Only one," he said again. "As far as I know, all our Black Hawks are fitted with DARPA's automation system."

"ALIAS?" Johnson asked. "I thought that was still experimental."

The guy managed a shrug.

"So what about the pilot?" Stacey asked, getting back to her question.

"Heard him whining about his great-grandparents being killed by the Bolsheviks or something."

Johnson took a step closer to him. "Radio him. Tell him you've got the boy, but that it was a trap. You're on your way with him now and will be coming in hot."

The guy chuckled.

"Or we can be sure to tell him how much of a help you've been. You may have never heard of Fedyenka Yevstigneyev, but I'm sure you've seen enough to know that the person running Osprey doesn't tolerate loose ends." He motioned at the guy's leg.

The guy raised his hands in a surrendering gesture. "Whatever you want." He worked the mic and relayed the message.

The pilot acknowledged.

"These other people you were fighting with... You know who they are?" Stacey asked.

"No. They dropped in and opened fire on us. Could've been FBI for all I know. The whole country is after you." He winced when he accidentally tried to move his leg. He was growing uncomfortable in the position he was in.

"You were tracking one of our phones?" Stacey asked, figuring names wouldn't mean anything to him.

He nodded.

"And how did these other people know where we were or who you were to start shooting?"

"No fucking clue. Can we get on with it now? That's all I know. And you know that's all I know."

"Alright," Johnson said. And he swung the butt of the rifle into the side of his head, rendering him unconscious. Then he looked to Stacey. "They were tracking a phone?"

"I'll tell you later," she said.

"Fine," but the look in his eyes said he already had a pretty good idea. "Take his clothes off," he said. Then he turned and went back into the tunnel.

Stacey began untying the laces of the man's boots. She had one off when she looked back and saw Johnson snapping pictures of the three men she'd put down at the bunker door. Then he was removing their clothing too.

45

JACK OPENED THE DOOR to the Honda and told Joseph to get in the back. He didn't have a plan, just knew that they had to be mobile. The key was still in the ignition. They shut the doors, and Jack started the car. He put it in drive and slowly started moving through the field, keeping the headlights off.

"Get down between the seats," Jack said.

Joseph slid out of the back seat and knelt on the floor in front of it, his backpack and the vest making it a tight fit.

Jack looked back to make sure his son was out of the line of fire. "Johnny Depp to Dwayne Johnson," he said, hoping that the trivia game might prove an effective distraction in these stress-filled situations.

Joseph answered immediately. "Johnny Depp was in *Sleepy Hollow* with Christopher Walken, who was in *The Rundown* with the Rock."

Crap, Jack thought. He knew Joseph was a movie buff and had no problem at all remembering everything he'd seen, but Jack had no idea that his library of knowledge went as deep as Christopher Walken. For a person Jack's age, sure (though he was beginning to forget a lot of things he once knew). But a fourteen-year-old? "Your friends know as much about movies as you?" he asked. He'd already told Brown as much, but he was trying to get Joseph's mind off his present circumstances—though he realized too late that bringing up his friends was probably not the best way to do that.

"Zane and Tommy," Joseph said.

And Jack could hear it in his voice, the pain and the frustration of not knowing if they were okay or not. As he drove slowly through the field, careful not to drive into a tree and praying they weren't rolling through a minefield, he addressed the unasked question. "We'll find out as soon as we can, I promise."

"Okay," Joe answered.

Then they were out of the tall grass and could see the house. The sky above it was lit up by a fire that he assumed was burning somewhere behind the house, and he wondered if it was from the explosion they'd heard earlier. He brought the car to a stop and stared out through the windshield, sweeping his eyes back and forth, looking for any signs of activity. Not detecting any, he pressed lightly on the gas, continuing to the house.

It came up on their right, and he aimed the HK-MP7A2 out the window, waiting to mow down anyone who might start shooting at them. But it was completely still, quiet. He brought the car to a stop twenty-five yards from the house.

"Stay down," he said to Joseph. "Think of one that'll really stump me." And he opened the door and slid out from behind the wheel, the rifle trained on the house.

Movement.

He swung the weapon in the direction of the front porch and almost pressed the trigger, when he heard Stacey's voice. It was her and Johnson coming out of the house and down the stairs.

"Thank God," he whispered.

"THAT'S THE SECOND TIME in two days I almost shot you," Jack said after Stacey was done hugging him.

"Where's Joseph?" she asked.

"In the car." He nodded behind him, then, "Where's Brown?"

She looked over his shoulder, glimpsing the old Honda sitting in the grass. Jack could tell she wanted to ask how they'd gotten out of the bunker, but there was apparently no time to get into it now. "He's dead," she said. And then added, "We have a plan."

She bent over to pick up the pile of black clothing that she'd dropped when embracing him. She handed it over.

Jack tried to push what she'd just said about Brown out if his head. He couldn't afford to be moved by that now. "What is this?"

"Just put them on." She pulled the earpiece from her ear and removed the vest. Then she pulled her shirt up over her head. Johnson did the same a few feet away.

"Okay..." Jack worked the Velcro straps on his own bulletproof vest, not quite sure what was happening. As he pulled on the black shirt, he had to keep himself from gagging. "Ugh. Smells awful."

She shrugged. "Guy died in it."

"Must've sweat through it all night first," he said. He looked at Joseph, who had gotten out of the car and was now standing beside it, barely a silhouette in the darkness. "What about him?"

She didn't answer with words, but she didn't need to. The look in her eye, made visible by the flames still dancing on the other side of the house, told him all he needed to know.

He sighed as he dropped his pants. Whatever their plan, it was a stretch, and it would involve Joseph being in harm's way.

Once dressed, Stacey and Johnson quickly explained the plan.

THEY RAN NORTH IN the direction the PMC had indicated, looking for the helicopter that could hopefully lead them back to some sort of Osprey headquarters and some more answers. It was hardly an ideal situation with Joseph in tow, but they'd deal with that later. Right now they could only hope that the operative hadn't managed to alert the pilot with some sort of emergency signal. They were banking on the guy believing that his best shot at survival was for them to take out his employer.

"You okay?" Stacey asked Joseph, who was jogging beside her in the dark, his pack slamming into his back every other step.

"I'm fine," he panted.

"Look," Johnson said, though it was too dark for anyone to see what direction he was indicating.

But then she saw it. A soft red light barely visible in the distance. And then they were in a field and could hear the chopper idling.

"Okay, remember what we said," Stacey said to Joseph, pulling the mask down over her face. She shouldered her MP15 and turned her hips, firing the Osprey rifle at some imaginary pursuers, selling the illusion that they were being chased. Jack and Johnson did the same. Stacey yanked on Joseph's arm, pulling him along for added measure. "Sorry," she said and squeezed off another few blind rounds. She hoped that the absence of muzzle flashes behind them would go unnoticed, or at least unquestioned, by the pilot.

They were close enough now to feel the air circulating from the spinning blades. The side door was open, the red bulbs visible in the interior. The helicopter looked like a utility chopper, most likely a UH-60 Black Hawk, just as the guy had said.

She'd been in Black Hawks before and knew they usually had two pilots and two crew chiefs along with enough room to seat an eleven-man infantry squad. But all she could see here was a single pilot sitting in the red glow of the cockpit, looking like some mantis alien with the helmeted night-vision goggles on. He was watching them as he reached up and hit buttons on the console above him.

When they reached the chopper, Jack and Johnson took up kneeling positions and began spraying the woods with suppressing fire. They hoped that the reports of the guns along with the thumping beats of the rotors and Joseph's fake crying would keep the pilot more focused on getting the hell out of there than on his passengers.

Stacey jumped into the chopper and pulled Joseph up after her. He was screaming and hollering about wanting his mom and dad, fighting against her as best he could without actually trying to get away. She pulled his backpack off and tossed it to the floor while dragging him down with her into the furthest two of the four forward-facing seats that had been assembled in a row across the middle of the cabin. The sliding door beside her was locked into an open position as well, and she had the briefest notion to grab Joseph and just continue right on out the other side and to forget this whole insane idea.

But then Jack was climbing in and shouting, "Go! Go! Go!"

The pilot didn't even turn around. He handled the controls, and the helicopter began to rise.

Johnson tossed the army bag that he'd taken from the house into the cabin and jumped aboard just as the black helicopter lifted off the ground. He threw himself into one of the two seats that sat back-to-back with the pilots' chairs, facing Stacey and Joseph and the back of the chopper behind them. Jack was already in the seat beside him, though there were no middle seats to connect them. As they ascended over the Ohio farmlands, Johnson turned his head and called over his right shoulder, "Comms went down. We got the boy. Only three survivors. Another team showed up and engaged us. Call it in!"

The pilot did so without question.

Stacey's heart was pounding in her chest as she took in their surroundings. The Black Hawks she'd been in before had been configured in various ways, most with four rows of seats, knees touching knees. She'd also been in one fitted with gunner chairs behind the pilots, two men operating 7.62 mm mini guns mounted to the cabin windows. There had only been a few other seats set up in that one. But in this setup there was only one row of four and two chairs across from them where the gunner chairs or the crew chief would've been. There was enough room between Stacey and Jack that they could stretch their legs a little, their calves touching in intersection. She didn't think there was anything behind their row of seats, which meant that other choppers must have been used to drop off the rest of the Osprey army.

She leaned her head back and tried to relax. So far so good. If the pilot was onto them, he sure wasn't showing it. They could only hope that this Osprey outfit was not as close as other military platoons or PMCs she'd known. If the pilot was close to anyone else on the team, he'd be making inquiries very soon and sure as hell would wonder why he didn't recognize their voices.

But the soldier she'd shot gave the impression that the Osprey operatives were not that close, that there were those there for the money and those who seemed to be in support of some cause or another. He'd said the pilot had mentioned the Bolsheviks, so this guy was probably one of Fedyenka's zealots, fighting for something most of Osprey didn't even know about.

She looked down below them but could only make out an occasional house light. Up ahead and to their left was a road lined with streetlights. The helicopter banked right and away from it.

She looked at Jack, wondering how he was holding up. She thought he looked good sitting there in commando gear and awash in red light. He was certainly not the man she'd married, the salesman from Philly who'd graduated from Temple. And though she found the new look in his eyes—the confident determination born of a soldier's skill set—sexy and impressive, she couldn't help but miss her innocent Jerry. She wouldn't trade one for the other, at least not now when she needed this Jack to help keep them all alive, but she hoped that someday he might be able to rediscover his old self again. Though after what he'd done yesterday morning, killing the intruders the way he had, she wasn't sure that it was possible.

He saw her staring at him, and he winked.

She winked back. Then she turned her attention to Joseph, wondering how much more he would have to endure because of her. How much more *could* he endure? She looked back at Jack, again noting the cold professionalism that she'd managed to shape into him over the last two years, and realized that she was probably looking at the future Joseph too. And that was something she'd never wanted for her son. To be like her. Like her KGB father. She'd wanted him to be free from that life. To be whoever he wanted without manipulation from some external force. Though life itself was manipulation, wasn't it?

A deep pang of sorrow shot through her, and she thought that if falling out of the chopper right now could save Jack and Joseph from all of this shit, then she'd do it in a heartbeat. But killing herself would accomplish nothing because the operative said that their primary mission had been Joseph, not her. She needed to live long enough to figure out what the hell was happening and to get her family out of it once and for all. She needed to find Fedyenka and put a bullet in his head.

She shifted her eyes from Jack over to Johnson. He was hunched over a cell phone, tapping and swiping away. It wasn't so long ago that she and Johnson had been together in another helicopter, yet so much had happened since then that it seemed ages ago.

She watched the screen's glow twinkle in his eyes as she thought of last night, of what he'd revealed to them. That he'd been watching her from the beginning. That he'd injected her with a tracker during their Appalachian flight. She wasn't sure what she thought of that. Ten years ago, she would've used a garrote on him and called it a day. But sitting there at the birthday party for the senator in a room full of people and ready to blow them all to hell had changed her. Had somehow resurrected her conscience and rendered her capable of sympathizing with other people's situations. Like Johnson's.

She moved her right leg away from Jack's and kicked Johnson's left foot to get his attention.

He looked up at her.

She lifted her mask to her nose and mouthed, "What are you doing?"

He turned the phone around so she could see the screen.

He was texting his pictures of the dead operatives to someone. She raised an eyebrow, though he wouldn't have been able to see that under the mask.

But he understood her concern and lifted his own mask, mouthing back three letters that she had no trouble understanding.

NSA.

She wasn't sure if he meant that he had a trusted contact at the NSA, or if he knew someone who had Level 15 clearance that could access the FBI database or maybe even the NSA and DoD servers. If they could run the faces through their facial-recognition software, maybe some of these guys would pop up in

Interpol's database. She could only hope. She pulled Brown's phone from her pocket and began going through the text thread he'd showed her.

She started from the beginning. An incoming text yesterday morning. It was a picture of a dead person lying in bed. The next two texts were also images of dead people. Then a message: CIA IS TAKING OUT YOUR TEAM. Then: ONLY WE CAN KEEP YOU AND YOUR FAMILY SAFE.

Brown: WHO ARE YOU?

Response: IF YOU DON'T HELP US, WE WILL KILL YOUR FAMILY AND LEAVE YOU TO THE CIA.

Then the image of his family.

After that, Brown had fired off some threats of his own, but as they went on, she could envision him starting to grasp the situation, and his responses started becoming more strategic and less emotional. She knew exactly what he'd been feeling. Same thing she'd felt when she picked up the phone and heard that synthesized voice on the other end telling her that Joseph had been taken. That was why she hadn't been able to kill Brown for it. Because she'd done the same thing.

She continued scrolling, seeing his updates telling them about the bunker. About Joseph. *Your son for my wife and kids,* was what his eyes had said in the firelight, full of remorse, regret, and dying hope.

Stacey leaned back against the seat and closed her eyes, taking it all in. Osprey had been the first group to arrive at the farmhouse. So who the hell was the second? CIA?

She leaned forward and handed the phone to Johnson. He looked at her questioningly, replacing his phone with the one she'd just given him. She watched his eyes through the slit in his mask as he took it all in too. Betrayal. Sympathy. Loss. Resolve. Worry. She watched his mind bend and stretch and contort in all sorts of unnatural ways as he tried to process the information, to quantify and explain it. To file it away into a drawer that hadn't before that moment even existed in his brain. And then, just like that, he blinked, and all the emotion was gone. In its place came an icy stare that he slowly lifted from the phone and placed on her. She shuddered and looked away, unsure how to interpret the expression. But she could certainly take a guess: blame.

She stared at Joseph instead, the sound of the rotors somehow transforming into a rhythmic lullaby that began to tug her into a dreamless sleep. The adrenaline rush from the shootout had drained her, and she let herself be taken. But as she drifted off, somewhere out there in the vague boundaries of consciousness, she felt a weight against her shoulder. A voice softer than a whisper told her that it was bad, but she couldn't figure out why anything would be bad right now. She dismissed the warning—if that was what it even was—and fell asleep, trusting Jack to watch over her and Joseph as she did so.

46

JACK OPENED HIS EYES. Had he fallen asleep? He looked around, trying to orient himself. Joseph was sitting across from him, his head leaning against the shoulder of a person in a mask and dressed in black tactical gear.

Stacey.

He continued to look around the interior of the chopper, wondering how he'd managed to doze off. He looked out the open side door and saw lights in the distance. A city, though he had no idea what city it could be. He looked over at Johnson and saw him staring down at his phone.

And then a deafening warning bell went off in his head as the sight that he'd awakened to finally registered in his brain.

He kicked Stacey's foot.

Stacey's head snapped erect, her eyes alert through the mask as she tried to take in everything all at once. Her gaze met Jack's.

Jack nodded his head ever so slightly toward Joseph, his eyes widening in a telling gesture as he did so. She looked over at their son, and Jack saw the realization suddenly explode in her eyes. She nudged Joseph with her shoulder, trying to get him off her. Jack knew it pained her to do it when all she wanted was to wrap her arm around him and hold him as tight as possible, but their lives depended on him moving in that very instant.

They could only hope that it wasn't too late.

As Joseph stirred, sitting up straight, Jack leaned over and whispered into Johnson's ear, telling him what had happened. Apparently, Johnson had been so engrossed in whatever he had learned on his phone that he hadn't seen it either. But had the pilot?

Johnson looked over a thread of texts and pointed out the time stamp on one of them, indicating his best guess as to when they'd drifted off and what time it was now. Ten minutes. Plenty of time for the pilot to see the kidnapped child snuggling with his captor.

The helicopter tilted into a bank, and Jack looked at the compass on his watch. They were transitioning into a westward heading. Was it a test? Was the pilot changing course to see if doing so would raise any questions? And should it?

Jack took a deep breath. *Calm down. You're overthinking it.* But he knew he wasn't. He glanced down at Johnson's lap and saw that he was slowly working the snap on the holster strapped to his thigh. They were both thinking the same thing.

* * * *

Stacey watched the pilot, looking for any sudden changes in his behavior, while in her periphery Johnson unsnapped the pistol she'd seen him take from one of the corpses in the corridor beneath the kitchen. She could only see the back left side of the pilot's head and his left shoulder from her seated position, but she could tell that he was speaking to someone through the mic on his helmet. She leaned forward, trying to hear over the turboshaft engine, and swore she heard something in Russian. She strained harder, closing her eyes and—

Suddenly, she flew to her feet, whipping out her auto-seared Glock, and lunged forward between Jack and Johnson. She thrust the pistol into the cockpit, leaning over the central console that separated the pilot sitting on the right and the empty co-pilot seat on the left. She pressed the muzzle against the back of his head.

"I speak Russian, asshole," she said. "Take the helmet off."

The pilot hesitated. Jack and Johnson stirred behind her, turning in their seats.

"I can fly this bitch too, so don't think I won't shoot you," she added. Though with the DARPA-made automation system engaged, she wasn't sure how true that actually was.

The pilot let go of the controls and held up his gloved hands, fingers spread. He began to raise his hands to his helmet.

"Slow," Stacey said.

But just as his fingers were about to touch the helmet, he dropped his hands back to the controls with lightning speed, slamming his right hand down onto the collective.

The helicopter dropped, and suddenly Stacey's feet were off the floor, her body slamming into the ceiling.

Then the pilot pulled on the collective, raising the Black Hawk and sending Stacey back down hard onto the center console, slamming her face onto the switches and knobs. The pilot elevated the nose, and Stacey went sprawling backward through the cabin, striking the row of forward-facing seats (her elbow just missing Joseph's face), and flipping up and over the top of them until finally coming to a painful stop against the rear wall.

She tried to regain her footing and was slightly aware that Jack and Johnson were bouncing around the cabin too. But when she leaned forward and gripped the back of Joseph's seat, pulling herself forward and peering over the top of it, she saw only an empty chair where her son should have been strapped in.

Still holding onto the pistol, she tucked it into her waistband and climbed back over the row of seats. "Joseph!" she cried. She looked around, even craning her neck to see if he had somehow ended up in the co-pilot's chair. Nothing. *Oh my god, he went out,* she thought.

She moved toward the open door and poked her head into the night, afraid she would see her son falling like a feather toward the earth. But it was too dark, and she saw nothing. "Joseph!" she screamed into the blackness.

The helicopter pitched, and she looked back to the cockpit. Johnson was climbing into the empty seat and struggling with the pilot. She glanced at Jack. He was lying on his stomach, his head, shoulders, and arms extending out the door as if he were doing some ridiculous Superman impersonation. She knew he needed her help, that she should pull him back inside, that if the helicopter banked again, he'd slide right out. But all she could do was stare out into the night.

Joseph was gone.

She closed her eyes and struggled to breathe. She thought of him alive in that moment, his heart beating, his lungs inhaling and exhaling, his brain functioning. How long before it all stopped in an instant? What was he feeling as he soared toward the ground? Was he scared? Was he calling out for her? Was he praying? "God, catch him," she heard herself whisper, though she wasn't sure how it was possible, because she still couldn't breathe.

She stepped back and collapsed into the seat Joseph had been in just moments before. She stared ahead, mind numb, body numb, barely even registering the fight taking place in the cockpit or her husband calling out for help down on the floor beside her.

47

WHEN THE HELICOPTER PITCHED, Joseph went flying from his seat and straight out the open door. And in that moment—which took one second at the absolute most—Joseph's mind did a funny thing. It filled with panic, but not really fear. There was no time for fear. Yet he realized that there would be. There would be plenty of time to be afraid while he fell through the sky. But not yet, not in this very moment. No, in this moment, he thought about his mom and dad and how he'd never see them again. Thought of all that he'd wanted to do in life and how he would never get the chance. He thought of his friends, wondering again which, if any, were among those who had died in the explosion. Priscilla's face flashed before him. And then he thought of Bethany, his baby sister. Then he wondered about some of the things he'd heard Scott's youth pastor say on the few occasions that he'd gone with him to his church's gym night. Though they weren't really "thoughts," as there was no time to be "thinking" in the general sense. Rather they were more realizations that came fully formed and in sudden flashes. As if a hundred thoughts had simply been downloaded all at once. Like a dream that covered years of events, but in reality had been confined to within a single second of sleep.

He flailed his arms as his world spun end over end in a wash of eerie red, the helicopter's lighted interior like blood clouding midnight waters. *Am I thinking of a shark movie?* he thought, getting closer to the door and his little sister. Jaws 4, *maybe?* And then he was sad. Sad for his parents, because if they managed to survive this, he knew they'd never forgive themselves. If only he could open his mouth and tell them it was okay, that it wasn't their fault. That he was going to be all right. But of course, he didn't even have time to open his mouth, let alone get their attention. He couldn't even see them, and for all he knew, they'd been flung out of the chopper themselves, already getting a head start to the ground.

His shoulder rammed into something, and despite the fire that exploded from the impact, he managed to wrap his arm around whatever it was and postpone his journey to the ground. He could feel his feet being pulled behind him, kicking into nothingness. He wrapped his other arm around what felt like a thick pole. He tried to pull himself into it, to hug it so tightly that his face would be pressed against it. But it was as if a hundred demons were trying to pull him away from the helicopter, and he just didn't have the strength to resist. So instead, he locked his right hand over his left forearm and just tried to hold on as long as he could.

He realized that his eyes were closed. Had been the entire time—which was really no time at all. He opened them and saw the earth straight below, streetlights like Christmas trees. Then, when he shifted his gaze back toward the helicopter, he saw that it was one of the rods connecting to the wheel that he had grabbed on to. How he'd managed to fall out toward the big wheel was a mystery to him, but it would all be moot in a second if he didn't find a way to further secure his grip. It was already starting to slip.

The wheel itself was right beneath him. Only about sixteen inches away. If he could maybe get his feet onto it...

He lost his grip on his forearm, but just before he was flung out into the night, he managed to grab the vertical strut. The pole was too thick to grip, and his fingers were already slipping off as his whole body continued to stretch out behind him. The pain in his forearm was incredible, the muscles burning in searing agony. The wind whipped at his face, making it hard to see. He figured he had about ten seconds left, but still he was not afraid. Still no time for that. Adrenaline and the need to survive blocked out all sense of it, and he thought that he understood how soldiers could still find a way to function despite knowing—

His fingers slipped off, and he was away.

JACK SAW JOSEPH GO tumbling across the back seats and straight out of the helicopter. "No!" he screamed. He tried to get his feet back on the ground and make a move for the door, but the pilot was moving the helicopter all over, and he was having a hard enough time holding on himself. Finally, after what seemed like an eternity, the helicopter leveled out, and he was able to plant his feet. He threw himself across the cabin and slid on his stomach across the floor, reaching his right hand out beside him and hooking his elbow around a bolted chair leg. Simultaneously, he thrust his left hand out into the night. Unbelievably, he caught a glimpse of a body dangling from the landing gear, sporadically blocking out the streetlights below.

He reached out further and could feel the material of Joseph's sleeve. He grabbed it just as the arm inside it began slipping away like something squeezed out of a tube. He let go of the seat and let himself slide forward until his entire chest was outside the doorway. He reached out with his right hand and managed to snatch Joseph's wrist just before it disappeared into the sleeve. He then got a better grip on Joseph's arm with his left hand, pulling him closer until he had a hand under his son's armpit, fully aware that if the helicopter was to suddenly bank left, he'd have nothing with which to secure himself, and they'd both be gone.

As Joseph clawed up his back, trying to climb up and over him, the helicopter did, indeed, tilt left.

* * * *

Stacey finally registered her name being hollered over the sound of the helicopter and the commotion in the cockpit. She snapped out of her stupor and turned her attention toward her husband just in time to see him start sliding out the cabin door.

She jumped to her feet and threw herself on top of him, landing across the back of his legs while grabbing his belt with her left hand. She wrapped her right arm around the leg of the seat, the metal bar positioned firmly in the crook of her elbow. She rotated her shoulders so that she could reach her right hand across her body and grab a handful of shirt at her left shoulder. As long as the fabric held and her grip on it stayed secure, she was hooked in. She started to pull on Jack's belt. Her bicep bulged, but nothing seemed to be happening as a result of it. She turned her wrist, taking a supinated grip on the belt, and screamed as she pulled with all of her might. She thought she felt his body slide toward her an inch.

And then another hand appeared, grabbing Jack's belt.

She blinked, confused.

The hand was upside down and pulling Jack away from her.

Another hand materialized...

Then arms, elbows...

Stacey squeezed her eyes shut and strained against this new person who was trying to pull her husband into the night. She didn't understand it. Where had they come from? When she opened her eyes again, she found herself looking right into Joseph's face. He was climbing up over Jack's body, coming toward her. Before she could fully register the sight, Joseph reached out and grabbed the arm that was holding onto Jack's belt, and used it to pull himself to her. He continued crawling up over top of her and back into the cabin. Stacey turned her head toward him and screamed, "Hold on!" She saw him wrap his own arms around the leg of a chair.

Free to use his hands now, Jack gripped the bottom of the doorway and used the leverage to slide himself back into the cabin. Stacey let go of her shirt and changed her grip on the chair leg, grabbing it with her right hand while getting to her knees and helping Jack back to his.

The helicopter banked again, and the three of them grabbed on to each other. This time Jack and Stacey had anchoring grips on the chairs.

Stacey looked back over her shoulder and saw Johnson pulling the pilot out of the pilot's chair and over the center console. He'd managed to get the upper hand and was now delivering blow after blow to the side of the man's head. Finally, the pilot's body went limp, and Johnson climbed over him and into the pilot's chair, trading seats.

Once Johnson had some semblance of control over the helicopter, he turned his head and called back, "Everyone okay?"

"Yeah," Stacey answered. She was panting, her chest heaving. She looked at Jack and Joseph, and a sudden uncontrollable burst of emotion sprang forth from somewhere deep within and expressed itself through an explosion of tears.

Jack grabbed her and Joseph and pulled them against him. Stacey squeezed them until her tired arms went numb.

48

Jack was helping Stacey drag the pilot out of the front seats and into the back. They'd both gotten rid of the masks, and Johnson was pulling his off now. "You sure you can fly this thing?" he asked Johnson again.

"I don't know," Johnson responded. He tossed the ski mask onto the copilot's seat. "I don't know how to disengage the DARPA shit."

Jack looked up to Stacey. "I got this. You go help him."

Stacey nodded and let go of the guy's feet. On her way to join Johnson in the cockpit, she found Joseph's backpack, one of its straps hooked over the handle of a fire extinguisher that was secured to the back of the co-pilot's chair. She unhooked it and tossed it back to Joseph. Then she climbed into the seat next to Johnson.

Jack dragged the guy by his armpits until he had him lying in front of the forward-facing seats. He smiled at Joseph, who had taken Johnson's seat, then took the shoelaces out of the pilot's boots.

"Good one," Joseph said, appreciating his dad's resourcefulness while he looked over his pack to make sure nothing had spilled out in the chaos.

Jack winked at him. He tied the guy's feet together with one string and then went to work on securing his hands behind his back. "Where we heading?" he called up to Johnson.

"No idea. I've only read about fully automated Black Hawks. No clue how this tech mimics a co-pilot and crew chief or how it functions differently than your standard autopilot. I don't see anything programmed into the GPS..."

Stacey bent over in the seat like she was tying her own shoe. When she sat back up, she had something in her hand. "A cell phone," she said. She held it up so they could see the map that was displayed. "He was using the GPS on his phone."

Johnson nodded. "Probably to make sure no one could find out where they were coming from if they crashed. Guessing it's SOP for these types of in-country missions. There a destination marked on the phone?"

"Yeah." She moved her finger over the screen, and the map moved north until finally settling on a red marker. "Looks like it's in the middle of a field in West Virginia."

"How much battery is left?" asked Johnson.

"Eighty percent," she answered.

Johnson looked back into the cabin and to the pilot. "Any chance of waking him up?" he hollered back.

Jack had just finished hog-tying him and was using the remaining length of lace to secure him to the leg of the middle seat, but even in the dim red light, he could see that the man's face was beginning to swell. "I don't know. You did a number on him," he yelled back.

"We need to find out what we're flying into," Johnson said to Stacey.

"You think he'll give us anything?" she asked.

"I think they want Joseph delivered to that location. His mission was to get him there. So yeah, I think he'll give us something. They want Joseph alive, and they won't do anything that will put him at risk."

Jack caught most of what Johnson had just said, and could see that Stacey was thinking about it, wondering if her attack on the pilot had even been necessary. "What was the pilot saying?" he called out to her.

She turned her head and yelled back, "He was reporting that they had the boy, but that the op may have been compromised. He didn't get much further than that."

"So could be that we land in the middle of an Osprey welcoming party," Jack said.

"I think," Johnson said, pointing at the phone, "that's going to be the case either way."

Johnson mulled that fact over. "We'll need to set down some-where else, then. Find me a place."

Jack sat down in the seat beside Joseph. He reached out and put his arm around his shoulders, pulling him close. He didn't care if Joseph resisted or not. He was still feeling the emotion of almost losing him, of almost dying himself. But Joseph didn't resist, and the two of them sat in silence for a minute.

"Where's Agent Brown?" Joseph finally asked.

Jack shrugged. "I don't think he made it, Joe."

Joseph didn't say anything.

Jack yelled up to the cockpit, "How much longer until we reach the marker?"

Johnson shrugged. "An hour, maybe."

Jack frowned. "You sure you can land this thing?"

"Why, you wanna try?" Johnson shot back.

Stacey handed Johnson the pilot's cell phone. "There. We can land there."

He took the phone from her and noted the new marker she'd set.

"Five miles south of the pilot's," Stacey explained to Jack.

Jack nodded.

"Chopper seems to be responding to my commands," Johnson said to Stacey as he course-corrected.

"Good," Stacey muttered.

Then Joseph's voice traveled over the whine of the engines. "Al Pacino to Liam Hemsworth."

Stacey turned her head back into the cabin. "What?"

Jack couldn't see her from his position, but he said, "I taught him the game while we were in the bunker."

Stacey looked at Joseph. "Your dad and I played that game the night you were born."

Jack frowned. "We did?"

"You don't remember?"

"No."

"You were trying to get my mind off the contractions," she called back over her shoulder. "I think it was Dolph Lundgren to Madeleine Stowe that got me through at least a dozen of them."

Jack smiled. "I do remember that." He looked over at Joseph. "*Rocky 4* to *Avenging Angelo*, easy. But your mother didn't know about *Avenging Angelo*, so she put together a string of, like, fifteen movies."

He turned in his seat and leaned forward so that he could see around the wall and into the cockpit. He managed to lock eyes with Stacey, who was still craning her neck back to see into the cabin. And there, in that brief sideways connection, was replayed that specific time of their lives. Back when things had been much simpler. Though, as it turned out, not as simple as Jack had believed it to have been, since during that time, his wife had actually been sleeping with her other husband... His smile must have faltered or something must've changed in his eyes, because Stacey broke the eye contact and looked away with what he could only describe as shame.

Jack looked back at Joseph and said, "Al Pacino was in *Scarface* with Michelle Pfeiffer, who was in *What Lies Beneath* with Harrison Ford, who was in *Paranoia* with Liam Hemsworth."

THEY'D MANAGED TO SET the helicopter down without crashing, and Johnson proclaimed, "Like riding a bike," as he shut the motor off. Though Jack could see the sweat on his forehead when he turned to look at them.

Johnson opened the cockpit door and hopped down into the grass. He walked back to the cabin door and reached inside for the unconscious pilot, using his knife to cut him free from the shoelace securing him to the chair. Johnson slipped the knife back into his pocket and then grabbed the guy, still hog-tied and on his stomach, with both hands. With a big heave, he slid him straight out of the helicopter. The Russian hit the ground, landing on his chest. Without waiting to see if the impact had jarred him awake or had knocked the wind out of him, Johnson grabbed him by the ankles and began dragging him a hundred feet across the dew-soaked grass to a tree. He cut the remaining string away and then propped him up into a sitting position against the tree.

Still standing next to the helicopter, Stacey said to Jack, "Maybe you two should try going to the bathroom. Not sure when we'll get another chance."

Jack understood her true meaning and nodded. "C'mon, Joe. Let's go drain the lizards."

Stacey started walking toward Johnson. She could tell that he was bent over the pilot, but it was too dark to make out what he was doing to him. Whatever it was, she didn't want Joseph seeing it. When she reached him, however, she saw that he wasn't pulling fingernails but just staring at his cell phone.

"What is it?" she asked.

He looked up. "Got some hits back on the pictures."

He handed her his phone, and she started scrolling. "Brad Stevens, Navy SEAL. Honorably discharged in 2014." She shrugged. "Osprey."

Johnson nodded.

The next one was a former Marine, the one after that Army. And then...

Stacey looked up. "Russian mafia?"

"Prison tats ID'd him."

"Osprey too?" Stacey asked. "He recruiting out of the gulags?"

Again, Johnson shrugged. "Keep going."

She scrolled down some more, her face frowning in the glow of the phone's backlight. She whispered the report out loud. "Interpol identifies as current SVR operative under the direction of Line S." She looked up. "So it was the SVR that showed up. They *are* operating on American soil—"

"They're trying to find Fedyenka. If they can't, then I guess their next best move is to take Joseph out of the equation." He nodded toward the phone. "There's one more."

Stacey looked down to the last picture, read the three words beneath it. Looking up at the West Virginian sky, she handed the phone back to Johnson.

"So what do you think?" Johnson asked.

"I think that a CIA asset embedded within Osprey broadens the possibilities." She squinted in thought. "I think the Agency *wants* Fedyenka to get Joseph. Because somehow, that's a greater threat to the Kremlin."

Johnson wondered aloud, "Could the FSB have known that the Agency was planning on blowing up the school, and got an agent in there to grab Joseph first?"

"If so, then they would've had to know our plan. That Monica would be on her way."

"Brown could've told Fedyenka, but..." He sighed, not liking it. "No, according to his texts, Osprey didn't contact him until after the explosion. So how would the FSB have found out?"

"The CIA could have tipped Fedyenka off. Given him a chance to get in there first and grab him."

Johnson nodded. "Would have been easy enough with an agent working on the inside." He nodded toward the phone, indicating the last picture Stacey had seen on it. Then he took it back and returned it to his pocket. "If the Agency knows about my team, then maybe it was Brady or Thompson who leaked our information to them like Brown said."

"What do you mean?" Stacey asked.

"The Agency got to one of my guys early on. That's how they knew about Monica. Then they leak Brown's information to Fedyenka..."

"So it was Fedyenka who came to the school for Joseph and the CIA that blew it up."

But Johnson sighed. "Could've been the Agency that did both." He looked at the pilot. "If they're tracking the pilot's phone, then they'll be coming up over those woods there pretty soon."

"Do you still have Brown's phone?" she asked.

"In my pocket, why?"

"Might want to get rid of it. They were tracing it. That's how they got to the farm so fast. Brown switched the secure phone for his and just pretended to call Monica."

He blinked. "That's why they didn't converge on the car," he realized. "The phone he tossed in it was the secure one." He stared at her. "Dammit, Stacey, if they thought Brown was in the chopper the whole time..."

"I think I have a plan," she said. "But we need to wake him up."

Johnson ran a hand through his hair and shook his head. "I hope you know what you're doing." And then he slapped the pilot in the face. "Wake up."

The pilot's eyes fluttered open, and he groaned.

"Hello, sunshine," Johnson said.

Stacey crouched down in front of the man. She began speaking in Russian, to which the man responded in kind.

After a few minutes of conversation, Stacey stood. "He says they want Joseph alive," she said to Johnson.

"Why?"

"He doesn't know. But he thinks it has something to do with the elections."

"He just gave you that for free?" Johnson asked, surprised.

"I don't think it's a secret."

Johnson looked down at the pilot again. Then back at Stacey. "How the hell does Joseph play into all this?"

Standing just two feet apart beneath the starlit sky allowed them to see into each other's eyes, and Stacey could tell that, even though he had asked the question, he now shared the same suspicion she had. Only she couldn't bring herself to say it out loud. She turned back to the pilot and began speaking again.

"Now what are you saying?" Johnson asked.

"I'm letting him know that whatever story Fedyenka sold him about a restored imperial Russia was just shit. That he's just using the story to build a following and gain enough power to push his true agenda."

"Did you tell him what that agenda is?"

"What it's always been. A war between Russia and the US."

Johnson fell silent. "Ask him about the marker on his phone."

"Marker is rendezvous point," the pilot said in English.

"Who's waiting for you?"

"Whole army." He smiled.

"And where is this army planning to go after you deliver the boy?"

"Alaska."

"Is that where Fedyenka is?"

"Fedyenka is everywhere. And nowhere."

"Why Alaska?" Stacey interjected. "Is that where Osprey operates from?"

Johnson leaned over and whispered into her ear, "He knows they're coming. He's just stalling."

Stacey nodded and changed her line of questioning. "What happened back at the farmhouse?"

"From what it sounds like, the FSB got there right after us."

"Do they want my son dead or alive?"

"Oh, dead for sure."

"Because Fedyenka's plans depend on him, right?"

"Right." The pilot blinked and looked up at her. "If you want your son to be safe, then you should hand him over. He will not be any safer than with us. We will protect him. We need him."

"You'll use him."

"Both things are the same."

Johnson leaned over and said, "But you don't know why?"

The pilot shrugged. "They said that all things will become clear once we have him."

"Sure they will," Johnson said. He turned to Stacey. "We need to go."

"Go where?" she answered. Then she placed a hand on his arm and moved him away so that they were out of earshot. "What if he's right? What if we surrender to them? They'll be protecting us from the Agency and the SVR, and they'll lead us straight to Fedyenka."

"Or they just shoot us all in the head and take Joseph like they've been trying to do from the start."

Stacey sighed. "If we run now, where do we go?"

Johnson hesitated.

"You know I'm right," she said. "You have the tracker still?"

Johnson blinked, and realization settled into his eyes. "This is your plan?"

"You'll know where they take me."

"Again, that's assuming they take you anywhere."

"Knowing Fedyenka like I do, he'll want to see me. And if he thinks that I know where Joseph is, he wouldn't dare kill me."

Johnson frowned. "Given what we know about him, he'll probably do worse to you."

She thought of his paintings, the rumors, and tried not to shudder. "He'd know that I would die before giving him up, so I don't think he'd try torturing me. He'll probably try to persuade me that Joseph will only ever be safe in his care. That he alone can protect him from the Kremlin." She could tell that Johnson wasn't buying her oversimplification of her idea. "Just get there as fast as you can," she said, reaching out and touching his forearm. "After Joseph is safe."

"You are insane," the pilot called out, evidently able to hear their conversation.

Johnson pulled the pistol from its holster and shot the man in the head. He turned and looked Stacey in the eye. "Good luck," he said. And then, before she could react, he struck her in the side of the head with the butt of the smoking gun.

49

JACK CAME BACK AROUND the Black Hawk with Joseph and saw a dark form heading towards them. The starlight suggested a large mass, maybe a bear, and he grabbed Joseph's shoulder, stopping him. He reached for his gun, but just then the form entered a portion of the clearing that was lit silver by the moon, and Jack saw that it was actually a person carrying another person.

"Jack," Johnson's voice called out.

"Yeah." Jack let go of Joseph's shoulder and ran forward. "What happened?" At first he thought it was the pilot he was carrying, the aftermath of the shot they'd just heard. But as he came up alongside Johnson, following him toward the chopper, he saw that it was Stacey. "What happened?" he asked again. He put his hand on Stacey's neck, feeling for a pulse.

"She's fine," Johnson said.

"What happened?" Jack asked for the third time.

"We have to put her back in the helicopter, and then we need to get the hell out of here."

Jack fell back a pace. "What?"

"It's her plan."

"Mom?" Joseph said, joining them.

"She's okay, Joseph," Johnson reassured him. They came to the helicopter, and Johnson stepped up into the cabin with her still in his arms. He laid her down on the floor, positioning her limbs to make it look like she'd been knocked unconscious during a rough landing. Then he pulled Brown's phone out of his pocket and slipped it into hers.

"No," Jack said, Stacey's intentions dawning on him. "No way."

Johnson hopped back down to the ground and faced him. "I can still track her." He motioned toward the army bag still in the helicopter. "Wherever Fedyenka takes her, we'll know."

Jack saw past him and to his sleeping bride. His eyes welled with water, and a tear fell when he finally blinked. "What if—"

Johnson shook his head. "Fedyenka will want to see her. She thinks he'll try to get her to turn Joseph over to him by convincing her that he's the only one who can keep him safe."

Jack swore out loud and began pacing, looking to the woods, back to Stacey's unconscious body, and back to the woods again. His mind raced, but arrived nowhere. They were out of options, and he had no better plan.

"We need to hurry, Jack," Johnson said.

"Dad, what's happening?" Joseph asked.

Jack looked at his son, then once more at Stacey. She had been willing to sacrifice her husband to keep Joseph safe before, and he knew that she'd expect him to do the same if needed. "We have a plan," he said, putting both hands on Joseph's shoulders and looking him in the eyes. "Trust me." He hoped that he wouldn't live to regret those words, that Joseph wouldn't forever resent him for saying them. But Johnson was right. They were out of time, and they couldn't be here when Osprey arrived. No bodily harm would come to Joseph, and they were pretty sure Stacey too, but in order to give Stacey the leverage she'd need to stay alive, Joseph would have to be outside Fedyenka's reach. As for Jack and Johnson, they would be gunned down on sight.

"Why are you crying, then?" Joseph asked, clearly not buying whatever plan they were about to execute.

Jack smiled and wiped his eyes with the back of his hand. "It's going to be okay," he said. It was the only thing he could think of to say, even if he didn't believe it. He took his hands off Joseph's shoulders and jumped up into the helicopter. He bent over Stacey, using his finger to hook a strand of her hair around the back of her ear. Then he whispered something to her, kissed her temple, and hopped back out.

"Find me a rock," Johnson said. He turned and jogged back toward the pilot.

"A rock?" Jack asked.

"Yes, now!" Johnson hollered back.

"Help me find a rock," Jack said to Joseph. He took his flashlight out and turned it on, sweeping the light back and forth across the grass.

"Found one," Joseph said.

Jack aimed the light at where Joseph was pointing and could see a jagged outcropping protruding from the grass. He bent down and tried to free it from the ground, but it wouldn't budge. "This thing could be the tip of a boulder."

Joseph took Hugh out and pushed the blade into the ground beside the rock. "No, it's not that big." He pushed down on the handle, leveraging the rock up out of the dirt.

"Good job," Jack said. It was about the size of a softball. When he stood with it, Johnson was already coming back, the pilot's body now draped over his shoulder. He could tell that either Johnson or Stacey had shot him. As Johnson passed by him, he held out his hand, and Jack placed the rock in it.

"Stay here," Johnson called back over his shoulder. Then he disappeared around the helicopter.

A moment later, a series of sickening thuds drifted along the silent night air. Jack thought of covering Joe's ears, but it was too late. It was done. There was the sound of cracking glass, and then Johnson was coming back toward them with the army bag and Stacey's Glock and M&P 15. He left the Osprey weapons they'd taken in the helicopter. "Okay, let's move." He started jogging south toward the trees.

Jack slung his own rifle across his back and grabbed Joseph's hand. "Ready?"

Joseph nodded, but he was staring at the helicopter. Starlight caught the wetness in his own eyes.

"C'mon," Jack said.

They jogged after Johnson, and as they ran, Jack looked to the dark outline of tall trees plastered against the night sky. Barely visible beyond that, he could make out the distant shadow of a mountain range. They were back to running through the woods in West Virginia.

He took one last look behind him, though he could no longer see the helicopter in the darkness. Would he see Stacey again? He couldn't be sure. What would Fedyenka do to her? He didn't know. But they could all be dead by morning anyway, so there was no use worrying about a future timeline that might not even exist. Her survival depended on him and Johnson living long enough to rescue her. And in order to do that, he couldn't be debilitated with an obsession over what-ifs. So he muttered a prayer for his wife and then forced her from his mind.

TWENTY MINUTES LATER, A helicopter swooped overhead, shining a searchlight down through the night and illuminating the forest to their left.

Jack was holding Joseph's hand. He knew they'd be better off running on their own, free to use both their hands to navigate the dark world around them, but he couldn't bring himself to release him. He had the gut-wrenching feeling that if he did, he would never see him again.

"Damn, they're right on top of us," Johnson said as he stumbled through some dense undergrowth beside them. They dared not use their flashlights.

"Think they have thermal imaging?" All Jack could imagine in his mind's eye was a bird's-eye view of their heat signature running plain as day over the terrain below.

"They wouldn't be using the searchlights if they did."

But Jack could read uncertainty in Johnson's voice. The operatives at the farmhouse had had night vision, so why wouldn't they? Maybe because they were only planning on taking into custody a boy already restrained? He could only hope.

The searchlight was actually helping provide a glimpse into their surroundings, allowing them to spot fallen trees and dead ends and to course-correct around them.

They continued to run, panting and struggling to breathe. With the helicopter overhead, they knew that men on foot or on ATVs were most likely right on their heels.

JOE TRIED TO PULL his hand out of his father's grasp, but his father had a vise grip on him that he couldn't shake. He understood his dad's concern, but running through a dark forest holding hands was ridiculous. Also, it made him feel childish. Had his dad forgotten that he'd already survived the West Virginian mountains all on his own?

The searchlight swept down at them and carved a wide swathe of silver light across their path, the trees five feet in front of them suddenly visible. *That was close*, he thought, still pulling against his father's hand.

"Keep moving," Johnson whispered through labored breath. "We need to get into the hills. We can lose them there."

They continued on, Joseph growing more and more annoyed that his hand was still being held. Then they came to a rise, and his dad began to pull harder on his arm, half dragging him up the incline. Joseph lost his footing and fell forward, nearly pulling his dad back down on top of him. "Dad!" he said, yanking his hand away as hard as he could. "I'm fine!"

His dad stopped and turned. Though it was too dark to see his eyes, Joe knew his dad was staring down at him. "Dad," he said. He didn't know why he was just standing there, not saying anything. It was like his dad had spaced out or didn't know where he was. Maybe he hadn't even realized that he'd been holding his hand this whole time. "Dad," he repeated.

His dad moved his head, shaking it a little as if waking from a daze. He wondered if his dad had been lost in thought, thinking about his mom. How they'd just left her there unconscious for the Russian guy to find. Joseph wondered how she'd gotten unconscious to begin with. Had the pilot woken up and attacked her somehow? That didn't seem likely, given what he now knew his mom was capable of. She was like Charlize Theron in *Atomic Blonde*—another movie he'd seen with Zane that he didn't tell his parents about.

He didn't know what was going on, only that his dad had asked him to trust him. But should he? On the one hand, his parents had been lying to him his whole life. His mom was the one who put him, his dad, and all his friends at school in danger. Why Sexy Sam was dead. Why he'd had to leave his old friends behind. Why he could never see his new ones again. Yet, despite all of that, the three of them were still alive. True, his grandmother wasn't. His dad's two friends weren't, according to what his dad had told him in the bunker, but his mom and dad had at least succeeded in keeping him alive this long. A few close calls along the way, but...

"Sorry," his dad said. "C'mon." And the vague outline of his body turned and began to recede into the surrounding darkness, scaling the incline.

Joseph climbed back to his feet and hurried to catch up just as the helicopter banked away from them and headed off in a different direction. He caught up to his dad and climbed the embankment alongside him, shifting his backpack into a more comfortable position.

As they climbed, he thought of what Johnson had shown his mom on the cell phone, and he thought of Wesley Snipes, how he was dead. But that fact didn't seem to register, and so instead, for the millionth time, he tried to guess as to why this guy from Russia wanted him so bad. He believed his dad when he told him that he didn't know, but there was something in his mom's eyes that made him question whether or not she was telling them everything. He could only hope that he'd have the chance to confront her about it.

When they got to the top of the rise, they were faced with a clearing. They circled around it, staying within the trees. The mountains loomed over them.

"Do you know where we are?" Joseph asked his dad.

"Not really."

"Are these the Appalachian Mountains?"

"All of West Virginia is considered Appalachia, remember?"

"So yes."

"Yes."

"Why did we leave Mom?" he asked.

"We'll talk about that when we get somewhere safe," his dad answered. "They'll be coming back this way again, and we need to be in the mountains when they do."

Joseph nodded and looked behind them. He couldn't see anything but shadows stacked upon more shadows. If there were people out there stalking them, he sure couldn't see them. And then came a mental picture of his head framed in some infrared scope, and a series of chills swept down his back.

They continued moving through the night, the sound of insects and nocturnal animals breaking through the distant sound of the rotors as the helicopter continued to search in the wrong direction. Soon, they couldn't hear the helicopter at all.

50

AN HOUR LATER, JACK, Joseph, and Johnson were out from beneath the trees and situated atop a rocky outcropping that overlooked the entire course they'd just taken. The moon glowed above and bathed the top of the forest in a silver sheet. There was no sign of the helicopter.

They walked off the outcropping and made their way to some bushes. The temperature had dropped, and when they sat down, Jack put his arm around Joseph, pulling him tight against his side, trying to keep him warm. A few minutes later, Jack could tell from Joseph's breathing that he had already fallen asleep. Jack leaned back against a rock and turned his eyes to the heavens.

"She'll be okay," Johnson said from a few feet beside him.

Jack looked over in his direction, but could barely make him out. "How do you track her?"

Johnson reached into the army bag beside him and pulled out what looked like a tablet. "With this."

"The range is good?"

"It's satellite, so we could track her back to Russia if we had to."

"She moving?"

Johnson turned the device on, and the screen lit up. He nodded. Then he turned the instrument around so that Jack could see the red dot slowly moving north over the map.

She's alive, Jack thought, and relief flooded his entire being. *Unless she isn't, and Fedyenka just wants to see her body for himself.*

"Here," Johnson said. He leaned forward and held out his cell phone with his other hand.

Jack reached out and took it. The screen was filled with a lifeless face. "What is this?"

"Those are some of the people who showed up at the farmhouse."

Jack moved his thumb over the screen, and the image moved. He continued to scroll, and more faces rolled on by. He read the messages that accompanied each one. "This is what you were showing Stacey?"

"Yeah."

Jack looked up. "FSB?"

"An SVR hit team. They showed up after Osprey. Turns out Fedyenka kidnapped Agent Brown's family and threatened to kill them unless he helped them out. They were tracking his cell. That's how they got there so fast." He pointed at the phone. "The CIA had an asset embedded within Osprey, so it looks like anything Fedyenka knows probably came via the Agency."

Jack thought about it. "So you do think you had a leak from the start."

"Looks that way. It wasn't Brown, though, because they only just turned him the other day. I'm sure whoever it was is dead now, so it's a moot point. No idea how the SVR showed up so fast though. Maybe they have someone inside Osprey too, or were at least tracking someone inside."

"They're trying to keep Fedyenka from getting Joseph?"

"We think so."

"Meaning they want him dead."

"Probably."

Jack glanced down at Joseph sleeping against him, and suddenly it didn't seem that long ago that he was just a baby. "Then they don't know where Fedyenka is either."

"Or they can't get to him where he's at," Johnson said. "Or they're coming after Joseph anyway."

Jack turned his attention back to the phone and scrolled through the rest. He handed the phone back. "So Fedyenka wants my son for some reason no one seems to know or no one will tell me. The CIA wouldn't mind him having my son as long as the rest of us are dead, and Moscow will do anything to keep Fedyenka from getting him." He looked up at the moon.

It seemed so alien right then. So indifferent. "If Moscow is so intent in keeping Fedyenka from getting him, then they must know why he wants him. And it's gotta be a pretty viable threat to them."

But Johnson didn't take the bait. Instead, he said, "And soon Fedyenka will have Stacey, and we'll finally know where the bastard is."

Jack stared through the thatch work of vines and plants and out across the tops of the trees. "The agents at our house..." He trailed off, turning his gaze to his hands. "They were real federal agents, weren't they?"

"Probably."

"They were just doing their job. They thought I'd blown up a school."

Johnson shrugged. "I'd bet a kidney that at least one of them had been told to make sure you didn't make it out of the house alive."

Jack knew that was true. The only reason he was still alive was because the sniper's first shot just missed his head.

"What difference does it make?" Johnson asked. "It was you or them. I appreciate that you feel bad about it. Proves you're human. But what's the point in letting those thoughts in? It's done. You can't undo it." He ran a hand through his hair. "And you're not the one who started it." He shook his head. "No, the fault is with the ones who put this whole thing into motion."

Jack nodded. He knew he was right, but it would be a long time before he felt it. If he *ever* felt it. "Are we going to get them all?"

Johnson smiled. "Not a chance in hell." He picked up a stone and tossed it in the direction of the forest below. "These people are weeds. You pull one out of the ground, and you just find that the roots keep on going and going, that they're intertwined with everything you see."

"So then there's no end to this."

Johnson shrugged. "To government corruption? Never. To your story? Maybe. But it's not going to be at some senate hearing where the director of the CIA is found guilty of unlawful operations against US citizens in the homeland. I can promise you that."

"At least not without a major change in the White House, anyway."

"Someone with a huge set of balls," Johnson agreed. "And someone smarter and shrewder than them who can avoid being JFK'd. But until that day comes..."

"I know," Jack said.

Johnson studied him, the whites of his eyes reflecting the moonlight. "We need to kill Fedyenka. It's the only real chance we have at getting out of this mess."

Jack nodded. "Where do you think he is?"

"The pilot said he's in Alaska. But who knows if he was telling the truth."

"If they take Stacey to Alaska, how the hell are we going to get there undetected and in time to stop anything..." He trailed off, not wanting to finish the thought.

Johnson set the tablet and his cell down beside him and leaned back, folding his arms across his chest. "No sense in worrying about it now. Odds are just as good that he's right here in West Virginia."

After a minute of silence, Jack asked, "What happened to Brown's family?"

Johnson shrugged. "No idea." Then he closed his eyes. "I'd suggest trying to get some sleep. May be a while before you get another chance, and you'll want to be fresh for when the time comes."

When the time comes. The time to kill this man who had been a scourge in his family's side for over ten years. He couldn't wait. It was tempting to start looking past that part, about what they would do next. But he wouldn't allow it. The cart before the horse and all that. He hoped to God Stacey knew what she was doing. He knew she could handle herself, but he couldn't stop himself from worrying. People who could handle themselves died every day. But he knew that worrying was pointless. Worse than pointless, it was debilitating. He'd had his fair share of being up shit's creek alone and without a paddle, and in those times, Stacey had always pressed on for Joseph's sake. Now it was his turn to press on. "She'll be fine," he whispered aloud, closing his eyes.

Johnson didn't respond.

JACK WOKE UP TO someone tugging on his arm. "Hey, time to move," he heard a voice say. He opened his eyes, unsure of where he was or how he'd gotten there. And then it all came rushing back in a flash, and he was wide awake. He sat up and saw the dawn sky awash in red and purples. Johnson was standing to his side. He came around, offered a hand, and pulled him to his feet.

"Where's Joseph?" Jack asked, looking around. And just like that, he was back in that tent two years ago.

"Just over there. He's taking a leak."

Jack tried to ignore his heart going from 60 to 250 bpm, and patted down the front of his clothes. They were wet with dew. He was cold, and his breath was clouding in front of his face when he talked. Eventually, the cobwebs of sleep disintegrated, and he finally arrived at attention in the present.

"Mist will cover us," Johnson said, indicating with his hand the wispy fingers running through the trees below.

Jack nodded. He looked at his watch. 6:50. "Where's she now?"

"Canada."

Jack blinked. "Is she still moving? Are they really headed for Alaska?"

"Yeah, they're still moving. By plane, it looks like. Moving too fast through the mountains to be anything else. We need to get out of here and find something to eat. Find some sort of transportation."

"You do think they're heading to Alaska, don't you? That he's been there all along?" Jack saw Joseph walking back toward them.

Johnson nodded once. "Hiding behind shell companies while building and recruiting his private army, propped up by various NGOs that are tapped into CIA dark money."

"I mean, it's gotta be in preparation for something huge, right? Something they're using Fedyenka for, but scrubbing past connections to avoid fallout blowing back on them."

Johnson didn't say anything. They'd already been through this to some extent.

Could it just be the same old story? Jack wondered again. Using Fedyenka to instigate a fight to the death with a divided and depleted Russia? If so, whatever the flashpoint they would need to justify it would have to appear to have Moscow's fingerprints all over it, clear for the rest of the world to see. A new "global" Pearl Harbor. Or...

Jack turned to Johnson as Joseph came up beside him and bent over to tie his shoe. "What if it isn't America that's made to look like the victim?"

Johnson scratched at the stubble on his jaw. "You mean, could Fedyenka be plotting a false flag on his own country? Blame it on the US?" He thought about it. "That would explain how seriously the FSB is taking him."

"But is the Agency so desperate for a war that they'd allow America to be seen as the bad guy?"

"Maybe. If it serves to get the war started. Then, in the aftermath, they can roll out evidence that it was an inside job that provoked Russia's attack and thus exonerate the US in the eyes of history." He shrugged. "Or maybe they have their own version of events ready to roll out, and they're playing Fedyenka for a fool."

"But what does Fedyenka get out of a war with America? Does he think that by helping the CIA, they will thank him by putting him in charge, him being a sort of ethnarch for the West?"

Johnson slapped him on the shoulder while flashing a patient smile. "No way."

Jack fell silent as his ideas ran out of road. Instead, he turned to Joe. "Sleep okay?" It was such a stupid question considering everything they'd just been through.

Joseph shrugged. "Sure, Dad."

They gathered their gear and headed north, walking down the back side of the mountain and disappearing into the mist.

51

STACEY CAME TO AND immediately felt the pain in her head. Whether or not it was the pain that had awakened her, she didn't know. In fact, she realized, she didn't know anything. *What the hell?* She opened her eyes but couldn't see. Maybe she hadn't opened her eyes? She blinked. Nothing. She could feel her eyelids touching, so she knew that she was blinking, yet only darkness. She winced. Her head was pounding, and it felt like there was an ice pick sticking in it. Was that why she couldn't see? Had someone hit her in the—

And she remembered. Standing there by the pilot of the Osprey Black Hawk... Johnson had struck her in the head with his pistol. *Dammit, Johnson.* Had that really been necessary?

She tried to bring her hand to her head, but found that her hands were restrained. She tried moving other parts of her body. Nope. She thought she was sitting up and tried to flex her glutes to see if she could realize the presence of something beneath her. She could tell that her arms were bent at the elbows, so whatever was restraining her had armrests.

Then she noticed the cold. It came suddenly, biting through the pain in her head and racing up and down her body. She started to shiver. There was an icy draft coming from somewhere, and for a second she thought that maybe someone had locked her in a freezer. But then a picture formed in her head, drawn by the feel of air against her skin.

She was naked.

It seemed Fedyenka's games had already begun. She tried to get a sense of her body, between her legs specifically. Had they done anything else to her while she was out? She couldn't tell, which was probably a good sign. Even with the piercing headache and the freezing cold, if a bunch of degenerate private contractors had had their way with her while she was out, she was pretty sure she'd be able to tell.

She took a deep breath and exhaled slowly, trying to calm herself. Wherever she was, she was exactly where she wanted to be. Where she had planned to be. But where was that? She tried to feel the space around her. It seemed empty, like she was in a void. And there was a vibration. She could hear it. The walls were shaking, *thrumming*. And now that she could hear it, she could feel it too. *Outer darkness*, she thought. And suddenly all Jack's Bible stuff rushed into her mind, and she wondered if she could be dead. Was this the atheist's eternity? Conscious in darkness, freezing, in pain, and unable to move forever? Had Johnson hit her too hard and cracked her skull, killing her?

Suddenly, there came the sensation that she was tilting. And the picture that snapped into her mind as a result was also the answer to her questions.

She was in an aircraft. That explained the vibrations and the cold. She imagined the cargo bay of a C-5M or an Airbus 400M and tried to home in on the noises, to try to detect the sound of propellers. Or maybe she was on the lower deck of a Boeing 747...

Damn, I'm thirsty, she thought. And then Jesus's words from the cross filled her head so loudly that she swore she heard a voice actually say them. "I thirst." She frowned. Why was her mind going religious on her? And again she wondered if it could be because she was dead. If she'd been wrong, if there really was an afterlife.

She winced as another sudden pain shot through her brain. Like the ice pick had been pulled out of her skull and then swung into it again. She took a deep breath. "Okay, God. Jesus. Whatever. If you're there, which I highly doubt you are, you probably don't respond to ultimatums or threats from the likes of us, but I'm gonna give you one anyway, because...well, here I am. Naked and restrained and heading to my own cross. Though you didn't even help your own son when he begged you for an out, so I don't know why you'd help me." She found her own whispered voice strangely comforting in the silence. "But if you get my family out of this mess, I promise I'll do whatever you want." Then she started to chuckle, realizing how many times that exact prayer must have been prayed throughout the centuries. But, like she said, what did she have to lose?

What good is it if you gain the whole world and lose your soul?

She blinked. She didn't even know what that meant or where it came from. It sounded biblical. She wondered if this was what had happened to Jack after he had been thrown off the cruise ship. Was she having a spiritual experience like he had, or was she just going crazy? Had her brain been scrambled by the strike, or had they given her some kind of drug?

She forced herself to relax, to steady her heart rate. She tried not to feel the cold, to imagine that she was warm and content. She thought of Joseph and Jack, back in the woods of West Virginia, and she let her mind slip into a string of prayers for their safety.

And she waited.

THEY MADE IT DOWN the mountain by 8:30 and with no issues other than their growling stomachs and sandpaper tongues. The mist had concealed their journey (in case anyone was still out there looking for them), and now they were in the foothills on the edge of a small town.

Joseph peered out from behind the tree line and could make out a few single-story buildings. By now, most of the mist had been burned off by the rising sun, and the only fog left was way off in the distance, hugging the tree-studded slopes of the mountain that rose behind the town. There was a road that passed in front of them, lined with telephone poles, long black wires sagging between them. He thought the town looked like something from a movie. *U-Turn*, which he'd only seen the trailer for, or *Last Man Standing* with Bruce Willis (he'd watched that with his dad when it came on HBO last year).

"What do you think?" his dad asked Agent Johnson, who was observing the scene with eagle's eyes.

"Well, we need to eat," Johnson said. Then he turned to them. "I'll go in and check it out. I'm pretty sure they don't have CCTV running through the Appalachian foothills, but I want to make sure. They may not be looking for me, but everyone is looking for you."

Joseph watched his dad nod in agreement.

Then Johnson slipped the bag off his shoulder and stood. "I'll be back," he said in a bad Arnold Schwarzenegger impersonation. He winked at Joseph. Then he was leaving the trees and walking toward the road.

Joseph looked over at his dad and saw how intently he watched Agent Johnson cross the street. Like he was expecting a sniper's bullet to take him out before he could reach the other side. In everything they'd been through together, Joseph only ever saw his dad look this way one other time—when Seth had put a knife to his neck. But then Joseph realized that it wasn't the fear of their present moment that had his dad's face set the way that it was, but rather worry for his mom. He was watching Agent Johnson with his physical eyes, but his mind's eye was elsewhere.

"Are you sure Mom's gonna be alright?" Joseph asked, deciding to breach the subject while it was so obviously on his dad's mind.

His dad blinked and seemed to snap out of whatever psychic channel he'd been observing. He looked over at him and forced a smile. "Are you kidding me? Have you seen your mom in action?"

It was a BS response that Joseph had no trouble seeing through, but what else was his dad supposed to say? Even if he didn't believe his own words, which he clearly didn't, could he ever make his lips say otherwise?

"You remember *Mission: Impossible III*?" his dad asked.

"Yeah."

"The beginning when they go to rescue Keri Russell?"

"The girl from *The Americans*? Yeah."

Yeah, The Americans, Jack thought, appreciating the irony. "Well, same sort of idea. We're able to track Mom, so we'll know where she is. And then we'll be able to go get her and finally get this guy off our back." He paused. "That's if Mom hasn't done it already, and she actually finds us first."

"Dad," Joseph said, "she dies. They put a bomb in her head."

His dad looked back across the street, watching Johnson continue to make his way to the old buildings that served as the southern edge of the town. "Yeah, well, besides that part."

Joseph could tell that what he'd said upset his dad. That now he was wondering whether or not the guy who had *Michael Strogoff* put into his son's locker was as insane as the late Seymour Hoffman's character in *MI3*. "Sorry," Joseph said.

His dad shuffled over on his elbows and wrapped an arm around his shoulders. "You have nothing to be sorry for," he said. "Nothing."

And as Joseph watched a single tear run into his father's beard, he could hear the unspoken second half of his dad's words. Something to the effect of all this crap being his and his mom's fault and the deep regret that they both shared at getting him involved in any of it.

Joseph turned his eyes to Johnson and swallowed the lump in his own throat. It sucked that this was his life, and he had no idea where all of this crap would lead, how it would end, but he couldn't deny the love he felt from his parents. There were kids at his school who he knew had nothing even remotely close to the affection that was shared within their family. So was it an even trade-off? Security and a stable childhood versus the unconditional and absolute love of his parents? He thought it might be. He turned his head back as his dad removed his arm from around his shoulders. "Sorry I was being such a dick before."

His dad frowned, obviously shocked by his word choice, but then he shook his head. "You don't have to be sorry. There's no playbook on how you're supposed to cope with any of this."

Joseph nodded. He wanted to say what he was thinking, which was that if his mom and dad had never gotten married, then he wouldn't exist. That though he couldn't choose who his parents were, his mom and dad had risked their lives to save his over and over again. So he could either thank them for putting him first, above even their own lives, or he could wish that his parents were different, which, of course, was a waste of time and energy and ultimately self-defeating. But he didn't say any of that. Maybe one day he would, but he couldn't make himself speak the words today. It was enough for him right now to have even realized it.

Johnson disappeared between two buildings, and his dad asked, "You think he'll bring us back breakfast again?"

"I hope so."

"Yeah, I'd do anything for a coffee right now."

And then almost as quickly as Johnson had disappeared from view, he was back and coming toward them. He crossed the road and walked up to the tree line.

"Okay, I think we're clear," he said. "The town is old, and I didn't see any cameras. If it weren't for the little diner over there, I'd question whether it even has a zip code."

Joseph stood along with his dad and tossed his backpack behind a tree beside Agent Johnson's gear. His dad set the weapons down next to the backpack and the other bag from the car.

"Just keep an eye out for anyone who seems out of place," Johnson said. "They're out there somewhere, still looking for us."

"Won't you look out of place in your new threads?" Joseph asked, pointing out the Osprey clothes they were still in.

Agent Johnson shrugged. "I think we'll be fine if we roll up our sleeves and untuck our shirts."

"Okay," Joseph said, obviously not so sure. He felt the familiar touch of Hugh in his waistband as he stepped out of the shadows and into the morning light.

THE THREE OF THEM sat at a table inside what Jack figured had to pretty much be the town's center. If not geographically, then certainly socially. The diner was like most small diners he'd seen in the movies. A long bar with stools all occupied by what appeared to be regular patrons. An old woman and a younger man who could be her son or nephew stood behind the counter and poured coffee, talking back and forth with the people sitting across from them.

Jack sat at one of the dozen tables that had been arranged in two long rows of six, his back to the bar. Joseph was sitting across from him, and Johnson was between them at the end of the table, where he could keep an eye on the front door and the street beyond. He was squinting into the sunlight that was coming through the windows, the only person in the place who was facing the rising sun.

There was a door in the back of the diner, a sign hanging above it indicating that it led to a bathroom and a telephone. A muted television hung on the wall up behind the bar. It looked like a news channel was on, though Jack couldn't tell which one. No one seemed to be paying any attention to it anyway.

He tried to stay calm, to act natural. In a place like this where they already stood out as strangers and dressed in what could be considered suspicious clothing, acting strange would only assert themselves further into the room's collective curiosity. Jack and Johnson had come up with a story if needed, similar to the one Jack had used on the guy who'd picked him up and taken him to breakfast after the storm in the mountains a couple of years ago. *What was that guy's name?* Jack couldn't remember. But the woman's name had been Bernice. Or Bernadette? Something like that.

He sipped his coffee. In fact, they'd already given the woman behind the counter their story when she took their order. They'd said they were on their way down from Ohio to catch the Appalachian Trail when their car broke down. They'd been walking for hours, looking for a place to eat. If the old woman bought it or not, he couldn't tell. She seemed to be a pretty savvy lady, years of stories etched into her face, their lessons sparkling in her eyes. She might not believe them, but then maybe she didn't care. She certainly didn't seem to be paying them any extra attention.

"Can I use the bathroom?" Joseph asked.

Jack looked at Johnson, who nodded his head. "Yeah, make it quick," Jack said.

Joseph pushed his chair out from beneath him and passed between two empty tables on his way to the door in the back of the room.

Jack kept his eyes on him.

"I hit her with my gun. Knocked her out," Johnson stated out of the blue.

Jack turned toward him and frowned, not sure of his meaning.

"I figured there was less chance of her getting shot by some hopped-up, trigger-happy ex-Marine if she was unconscious and couldn't possibly be perceived as a threat."

"Stacey?" Jack felt the heat of anger flush his face. Yet at the same time, he knew that Johnson's actions could've saved her life. If the Osprey operatives knew her background and had come up on her in the dark, then there's no telling what they might have done—whether Fedyenka wanted her alive or not.

Johnson nodded. "She believes that he wants her alive, to see her, to get Joseph's location out of her." He shrugged. "I think she's right, but I didn't see the need to take any chances."

"It was her idea?" Jack asked.

"To let herself be taken? Yeah. I tried to talk her out of it, but again, I think she's right. It's our best chance of ever finding him."

"And where does your tracker show her now?"

"I left it with the gear," Johnson said.

"Do you think they'll do anything to her?"

"Whatever they might do to her, she's been trained for it. She'll be fine. And we left the helicopter on foot while she was out, so he should know that she wouldn't have a clue where we went."

"I hope you're right," Jack mumbled, having no trouble imagining a steel case being open and all kinds of sharp instruments gleaming under fluorescent lights.

Johnson leaned forward onto his elbows while lifting his coffee mug to his lips. At the same time he turned and looked back over his left shoulder, toward the counter and the backs of those sitting at it. His eyes narrowed as he focused on something. "Holy shit," he suddenly whispered, and turned to look back down at his coffee.

"What?" Jack asked.

"You're on television."

Jack looked up to where Johnson's eyes had been. There he was. Even from this distance he had no trouble recognizing himself. It was the same picture he'd seen on CNN, only now the picture wasn't just framed in a small box up in the corner of the shot but filling the entire screen. Then his picture disappeared and was replaced by some kind of CCTV footage. He couldn't hear the monologue and had no idea what was being said of him, but he did know that the person in the collage of moving images couldn't possibly be him because he'd never been to any of the places in the footage before.

But then more CCTV footage began playing, and now Jack did recognize the location. As the parent of an enrolled student, he'd been on the school grounds plenty of times. But never alone at night. Never with a large duffel bag slung over his shoulder. And certainly never breaking into a classroom window. "Holy shit," he echoed, casting a quick glance at Johnson. And for just a split second, Jack thought he detected a slight flicker of doubt dance across the secret-agent man's eyes. As if he was seeing something differently all of a sudden. Like maybe Jack had been recruited by Stacey and was now helping her run black ops for the Agency, the footage on the TV absolutely real.

Jack shook his head, no.

A guy sitting at the bar looked up at the screen. Jack heard him say, "When they find that psycho, they should just let the parents have their way with him." A couple of the others agreed.

"Stay calm," Johnson whispered. "That's not you."

"Damn right it's not me," he said, and he sounded a hell of a lot more sure about it than Johnson had.

Jack's heart was racing now, and he looked over at the back door, hoping that Joseph's picture wouldn't flash up on the screen next. He took another sip of coffee.

Joseph came back to the table.

"Feel better?" Jack asked.

"Oh yeah," said Joseph.

Jack forced a smile and noticed that the story on the TV had finally changed.

Johnson leaned back in his chair and did his best to yawn like a guy who'd only spent the last few hours walking from a broken-down car and not like a guy who was being hunted by Russian Special Forces, private contractors, and every law enforcement agency in the country.

Jack tried to act the part too. But when he turned his head toward the front windows, his blood froze.

A black Chevy Suburban with tinted windows was rolling slowly down the street and passing the diner.

Jack snapped his head back and lifted the menu off the table, holding it up and pretending to show something to Johnson while using it to block his face from view of the street. Jack saw Johnson register the vehicle too.

"Stay calm," Johnson said, reaching into his back pocket and pulling out his wallet. "Was there a back door by the bathroom, Joseph?" he asked, smiling at the boy.

Joseph nodded and almost turned to look behind him, to see what had spooked them.

"Don't look," Jack said.

Joseph paused, then looked back down to the table. "Yeah. It was propped open. I think someone was smoking outside."

"Excellent," Johnson said as he placed some bills on the table. He looked back at Jack. "I'm going to go take a look. If I'm not back in sixty seconds, you and Joseph follow after me."

He nodded. "Do you think they saw us?"

"I don't know," Johnson said. "But *she* sure as hell did." He nodded to the woman behind the counter.

Jack turned one more time and saw the woman staring right at him, phone held to her ear. Jack smiled and turned back, his heart beating like a war drum in his chest.

Johnson stood and casually made his way toward the bathroom. No one at the other tables even batted an eye in his direction. Jack wanted to know what the woman was doing. Was she reaching for a shotgun? Was she whispering to all the men at the counter, coming up with a plan to take him down? But he didn't dare look. To look was to give them away, and there was still a chance that she hadn't made the connection, that she was just talking to a friend or a customer while curious about new faces.

He looked at his watch. Sixty seconds and no sign of Johnson. He caught the reflection of the outside street in the glass of one of the framed pictures on the wall and saw another SUV glide across it.

"I have to use the bathroom, too," he said just loud enough to be overheard by anyone paying attention. He stood. "C'mon,

I don't want you to stay here by yourself." He put his hand on Joseph's shoulder and let his son lead him past the empty tables and through the back door.

He held his breath the entire way, waiting for someone to shout at them, to tell them to freeze. To hear the sound of a shotgun shell being pumped into a chamber. But none of that happened, and before he knew it, they were standing next to Johnson, who was peering out the back exit and into an alleyway, the back of a red-brick building across from them.

"C'mon," Johnson said. He stepped out through the propped door and turned left.

Jack grabbed Joseph's hand and followed.

They took the alley to the corner, where a cross street separated them from more buildings.

Johnson peered around the diner and up the street.

"See anything?" Jack asked.

Johnson shook his head.

The alley continued across the intersection and between more buildings, preserving a view of the mountains in the distance. "We need to get back to our stuff," Jack said.

And then Johnson whipped his head back behind the wall. "They just pulled up to the front door."

The unmistakable sound of car doors being shut echoed down the street.

"They'll send someone to cover the back," Johnson said. He turned back toward the door they'd used to exit the diner and pointed to another door farther down at the back of the red-brick building. There were trash bags piled alongside it. "Let's go," he said, and sprinted for it.

Jack and Joe followed.

"Shit," Johnson whispered, getting to the door just half a second before them. There was no handle on the door. It could only be pushed open from the inside.

Johnson pulled out his pistol. "Stay here," he said, and ran northeast down to the other end of the alley, taking up a position at the opposite corner of the diner. He crouched low, this time his right shoulder leaning into the wall, and held his palm up to Jack and Joseph. He wanted them to stay where they were.

Which was in plain view of whoever would be coming down the side of the diner or out the back door.

Jack knew what Johnson was doing, and though he realized it might be their best shot at getting out of the alley alive, he didn't much appreciate it.

Then a shadow appeared on the ground beside Johnson. Someone was on the sidewalk next to the diner, the sun striking their back and throwing their dark form out past the side of the building and into the alley. Jack knew that the operative would want to clear the alley before stepping into it, which was why they'd stopped. But it didn't matter. Because from their position, they still had enough of a peripheral view to see the trash bags and Jack and Joseph crouching down beside them. And—just as Johnson had hoped—the sight of them distracted the guy from clearing the corner, and he came straight around it, his weapon coming up and settling on them. But the guy hesitated, didn't shoot. Which told Jack that it was not an SVR kill squad that had found them. Probably not the CIA either.

The hesitation to shoot gave Johnson the window he needed. Seeing the gun's shadow stretch past the side of the wall and then swing toward Jack and Joseph, he spun, still crouched low, right onto the sidewalk, pulling the knife from his belt and ramming it into the man's groin while swatting the barrel of the gun up and away at the same time. Then, with lightning speed, he removed the knife and shot to his feet, jamming the blade into the guy's chin and then into the side of his head. Johnson lowered the lifeless body to the sidewalk and dragged it into the alley, out of sight from the roads. He waved Jack and Joseph over to him.

By the time Jack reached him, Johnson had taken the man's pistol and earpiece. Thankfully, they were only wearing vests and not helmets or other body armor. He handed Joseph the vest and Jack the pistol. He took the rifle for himself.

"Back to the other end of the alley," Johnson told them. "Go!"

Jack didn't ask any questions. He pulled Joseph after him and ran back down the length of the alley, passing the trash bags and then the back door of the diner. He could hear Johnson's feet pounding the pavement behind them. When they reached the street, Johnson called out for them to go right. They did, running west alongside the brick building and approaching another intersection.

This is no good, Jack thought as his eyes surveyed the town. It was too open. The buildings were few and far between with too many empty parking lots scattered around them. Maybe if it was just the one SUV that Johnson had seen, they might stand a chance of making it to the hills without further detection, but if there was more than one—

"Right! Go right!" Johnson again called out behind them.

They turned at the intersection and found themselves on a sidewalk that ran across the front of the brick building—which Jack saw was a grocery store. A gas station and a convenience store stood across the street on their left.

"Keep going!" Johnson yelled. "Cross the street! To the bank!"

Jack looked back over his shoulder and saw Johnson waving ahead of them. When he faced forward again, he could see another building standing on the next block, across the street. There was a sign on its side that read BANK. But across the side of the building some smart-ass prankster had spray-painted, "Guns, Ammo, and Baby Needs."

Not seeing traffic in either direction, they crossed the street and ran to the front of the bank. It didn't appear to be open yet, if at all, and Jack was glad for that. The storefront was all glass, and anyone inside would have clearly seen Johnson standing there with an assault rifle, which probably would have led to an alarm being sounded, pictures being taken, and the whole world finding out where they were in minutes.

But then Johnson stepped up to the glass doors and began smashing them with the butt of the rifle.

"What are you doing?" Jack asked.

It took a few blows, but the glass wasn't bulletproof, and it eventually cracked and then broke. Alarms began to sound so loud that they had to cover their ears. The noise seemed to fill the entire town, reaching all the way to the distant hills before echoing back.

"If they're Osprey, then they won't want to be around when the authorities show up," Johnson yelled over the alarm.

"You hope," Jack said.

"I hope."

Jack knew that if there were more operatives wandering through the town, they'd be more than capable of taking out the local sheriff when he rolled to a stop in front of the bank. The question was whether it was worth risking the mess that would come in the aftermath. "How long do you think they have?" Jack asked.

Johnson held up a finger with one hand while cupping his other over the stolen earpiece in his ear and listening to something that Jack couldn't hear. "They're pulling out before the police can get on the scene." He kept listening. "But they're going to cover the roads to and from the town." Then his eyes rose to Jack's. "The woman at the diner identified us. They know we're here."

"Where do we go?" Joseph asked, his eyes darting up and down the street.

"We have to get back to the woods," Johnson answered. "That way." He pointed east.

Jack knew that meant having to cross the main street that the diner was on. The street their pursuers had stopped on. Were they still there, in front of the diner? Or had they already moved to get out of town?

A black SUV suddenly appeared to their left, coming down the very street they'd need to cross to get to the woods, and heading toward the diner. If it was the same vehicle that had stopped in front of the diner before, then they must have circled around the town and were now on their way out.

From its position facing the diner, anyone on the passenger side of the vehicle would need only to turn their heads to the right and toward the sound of the alarm as they passed by, and they'd see all three of them standing on the sidewalk in front of the bank.

And apparently, that was exactly what happened.

The SUV came to a screeching stop, its brake lights glowing red through the smoke sent drifting up from the tires.

Johnson swore. "They see us. Go!" He ran across the street and back in front of the grocery store. Jack and Joseph went after him as the SUV reversed with screeching tires and swung to face them.

Johnson veered right toward the convenience store and the gas station just as another SUV turned onto the street two blocks ahead of them, and the other came skidding around the corner behind.

They were being pinched.

"Split up!" Johnson's voice echoed as he ran for the gas station.

When Jack reached the end of the block, the oncoming SUV just about on top of them, he grabbed Joseph and pulled him left down the side street and back toward the diner. When Jack looked over his shoulder, he saw both SUVs converging on the road behind them. One from the left and one from the right, nearly ramming into each other.

"Go left into the alle y, and I'll go right across the street," he yelled to Joe, pointing. His heart heaving in his chest, he added, "Get back into the diner! We'll meet you there!" Then he veered right and crossed the street, heading for the shadow of the buildings across from him. He saw Joseph turn down the alley and head for the back door of the diner.

Jack knew that one of the vehicles would turn after Joe, but after neither had gone after Johnson, he was afraid both would.

And both did. They cut hard to the left, their backsides fish-tailing and kicking up dirt as they entered the narrow alley.

No, no, no! He pulled the pistol and fired at the tires, hoping to cause a flat that might spin the vehicle into the side of the building and give Joe more time to get through the back door and into the diner. But he wasn't so lucky, and they didn't stop. As he crossed back over the street, now heading to the front of the diner, he saw that Johnson was on his way to them, rifle held tight to his shoulder.

More sirens sounded in the distance.

53

SOMETHING JOLTED STACEY AWAKE. She blinked, but it did no good in the darkness. She was disoriented. She didn't remember drifting off to sleep again and had no idea what had awakened her. And then she understood. They'd landed.

She could feel the aircraft begin to slow, its wheels rolling over the ground. It was smooth enough to know they'd touched down on a paved runway. She had no idea where though. Had no idea how long she'd been out. Hell, she could be anywhere in the world. Even Siberia. It would certainly explain the cold.

The plane stopped moving. Time seemed to come to a standstill, the darkness pressing in on her and taunting her sanity, one minute seeming like thirty. She waited in anticipation for something to happen. But nothing was happening. Just the cold nibbling at her bare skin.

Then, finally, a line of light appeared. At first, she wasn't sure if it was something far away from her, or if it was somehow right in front of her face. The sudden radiance of it forced her to shut her eyes and turn away.

A loud mechanical noise started singing, and she could feel the metal beast vibrating around her. She looked back at the light and, her eyes a little more adjusted, saw that what had been a thin line was now yawning into a widening rectangle. Depth and perception came back to her with the light, and she gained a sense of her surroundings. And though she was glad to have escaped the outer darkness, she felt like a vampire forced to face the rising sun for some long-overdue execution. Only she felt no relief from the cold, none of the sun's heat against her body. For a second, she wished she would just go up in flames like a candle if it meant putting an end to the aching, throbbing cold for a minute. Her teeth chattered so hard, she thought they might break, and no matter how hard she tried to stop her jaw from moving, she couldn't.

She closed her eyes and listened to the cargo door continue to lower. Once the psychedelic explosions in her blinded eyes subsided, she tried once more to look at the light, this time slowly and with just one at a time.

It wasn't natural light. Not the sun. Rather, she could see at least two large spotlights that were aimed directly at her.

It was still dark outside. Though she realized "still" might not be the appropriate word, given that she had no clue how long she'd been out. She struggled against the restraints, but her body was numb, and her brain didn't register the feeling.

A silhouette appeared within the triangle of light that was the open cargo bay. Like an alien in some sci-fi movie, it moved up the ramp, its right arm elongated, its head swollen. For a moment, she thought she must still be dreaming, because the first thing that went through her mind was that they must have landed at Groom Lake. But as the figure got closer, the exaggerated features subsided, and by the time the form was standing right in front of her, she knew that the illusion had been created by the hat the man was wearing and the radio in his hand.

She stared at him in the light, watched as his eyes traveled up and down her body. He was wearing jeans and a high-neck sweater under a white parka. A black aviator hat lined with fur covered his head. She could tell that he had broad shoulders and a thick, muscled neck even with the sweater and coat. He looked like Special Forces. His cold eyes continued to take her in, obviously liking what he was seeing. Stacey had no trouble imagining what was about to happen, and she was suddenly thankful for the cold, that she wouldn't be able to feel anything. With any luck, she'd pass right out.

The man transitioned the radio to his left hand and then pulled the glove off his right before reaching out and pressing his bare fingers against her face. He leaned close and whispered into her ear, "Isn't it funny how cold you can be on the outside—" He traced his fingers down her neck, over the curve of a breast, down her ribs, and past her navel before stopping at her pubic bone. She felt the pressure he was applying there. "—while being so warm on the inside?"

She closed her eyes and waited for him to proceed.

Only the pressure beneath his fingers didn't move to where she'd expected it to. Instead he was touching her head. Then her wrists. Then he was kneeling down in front of her and working on her ankles.

He'd just freed her.

She looked up but couldn't see anything past the lights. Should she try to make a run for it? If she did, she might find that the only thing beyond the lights was a frozen lake. Or a firing squad.

Her body slumped forward.

No.

It didn't matter. She couldn't move a muscle, anyway. Couldn't even hold up her head. Her body toppled, bending at the waist and landing over the man's shoulder. Then he was standing up, and she was in the air. His right arm was across her thighs, his left on her ass. He walked her down the ramp and into the open air.

She shifted her eyes, trying to take in her surroundings, but it was still too dark. As the man continued to carry her, she began to notice other lights to her left—the man's right. As they got closer, she saw they were illuminating another plane. But this one wasn't a Hercules or an Airbus or a Super Galaxy. This one was a midsized jet. Maybe a Challenger 300.

Eventually, the light revealed men with automatic weapons standing around it, and she thought the whole scene looked a lot like the set of some James Bond film. In her delirium, she imagined a director yelling, "Cut!" and the late Roger Moore walking over, taking in her nudity, and then holding out a vodka martini.

She squeezed her eyes, tried to clear her mind. The effects of whatever drug they'd used must still be lingering. She wondered why her subconscious had chosen Moore over Connery and Craig, Brosnan and Dalton. She'd slept with a guy who looked like Dalton once, back in some seedy hotel the Agency had—

The sound of the man's boots crunching across the frozen concrete suddenly stood out to her and halted her train of thought. As they approached the other plane, and yet another man standing by its open door, she tried to fight through the fog in her brain, to weigh her options.

She stared at her limp arms hanging down the man's backside. They flopped back and forth, bouncing harmlessly off his parka. She hoped her nipples were being rubbed raw on the same nylon material. If only she could use her hand, she could slip it between his legs and grab his balls. Squeeze them until they burst like Cadbury eggs. He'd let go of her, and she'd slip face-first down his back, where she'd break her fall with her forearms and roll gracefully onto her back and come up onto her feet...

Only her hand wouldn't move. It just hung there, flapping like a dying fish.

Maybe if she could manage to get her head in line with his neck, she could take a bite out of his jugular or the external carotid artery. Though his neck was so thick, she doubted she'd do much more than break the skin before he had her on the ground. In all the zombie shows, the undead were able to use their teeth to rip people's throats out. However, the amount of force it would take to produce the blood geysers portrayed was probably more likely to dislocate their decomposing jaws and shatter their rotting teeth.

But then...she didn't want to get away, did she?

No, she told herself, the thought breaking through the fog like a lighthouse. This was all part of her plan. To get to Fedyenka. She had Johnson's tracker in her, and Jack would find her. She began to relax.

But then she wondered if they'd be able to find her in time. How would they get to wherever it was they were taking her? They couldn't use the airport or rent a car or buy a train ticket. When she'd given Johnson the idea, she had assumed she'd be taken to some secret compound in the Appalachian Mountains. But she didn't think this was anywhere near Appalachia, and if this other plane was a Challenger, then it was intercontinental, and she could be on her way to just about anywhere in the world.

"You've got a fantastic ass," she heard the man say, and she could vaguely tell he was smacking it. "Pity we were told hands off. I think you would've enjoyed some of my specialties."

So that was it. Fedyenka had told his crony henchmen that she wasn't to be molested. Embarrassed and humiliated, frozen nearly to death, yes. But she wasn't to be assaulted sexually. And she knew why.

He'd want that pleasure all to himself.

The man walked her up into the plane and dropped her down into a seat. He then zip-tied her wrists and ankles to the arms and legs of the chair. Then he reached up and positioned one of the overhead nozzles so that it was blowing warm air on her.

"Let's get some color back into you, shall we?"

He stood over her, staring at her chest, and she knew he was weighing the pros and cons of disobeying Fedyenka's orders. She stared at him with all the resolve she could muster, daring him to try. And hoping at the same time that her boldness wasn't just turning him on even more.

He leaned down in front of her and put his mouth over hers while grabbing a huge hand full of breast. Then he stood, visibly shivered, and walked to the doorway where he said something to the man standing there. Then he left the plane. She watched him walk across the runway and back toward the other plane. Halfway there, he stopped and turned back toward her, giving her one final look through the window while adjusting his pants.

She turned away from the window in time to see the man from the doorway sit down in the seat across from her. He had a pistol in his hand, resting on his thigh.

The door closed.

The pilot looked back and asked if they were ready.

The man nodded.

The plane began to move.

Stacey closed her eyes.

Once they were in the air, the man stood up and retrieved a blanket from a cabinet behind him. He laid it across her body, though making sure that it didn't conceal her wrists and ankles.

She thanked him with her eyes, not knowing if he was trying to avoid temptation, or if part of him actually cared. As the cold slowly fled her body, she looked back to the darkness outside the window.

Before she knew it, she was back asleep.

54

JOSEPH WENT THROUGH THE propped door, running past the bathroom and into the diner. He heard the car doors open in the alley behind him and knew they were just feet behind him. But he also knew they wanted him alive; otherwise they would have just run him over before he reached the door.

Everyone in the diner turned and looked at him. He stood there in the middle of the tables, chest heaving, not knowing where to go or what to do next. He turned and looked behind him, saw the men walking through the back door. They were taking their time, like they knew he had nowhere to go, so why work up a sweat about it? Without thinking, Joseph raised his finger and pointed down the hall at them. "Help! They're trying to kill me!"

Some of the men at the bar began slipping off their stools, turning their eyes toward the hallway.

"Wait," the lady behind the counter yelled. She pointed back at the television behind her. "He's the kid from the school! The man he was just with is the bomber!"

Everyone looked at the woman and then up to the television. But before they got a chance to turn back to Joseph, the three men in black fatigues and armed with automatic weapons stepped into the room.

"That's him," the woman said to them, thrusting a big finger in Joseph's direction. "That's the kid from the school! That's who you want. I'm the one who called!"

The sirens were getting louder.

One of the men began scanning the ceiling. "You have cameras in this place?" he asked calmly.

The woman blinked. "Cameras? No. Why?"

And without another word, there was a loud crack as the woman's face turned red, and pieces of it smacked against the wall behind her.

The men standing next to the bar stools flinched at the sounds and then watched the woman who had served them for who knew how many years topple, faceless, to the floor. If any of them were armed with pistols of their own, none got a chance to use them. A volley of gunfire, a moment later, blew them apart. Blood flew everywhere.

Joseph dove beneath a table and covered his ears with his hands. The sound was deafening, and it felt like someone was punching him in the head. A body landed on the floor beside him, a lifeless hand flopping against the floor just inches from his face. Another body fell, and this one had a face that he recognized from the bar. Joseph stared into his open, vacant eyes.

The shooting continued, and the room shook, pieces of it falling like rain all around him.

Finally after what seemed like an eternity, the shooting stopped. His ears were ringing so badly that it took him a moment to notice that the siren outside had gotten much closer. Then a voice said, "Come on, kid. Don't make us drag you out of here."

Joseph knew they wouldn't shoot him. They might hurt him, but they wouldn't kill him. He rose onto the balls of his feet and got ready to make a run for it.

Red and blue lights began strobing through the shattered room, and Joseph peeked up over the table and out the front window. A police car screeched to a stop in front of the diner. The men in the room—he counted six of them now—all turned to face it. They raised their rifles and began shooting through the diner's front windows, peppering the vehicle with automatic fire.

Joseph crawled over a dead body and slid beneath another table. The men's booted feet were standing around him, and empty shell casings danced across the floor, one landing on the back of his hand, burning his skin. He made a run for it, sprinting back toward the bathrooms, the deafening noise of the guns masking his pounding feet.

JACK HEARD THE GUNFIRE erupt from inside the diner just as he reached the corner of the building. His paternal instincts told him to run for the front door, to get in there as soon as possible, but he knew that would only result in Joseph witnessing his dad getting mowed in half by automatic fire.

He crouched low, unsure what to do, when a police car came screeching to a stop in front of the diner. Jack quickly tucked the pistol into the back of his waistband, not wanting the sheriff to draw on him when he stepped out of the cruiser. But before the cop could even open his door, another barrage of gunshots rang out, exploding glass all over the sidewalk and into the street, punching holes across the passenger side of the car.

The sheriff flung the door open and tumbled out of the cruiser, frantically crawling behind the front wheel where the engine block would provide cover from the assault. The strobing red and blue lights on the car's roof shattered.

The *thunk-thunk-thunk* of the bullets sinking into the cruiser echoed up and down the street like a frantic bass line played beneath the savage chaos of the rapid-fire shots, the breaking glass clanging cymbals.

Jack peered around the corner and could see the sheriff crouching down in a sea of cubed glass, his service pistol in one hand, a radio in the other. Then he raised the pistol and fired blindly over the hood of the cruiser while yelling into his radio.

There was a lull in the gunfire, and Jack heard the distinct sound of an engine roaring from the alleyway behind the diner. He turned his attention in that direction and watched as one of the SUVs shot backward out of the alley. The driver cut the wheel while slamming on the brakes, and the vehicle swung around, its headlights pointing right at Jack.

"Crap," Jack whispered.

The SUV's tires spun on the asphalt and charged.

The men in the diner had resumed the shootout with the cop, so there was no way Jack could run in that direction. He was out of options. He pulled the pistol and aimed at the approaching windshield, knowing full well that it would be bulletproof. But as he aimed, wondering whether they were going to shoot him or run him over, the face behind the wheel came into focus. He released the trigger just before firing off a round, and jumped out of the way. The driver stopped and lowered the window.

"Get in," Johnson said.

Jack reached out and grabbed the handle, yanking the door open. "What about Joseph?"

"I'm right here," Joseph answered, leaning up from a seat in the back.

Jack climbed in and shut the door.

Johnson hit the gas and turned right, away from the diner. "I was about to go through the back entrance into the diner"—he explained—"when Joe came running out. The truck was just sitting there running, so…here we are."

Jack turned in the passenger seat and reached back, patting Joe's knee. It seemed a ridiculously inadequate portrayal of the emotion he was actually feeling, but the situation didn't allow for anything else. He turned back around and glanced into the rearview just in time to see the sheriff go sprawling backward onto the street.

"Our stuff is back there," Jack whispered, shifting his eyes to the sideview and watching the sheriff's body grow smaller. *Another death added to our account*, he thought. He wondered how many in the diner had died, what Joseph had just witnessed.

"I know," Johnson answered. "We'll circle around. Hopefully, they'll clear out by the time we get there."

Johnson turned right at the next block and raced south one street over from where it seemed they had been running in circles all morning. Though "all morning" had really only been about ten minutes, hadn't it?

Johnson swore.

Jack turned and saw the other SUV turn onto the street behind them. It was coming at them fast.

"Any ideas?" Jack asked.

"Maybe," Johnson said, and he made a hard left down another road, sending Jack and Joseph slamming against the passenger doors. They were heading toward the mountains now.

Johnson threw a thumb over his shoulder. "See what's in the back."

Jack turned and climbed into the middle seat next to Joseph. "You okay?" he asked him.

Joseph nodded, though his eyes betrayed him. There was no time to get into it now though, and Jack was just glad his son had escaped the diner without any holes in him. He looked over the back of the seat and saw two long storage lockers. He reached down and worked the clips on the closest one, flipping the lid. He blinked.

"Anything?" Johnson yelled back.

"Yeah," Jack answered. He reached down into the crate and pulled out its contents. He turned in his seat and held it up so that Johnson could see it in the rearview.

Johnson acknowledged with a slight head nod.

They were in business.

"Do you know how to use one of those?" Johnson asked.

"Never fired one before." Jack looked over the tubular device, knowing that it was a shoulder-mounted rocket launcher. It was a little longer than one of his arms, seemed to weigh around ten pounds, and was a familiar metallic green.

"Are there rockets?"

"No," Jack called back.

Johnson turned his head and took a closer look at the thing. "An M72," he said. "The rocket is already in it. Probably 66mm, prepackaged. It's single use, so we'll have to make it count." As he maneuvered the Suburban around a couple of sharp turns, trying to put as much distance between them and their pursuers as possible, he walked Jack through how to use the thing. Jack noticed the instructions were also written along the launcher's side.

"Shouldn't you be the one to do this?" Jack asked.

Johnson nodded. "But just in case I can't." He pointed to the floorboard in front of the passenger seat as he glanced in the rearview. "Put it up here."

Jack set it on the floorboard, leaning it against the seat. The SUV hit a bump, and Jack hit his head on the ceiling.

"There," Johnson said, pointing out the windshield.

"There where?" Jack asked, not seeing anything but woods ahead.

"That ridge."

"You're going up into the trees?"

"We're gonna double back. The turn should buy us enough time."

"Enough time for what?"

Johnson pushed the gas pedal all the way to the floor.

Jack looked behind them and saw that the other SUV was about twenty yards behind. He forced a smile at Joseph. "Crazy day, huh?"

The absurdity of the question made Joseph laugh.

The road ahead ended at a T. Beyond it was a tree line. The ridge Johnson had pointed out started about fifty feet into the trees and gradually rose until stretching out of sight to their left. The SUV shot across the street and onto the grass with another jolting bump. Johnson maneuvered through the trees and passed three of them before one clawed the side of the vehicle with branched fingers. Then another tree took out the driver's side mirror. The SUV bounced over the uneven terrain, its wheels spinning over roots and fallen branches, crushing saplings and flattening grass.

The other Suburban followed them into the woods.

"Hold on," Johnson said as he turned the wheel to eleven o'clock and headed up the incline.

The sky above the trees filled the windshield all the way up the slope.

"Damn," Johnson grumbled when they reached the top of the ridge. What little level ground there was immediately receded down another steep slope, leaving just a narrow plateau that was barely wide enough for the SUV's tires.

Johnson turned left and rode along the tight peak, trying to keep the vehicle on the tightrope and from spilling into the ravine on their right or sliding back down the ridge and into the trees to their left.

The other SUV came roaring up the embankment so fast that it almost flew straight over and down the other side. But the driver was able to recover in time and had them right back on their tail.

"Screw this," Johnson said when the ground became so narrow that the right-side tires slipped off, and they started to slide. He cut the wheel and took the ridge back down, riding it like a wave while dodging trees. The truck bounced and rocked all the way down, but Johnson was able to get them to the bottom without overturning the vehicle or crashing into a tree. A few moments later, they were out of the woods and back on asphalt.

"I don't see them," Joseph said, looking behind them.

"Good," Johnson muttered.

"Never mind," Joseph said. "There they are."

Jack saw them shoot out of the trees behind them. "Fifty yards," he called up to Johnson.

They came to an intersection, and Johnson turned left between some buildings. Then, before their pursuers could follow down the same street, he made a quick right down another. Working the wheel with one hand, he reached over and grabbed the rocket launcher from the passenger seat with the other. He laid it across his lap. "Get ready to climb up behind the wheel," he said to Jack. "Stay on this road, and put as much distance between you and them as possible without losing them." Then he took his foot off the gas, and the SUV began to slow. Without another word, he opened the door, tossed the launcher into the street, and then flung himself out after it.

Jack swore under his breath and quickly climbed up into the seat, dropping down behind the wheel and grabbing the wheel before the truck could veer off the road. He closed the door while trying to catch a glimpse of Johnson in the sideview mirror, but there was no sideview mirror anymore. He hit the gas. "Do you see him?" he asked Joseph. In the rearview, the road behind them looked empty.

"Yeah," Joseph said. "He ran behind the building."

The speedometer read sixty, and they had a straight line all the way to the end of town. They only needed the other Suburban to turn down the same street. *But what if they don't?* Jack thought. And he took his foot off the gas, not wanting to get too far away from the intersection.

"There they are," Joseph said.

Jack glanced into the mirror and saw the Suburban take a late turn onto the road behind them. He hit the gas, but it was unnecessary. Almost a hundred yards separated them, and the other Suburban would be in Johnson's kill zone within—

A flash in the passenger and rearview mirrors made Jack turn in the driver's seat and look past Joseph and out the back window. A loud explosion rocked the morning air as a massive fireball sent the back of the SUV up into the air. The whole vehicle somersaulted, flipping up onto its roof and skidding across the street for twenty yards in a flaming heap.

Jack stomped on the brakes, bringing the SUV to a stop. He grabbed the rifle Johnson had left behind and stepped out into the street with it. He could see a few faces in the windows of the buildings that lined the street, but he ignored them. He raised the weapon to his shoulder and trained it on the burning wreck as he began jogging toward it. He heard a door open behind him and feet hit the pavement. "Get back in the car, Joe," he said without taking his eyes off the flames.

"I want to stay with you," Joseph replied, running up alongside him.

"Dammit, Joe—"

Gunshots rang out, echoing down the street.

Jack reached over and snatched Joseph out of the spot he was standing in, quickly turning to put his body between the shots and Joseph even though Joseph was the one still wearing a flak jacket. He took his boy to the ground and covered him with his body. But when he turned back, expecting to see someone climbing out of the overturned truck and shooting at them, it was actually Johnson he saw. The agent was crouching low beside the Suburban and firing a pistol through its broken windows.

Johnson stood. "All clear," he called out. And then he began jogging toward them, his eyes scanning the street and the surrounding buildings.

Jack got to his feet and helped Joseph up. "You okay?"

Joseph nodded and brushed himself off.

"Listen," Jack said, looking him straight in the eye. "When I tell you to do something, I need you to do it. No arguing, no debating, okay?"

Joseph nodded, and it was clear he understood that his disobedience could have just cost him his life.

Jack gripped the back of his neck and pulled him into himself, hugging him tight.

Johnson came up beside them. "Put your heads down. I saw at least one person with a phone, so it's a pretty safe bet that this'll be all over TikTok."

Joseph frowned, looked around.

"Okay," Johnson said. "Maybe not TikTok, but possibly Facebook." He ushered them back to the Suburban. "Don't let them get a clear view of your faces."

"You think it matters?" Jack asked, lifting his shirt up over his nose and motioning for Joseph to do the same.

"Probably not," Johnson said. "But why make their job easier for them? With actual footage of you on the scene, they can slap any caption they want on it."

They climbed into the SUV, Johnson back behind the wheel. "Let's get our gear and get the hell out of here," he said. He hit the gas.

55

STACEY OPENED HER EYES, waking once again, and immediately realized the wonderful feeling of warmth tightly embracing her body. She looked down and saw that the blanket still covered her. She closed her eyes again, blocking out any thought of the future or past, and just tried to appreciate that one single moment, to experience the heat radiating in her bones, in her muscles, warming her skin. The physical relief of it was indescribable, though she related it to savoring the first sip of a fine wine or soaking sore feet, or feeling a pair of strong hands massage away stress in her neck and shoulders.

She could feel her fingers again and moved each one. She curled her toes. Even with her hands and feet still zip-tied, she could cry with relief and fall back into a rather comfortable sleep if she allowed herself. But, no. She fought against that temptation and reminded herself that she was on her way to be raped and tortured by a megalomaniac.

She turned her head to the window and saw that the sky was a few shades lighter than the pitch black it had been before. The sun would be coming up soon.

She looked around the cabin. The man who had given her the blanket was still sitting there. He had a toothpick protruding from between his pressed lips, his eyes holding her in an unwavering gaze. She met those eyes, expecting to see in them the same lust she'd found in the others, but that was not what she found there. There was something gleaming in his eyes, but it wasn't lust or desire. It was something more...paternal. But he had to be her age if not a little younger, so maybe *familial* would be a more appropriate description, like the concern of a brother she'd never had. Could it be sympathy she was detecting on that weathered face?

She decided to test the waters. "Where are we?" Her voice was hoarse, and after not hearing it since speaking with Johnson (however long ago that was), the sound of it surprised her.

"About to enter Alaska," the man replied.

"Alaska," she repeated, looking out the window again. Behind them, she saw a faint glow on the horizon, which meant they must be heading west. "Fairbanks?"

"At first." He was speaking softly, obviously not wanting the pilot to overhear them.

"Then Siberia?" she asked.

The man actually smiled. It wasn't a devilish smile, but one that actually found her question to be humorous. Or was he trying to flirt with her?

He took the toothpick out of his mouth with calloused fingers. "I don't think anyone's takin' ya to Siberia."

She focused on his voice. He had an interesting accent, one she wasn't all that familiar with. It had a Southern tint to it, but it wasn't Texan or even Delawarean. It was more exotic than the typical Southern twang, though "exotic" probably wouldn't be the word most would use. "Fedyenka isn't in Siberia?" She had ventured out onto the ice with that, and she was about to find out just how thick that ice was.

Another smile. At first the man didn't answer, just continued to stare at her. Then he said, "No, he ain't in Siberia."

"But you are taking me to him?"

He tilted his head, eyes searching hers. "Do ya want me to?"

She paused. Was this some kind of interrogation tactic? Some good-cop routine mixed with the drugs to get her talking? Was he going to offer to help her escape? Earn her trust in the hopes that she'd tell him where Joseph was? If so, how far would Fedyenka allow the illusion to go? Would this guy be authorized to kill some of his own colleagues in order to sell such a fiction?

"What if I told you I could get ya outta here," the man said softly.

"I'd say you're a fucking moron if you think I'm going to play this game with you."

He leaned forward, his face becoming serious. "It ain't no game."

"I'll never tell you where my son is, because I don't know where he is. I was unconscious when you found me. I don't know where they went."

"Joseph," the man whispered. He looked over his shoulder toward the pilot, then back at her. "I ain't interested in finding your son."

"Then what exactly is it that you're interested in?"

He leaned back. "Helpin' ya get done what it is ya came to do."

"And what is that?" she asked.

"You tell me."

"You know what he's going to do to me. You think that's why I came here?"

"I'm thinkin' he ain't gonna get the chance to do any such thing."

She stared at him, trying to read him. It had to be a ploy. Maybe this guy wasn't just an ex-Marine working for a paycheck. Maybe he was ex-intelligence, and this was a psy-op.

He seemed to read her thoughts. "I know you," he said.

That seemed to hit her between the eyes. What the hell did that mean? Had he seen her picture on the news? Or was he referring to something else? Could he have been a mark, one of the people she'd fucked for God and country? Couldn't be. She'd only engaged with people of influence, people who had dirt to spill or information to give or power to lose. This guy didn't seem to have any of that. And she sure as hell hoped that she'd be able to remember if this guy had been inside her. *God*, she thought, *is it possible that I wouldn't know?* Not that she tried to remember such things. On the contrary, actually. But still... "What do you mean, 'you know me'?"

He leaned forward and dug something out of his coat pocket. It looked like a black bullet, the size of a .357. It had a little string on the end. He glanced back toward the cockpit again, and then when he was sure no one was paying them any attention, he reached his hand out and moved it beneath the blanket. Using his other hand, he pushed her right knee to the side, forcing her legs apart.

"You're gonna have to trust me," he whispered. He leaned forward a little more and slid his hand between her legs.

And for some reason she could never explain, she let him do it.

56

JOSEPH WATCHED FROM THE back seat of the SUV as Johnson hopped out of the vehicle and disappeared into the woods.

His dad turned around in the front passenger seat and looked him over. "You sure you're okay?" he asked for the dozenth time.

"I'm fine, Dad." And he was. For now. Though he wondered if he was in shock, because he realized that he should definitely *not* be okay. He'd seen a woman he liked very much shot in the head, wasn't sure how many of his friends were still alive, had lost his dog, his house, and all of his possessions. Had his entire life flash before his eyes while dangling from a helicopter, had just witnessed multiple people being murdered all around him while his mom was being held captive by the very people responsible for it all. He should be the furthest thing from *okay*. He could see that his dad knew all that, and figured that what his dad was really asking was whether or not he had it in him to go on. Which he did. What other choice was there?

His dad nodded, getting the message, and turned back in his seat.

Joseph watched out the window and saw Agent Johnson reappear with their gear in hand. He came around to the driver's side and tossed it to his dad, then climbed back behind the wheel.

"Well?" his dad asked.

"She's in Alaska." He had the tablet in his hand.

There was silence for a second, and then Joseph heard himself ask, "How the hell are we going to get to Alaska?"

This time it was Johnson who turned and looked him in the eye. "You're not."

"What?" Joseph asked.

"We can't take you straight to the person who is trying to find you. Besides, you'd attract way too much attention." He pulled out a cell phone and dialed a number. After a few seconds, Joseph could hear a faint voice come over the other end.

"Hello?"

"It's me," Johnson said.

"Shit, man. What the hell is going on? I saw—"

Johnson cut him off. "I'm on an unsecured burner. Let's keep this short."

"Got it," the voice said. *"What do you need?"*

"I need to get to Anchorage."

"And where are you?"

"West Virginia."

"Okay. Give me five."

The line went dead, and Johnson placed the phone in the cup holder. He turned to Jack. "We need a new car, fast."

"I think I saw a gas station in town," Jack said.

"Me too," Johnson agreed. He put the SUV in drive and turned the wheel back toward the town. "Keep an eye out," he said. "The Russians will be here any minute."

"Or more Osprey," Jack said.

"Or more Osprey," Johnson repeated. He hit the gas, skirting the edge of town, and headed toward where they all hoped would be another working vehicle.

Joseph reached forward for his backpack. His dad handed it to him.

"THERE," JOSEPH CALLED OUT, pointing to his right.

Jack squinted, peering down the street and looking for pumps or signs advertising gas prices. But Johnson saw it before he did.

"I see it," he said, and made a hard right down another street.

As they rolled forward, the sign Jack had been searching for emerged from behind the building next to it. "Good eye, Joe," he said.

"Looks closed," Johnson said as they drove near. "See any cars?"

Jack didn't see anything other than four empty pumps in front, but he saw a fender peeking out from behind the back of the building. "Behind."

Johnson pulled the Suburban into the lot and drove past the pumps, circling around to the back of the station. There was a little garage back there, its old doors closed, three cars parked in front of them. One of the cars was up on blocks and had no tires. The other two had potential.

Johnson pulled in between the two with wheels—a black 2000 Grand Prix and an even older teal Ford Taurus. He put the vehicle in park, but before he could open the door, the phone in the cup holder began to vibrate. He answered it. "Yeah?"

All Jack could hear on the other end was a string of numbers. He figured they were coordinates.

Johnson pulled a pen from his coat pocket and began writing them along the inside of his left forearm. "Thanks."

"*You take care of yourself,*" the voice responded.

"You too." He hung up, dropped the phone back in the cup holder, and swung the door open. He stepped out into the lot. "Stay here," he said, and then closed the door.

Jack watched him walk to the two-door Grand Prix and try the door. When it didn't open, Jack assumed it was locked. Johnson walked around to the other side and tried the driver's side door. Nothing. He leaned forward, placed his face up against the glass and cupped his hands around his eyes, trying to see into the car's interior. Then he walked around the side of the building and out of sight. Jack slid over into the driver's seat just in case they needed to make a quick getaway. "Keep your eyes peeled, Joe," he said, scanning the streets.

There was the sound of breaking glass, and Jack's heart skipped a beat. He sat forward, his hand instinctively going for the gearshift. Sixty seconds later, Johnson reappeared holding something in an outstretched hand, aiming it at the Grand Prix.

He was trying to unlock the car with a keyless remote, but the car just sat silent and dumb. Johnson went to the door and put the key in the keyhole. When he lifted the handle, the long door swung open. He slid behind the wheel and slipped the key into the ignition.

Jack held his breath.

The engine turned over, and a cloud of smoke billowed from the dual tailpipes. Johnson hit the trunk release and jogged to the back of the car, lifting the trunk by the spoiler. "C'mon," he called to Jack, waving them over.

"Let's go, Joe," Jack said, shutting down the SUV and tossing the key.

Joseph hopped out of the Suburban and ran for the Pontiac.

"Get in," Johnson said. He took the gear from Jack and tossed it in the trunk.

Joseph tossed his backpack into the back seat and slid in after it.

Johnson slammed the trunk closed and handed Jack the tablet. They were both about to get into the car when they stopped.

"You hear that?" Johnson asked.

Jack nodded. "Car's coming."

"Get in." They both hurried into the car and shut the doors. Then they sat, waiting to see what was coming.

Jack looked into the sideview and could just make out the faint whispers of smoke slithering from out of the car's tailpipes. He wondered if it was enough to draw attention to themselves. "Sign on the door says the station opens at nine. Which is in fifteen minutes. Could just be the attendant."

Two pickup trucks appeared down the road. The people were driving slowly, like they were looking for something.

Johnson gripped the wheel with his left hand and palmed the gearshift with his right, ready to put the car to the test. Finally, the two trucks passed the gas station and continued down the road and out of view.

Johnson put the car in reverse and backed away from the garage. "Got three-quarters of a tank," he said. He drove slowly across the lot and back out the way they'd come in, his eyes on the rearview the whole time.

"You think they saw the Suburban?" Jack asked.

"If they didn't, they will on their second pass." Once onto the road, he floored the gas, and the Pontiac's V6 engine growled as they shot north out of the valley.

"Where are we going?" Jack asked.

But Johnson just told him how to enter coordinates into the device. He read him the line of numbers from off his arm, and Jack punched them in.

Jack looked up.

"Well?" Johnson asked.

"Looks like a small airport."

"Where?"

"About two hours west."

Johnson nodded. He had the Pontiac going seventy over a small bridge when he rolled down the window and tossed the burner phone into a creek bed below.

JOHNSON WAS TAKING BACK roads, wanting to avoid the possibility of any surveillance cameras. He kept the Pontiac at a steady 80 mph, always searching for signs of traffic cops. But just twenty minutes into their getaway, they had learned why the car had been at the shop. Something was wrong with it. An intake valve or a sensor or maybe the transmission, they weren't sure. Only that the car seemed to hiccup and threaten to stall every once in a while.

Johnson had to keep playing with the gas pedal, manipulating the engine into a certain sweet spot, and then try to keep it there. Too much gas, and the thing would start to choke. Slow down too much, and he'd have to try accelerating again but without causing the gears to shift too drastically. But they couldn't continue to bank their lives—Stacey's life—on something this unreliable. They'd need to find another ride as soon as possible.

"The video footage," Jack started to say, referring to the news program that had come on in the diner. "How could they do that?"

Johnson looked over at him. "Do what?"

"Put my face on it?"

Johnson stared ahead. "Deepfake crap." He shrugged. "AI-image-generation tech. They've probably been taking pictures of you. They run them through the AI program, and you've got *Wag the Dog* part two."

Jack recalled an episode of the *X-Files* where a young Cigarette Smoking Man and J. Edgar Hoover were proposing plots to undermine Martin Luther King, one of the ideas being to doctor images of King having sex with other women. The show was from 1996, and the time in which the episode was supposed to be taking place was 1968. Jack had often wondered if the CIA had ever manipulated history in such a manner before. Could some of the most famous pictures in history books actually be fake? Not just staged photos, he knew those were a dime a dozen. But actually fake pictures. Or videos. Like the movie *Wag the Dog* that Johnson just referenced, whole geopolitical scenarios and events shot in front of a green screen. Well, here he was, all these years later, the answer to his own question. "Who could have done this?" he asked.

Johnson shrugged. "This tech is out there now. Just go on social media and you'll find hundreds of manipulated videos, some better than others. Of course Hollywood's been doing it at least since *Forrest Gump*. Hell, all the White House has to do now to refute video evidence it doesn't like is to just announce it as fake. Have their Ministry of Truth fact-check it wherever it pops up. The technology has opened the door to both create history and to sidestep history."

Jack understood the implications, and he was sure his mind would be blown by it later, but right now he was more concerned with his own role in it. "Okay, so anyone *could* have produced the video. But who would have directed it? Who set the whole thing up?"

"My guess would be the same people who put you on the news earlier."

"So the CIA."

"I don't see how it could be anyone else."

"*Could* Fedyenka do it?" Jack asked.

Johnson shook his head. "Not on his own. I'm sure he could have someone put your face in the video, but to make the video in the first place? To get the national media to run it? He would've had to know about the bombing well in advance."

"Maybe he did. Maybe the Agency tipped him off. If it was his people who went to get Joseph, then he'd have to have had prior knowledge."

"Or, like we said before, the Agency could have done both."

Jack looked out the window. "Neocon psychopaths," he mumbled. "You really think Ukraine is just the primer for whatever this whole thing is? So that when we enter the ring, the Bear is already weak and malnourished?"

"Could be."

"At the expense of an entire generation of men. Disgusting."

"Hey, Dad?" Joseph asked from the back seat, interrupting them.

Jack turned. "Yeah, buddy?"

"Our history teacher said that Russia invaded Ukraine because they want to take over the world."

Johnson laughed.

"War propaganda, Joe," Jack said. "That's all that is."

Johnson nodded. "It's a complicated situation."

Jack turned more completely, putting an arm around the headrest and facing the back seat. "Speaking of JFK," he said, "have you learned about the Cuban Missile Crisis at all?"

"I watched *Thirteen Days*."

"Good enough. So the whole thing was over Russia moving missiles into Cuba. And the US would not stand for that. But the US had put missiles on the Turkey-Russia border first. And so JFK made a secret deal with Khrushchev that we would remove the Jupiter missiles from their border, and they would remove their missiles from Cuba."

"Okay," Joe said, not seeing what it had to do with Ukraine.

"Then, in 1990, Russia agreed to let NATO reunify Germany—Russia had about four hundred thousand troops in East

Germany—but on the condition that NATO didn't move any far- ther east than that. The US Secretary of State famously promised Gorbachev that Western forces wouldn't move an inch closer to Russia. Since then, NATO has brought in fourteen more coun- tries and moved a thousand miles closer, every time assuring Russia that they're not being hostile, that they shouldn't be concerned. They've talked about bringing Ukraine into NATO before, and everyone knew it was a bad idea, that it would put Russia in a very dangerous spot. Everyone agreed on this. And now they're trying to push it through anyway. And if that happens, Western missiles could go into Ukraine that would be capable of reaching Moscow within three minutes. Not to men- tion the fact that Russia has been invaded three times through Ukraine."

"So it's like *Thirteen Days* in reverse. We wouldn't let Russia put missiles in Cuba, but now we're expecting them to let us put missiles in Ukraine."

"Right. Russia is never going to allow Ukraine to become part of NATO, and that's basically what this whole thing is about. That and the 2014 coup we helped orchestrate against Yanukovych."

Johnson added, "Then Minsk 2."

"Voted by the UN Security Council, signed by the Ukrainian government, and guaranteed by France and Germany. But the United States would have no part of it."

"Really?" Joseph asked.

"More or less," Jack said. "I lot more, actually."

Joseph leaned back against the seat and crossed his arms. "Oh," he said, rethinking the last few years of media propaganda spoon-fed to him by his teachers. "But how can Ukraine win a war against Russia? Isn't that like Cuba trying to win a war against the United States?"

"Yup. That's what I was just asking Agent Johnson, if he thought globalist forces were just using Ukraine to weaken Rus- sia, trying to turn it into their new Afghanistan."

Joseph smiled. "*Rambo III*."

Jack chuckled. "Yeah, well, that didn't really turn out too great for us either. Blowback and all. Don't get me wrong," he said.

"I'm not saying Russia is good. But I hate seeing human life wasted for no reason, used as expendable chess pieces on some political map. And I would really like to avoid a nuclear war with a country that has twelve hundred more warheads than us, electronic warfare a generation ahead of us, and that can apparently exist on a parallel economy independent of the rest of the world."

A new thought struck Joseph, and he frowned. "Wait. Are you saying that the US government is blaming *you* for the bombing at the school?"

"Yeah, Joseph. That's what it looks like." It sounded absurd. But then again, so did Operation Northwoods and the Stargate Project. He turned back around in his seat.

Jack thought the next, obvious question from his son's lips would be why. But it wasn't. Instead his son asked, "What are we going to do?"

It was a question about the long game. Not what they were presently doing, but about what they would do after their current goal had been accomplished. But of course, the real question was, what *could* they do? Jack forced a smile. "I don't know, Joe. But we'll figure it out." And Jack watched, reflected in the rearview mirror, Joseph comprehend the fact that he was never going to see his friends again. That his entire life would be reset yet again. And this time, they wouldn't be hiding from one crazed Russian, but the entire United States government.

"It'll be okay," Jack said, and he tried to believe it himself. "First let's just get Mom, okay?"

Joseph nodded and put an earbud in his ear.

57

STACEY STOOD AT THE top of the boarding stairs and pulled the blanket tight against the cold morning air. The man had just reached the bottom of the steps and was motioning for her to come down after him. She quickly looked around, wanting to capitalize on the high vantage point.

To the east she saw a mountain range. It ran along the horizon, the sun climbing up its back and setting on fire the bottoms of low-hanging clouds. It would only be a few minutes before the orange dome itself broke over the jagged, snow-stained teeth. In the north, tall evergreens rose like green waves for as far as she could see. She couldn't tell if the blue behind them was sky or distant mountains. To the west was a large body of water, and small waves lapped at its rocky shore. It was beautiful, straight from a painting or a postcard. But the caravan of black SUVs awaiting her on the ground dimmed her appreciation of it. A line of suited men stood by them, waiting to escort her to Camp Fedyenka.

She forced herself to move before someone else felt the need to do it for her. She descended the stairs, the entire time conscious of the thing inside her. It was small enough that it felt little different than what she'd endured every month since she was thirteen, and it was certainly less encroaching than other things she'd experienced over her career as a female spy. Still, she was naked and self-conscious about it, afraid it might fall out while she walked barefoot across the frozen runway. She concentrated on the muscles down there, remembering some of the strengthening exercises she'd made routine after Bethany's birth had ripped her wide open.

"There's a boat waiting for you," the man said under his breath once she joined him on the ground. "It'll take ya to him." Then he added, "I hope ya know whatyer doin'."

She didn't understand who this man was or where he'd come from. The transfer—if you wanted to call it that—had been strangely anti-sexual. Though how spreading her legs for a man and letting him use a finger to "open port" could be anything but sexual, she didn't know. But there had been no glint of desire in his eyes as he'd worked the thing into position. And even if she'd spotted a bulge in his pants, the physical reaction wouldn't have matched the stoic expression on his face. Like an ob-gyn performing a routine exam on a patient. Though what he'd put in her, she had no clue.

The pilot had turned and started talking to him as soon as he'd finished, and they hadn't been able to talk again. She wondered if it was part of Fedyenka's game, returning to the theory that he was just trying to earn her trust. Had he loaded her with a vagina bomb, and Fedyenka would use a remote detonator to blow her legs off? "Who the hell are you?" she whispered. "And what did you put in me?"

But he didn't answer. Instead, he gripped her elbow and began leading her toward one of the SUVs. His touch was firm, but not hard. And she got the sense that he was actually being rougher than he wanted to be. Which made her think he was acting a part. She wondered if Johnson could have someone on the inside of Osprey. But if so, wouldn't he have told her?

When they got close to the vehicle, one of the men standing beside it stepped forward and pulled the blanket off her. She could feel all the men's eyes on her breasts, but she wasn't going to give them the satisfaction of trying to cover them. Instead, she glared at the man before her with all the confidence of a guest porn star stripping at the local titty bar. *Look all you want,* her eyes said. *But we both know you can't do a damn thing about it.*

When he finally managed to peel his eyes off her nipples, he threw the blanket to the man from the plane. Then another guy stepped forward and pushed her against the SUV. Her breasts flattened against the cold window as her arms were wrenched behind her back and new zip ties were applied to her wrists. She could feel the man pressing his body against her ass.

"Get in," he said after finally backing up and opening the door.

She climbed in, and just before the door was shut on her, she caught the eye of the ob-gyn. There was a strange look in his eye that didn't fit the scenario. An affirming look. One that you'd expect to be accompanied by a head nod (which he obviously wouldn't do even if he'd wanted to). Like they were on the same page of some secret plan and everything was going according to plan. But what plan? And then more men filled the seats around her, and she lost sight of him.

The driver turned the SUV away from the jet and took off down the remaining stretch of runway.

"Well, hello, boys," she said. She leaned back and spread her legs, getting comfortable and putting on a show. "How we doing today?"

One of the men stared unabashedly while two others looked uncomfortably out the window. Either way, she had them distracted and off-balance. She could tell that at least two of the men were sadists, getting pleasure out of her discomfort, her vulnerability. Seeing her naked and afraid aroused them. They fed off it. If they were allowed, they'd torture her, soaking up her screams and pleadings the same way normal men would respond to a strip tease. She wasn't going to fuel that fire. Instead, she would try to put it out. Not give them the satisfaction of showing fear, but rather convince them that she was perfectly okay with them looking at her—even wanting them to. She wasn't just letting them see her, she was *showing* them. And that robbed them of their power. Gave it to her, in fact. And it was working already, because they clearly didn't know what to do about it.

She wasn't arrogant enough to think that she could overtake them within the confines of the SUV. Maybe two of them, she could. Three at the most. But what would be the point? She needed to get to Fedyenka, and they were taking her to him. She crossed her legs and looked out the window, trying so very hard to keep up the facade and to keep from shivering.

58

JACK LOOKED AT HIS watch again. It was just past noon, and he was beyond restless. He felt like a quarterback standing on the sideline, watching helplessly as the defense tried to get him the ball back with enough time for one more shot at the end zone. But they only had one time-out left, and the other team, sitting on a four-point lead, just needed to gain a couple more first downs.

How things played out over the next few hours would determine whether or not he'd ever see his wife again. Even if they got the ball back with enough time, any delay of game penalty could move the end zone out of reach. One red light. One more encounter with Osprey or an SVR kill squad. A bathroom break. A flat tire. A wrong turn. He wanted to jump out of his skin.

They had left the Pontiac parked behind a boarded-up convenience store and had walked across a field and into a Walmart parking lot, where Johnson quickly got them into a rusting Ford Fusion. The car was filthy and smelled of cigarettes and cat piss. Even with the windows down, it was difficult to breathe. They had the heat blasting out of the cracked dashboard, trying to counter the cold air coming through the windows at sixty-five miles per hour.

"How much longer?" Jack asked.

"Ten," Johnson said as he followed a road sign.

After a few more minutes, they came upon a sign that announced a nearby airfield. A minute or two after that, Jack spotted a small plane sitting on a runway, dotting the horizon. He checked the tracker. Stacey was moving farther and farther away from Anchorage. "Where are they taking her?" he wondered aloud.

"Listen," Johnson said. "We'll land in Anchorage and get a motel. Joseph can stay there." His eyes went to the rearview as he spoke, settling on Joseph's reflection.

Jack frowned, but nodded. What other option did they have? There was no one to watch him, and they couldn't take him with them. "It'll be okay," he said to Joseph. He seemed to be saying that more and more, and every time he said it, it seemed less and less sincere on his tongue.

Joseph nodded, understanding the situation. "I'll be okay," he said. "If they're looking for me, they won't think to look for me in Alaska."

"Nope," Jack said. *Let's hope not.*

Johnson turned onto a long road that cut between two large fields. The runway sat on their left, a helicopter pad to their right. Chain-link fences ran up and down both sides of them.

JOHNSON DROVE THROUGH AN opening in the fence and followed an asphalt road to a hangar. The hangar doors were open, and he drove straight through, coming to a stop beside a white, midsize jet. The steps were down, and two men stood at the bottom of them, their posture indicating that they'd been waiting for some time.

"Here we go," Johnson said. He shut the car off and opened the door.

"Ready?" Jack asked Joseph.

Joseph nodded.

Jack turned his hands into guns and mimicked a quick drum roll while saying, in his best Nick Cage, "Let's ride."

Joseph smiled and threw the door open. "*Gone in Sixty Seconds*," he said, pulling his backpack over his shoulders. He'd left the flak jacket in the Grand Prix.

"Hopefully," Jack said. And they both stepped out of the smelly car and walked over to where Johnson was already talking with the two men.

The pilots looked Jack over as he approached them. Then their eyes went to Joseph. And again back to Jack.

Jack saw the recognition click in their eyes just before both their heads whipped back to Johnson in comical synchronism.

"What is this?" the taller one whispered.

Johnson reached into his pocket and pulled out a stack of green bills. "What is what?" he asked. "This is my brother and his son. We're acquiring your services to fly us to Anchorage so that we can pay a visit to his dying wife. Recently estranged, yes, but with the end so near, anxious to make amends."

The other pilot leaned in. "Peterson didn't mention anything about this. He just said   "

Johnson waved a hand.

Jack didn't know who Peterson was, and he didn't care. Probably someone who owed a favor to the person Johnson had contacted. Or maybe a person who owed a favor to him. That was how all this stuff worked, right? Everyone in debt to someone else and each one pulling their own unique levers of influence when it was time to pay the piper? Jack wondered just how many of those cards Johnson had up his sleeve, and how many points of contact each one took to get what he wanted.

"Look," Johnson said, cutting him off. "I can explain this all to you on the way, if you'd like. But it'd be much safer for you if you happened to have been too busy to catch the news over the last few days."

"The less we know, the better," the tall one mumbled.

"Exactly," Johnson said with his best Tom Cruise smile.

The pilot who had taken the cash began turning it over in his hands. His expression revealed a desperation that this Peterson fellow must have known could be exploited. "It would pay for Mary's procedure," the pilot said, looking up from the money and then down to his shorter partner.

And that's how the game is played, Jack thought. Pinpoint a vulnerability and throw money at it. Desperate people and all that.

The shorter one stepped toward Jack. "You running to Alaska? Trying to disappear?"

Jack shook his head. "No. Actually, I'm going to Alaska to rescue my wife from the man who blew up my son's school."

That seemed to stiffen the pilot's spine, and he stood a little straighter. He looked at Johnson for confirmation, and Johnson nodded. Whoever these men were, however they knew Johnson, and whatever their life experiences, it was clear they had no trouble believing what Jack was inferring. "Well, Mr. Thomas," he said to Johnson, reading the name off the manifest, "let's not keep your sister-in-law waiting." And he turned and walked up the steps and disappeared into the plane.

The taller pilot nodded toward the Fusion. "Park that back there." He pointed to the back of the hangar where a large blue tarp sat in a pile. "Then cover it." He looked at his watch. "Wheels up in five."

Jack went to the trunk of the car and lifted the duffel bags out of it. As Johnson parked the car in the back and struggled to get it covered with the tarp, Jack carried the bags first to the bottom of the stairs, then up into the aircraft.

Joseph took a seat in the middle of the cabin and looked around. "Jamie Foxx and Dane DeHaan," he said, his eyes tracing the ceiling.

"What?" Jack asked, sitting down across from him after helping the shorter pilot get the gear into the storage compartment behind the cockpit.

"Jamie Foxx and Dane DeHaan," Joseph repeated.

Jack squinted. "Who is Dane DeHaan?"

Joseph smiled.

"Oh, come on. You have to tell me who it is. Unless you want me to start throwing out names like D. B. Sweeney or Erika Eleniak."

"Okay, okay," Joseph said. "He was the guy in *Valerian*."

"The main guy?"

Joseph nodded.

Jack leaned back into the seat and saw Johnson sprinting back from the blue blob that was now hiding the car they'd stolen. He had no idea what sort of arrangement Johnson had made and with whom, but he couldn't help wonder where the car would end up. And how much they'd just screwed up the owner's life. He turned away from the window. "He was in *Lawless*." And he began following Joseph's eyes around the interior of the plane. "Ah!" he said, understanding where the question had come from. "*Amazing Spider-Man 2.*"

Joseph smiled and nodded. "It's, like, the same exact plane."

Jack took it in. He figured most private jets probably looked the same, but he'd never been in one before, so what did he know? He only hoped that the opening scene Joseph just referenced wouldn't turn out to be their own experience.

With six seats, a sofa, and a kitchenette, the plane looked like it could comfortably seat a dozen passengers. The six seats were in three pairs, all facing each other on their respective sides of the aisle. Jack and Joseph were sitting on the right side of the plane, across from the sofa. A bathroom was behind them at the rear of the cabin. Seven oval-shaped portholes lined both sides of the plane. Jack wondered what VIP passengers might have graced these seats before. Who had these pilots scurried across the continent? And then an image of Stacey sitting on the sofa in some revealing dress popped into his head, a martini in one hand and some politician's cock in the other. He shook the thought loose, and it fell back into the rabbit hole.

Hearing Johnson enter the plane, he turned around and saw him duck his head into the cockpit and ask the taller pilot a question. Whatever the question was, the answer seemed to be a yes, the pilot nodding his head in response. Then Johnson left the cockpit and sat down on the couch across from them.

"Once we're airborne, I'll need your help with something," Johnson said.

Jack nodded.

The door closed, and the jet started rolling out of the hangar.

A few minutes later, Jack studied his son's face as he stared out the window and watched the ground fall away.

59

THE SUV PULLED INTO a gravel lot. The doors opened, and Stacey was shoved back out into the cold. Her feet had thawed during the ride, and a jolt ran up her legs when they landed on the frozen stones. She did her best to hide the shock, clenching her teeth and staring out over the vast lake that lay before her.

There was a wooden dock that stretched away from the shore about forty yards ahead. At the end of it was an inflated dinghy that looked capable of transporting four people. Out beyond it, floating on the glass surface, was what looked like an NSA spy boat. Sharp angles, matte-black finish, bouquets of radar dishes and antennas. She wondered what Fedyenka was trying to communicate by showing it off. Was it his way of displaying just how well equipped his private army was? That Osprey Inc was into far more than just providing security for Hollywood celebrities and their freak parties?

She heard a blade snap open behind her and felt the zip ties being cut from her wrists. Then someone nudged her forward, and she winced again, her bare feet chewed on by the cold gray rocks underneath. She rubbed her wrists while trying to walk as gingerly as possible, knowing that she must look ridiculous trying to defy both gravity and pain with her awkward, naked steps.

Then, feeling like a hundred bee stings, a gust of wind came off the lake and slammed into her flesh. She stopped and wrapped her arms around her chest in an attempt to fortify herself against the numbing cold.

"Keep moving," one of the men said, and pushed her in the back.

Out of reflex, she extended her right leg forward to balance herself, but her foot landed on the sharp apex of a stone pyramid. Her ankle rolled in an evasive maneuver, slipping her foot off the stone to relieve the pain, but sending the rest of her body pitching forward and onto her side in the process.

She felt the impact all along her side, from her hip to her shoulder, but was too numb to feel the sting of scraped flesh. Lying there, sprawled naked in front of all those men, she felt the dam of resolve she'd been sustaining finally start to crack with humiliation. She almost cried. Almost. Instead, she gritted her teeth and pushed herself up off the ground. She couldn't feel her hands at all, but she wasn't about to give them the satisfaction of knowing that.

"Sorry, doll," one of them said as he bent over and hooked a hand under her armpit, his fingertips on the swell of her breast.

Again she was tempted to strike out. His crotch was right there in perfect alignment for a left-handed grab. She could squeeze until things started to burst, and oh, wouldn't that be satisfying? But then the others would be on top of her, and this stony beach was not the wrestling mat she wanted to spar on.

So she let herself be picked up and escorted onto the dock. As her feet passed over the slatted wood, she asked them, "Just out of curiosity, any of you boys family men?"

No answer.

"Wives back home who think you're serving God and country? Protecting freedom? You got kids you tuck in bed at night? God, I hope you don't have daughters."

Still they didn't respond. Only ushered her into the boat.

And there was that hypocrisy again. Her judging these men for being able to disassociate their home life from their work. Something she'd spent a good part of her own life doing. Yeah, these bastards were trying to humiliate and break a woman, but had any of them done what she'd done in Trenton? And really, she couldn't be too upset about the way they were treating her because she'd have done it the same way. To men *and* women. *Had* done the same. But again, it was all irrelevant because *she* was the one already in control. She was the one using *them* to take her to her target. This was *her* operation. Not theirs.

One of the men pushed down on her shoulder, forcing her to sit her bare ass on the raft's floor between the bench seats. A little pool of water had settled there, and as the sensitive folds of flesh submerged, she discovered that she wasn't as numb as she thought. She bit the inside of her cheek to keep from shouting, and focused on squeezing her carry-on.

Three of the men entered the raft with her, leaving the others standing on the dock. When they started the engine and began motoring for the super yacht, icy spray began to pelt her face, chest, and side. She wondered for the first time if maybe Fedyenka preferred her to be half dead for their reunion. She wished she could lean back and stretch her arms out across the sides of the raft, to give them all a full view of her bouncing tits as a psychological middle finger, but she couldn't. Instead, she leaned forward and brought her knees to her chest, wrapping her arms around them and squeezing as hard as she could.

She caught a glimpse of the man sitting on the bench in front of her. He was looking at her and smiling.

A point for the bad guys.

THEY TOOK HER INTO the boat and sat her down beside a window that she could see out of but that no one could see into. They handcuffed her to the chair, which was better than she'd expected—at least they hadn't made her into the boat's nude figurehead by tying her to the bow.

She thought they would have blindfolded her, but they were letting her see everything. Which meant that Fedyenka had no plans to ever let her go. The question was whether he was planning on killing her or making her his slave Princess Leia.

A man walked over to her. He hadn't been on the dinghy, so she figured he was part of the yacht crew. He was wearing black fatigues, his pants tucked into combat boots. He threw a blanket at her. "Cover yourself up," he said, as if this were her preferred attire and he disapproved. She snatched the blanket out of the air with her free hand and slung it around her shoulders. It was long and covered her all the way to her calves.

The man turned and walked away.

Now that the blanket concealed her body, she carefully slipped her free hand beneath it and probed between her legs. The object, whatever it was, was still there. Again, she wondered what the hell it could be. A weapon of some sort? A tool that would help her escape? Was it information, like a microdot? Without knowing the purpose of it, how was she supposed to know when to use it? But then, the man would have known that. Which told her that he was expecting her to get at it the first chance she had. When she was in clothes or perhaps alone. She thought of asking to use the bathroom, but then couldn't be certain they wouldn't watch her go. Or worse, maybe they'd make her go over the side of the boat. She couldn't risk that. She'd just have to wait it out for now. Instead, she'd concentrate on regaining as much strength as she could.

She turned her attention out the window. Alaska, the man on the plane had said. She had no reason to doubt him. If this was where Osprey headquarters was, then maybe that was why no one had been able to find Fedyenka. Maybe he'd been on the Diomede Islands, sitting right in the middle of the Bering Strait, skating back and forth through what one of Gorbachev's spokespersons had once called "the Ice Curtain." Little Diomede was owned by the US and was only two and a half square miles with no more than ninety inhabitants occupying a single settlement. So unless Osprey's headquarters was located beneath the island, someone surely would have noticed it.

Her imagination spawned a preposterous underwater facility that ran beneath the two, complete with a shark-tank-like secret tunnel that Fedyenka could walk through without ice skates. Or maybe he had some kind of submarine that he traveled in. *Yeah,* she thought, *and maybe he's bald and wears a ring on his pinky finger and has a pet cat, too.*

The International Date Line ran between the two islands, putting Russia twenty-one hours ahead of Alaska—which resulted in the islands being referred to as "Yesterday Island" and "Tomorrow Island." But was it possible that Osprey could operate from Tomorrow Island or somewhere just a little farther west? She didn't think so. If the SVR was this serious about hunting Fedyenka down, then surely they would have found him if he'd been in their own backyard all this time.

She shook the thoughts of underwater bases out of her head. There was no use speculating about it now. She would find out soon enough. Instead, she thought about Jack and Johnson, wondering if they were still tracking her. She'd never counted on them actually showing up to save her. She'd known it was a pipe dream when she told Johnson her plan, and she knew that he'd known it too.

But now it was beyond a pipe dream. The way she saw it, there was zero chance of them making it from West Virginia to Alaska undetected before she'd have to do what needed to be done. And that was fine. She always figured it would be a suicide mission that triggered her end credits.

And at least this suicide mission would be better than the last one. Because last time, when she was supposed to blow herself up at the senator's birthday party, she had to trust that the captors would follow through on their promise and release Joseph after she was dead. This time, however, Fedyenka himself was the target, and if she could take him out with her, then she would die knowing that Joseph would be safe. If she could kill the bastard, then her family would be free of the FSB, and if she died in the process, they would also be free of the CIA, and Joseph could live out a normal life (assuming, of course, there was a way to clear Jack's name of the school bombing). No more false identities. No more switching schools.

No more mommy.

Her eyes glazed and started to burn.

She would hold out as long as she could, of course. But she would have to make her move while she still had strength enough to make it. Which was how she knew that Jack and Johnson wouldn't reach her in time. She took a deep breath and began to mentally prepare herself for that moment. Because there could be no hesitation when it came.

She lifted her eyes from the passing water and set them on the approaching shoreline. It was still just a line along the horizon, but they were close enough now to see that the line was actually a cliff. She squinted, thinking she could just make out trees. She was about to look away when, like an explosion, a bright orange glow suddenly materialized over the shoreline. It gleamed in the distance like a second, smaller sunrise and cast a line of fire from left to right across the frigid water. She turned right, to the east, and saw the sun hovering above the snowcapped peaks. The sun was being reflected by something resting atop the northern cliffs, she realized. "That where we're going?" she asked out loud.

The nearest of Fedyenka's thugs just looked at her.

Stacey crossed her legs beneath the blanket and studied what would be her final destination. *How interesting*, she thought. She never would have guessed an Alaskan hilltop for her departure. She supposed there were far worse places to die, places that, given her profession, would've seemed much more likely. *Silver linings...*

She relaxed her breathing and, just like in the early days, imagined herself as Lyudmila Pavlichenko, the Lady of Death, getting ready to pull the trigger on an unsuspecting target far away.

I'm coming for you, you son of a bitch.

60

"CAN YOU GIVE ME a hand for a second?" Johnson asked Jack.

Jack watched him get up and move toward the front of the plane and open the storage closet. "I'll be right back," he said to Joseph.

"Don't get lost," Joseph said.

Jack smiled and gave a reflexive look out the window, noticing the rectangular grids of farmland below. He got to his feet and walked the few paces to where Johnson was pulling a crate out of the closet.

"Look," Johnson said. He flipped the crate's lid open.

Jack's brow furrowed as he squinted at its contents. "What—"

But Johnson cut him off by placing a finger over his lips, instructing him to lower his voice. "We aren't landing in Anchorage," he whispered.

"What do you mean?" Jack whispered back.

"There's no time to land, get to a hotel, and then find a way to Stacey. And leaving Joseph alone at a hotel has its own risks."

"So where are we landing?" Jack asked.

"We're not." He grabbed one of four backpacks out of the crate and set it aside.

That was when Jack noticed what they were. "We're *jumping*?" He looked back at Joseph, but he was staring out the window and not paying attention to them.

"Have to. It's the only way. We splash down and swim to shore."

"Then what?" Jack asked, incredulous.

"Then the pilots will fly to an airport in Washington, where they'll sit and wait things out."

"The pilots?"

"And Joseph."

Jack tried to compute what Johnson was telling him. "So you and me are parachuting into Alaskan waters like we're in some Chuck Norris '80s movie while Joseph flies to Washington and hides in the plane until…" He trailed off, wondering what would become of his son if they never made it back.

Johnson understood the hesitation. "Arrangements have been made."

"What kind of arrangements?"

"If we don't contact them by tomorrow night…" He shrugged. "Joseph will be taken care of. Not the ideal life anyone was hoping for, probably, but he'll be okay."

Jack glanced back at Joseph, who was now putting his earbuds in. After a long sigh, Jack looked down at the parachute packs. There was no use in trying to pull out of Johnson just what "he'll be okay" looked like. If they were going to avoid that scenario altogether, then there were more pressing issues that needed to be discussed. "So what's the plan?"

Johnson reached over and grabbed the tablet, flipping it around so that Jack could see the display. The little dot that was supposedly the tracking chip in Stacey's shoulder was glowing strong against an aerial map. The dot looked like it was right along the west coast of—

"Where is that?" Jack asked.

Johnson pinched his fingers on the screen and minimized the image, suddenly bringing to view the shape of Alaska, specifically the state's familiar tail that curved into the Pacific like a smile—or scythe. Stacey was near the right corner of that smile, up at the north end of the Alaskan Peninsula. Jack frowned. "So Fedyenka is there, right on the Bering Sea?"

"Well, Stacey is. We're assuming Fedyenka is too."

Jack pointed at the water on the screen. "We're landing in the water and swimming to shore?"

Johnson nodded and threw a thumb over his shoulder back to the closet, where another duffel bag was leaning on-end against the wall. "They got us snowsuits, parkas, gloves… It will help against the cold. And we'll use the plane's inflatable raft."

"So you knew we'd be landing in water when you contacted them. How did you know that? How did you know that's where they were taking her?"

"Educated guess."

Jack leaned forward. "You're gonna have to fill in a few of those blanks."

"Osprey Security Services Inc. I told you they're a legitimate private security company. They have a dozen locations throughout the world, all of them in plain sight. Once we found out Fedyenka was behind it, we tracked down all their known locations. We were in the middle of putting together a plan to infiltrate Osprey when all this crap happened."

"And that's one of their locations?" Jack asked, again pointing to the screen.

"Yeah. It's just inland, at the base of a bay. We can splash down in there, take out the guards, and infiltrate the fortress."

"Fortress?"

He shrugged. "All we have are some preliminary satellite photos. Whatever it is, it's big. But we didn't get far enough into the investigation to know anything else." He clicked the screen off and slid the tablet back into its case. "Frankly, this was last on our list to check. We assumed he'd be underground, not operating on US soil in broad daylight. Someone in the government must've been running interference for him."

"If he *is* there."

Johnson nodded. "If he is there. Could just be a staging point. Hold her there until he's ready for whatever else he has going on. Or maybe he won't come to her at all. Maybe he's just using Osprey to get what he wants from her."

"Joseph," Jack mumbled.

"Looks that way." He put the chutes back in the case and closed the lid. Put the tracker on top of it. "Regardless, the plan is to get Stacey back, and we know where she is."

"But that's not *her* plan," Jack said.

Johnson rubbed his chin. "It'll be around 3:30 Alaska time when we splash down."

"Shouldn't we wait until dark?" Jack asked, though he knew the plan had already been set.

"Do you want to?" Johnson asked.

Jack imagined all the things that could be happening to his wife at that exact moment, and shook his head. "No."

They both stood.

"Hey," Jack said. "Thank you." Johnson started to walk back to his seat, but Jack grabbed his arm, stopping him. "I'm serious. Thank you. If it weren't for you…" He shrugged. "Hell, if it weren't for you, we probably would've been dead a long time ago, but I mean—" He looked around the plane. "All this… And you risking your life to help us?"

But Johnson just nodded. "You should get some sleep while you can." Then he went and sat back in his seat.

Jack thought about the plan Johnson had just relayed to him. He'd never gone skydiving before. He felt his guts begin to tighten.

61

BY THE TIME THEY reached the dock, Stacey was almost feeling back to normal. Despite being hungry, her mind was sharp, and she could feel all of her extremities.

"Let's go," one of the men said to her. He pulled the blanket off her and unlocked the handcuff from the chair. Then he grabbed her arm and pulled her to her feet. "Boss said you weren't to be trusted. Not even with clothes."

She thought about that. Could it be true? Was her nudity less about humiliation and more a security measure? If so, then Fedyenka was certainly not underestimating her. If he intended for her to be naked at all times, then her mission was going to be a lot more difficult than she'd hoped. But maybe that was what the guy from the plane had anticipated, slipping her a weapon that wouldn't be visible to the eye.

Other men took up positions around her. The one who had given her the blanket stared into her eyes. She stared back at him, holding his gaze and praying they weren't about to bend her over. If Fedyenka was so concerned about her ability to conceal a weapon, then it would only make sense that he'd order a cavity search too. But instead of reaching between her legs, the guy reached for her shackled wrist. He stepped to her side, bringing her arm with him, and then to the small of her back. He reached around and took her other hand, cuffing both behind her. *And now is the part when they're going to—*

But they didn't. The man just nudged her from behind to get her moving forward, and they all walked out onto the deck.

THE WIND SEEMED TO howl off the water and slam into the cliff face that rose above them. With her hands cuffed behind her back, she had no way to shield herself from the freezing air, and it struck her full in the face, chest, and thighs. In just a few seconds, her skin turned bright pink. The steps beneath her were metal and like ice against her bare feet. Her hair whipped across her face and into her eyes and mouth. As she climbed the stairs, which were assembled more like scaffolding and bolted into the rock itself, she was fully aware that the men following had a full, 4K UHD view of all her most intimate parts. But she was past caring about any of that, so long as her secret remained in place.

When they finally reached the top of the stairs, tears were dripping off her jawline from the cold, stinging air. No matter how many times she blinked, she just couldn't manage to clear her vision. Everything was a watery blur. She turned her back to the wind and the water below, her legs burning from the climb, and blinked more tears as she tried to get a glimpse of her new surroundings.

The building she had seen from the boat stood before her. She figured it had to be about twelve stories tall and fitted with floor-to-ceiling windows that were still reflecting the sun and the sky to the east of them. She could make out, through her tears, a plethora of radar dishes and satellite antennas tracing the near side of the roof. A Pantsir missile system was hiding among them.

She turned her gaze to her left, away from the concrete structure, and saw open grass for maybe a quarter of a mile before ending against a tree line. She noticed a distant flag, just visible from her vantage point, and knew it was a wind marker. Which meant there was a helipad somewhere behind the building.

To her right, she could only see open sky beyond the building and figured the cliff must cut inland along that side of the structure.

A hand landed on her bare shoulder and pushed her forward across a slab of frozen concrete and toward a pair of sliding doors. "We have the girl," she heard him say into his mic. He swiped a card over a card reader, and the doors split at the center, moving away from each other and disappearing into the walls.

If getting into the building required a card, Stacey wondered how Jack and Johnson would infiltrate the place themselves. *They won't,* she reminded herself. *Because they'll still be thousands of miles away when I make my move.*

They passed through the doors and entered the building. The doors slid shut behind them.

Stacey looked around. The walls were either gray concrete blocks, or they were just panels fastened to drywall and meant to look like concrete blocks. They were each two feet long and about a foot high, giving it the feel of a military base or a bunker. But then she noticed the lights and the furniture and the pictures hanging on the walls and wondered if the place was trying to pull off some kind of modern style. It reminded her of Pierce Brosnan's house in that movie she'd seen with Jack forever ago—*The Ghost Writer.* Based on the Robert Harris novel. She remembered because she'd been halfway through the novel (reading it for reasons other than just entertainment) when Jack talked her into watching the movie with him.

They escorted her across the space and into a waiting elevator. The elevator's walls were mirrored, and she could see her nude body reflected in the glass along with the men around her. Her skin was almost purple, and for the first time, she began to feel self-conscious. Naked outside in the elements was one thing—primitive, native, hippie, whatever. But here? In this building? This was more along the lines of being naked while wandering the halls and looking for homeroom on your first day of high school than stripping at the club or frolicking around at some nude beach. The endless reflection of herself—back to front to side to back to front to back to side to... Her ass went on forever; her breasts doubled into infinity.

She wondered what practical purpose such a configuration of mirrors would serve. It seemed more fitting for a fun house than a corporate building or stronghold. Though for all she knew, this entire building could be a fun house, Fedyenka's personal fantasy island with a red room on every floor.

She shuddered.

When the elevator stopped, they led her out into another foyer with the same gray walls. There were larger paintings hanging on these walls, strategically spaced out in perfect proportion as if they were being showcased. She didn't recognize any of them. Maybe they were pieces of Fedyenka's own work. If so, they weren't terrible, and they certainly weren't along the lines of the ones she'd heard about way back when.

The men escorted her down a long hallway lined with doors. Stacey didn't know if they were offices, suites, closets, or cells. And then they stopped before one, opened it, and pushed her in. One of the men entered behind her and removed her handcuffs. Without a word, he then turned and left, shutting and locking the door behind him.

Stacey looked around. The room was about fifteen feet long and ten feet wide. The walls were more of the same, the ceiling too. There was a long rectangular window about eight inches tall that ran across the whole back wall, letting in daylight from outside. It was just below the ceiling though, and she'd have to jump up to try to get a glimpse of what was on the other side. Five circular LED lights sat recessed in the ceiling. An air vent was positioned up in the corner of the room and there was a return vent near the floor on the adjacent wall.

A folded red robe sat in a neat square in front of it. It was the only thing in the room. She bent over and picked it up. Silk. She slipped into it and tied it shut at the waist. It was long and did very little to conceal her figure, but it was better than being naked.

She began walking around, searching the walls and the ceiling for the camera she knew had to be in the room. Not finding anything obvious, she knelt before the metal return grate and tried to peer through the slats. There was no red power light blinking in the darkness, but then they wouldn't use something so noticeable. She turned and look back over her shoulder, up to the vent in the ceiling. With no furniture in the room, there was nothing to stand on and no way to reach it. She figured that was where the camera was. Or at least one of them.

She stood and walked to the other side of the room, turning her back to the ceiling vent so that it was positioned up over her left shoulder. She needed to know what the guy had given her, and she needed to know right now. Before Fedyenka found it himself. There was only one way to do it.

She turned her head and looked up at the vent, letting whoever was watching know that she knew they were watching. Then she hiked the robe up to her thighs and assumed a squatted position in the middle of the floor. The robe pooled on the floor around her feet like a red puddle. Trusting that the position of her body concealed her right arm from the camera, she then pulled her arm into the robe's sleeve, tucking her arm tight against her body. Carefully, she removed the smuggled object and as discreetly as possible began to probe it with her fingers.

It was tubular. About an inch and a half long, three-quarters of an inch wide. There was a crease near the tip, and she knew it had to be a screw-on cap. She gripped the thing like she would a joystick and tried using her thumb and forefinger to unscrew it.

The cap turned. And then it fell off. It landed on the floor between her feet but stayed under the tent of the robe.

She pressed her finger against the opening and turned what she now knew was a capsule upside down. Its contents tapped against her skin. Whatever it was, it was hard. Not a powder or a liquid or something else that would be wasted if she was to accidentally spill it.

She moved her finger from the opening and emptied its contents onto the floor. Quickly, she set the capsule aside and, still using her one hand inside the robe, touched what had fallen out of it. She frowned. It felt like... She spread her fingers away from it, knowing instinctively what it was. There was something else there too. Something that felt like a rolled joint. Paper. Was it a note? If so, how was she going to read it without the cameras seeing it?

Damn. How long had this already taken? It felt like forever, and she knew she was running out of time.

She picked up the capsule and its cap and lifted the robe just enough so that its edges were off the floor. Then she relaxed her bladder. As the warm liquid formed around her left foot and began to move across the floor behind her, she quickly thrust her right arm back into the sleeve.

She leaned forward, holding her hand close to her stomach, and opened it. It was as she suspected. A tightly rolled piece of paper the size of a fortune cookie note and what looked like an engagement ring. She unrolled the paper and saw two words scribbled across the paper. POISON RING.

She looked at the ring and noticed that the diamond was fastened to the inside of the band. She turned the paper over and saw a crudely drawn picture that showed a needle inside the diamond. Feeling the diamond, she could tell that it was plastic, just a cover for the needle. She carefully tried to move the plastic diamond, and it popped free of the band. There was a square hole in the ring that the diamond cap fit in, clicking into place. She connected it to the top of the band and quickly went about replacing her own engagement ring with it. It was a little loose, but her wedding ring would keep it in place.

Quickly, expecting the door to open at any moment, she screwed the cap back onto the capsule and let the robe fall back around her feet. She pulled her right arm from the sleeve again and returned the tube to its hiding place.

She heard footsteps coming down the hall. And they were coming quickly, no doubt responding to her urinating on the floor. Which proved that they had been watching.

As fast as she could, she wrapped the paper around her engagement ring, thankful Jack had only been able to afford a small princess cut, and shoved it in her mouth. There was no other option. Because the diamond was on the outside of the band, it wouldn't fit in the capsule, and she didn't have time to figure out how to make it stay anywhere else.

Shadows beneath the door. The handle moving.

She stood tall and faced the door, taking a step back from the yellow puddle at her feet. Using her tongue to maneuver the ring so that the setting was facing her teeth, she gathered as much saliva as she could and swallowed.

And then the door opened, and two men came rushing in, their eyes immediately finding the puddle and then darting to her face. The look in their eyes was neither revulsion nor satisfaction. Or at least not one in exclusion to the other. It was suspicion, as if understanding that pissing on the floor had to have been a tactical maneuver but not understanding how.

She swallowed again, feeling the ring sitting halfway down her throat. Thankfully, the diamond had gone down like a tail and not sideways. She offered the two men the reason they seemed to be looking for by raising both hands and flipping them her middle fingers.

They stepped around the yellow lake, one going around to the left, the other to the right, each coming up behind her and grabbing her arms. As they dragged her across the floor and out the door, she swallowed again.

62

JOSEPH ADJUSTED THE HEADPHONES as he looked out the window and put the trading cards from Bryan the Tall back into his backpack. It was strange to think that all those little ants down there were people—individual people with beating hearts and thoughts in their heads. It was even stranger to think that most of them were looking for him. Well, maybe not each one of them, but as a whole, the entire country was on the lookout for him and his family.

A rock song from the early nineties played into his ears. He and his friends enjoyed rock, even though it seemed that everyone else in his school preferred country and rap. He didn't get it himself. He turned away from the window, leaned back in the oversized chair, and let the music carry his mood away to some distant fantasy—the chords a river, the lyrics the boat transporting him.

As he drifted off, his mind tried to hold onto the image of his dad and Mr. Johnson talking up by the cockpit. It was clear they had been making plans. Plans they didn't want him to know about. That was apparent from their hushed tones and the conspiratorial glances he kept getting from his dad. But Joseph didn't really care right now. Right now, so far up in the sky, he felt safe. All the problems that were after him were thousands of feet below them. No one could touch them up here. So he'd take advantage of the peacetime while he could. They'd be landing eventually, and then he'd be sitting in some hotel room alone and waiting for more guys to come kicking down the door. Like at the bunker and the diner.

His thoughts turned to Agent Brown. It was strange to have just met someone that was no longer alive, and it still wasn't registering. It all felt like a strange dream. Even stranger than the one where he'd been kidnapped by hillbillies and held up in the mountains.

He wondered what would happen if his mom and dad didn't come get him at the hotel room. If no one ever showed up. What would he do then? How long would he wait to decide?

He turned his head and watched his dad as he slept, wondering what the point of surviving the woods had been if they were just going to putter out here and now. It seemed like a waste. He closed his eyes and let the electric guitar take him to the other side of consciousness, no idea what things would be like when next he opened them but too tired to care. He'd deal with whatever it was then.

63

THEY MOVED HER DOWN another long corridor and into a second elevator. One of the two men hit a button, and the floor began to move. Stacey could tell from the sudden pressure in her heels that they were ascending. Her mind began to spin. This was finally it. After all the years of running, hiding, and then searching, the moment had finally come. And it was about damn time. And yet, she was nervous. Nervous because she knew that whatever it was Fedyenka had in mind for her was just moments away from being her new reality, and she wasn't sure how long she'd be able to endure it.

She played with the ring on her finger, trying to draw some courage from it. She wondered what kind of poison the needle was coated with. Cyanide? Novichok? Would its effect be immediate, or would he have time to kill her first and then die hours or even days later? She had no way of knowing. So she would only use it if no other options (with more immediate and certain results) failed to present themselves.

She felt the wetness of the robe as it brushed against her calves and could smell her urine. But she refused to let herself be dehumanized by it. Instead, she considered it a measured tactic designed to keep her captors off-balance. She looked up for the floor numbers, but there were no glowing digits displaying the progress of their journey. Perhaps this elevator only had one destination.

The elevator stopped, and the doors opened. She had no idea how many stories they'd just traveled, but if she had to make a guess, she'd say three. The men, neither one of them breaking their silence, moved her out into another corridor with concrete-paneled walls. At the end of the hall was a large room with a black marble floor.

As they approached it, Stacey saw a large blue-gray rug covering the center of it. It looked like a giant geode, and leather furniture sat positioned around it. A large silver chandelier hung from the ceiling. A floating staircase extended from the left wall, each step a long piece of walnut leading to another floor.

The men directed her to the stairs, and she climbed to the next room. Wall-to-wall red carpet covered the floor, and more pictures decorated the walls. A pair of sofas sat around a long coffee table. At the back of the room were large double doors, two men in suits standing on either side of them. Floor-to-ceiling windows ran along the outside wall and offered a view of the water out on the horizon.

As Stacey approached the doors, the men positioned on either side of them pulled them open and gestured her through. She stepped into the room and felt as if she'd stepped through a portal to another time. The room resembled a king's chambers in some medieval castle. The doors closed behind her, and she glanced back over her shoulder, seeing that none of the men had followed her in.

A fire roared from within a large fireplace over in the corner of the room, which was some fifty feet to her right. She could feel its heat even from where she stood. There was furniture scattered around the room. Large sofas and reclining chairs, mostly. A large window looked out to the mountains, and a table stood in front of it. Bottles filled with red and clear liquids—vodka and wine, she guessed—were arranged at its center.

Pictures on the wall caught her eye. Paintings, all of them. Nude women posing erotically, some even seeming to be captured within the throes of pleasure. Or pain. It was hard to tell the difference. An icy finger ran up her spine, and her flesh broke out in goosebumps.

In the back of the massive room, thirty yards away and centered against the wall, she could see a bed fit for an emperor. A pillar rose from each corner, supporting a canopy from which hung velvet curtains, each one tied to a post with a gold, tasseled rope. Sitting on the end of the bed and facing her was a man she had not seen in many years. Not since the day she'd shot him in the head. But his form was all she could make out in the shadows cast by the bed's canopy, though she could tell he was leaning forward, elbows on knees, his large hands together, fingers interlaced.

"Hello, Anna," Fedyenka said. He stood up and into the light coming from the window.

STACEY WAS STRUCK FIRST by the size of him. He had always been a big man, powerful, but this was something else entirely. As if he'd spent the last ten years bodybuilding. The gray suit he wore swelled over top his shoulders, biceps, and thighs. And then he took a step forward, and the light revealed his face.

If age, stress, and whatever Siberian winters he'd endured over the course of their estrangement had taken any toll on him, then it didn't show. What did show, however, was the damage that had been done to the right side of his face. Either he'd gotten into a fight with a Kodiak bear, or the scars were from the bullet she'd sent through the back of his skull and out his face.

"You are even more beautiful than I remember," he said, his voice traveling softly throughout the big room and against the crackling fireplace. If not for the events that led her here (and their audience of obscene pictures), Stacey might be tempted to misconstrue the atmosphere as soothing.

"You're a lot uglier," she said.

He smiled, and the scarred flesh flexed beside the corner of his mouth. He walked toward her, crossing the thirty feet between them. The closer he got, the smaller she felt.

Is this the moment? Stacey thought. She put her hands behind her back and puffed out her chest, feigning defiance while her fingers worked the false cap off the ring. Getting it free, she transferred the fake diamond into her right hand, then rotated the ring on her finger so that the needle was facing inward. She would slap him open-handed rather than try to throw a punch at him. Though with the poisoned needle extending from the underside of her ring finger, if she closed her hand now, she would prick herself.

Fedyenka's growing presence continued to overwhelm her, seeming to engulf her altogether as he glided across the room in strong, fluid strides. He was surely not the crippled man she had hoped to find.

She stared at his neck. It was like a tree trunk, and she began to wonder if the needle would even penetrate the skin or if it would just snap off. Would she only need to scratch him, or would the needle need to plunge into the muscle? Perhaps now was not the right time. She started to shake.

He walked right up to her and then moved past, his bicep brushing against her shoulder. He circled, coming to a stop behind her.

She moved her hands in front of her, trying to conceal the ring while careful not to poke herself. She stood ramrod straight and held her breath, waiting to feel his icy touch on her body. He reached around the front of her and ran his fingers across the front of her neck, brushing her neckline and hooking a finger beneath the robe.

"I trust the trip wasn't too uncomfortable for you," he said as he pulled the robe off her shoulders.

She felt it glide down her body and pool at her feet.

"I know you probably enjoyed the attention," he continued. "You always did enjoy the attention." Still behind her, he reached around and cupped her right breast, gently thumbing her nipple. Then he leaned down and pressed his nose into the side of her neck and took a long drag of her scent. "All these years you have been the CIA's whore." He moved his hand to the other breast and lifted it, feeling the weight of it in his hand. "Now you will be mine."

She tried to divorce herself from what was happening to her. It was a skill she had learned over the years, letting her body be enjoyed by someone else while her mind teleported her some- where else. She swept her gaze around the room, absorbing every detail she could, looking for something she might be able to use as a weapon in the event that the ring didn't work or didn't work right away. But it was the pictures that ended up capturing her attention.

Fedyenka's hands brushed down her ribs and to her hips. She worked the plastic cap back onto the needle as he walked around to face her, tracing her waist with a finger. He stood there and stared at her body for what seemed like an eternity. "You put out to anyone who came across your path. Even married Vadim. But you always deflected my advances." He shook his head. "I would have treated you like an empress." He lifted his eyes off her body and noticed that she was looking, not at him, but at the pictures. He followed her gaze to one particular painting. "Ah. You have noticed my lady friends."

"You painted them?" she asked.

He nodded. "I did."

"And did you treat them like empresses?"

"Not exactly," he admitted. He cast a sweeping gaze over all of them. "Consider them my conquests. Each and every one a masterpiece of female anatomy and sexual deviance."

"A metaphor, then?" she asked. "This supposed to show how you always get what you want?"

He scratched at his chin. "I suppose. Some men hang the heads of their great victories over their mantels, whereas I like to paint mine."

Stacey moved her eyes to his. "So when your dream of ruling Russia begins to wane, you come in here and stare at all the women you have ruled, and it inspires you to press on."

"Something like that, I suppose."

She noticed that one of the hanging pictures was blank. "Hmm... Looks like one got away."

He smiled again. "Until now."

"I see," she said. "And will you have my hands over my head?" She nodded toward one of the other pictures. "Or wrists bound to my ankles?"

He put a finger under her chin and lifted her face so that it was angled up toward his. "We have plenty of time to figure that out. After all, it is through trial and error that such perfection is to be discovered." He leaned closer, the grotesque scars on his face mere inches from her. "Lots and lots of trial and error."

"Okay, Fedyenka," Stacey said, spreading her arms. "I'm all yours. You finally got the one who got away. You win again. Do whatever you want to me. I'm sure it's all been done to me before. But first, tell me...what in the hell do you want with my son?"

He looked down at his polished wing-tipped shoes and seemed to consider the question before ultimately dismissing it. "You do not seem very comfortable at the moment. Perhaps you are still cold? You smell like piss."

"That's because I pissed myself."

He smiled again. "Such a thing is not so much a turnoff to me as you might expect. But again, we will have plenty of time for all of that. Right now, I think you should go freshen up so that you can join me for lunch."

She shook her head. "Tell me now, you piece of shit. What does Joseph have to do with this Romanov plot of yours?"

He blinked in surprise. "I'm impressed. Did you learn this from the CIA or from the SVR? Or perhaps from your friend Johnson?"

Now it was her eyes that showed surprise.

"Oh, yes. I know all about Mr. Johnson. He has proved to be somewhat of a nuisance. The raids in West Virginia alone could have ruined me."

She bent over and grabbed the robe off the floor and pulled it back on. "Are you the one who took out Johnson's team?"

He turned toward the window, ignoring the question. "Do not worry about your son. No harm will come to him."

"You mean like with those maniacs in the woods you hired?"

"Yes, well, your American husband has been a fly in the ointment, that is for sure. None of that was supposed to happen."

"You're right," she said, mocking him. "It's all Jack's fault. He should have just let them take our son. How incredibly inconsiderate of him."

He studied her for a moment. Seemed to chew on her words.

"You are mine now. The sooner you accept that fact, the better things will go for you." He turned back to her and pulled his hair off his head. Standing there with the wig dangling at his side, and the sunlight catching his melted scalp, he glared at her. "Many surgeries it took to repair the damage from your bullet and the explosion."

"Is that what all this has been about?" she asked. "You getting back at me?"

"I will not deny that I have gotten some personal satisfaction out of it, but no. It is about something much greater, which we will discuss at length over lunch." He motioned for the door she'd come through, ushering her toward it. "All you need to know right now is that you can put yourself at ease concerning Joseph. He will be safe with me, and you can live to watch him grow."

"Unless the SVR gets to him first," she said.

"Well, yes. That is true. Which is why you should really hurry up and tell me where he is."

"And what about Jack?"

"Oh"—he waved his hand dismissively as he opened the door—"Jack has to die. One way or another. He just does not fit into anyone's plans. He never has."

The men who brought her into the room were still standing outside the doors, waiting for her.

"Take her to her room," he said to them. "See that she showers."

They nodded, and the one on her right actually touched her elbow and gestured forward with his free hand as if he were a host at a restaurant politely showing her to a reserved table.

"You are my guest now, Anna. No harm will come to you," Fedyenka said. Then he added, "Well, no harm you will not learn to enjoy, anyway."

She looked back over her shoulder and to the pictures behind him. *Not a chance in hell,* she thought.

64

JACK OPENED HIS EYES and yawned, not realizing he'd fallen asleep. He looked over at Joseph and saw him sleeping with his earbuds in. He could just make out the soft, tinny clang of cymbols in whatever song was playing. Johnson was sitting in his seat and looking out the window, seemingly deep in thought. Jack took a glance out the window himself before leaning back and shutting his eyes again. He tried to jump back into the nap he'd been in, but his mind was too awake now and wouldn't let him. He fought it for a while, but then gave up, surrendering to the cerebral hamster wheel.

Again he thought of what Stacey could be going through in that exact moment. And when he couldn't take that idea anymore, his mind took him to the imagined windows of Samantha's house. He saw her husband there, sitting in a recliner, glass of scotch in one hand, red eyes staring into nothing. Then he was whisked away to other homes of other parents. They were all pissed. Most were close to their children, obviously thankful for another day with them, but there was another who was standing in the doorway of a child's bedroom and staring at the empty bed, tears running down their face. And then, when that became too much, he got to witness the massacre of all those patrons at the diner. *The destruction we have left in our wake,* he thought.

And just like that, the Stacey Green/Anna Aleksandrov rabbit hole opened and began filling his mind with accusations. It was all *her* fault. *She* was the one who had brought this death to their doorstep, who had literally tried to kill him, who had put their child's life in danger over and over again. It was *her* past that had made them a target of Moscow and of the CIA. Johnson was in their lives because of *her*, his team dead because of *her*. Donny and Ivan. And now Samantha and whoever else had died in the explosion. The sheriff and the people in that town... And as he stared into the windows of all those broken homes, he could see himself standing there in the reflection. And he could see Stacey standing behind him, her face over his shoulder.

The hamster wheel spun so fast that it started to smoke, ultimately spinning off its track and spiraling away, freeing his thoughts from their endless prison.

It was true, he knew that. It *was* Stacey's fault. Or at least she was the magnet that had attracted all of it. He supposed he couldn't blame her for being who she was before he met her. Though he could certainly hold a grudge for being deceived by her afterward—and everything else that she'd done for country while they were married. God only knew what all that entailed. He slammed the rabbit hole shut again. He didn't want to think about it. It didn't matter. He loved her. Joseph loved her.

He nudged his thoughts down a different avenue, one that wasn't so emotionally draining. One that he could navigate objectively. It was Deep Fake Street. And as he walked down it, he looked around, seeing the AI-generated footage that had played on the news program. He didn't understand it. Didn't know why someone would go through that much trouble to set him up. What did any of it really have to do with *him*? He had always just been an inconvenience that they'd tried to get rid of. The cruise ship, then the guy in his house, Ham's gang, and the sniper in the woods... All of them had simply been trying to kill him. So what would anyone gain from setting him up for the bombing? It had to be about Stacey or Joseph. Like it always had been.

Again, he pondered that morning, guessing at what the initial plan could have been, where things would be now if they'd succeeded. They seemed pretty confident that the CIA had to have been the ones who had orchestrated the bomb, but what if it had been the SVR? Maybe some Spetsnaz unit, assassins under the chief of Line S or something. What if the Agency had known about it and had allowed it to happen? Had used the explosion to their advantage, knowing they could control the narrative in the aftermath? They only needed to remove Joseph from the situation first.

Jack sighed and ran a hand through his beard. Was the plan always to grab Joseph and then blow up the school, or did they blow up the school after failing to get Joseph? Or, again, was the bomb not the work of whoever killed Mrs. Hatfield? And what about the Audis? If Fedyenka wanted Stacey alive, then that would make them SVR, right? And if the SVR was around that morning, then they had to at least know something was going down, either involved in it or monitoring someone who was. And what about the FBI agents? If they were operating on real orders, believing they were looking for some kind of bomber prior to the explosion, then they had to have been operating on some "tip" that the bureau deemed credible. And who had the ability and influence to convince the feds that he was an imminent threat?

But again, why would someone go through all this trouble to set him up? Were they using him to oust Stacey? To blow her cover? Both their names were all over the news now, Stacey's involvement with both the CIA and Moscow public knowledge, leaked by someone who knew about her past.

He still couldn't make sense of it. And why Fedyenka wanted Joseph so bad made even less sense.

65

STACEY LOOKED AROUND THE new room the two men had brought her to, ignoring their watchful eyes as she did so. They were standing in the middle of the room, feet spread shoulder-width apart, their hands grasped in front of them. Their faces looked to have been carved from the East Siberian Highlands, the eyes that stared out of them, cold shark eyes. One of them had a deep scar at his temple, visible just beneath the hairline. She'd seen scars like that before and guessed it had been formed by a piece of shrapnel. They each had a MAC-11 slung over their shoulder. Stacey knew not to mess with them. At least not physically.

The room's walls had the same gray paneling she'd seen everywhere else, but the floor was wood planking. There were sofas, a fireplace, and even a bar off in the far corner, a little kitchenette across from it. It was an apartment, she realized. Was this to be her new home, then, she wondered. Had all the women now hanging on Fedyenka's bedroom walls lived here too? Probably not, she thought. There were too many of them, and this place didn't seem that old. But perhaps a couple had, depending on how long he kept them around.

She turned behind her and studied the bathroom. There was no door to the room. She walked into it and saw a vessel sink bowl positioned beneath a back lit mirror to the immediate left. Next to that was a toilet. A tiled, walk-in shower comprised the entire back half of the room, a large rectangular showerhead hanging suspended from the ceiling at its center.

She looked back over her shoulder at the two men. They were still standing there watching her. They nodded to the shower as if to say, "C'mon, let's go."

Okay, then. So she untied the robe and let it fall. Naked, she stepped onto the tile. Getting beneath the showerhead, she reached for the knobs on the wall, hardly caring what was going on in the basal forebrain of her audience. If she wanted to further toy with their alertness, she could put on a show for them that would rival the most erotic strippers they'd ever seen. But after what she'd been through, the simple expectation of a hot shower was all she was concerned with, audience or no audience.

She moved to the side of the faucet, and the water came down like rain, pitter-pattering against the tile beside her, swirling at her heels before disappearing down the drain. Stacey stuck her left hand into the stream to check the temperature. It was cold. She waited a few more seconds and then tried again. Warm enough.

She stepped beneath the flowing water and closed her eyes. The water matted her black hair against her head and face, splitting it over her shoulders so that half fell down over her breasts and the other half covered her back. She leaned forward against an outstretched arm and rested her chin on her chest, letting the water run down her face. She could feel the coldness in her bones packing up and leaving as everything else melted away with the water. The whole of reality, it seemed, washed off her, circled at her feet a few times, and then disappeared.

She stood there with her eyes closed long enough to start nodding off. Turning her back to the wall so that she was facing the doorless entryway and the open room beyond, she saw that the two men were still watching her. And she saw exactly what was going on in their nucleus accumbens, because though their faces were trying to hide it, their pants could not. She didn't care.

She sat on the tiled floor, her legs outstretched, ankles crossed, and leaned her head back against the wall. She closed her eyes again and concentrated on the hot water falling over her legs, letting the steam engulf her head and shoulders. She didn't know how long the men would let her stay in here, though judging from how much they were enjoying themselves, she figured they'd let her stay as long as they possibly could. She'd gladly let them stare at her if it meant prolonging the shower.

She drifted off to sleep, the water massaging her sore body, nothing else ever seeming to have felt so good.

THEY'D LET HER SIT there somewhere between ten and fifteen minutes. And though they were probably willing to let her spend the rest of the day in the shower, they knew they couldn't keep their psychotic boss waiting too long.

"Time to get dressed," one of the men said, readjusting the submachine gun so that it hung in front of him.

She stood, turned off the water, and walked over to a shelf that hung on the wall across from the toilet. She took one of three folded towels from it and began to dry herself off. When she was done, she wrapped herself in it and went to the sink. Since there was no door to trap the steam, the mirror above the sink hadn't fogged that much, and she could still see her reflection.

The man with the scar walked away and out of view. Stacey began to brush her hair with a comb that had been left on the corner of the sink. Again, she wondered if it might have belonged to one of the painted girls.

Her guard reappeared with a dress over his arm. He stepped into the bathroom and held it out to her. She took it from him, wondering what Fedyenka had in mind. It was a silver bodycon minidress, sequined, made of aluminum and rhinestone. It had a plunging neck line and a low back. The sides had long slits that would almost reach her waist, allowing her the ability to spread her legs. Which was a good thing, tactically. And a bad thing for other, obvious reasons.

"Ten minutes," the scarred man said. Then, knowing the show was pretty much over, he turned and went over to the fireplace, taking a seat on the sofa. The other man gave him a worried look, but the man just shrugged. "She's not going anywhere," he said. But the other guy didn't seem so sure. He remained where he was, the MAC-11 ready if needed.

Stacey ignored him and dropped the dress onto the floor. Then she threw off the towel and stepped into the silver pile, bending over to pull it up over her body, slipping her arms through the straps and pulling them up over her shoulders. She looked down at herself, surprised that she actually did like the thing—if she were wearing it under different circumstances. She looked up at the man still standing outside the bathroom and could tell that he approved too.

She retrieved the towel and began drying her hair.

Ten minutes.

Ten minutes to live, she thought.

66

THE SOUND OF JOSEPH unzipping his backpack caused Jack to open his eyes. Blinking, he looked out the window and took notice of the clouds still below them. For a split second, he'd once again thought the last ten plus years must've been a dream, that he must've fallen asleep watching some '80s spy thriller on his way to... *To where?*

Alaska.

And just like that, the momentary relief he'd felt upon waking—that everything from the cruise ship to the farmhouse must have been a dream—was replaced with a sudden, terrifying panic. *Stacey.* He rubbed his eyes as he tried to recover from the unexpected seesaw of realities.

"You okay?" Joseph asked him.

He nodded. "Yeah." Then he opened his eyes and met his son's concerned stare. "How 'bout you?"

"Okay," Joseph said.

"Come here." Jack patted the seat beside him.

Joseph set his bag aside and moved over.

"Listen," Jack said, looking down at his hands while he talked. "You're not going to a hotel."

Joe squinted. "What do you mean?"

Jack relayed the plan exactly as Johnson had explained it to him.

JOHNSON LEANED INTO THE aisle and said, "Two hours."

He'd apparently been listening to Jack explain things to Joseph and knew there was no need to continue hiding things.

Jack nodded. He had his arm around Joseph, the boy's head resting on his chest. Jack couldn't recall the last time he'd held Joseph like this. Had to have been a few years ago, at least. Even after all that had gone down in the mountains, they hadn't had a moment like this. Similar moments. Comparable moments. But not anything quite as vulnerable as this.

Suddenly, an endless parade of memories started playing across Jack's mind's eye, transporting him back to life before. Before the cruise ship. Back to when Joseph was just a little child, always reaching to be held, always sleeping in his daddy's arms. And with those memories came the feelings associated with them. Feelings that seemed so precious now, but that had been completely unappreciated at the time.

Jack missed those days. And not in your typical "if only I had held on to those moments a little tighter" sort of way that most parents felt about the younger versions of their offspring, but something deeper, something more acute. No, he actually mourned the loss of them. It was a strange thing, Jack thought, to mourn the death of a child who was alive right beside you. Because that was what it felt like in a way—a death. And, god, he didn't mean to undermine the pain that parents went through who actually lost a child—hell, he knew what that was like, too, having lost Bethany.

But in a sense, standing on the threshold of time and watching little three-year-old Joseph curling his hair with his forefinger (Jack had forgotten he used to do that), it was impossible not to feel that kick in the gut that came with the realization that those days were gone. That that boy was gone. If only Jack could climb through the window of time and relive just a few moments of those days, to appreciate them for what they were in that moment. And that was the cruelty of it, wasn't it? That time had so slowly and gradually robbed him of that little boy that he hadn't even noticed it happening. Hadn't even known that it *had* happened until one day looking up from the daily grind and trying to find the little boy who liked to be flown like an airplane around the yard, who liked to somersault across the living room floor, who talked to himself in the mirror for hours. Who loved to play with the toy boats in the bathtub and line Matchbox cars up from one end of the driveway to the other. Who loved to sleep on his dad's chest during the Phillies games. Only then, when that boy was nowhere to be found, had Jack realized the awful truth. That Joseph, when Jack wasn't looking, had been switched out with an older, different version of his boy. It wasn't that he didn't love the ten-year-old version of his son. Or this fourteen-year-old version of his son. It was just that he so badly missed that other little boy.

Yet, Jack knew he would soon feel the same way about this version of Joseph, too. If given the chance, years from now, Jack would miss this kid just as much as he missed the three-year-old. So then what was the lesson for him now? He supposed it was to enjoy *this* moment and to appreciate it as best he could. To turn around and look the other way through that window and to give his future self a big thumbs-up, knowing they had at least done this part of Joseph's life right.

Jack blinked and looked back to the clouds. He knew that he could've never kept Joseph trapped in his three-year-old body. It wouldn't have been fair to him. No, Joseph needed to grow up so that he could experience for himself all the same moments that Jack now missed so badly.

But would he?

Jack ran his hand over Joseph's hair, hoping and praying that they would find a way out of all this. Jack wanted his son to be able to experience all the wonderful things life had to offer, even if the backdrop of such wonder would be a world going to hell faster than a speeding bullet. But there was nothing Jack could do about that part of it. That would be on Joseph to navigate. On Joseph's own children to navigate. And so forth and so on, just as it had always been.

If there was a future in store for Joseph, then Jack wanted to be there for as much of it as possible, and the thought of getting up from this seat and jumping out of the plane, never to see his boy again... It was too much.

His heart started to hammer harder, and suddenly he was having a hard time catching his breath. He closed his eyes, the reality of the situation bringing him to the edge of an anxiety attack. He wasn't sure if it was staring death in the face or the fact that death would rob him of knowing Joseph's own fate that had burning hot tears filling his eyes. He didn't want this moment to end. Yet he knew it would. In two hours. But two hours was not enough time. Not enough time at all.

He held Joseph tighter, and Joseph let him.

67

THE TWO MEN WHO had watched her shower and dress led Stacey back the way they had come. But though they took her to the same room with the geode-like rug, they did not escort her up the suspended walnut steps this time. Instead, they took her past the stairs, through the room, and all the way to a door at its back. The man with the scar opened the door, and the other nudged her through it.

As she stepped past the guard holding the door, she quickly considered making her move then. He would be completely taken by surprise, and she had no doubt that she'd be able to use his MAC on both him and the other guard before either of them knew what was even happening. She could then charge into the room with gun blazing. She wouldn't even have to worry about the ring. Then again, Fedyenka might shoot her before she got three feet into the room. No, she knew she only had one real chance at doing it right. And that she had to wait for it. She walked into the room.

She was greeted by a large table that had been set for two. The spread seemed a little obnoxious, like maybe Osprey Inc had its very own chef. Whatever it was, though, she couldn't deny that it smelled amazing. Her mouth watered, and her stomach growled so loud, she wondered if Fedyenka heard it.

He was standing directly ahead, facing her at the head of the long table. He had replaced the gray suit with another—this one a three-piece with a black shirt beneath. No tie. He wasn't that stupid. He watched her body move beneath the sequined dress, and Stacey could tell from the blatant lust gleaming in his eyes that he was enjoying what he saw. It became abundantly clear to her that all this food was just the appetizer, his real meal to come later.

"You look stunning," he said, motioning for her to take a seat in the only other chair at the table. He sat down in his.

She didn't respond, but she did sit.

Seven feet apart from each other and at opposite ends of the long table, he was taking no chances. Perhaps he thought that if they were to eat within arm's length of each other, she might try to surprise him, to get him all worked up and then slide into his lap, wrapping her arms around his neck and... *And what?* she thought. He didn't know about the poison, and she didn't see any knives on the table. No, he wasn't afraid of her. This was just his way of teasing himself. Foreplay.

She looked behind her just in time to see the doors close, the two men out of sight behind them.

"It must be four o'clock in the afternoon to you, and you probably haven't eaten anything since last night." He gestured at the spread. "Please help yourself."

Had she even eaten anything last night? She couldn't remember. She watched him pull a silver dome off the plate in front of him, revealing some kind of roasted meat atop vegetables in a kind of pastry bowl.

"What is it?" she asked. Not that she cared what it was. She'd happily scarf down raw goat testicles right now. She would let him feed her, and she would regain her strength. And it would be his own undoing.

"You do not remember?" he asked.

She frowned. Then she did remember. "Ratatouille tartlet with lamb." The three of them—she, Vadim, and Fedyenka—had gone to a restaurant in Moscow the night before she left for the States. There was a French menu the chef had put out, and they had all tried something new.

He smiled and put a forkful of meat in his mouth. As he chewed, he reached for a bottle of red wine.

Stacey shook her head. "And here I expected solyanka and vodka."

"Oh yeah? What else did you expect?" He poured the wine into a glass.

Stacey removed the lid off her own plate. "Oh, I don't know," she said, looking around the room. "Maybe something more along the lines of St. Petersburg, given your recent tsar obses-ssion."

"Rubbish," he said.

She reached for the bottle of wine that was set on her side of the table. "You know it, and I know it."

He took a generous sip from his glass and watched her take a bite of the lamb. It was just about the best thing she'd ever tasted, and she had to try very hard not to show it. She didn't want to give him that satisfaction.

She let him stare at her as she ate but knew that it would not be too long before he grew bored of using his eyes. She lifted the wineglass to her lips and drained its contents in one gulp, recall-ing as she did so those days between the three of them. Days that seemed forever ago. Like a dream, even. She recalled once more Fedyenka's subtle advances back then, behind Vadim's back, and again, as the wine went to her head, she shivered in the sequined dress, chills racing up and down her bare spine.

She poured herself another glass.

ABOUT TWELVE MINUTES, IF she had to guess, turned out to be the answer to her question—how long it would take him to become bored just looking at her.

Fedyenka got up from the table, most of his food eaten and two glasses of wine consumed, and walked over to her, tracing the fingers of his left hand along the length of the tablecloth as he approached.

His hands were huge, fingers like dildos. She thought that was a strange thought, and then she recalled that he used to joke about how the girls enjoyed them so much. In fact, she was pretty sure that one drunken night, he had held out his fingers and hollered out, "Edward Scissorhands, ha! The women call me Comrade Dildo Fingers!" Then he had stared at her as if hoping she would want to find out why. She had turned away from him, disgusted, but now here she was all these years later, probably about to find out anyway.

He had taken his jacket off when he stood, and she could see how muscled his forearms were even beneath the long sleeves of his shirt. If he got his hands on her throat, there would be no prying them off. She made a mental note not to waste her time trying to wrestle his fingers apart, but instead to go straight for his eyes, or to break his nose with the palm of her hand, or to grab his testicles. Anything other than the futile reaction her body would want to default to.

He stopped at the edge of the table, just three feet away.

Stacey played with the fork in her hand, contemplating whether or not there was anywhere other than an eye she could stick it. His neck was all knotted muscle, and she doubted she'd be able to puncture the artery. Besides, he'd already survived a bullet to the head, and she wasn't going to trust a fork to do what a bullet and an explosion couldn't.

"Take your best shot, if you must," he said, looking at the fork. "But I will fight back this time."

"Oh, I believe it," she said, laying the fork down next to her cleared plate. She looked up at him. "So what now?" And though she wanted to know why Fedyenka wanted Joseph so bad, she wanted to kill him even more. The answer to the question wouldn't really matter after he was dead, anyway. And she just wanted to get it over with.

He walked behind her and placed his hands on her shoulders. His palms seemed to swallow them. He squeezed and lifted, pulling her up to her feet. As soon as she was vertical, her head began to swim. She'd gotten up too fast. She stepped forward involuntarily, putting a hand out against the table to steady herself. The dinnerware rattled. She looked down at her feet, and watched the two of them blur into four.

She felt his hands slide down off her shoulders, taking the straps of the dress with them. Then she felt his hands on her breasts. She turned around to face him and looked up into his eyes, the dizzy spell subsiding for a moment. She looked down at his hands and watched as they squeezed her body. She let him. Better his hands were there than around her neck. Better they were filled with her skin than with a knife or a gun or a stick or whatever the hell else he might get pleasure out of using on her.

She put her hands on the table behind her, steadying herself and arching her back, puffing out her chest in open invitation. He made some kind of noise she thought was pleasure, and he began to squeeze harder. She moved her hands together and tried to get the cap off the ring. She wanted to have the needle exposed before he ripped the rest of her dress off. As soon as he bent down, she would whip her hand around and slap him right in the neck. Not down by his collarbone where it was all hard muscle, but by his jawline where she imagined his pulse could be felt.

But something was wrong.

It wasn't the wine that was making her dizzy. She leaned forward and tried stepping away from the table. "What did you pu—"

He shoved her backwards, hard. She landed on top of the table, sprawled out on her back and staring up at the ceiling. She could hear plates and glasses shattering against the floor, but it sounded like it was coming from another room. She tried to sit up, but couldn't. Couldn't do anything but look straight ahead. And then Fedyenka's face blocked the ceiling, filling her vision. He was looking down at her, a grin stretched across his scarred face.

BRIGHT LIGHT SHONE IN her face, and she closed her eyes. It surprised her because she hadn't even known that her eyes were open. She realized that she was on her stomach and wondered if she was still on the table or if she'd fallen onto the floor. She moved her fingers and was surprised to find them clutching what felt like fur up by her head. The tablecloth was not fur, so she couldn't be on the table. Had there been a rug on the floor? She didn't recall one.

She squinted into the light, and her brain told her that she was staring into windows across the room. Only there weren't any windows in the room she'd just been in. She blinked and managed to pull her elbows down to her sides. Her elbows seemed to sink into the floor a little. She slowly turned her head in the other direction, but ended up wrapping her face in her hair as she did so. She tried to see through it, but everything was a blur.

She heard movement beside her and felt the floor shake.

No, not a floor, she realized. She was in a bed.

And with that revelation came sobering clarity. Suddenly she was sore, her whole body aching. Her head, her chest, her back, her legs. Between her legs.

She used a hand to move her hair out of her face.

She saw a man sitting on the edge of the bed, his massive back facing her. His flesh looked to have been melted off his body and then slapped back on.

Fedyenka stood, naked, and walked over to a chair that contained his clothes.

Stacey rolled onto her side and cast her eyes down at her own body. She was naked, and the pain radiating from her lower half let her know all she needed to know about what had just happened. "You fuck," she murmured, pulling herself into a fetal position.

He turned and faced her. Smiled. She could see that he was still excited and could also see why she was so sore. The thing extended from him like William Wallace's broadsword in *Braveheart*. She closed her eyes, swearing to herself that the last thing she did to him would be to cut it off and ram it down his throat.

"I cannot say that you enjoyed that," he said. "Which surprises me, given all the fat politicians you must have had to screw over the years. Surely, you let yourself enjoy it a little." He shrugged. "Why would you not?" Then he turned back to his clothes. "It does not matter. You will learn to like it. They all do."

"Hey, Fedyenka," she said, her eyes barely open.

He stepped closer. "What is it, my dear?"

"You have the ugliest cock...I've ever seen in my life."

He looked at her for a second, and then his fist came crashing into her temple, and after a flash of white, everything went black.

68

JACK RAISED HIS CHIN to the ceiling and zipped the wet suit all the way to his Adam's apple. Johnson had his on already, along with the black snowsuit, winter parka, ski mask, and gloves that the pilots had gotten them. Apparently, skydiving in Alaska would be cold. Johnson was inspecting the soft valise that held the plane's inflatable aviation raft. A Kodiak would have been better, he'd said, but there hadn't been enough time for the pilots to make those kinds of arrangements.

The pilot on the right side of the cockpit leaned into the center console and looked back into the cabin at them. "Once you're out, we'll head south down the coast. We'll keep the plane in the hangar and watch over the boy for as long as we can."

Johnson gave the man a thumbs-up, then pulled a stack of green bills from the army bag they'd been carrying around. He stood and went to the cockpit, handing it to the pilots. "Thanks."

"I sure hope you know what you're doing," the pilot on the left said.

Johnson put a hand on his shoulder. "Yeah." Then he looked at his watch. "How much time?"

"We'll start descending in about five minutes."

Johnson nodded and walked back to Jack and the raft.

"You sure you're sure about this?" Jack asked.

Johnson smiled. "Why, do you have any other ideas?"

Jack shook his head.

"Then yeah, I'm sure. And you should be too." He slid the raft over against the door. "Finish getting dressed and then say goodbye to Joe. It's game time."

Jack swallowed.

As Johnson continued to get the rest of the gear together, Jack finished pulling on his own snowsuit and then slipped into the heavy coat. He went over to Joseph and said, "Mind helping me with these gloves?"

In a clear role reversal from what had been normal in the past, Joseph took one and held it out so that Jack could slide his hand into it. Jack smiled as he recalled Joe in a big marshmallow snowsuit, barely able to lower his arms to his sides, and asking for help getting his gloves and boots on before heading out into the snow. "Thanks," Jack said. He sat down next to Joseph.

Both of them sat in silence, neither knowing what to say. Maybe everything there was to say had already been communicated in their embrace.

Finally, Jack managed the dreaded words. "Guess it's that time." A hot tear leaked from the corner of his eye, and he felt it glide over his cheekbone. He struggled to find something to say, knowing that whatever words he settled on could very well turn out to be a father's last words to his son. Words that Joseph would carry with him for the rest of his life.

And then all the important conversations Jack had dreamed about having with Joseph over the next twenty or thirty years began flashing through his mind. In retrospect, perhaps he should have thought ahead and put all these conversations down in a journal, given them chapters for easy referencing. Like "Dating." Or "When your wife is pregnant." Or "Don't believe the news." Or "Always be there for your friends." Or "How to apply for a job." Or "How to pick the right college." There were so many.

Jack felt the plane descending and with it the realization that there might not be any more birthdays, Christmases, Thanksgivings, movie nights, baseball games, Stratego marathons...

"It's time," Johnson said.

"Wow," Jack whispered, looking at Joseph and smiling while he wiped his eyes with gloved fingers. "Five minutes already?"

Joseph leaned forward and threw his arms around Jack's neck. "I don't want you to go."

Jack felt his son's tears against his skin, and they triggered more of his own. "I don't want to either. But I have to. I have to get Mom." He felt Joseph nod his head in understanding.

"I know," Joseph said.

"We're going to get Mom back, and we're going to go somewhere safe, where we won't have to worry about any of this ever again." He pulled away from Joseph and saw the burning questions in those teenage eyes.

What about Priscilla, Tommy, Zane, Moses?

Jack didn't have an answer to that. At least not one he was going to articulate right now. He didn't want the last words to his son to be, "You can never see your friends again." Even if they both knew it.

Johnson walked over to them and held a parachute out to Jack. "Let's go."

Jack stood and slipped his arms through the straps, watching Joseph the whole time, absorbing every detail of his face.

"You'll be okay, right?" Johnson asked Joseph.

Joseph nodded. "Yeah."

"Good. So will we. We'll see you soon."

The pilot turned in his seat. "Sixty seconds."

Jack could see water instead of clouds out the window. He pulled Joseph up and gave him one last hug. "I love you."

"I love you, too," Joseph answered, squeezing as tight as he could against the big parka.

"Now buckle in," Johnson said to Joseph. "And get ready. It's about to get very cold in here."

Joseph sat back down and buckled himself in while Jack took the ski mask out of the coat's pocket and pulled it over his head.

Johnson made sure that Jack's pack was secure and then went to the door. He opened it, and freezing air came into the cabin like a hurricane. He looked at his watch. Then he looked at Jack. "You come right behind me," he shouted over the wind. "And you pull your chute as soon as you see me pull mine. Remember what we talked about. And remember your form when you hit the water."

Jack nodded.

Johnson picked up the case that held the raft, the army bag strapped to it, and jumped out of the plane. Jack stepped into the doorway next and turned his back to the open air, holding on to the sides of the plane and taking one last look at his son.

"Catch you later, dude!" he said in his best Ted "Theodore" Logan impersonation while playing a riff on his air guitar. Then he fell backward and into the blue.

JACK FELL THROUGH THE sky, wishing for the one piece of equipment the pilots seemed to have overlooked—goggles. He was squinting into the freezing air and could feel tears streaming into his hair beneath the ski mask. Soon his eyes were completely dry, and he was having trouble seeing Johnson below him. He kept blinking, but it didn't seem to help. He was waiting for Johnson to pull his chute, his eyes begging him to put an end to the crazy free fall. All below them was water, but he could make out a blur of land in the distance.

His heart was racing, but he could hardly feel it over the terminal velocity. *Terminal Velocity*. Another movie he'd have to subject Joseph to when this was all over. He was sure his son would enjoy a Charlie Sheen movie about former KGB agents, a Russian mobster, and a plot to overthrow Russia's new democratic government. *Damn*, he thought. If it weren't for the skin on his face feeling like it was being shaved off with frozen razors, he would have pondered the irony of the connection...and considered whether it was a glitch in the matrix.

Sixty seconds of free fall was what Johnson had told him, but he'd forgotten to count. Had it been sixty seconds? It felt like it had been six minutes. Johnson had explained that they were jumping lower than usual due to how cold the atmosphere was, so it was imperative that he—

Suddenly, a giant blue and yellow, squid-like creature jettisoned from Johnson's back, racing up and away from him but still clinging to his body with its long tentacles. The parachute opened and ballooned beneath Jack, flinging Johnson to the left with the wind and out of sight.

As Jack reached for his own cord, a sudden surge of panic hit him as he imagined his chute refusing to deploy. He'd have to try crashing into Johnson and grab hold of him like he'd seen in all the movies.

But then, suddenly and seemingly out of nowhere, someone hit the brakes and abruptly slowed his 120-to-150-mile-per-hour descent. He looked up and saw a similar dome hovering over him, though his jellyfish was red and green. *Holy crap*, he thought as he glided through the sky, *it worked.*

Now he just had to follow Johnson into the icy bath below. He tried to see up around the parachute, to get one last glimpse of the plane, but he couldn't spot it against the clouds.

He looked down at the water, and the panic returned. It wasn't the calmest body of water, and it looked freezing cold. He gritted his teeth and clenched every muscle in his body as the lapping water flew to meet his feet.

Splashdown.

Had he hit the water as Johnson instructed? He had no idea. All he knew was the freezing cold and a growing weight at his back. He couldn't move, couldn't think. He was paralyzed.

An old memory flashed before his mind's eye. Little League. Eight or nine years old. He'd finally gotten his first hit late in the season, every at bat up to that point had been a strike out. And then, finally, he'd smacked the ball with the aluminum bat, felt the ball fly off the barrel, and had somehow been aware of the ball skipping out of the infield and into right field. And then the next thing he knew, he was at first base. Only the first baseman was standing there with the ball already in his glove. He had no idea how that had even been possible, and as he turned to head back to the bench, completely missing everything that had happened between smacking the ball and then seeing it in the glove of the first baseman, his coach had patted him on the back, saying, "Good hit. Next time, try running to first base."

He was experiencing a similar sort of blackout now, his mind sort of numbed by what was happening. He tried to think, to get his brain moving again. To recall Johnson's instructions. There was something important that he was forgetting, but what? He got his feet kicking and concentrated on keeping his head above the water. That was a start. And then something tugged at his back, jerking his head beneath the water, and he remembered.

Quickly, he moved his hands to the pack, desperately trying to free himself of the parachute. Either it would fill with water and start to sink, pulling him down with it, or it would get caught in the current and drag him away from Johnson. Or he'd find himself tangled beneath it and drown. None of those scenarios were any good. He fumbled with the gloves' waterlogged fingers, beginning to lose the feeling in his hands. Finally, he was able to slip out of the pack. He swam away from the giant jellyfish and its dangling arms.

Where was Johnson? He looked around, the waves lapping up and into his eyes, but couldn't see him against the horizon.

A loud hissing noise erupted nearby, and he spun around, looking back across the floating chute. He saw a flash of yellow and knew it was the raft inflating. He must've gotten turned around and started swimming off in the wrong direction. Because Johnson was on the other side of the chute. It would take forever in the parka and snowsuit for Jack to swim around it, so he started waving his hands over his head and waited. He tried to float on his back, but his boots kept pulling his feet down. His body was growing numb, and the waterlogged clothes were getting heavier.

He heard splashing and knew it was Johnson paddling toward him. He took one last desperate look into the sky, but of course there was no sign of the plane. Of Joseph. He was gone. Maybe forever.

"Hang on," he heard Johnson shout over the waves.

Jack saw the yellow raft coming for him overtop the parachute. He couldn't feel his legs anymore and wasn't sure if he was still kicking or not. Then, suddenly, he was under the water and looking up at the surface. The daylight shimmered in distorted fun house mirrors. He could see his own arms stretching up past his head as if trying to grasp another world just out of reach.

And then a shadow blocked the light, and Johnson's distorted face appeared, his hands breaking through the Jell-O-like glass divide and grabbing onto Jack's left hand.

"We don't have time for this," he heard Johnson mutter as he pulled him up and into the raft.

69

STACEY OPENED HER EYES and could immediately tell that her position had changed. She was sitting now. Maybe standing. She knew because her chin was resting on her chest, and she had to use the muscles in her neck to lift her head.

It was a chair.

She could tell by the way her arms were bent, could feel her forearms running along cold metal, her wrists bound. She blinked her world into focus and felt the pain where Fedyenka had struck her. She looked ahead and squinted, unsure of what she was seeing. Then she understood. She was looking at herself.

The room she was in now was lined with mirrors, just like in the elevator. Moving her head around and taking in the room, she wondered if this was some other sex thing. Was round two about to commence with every available angle on display?

She examined the reflection in the mirror, attempting to grasp her situation. She was naked, which was no surprise. She was still sore between her legs, but the coldness of the metal chair was soothing. She still had the ring on. Her ankles were strapped to the chair legs, but the chair itself didn't appear to be fastened to the floor in any way. But...

She leaned forward, feeling the restriction around her neck even as she fought to get a good look at it in the mirror. *What the hell...*

She was wearing some kind of collar. *Dammit, Fedyenka...* Was it a bondage thing? An act of dominance? Would he have her walking around on her hands and knees like a dog? She tried to figure out just what kind of collar it was, hoping it wasn't a choker.

"Do you like it?" Fedyenka's voice boomed from behind her as he entered the room.

She watched him walk toward her in the reflection. He was fully clothed.

"I can't believe you drugged me," she said, perhaps attempting at some subconscious level to appeal to their earlier, friendlier days. "Pussy."

He smiled. "That was just to break you in. You won't always be unconscious. Believe me, I prefer it better when you fight. And even more when you no longer bother."

"That'll be the day."

He reached over and grabbed a handful of her hair, yanking her head back before thrusting it forward toward the mirror. He bent over so that his cheek was rubbing against hers. "Look."

She met his stare in the mirror and watched as he brushed the collar encircling her neck with his other hand.

"It's a bomb collar," he said.

Stacey's stomach dropped, and her asshole clenched involuntarily.

"That's right," Fedyenka said, able to sense her reaction. "It can only be released by a combination, and I am the only one who knows the combination. So if you were to kill me..."

She swallowed, feeling the swell in her throat press against the collar.

"It is also calibrated to a specific frequency. Stray too far from the transmitter..." He shoved her head forward again, releasing her hair. "Boom."

At first, Stacey thought that she'd underestimated him, and she cursed herself for being so stupid. He had trapped her. But as the fear and initial panic melted away, she saw things more clearly, and she had to fight to keep from smiling. "What happens if I try to take it off?"

"Without the combination, it is impossible." He traced the soft skin of her neck with his fingers. "Though I suppose if you were truly desperate and had a metal grinder or a torch, you might try removing it that way. If you were not too concerned with destroying your lovely neck."

"And if I enter the wrong combination?"

"I have ensured that a wrong combination would be quite deadly."

Inwardly, she did smile. It was Fedyenka who had miscalculated, underestimating her commitment to her son. Perhaps he was misinterpreting the situation with the senator, thinking the reason she hadn't tried blowing herself up as instructed was because she didn't want to die. And at the time, he was probably right to assume so. Hell, until that moment when her conscience decided to rise out of the permafrost, she would never have disregarded her instructions for the reasons she had. But it wasn't because of self-preservation that she wouldn't sacrifice herself for her son, it was because, suddenly, she hadn't been able to sacrifice all the innocent people around her *for* her son—something that was apparently as improbable to Fedyenka now as it had been to her moments before she'd realized it herself. No, she had no problem sacrificing herself for her family if she knew that her sacrifice would truly set them free. And Fedyenka had given her the perfect weapon to do just that. She thought it slightly amusing that her story would end with a suicide bomb after all.

She tried to get a better look at the device, but couldn't make out anything across its front at this distance. She guessed the buttons were in the back, at the base of her neck. Or at least she hoped they were. If the thing operated like a garage door, and the code had to be punched in via remote, then she'd have to find the remote.

She closed her eyes, deciding there was no sense in thinking about it now. Not until her hands were free and she could feel the collar with her fingers. She still had the ring and figured that should be her plan A, if only for the sole reason of watching him die. It was possible that the explosives in the collar were only strong enough to sever her neck. She'd have to find a way to have his face pressed against it when and if the time came. Given what he had in store for her, she didn't think that should be too difficult.

She opened her eyes and steeled herself for whatever the next mode of torture was to be.

"As much fun as it has been and will be," Fedyenka said, again reaching down and groping a breast, "I really must know where your son is." He squeezed, his huge hand like a vise. Or a malfunctioning mammogram.

"I don't know where he is," she hissed, fighting against the pain.

He squeezed harder.

"Do you think I'd put myself in that position?" she asked. "To even know?" But that was the drug talking, wasn't it? She cursed her mental slip. She should be convincing him that she *did* know where he was. If she didn't know, then she was no good to him, and the only use he'd have for her would be personal in nature and only for so long as it interested him. If he decided that he believed her and killed her before she could get close enough...

He released her breast, and she could see in the mirror his handprint still lingering. It was bright red, but would certainly turn yellow and purple later on.

Fedyenka walked around in front of her, facing her. He stood there staring. First into her face, and then all over her body. She could tell he was growing excited again.

"It really is a fair offer," he said. "I would protect him. Raise him as my own. He would be safe." He shrugged. "What is the alternative? Either the CIA or the FSB will eventually find him and kill him. Even if you want to dream of some sort of escape, surely that escape would be from me in some future he is still alive in." He stepped closer to her and bent over, resting his hands on her knees. He knelt down in front of her and pushed her legs apart. "I really don't see how you have a choice in this." He ran his hand down the inside of her thigh.

Suddenly, she thought of something. And her eyes must have betrayed it, because Fedyenka stood and smiled as a result. He reached into his pocket and pulled something out of it. "Yes," he said. "Look what I found." He held up the capsule the man on the plane had given her.

She swallowed, part of her relieved that the thing wasn't still in her and requiring a surgical procedure to extract. Then again, she wasn't planning on living long enough for that to be a problem, anyway.

"It is empty," he said. "But I wonder if it was not always empty."

It was a good thing she'd swallowed her paper-wrapped engagement ring. If she had put the paper back in the capsule… "It's where I keep my blow," she said.

He grinned. "Sure it is."

"Why do you want Joseph?" she asked again.

He looked down at her, his expression suddenly growing bored. "Oh, stop it already." He looked around and gestured to their surroundings, to the audience of only their reflected selves. "There is no one here you need to pretend for, and you know that I know. So how about we stop with the games, okay?"

Her brow furrowed in confusion, but at the same time a knot began to form in her stomach. "I don't know what you think you—"

But her words were cut off by the sound of a loud bang somewhere in the compound. The floor shook. One of the mirrors cracked. Dust drifted down from the ceiling.

Without another word, Fedyenka turned and quickly left the room.

Another explosion sounded, and the mirror in front of Stacey splintered, fragmenting her naked image into a kaleidoscope of confused faces.

70

JOSEPH TRIED NOT TO think of all the things that could've gone wrong with his dad's first ever skydiving experience. Instead, he wondered how long he might have to stay in this plane before someone realized no one was actually coming for him. But that wasn't a thought he wanted to dwell on either, so he reached for his earbuds. But just before he pushed them into his ears, he heard a few stray words drift into the cabin from the cockpit. He couldn't make out exactly what the two men were talking about, but something about their tone of voice set his Spidey senses tingling.

Then he felt the plane start to turn and looked out the window. The left wing was dipping. They were turning. But they had already turned right after his dad had jumped and they closed the door. They'd turned south and were following the coastline down toward Washington with the ocean on Joseph's right. So if they had turned left before in order to head south, and they were now turning right...

He watched the ground below until the plane leveled out. Now the ocean was to his left, land to the right. Which meant they'd just turned around and were now heading north. Or maybe northwest. But why would they be heading in that direction? The last thing the pilot had told Agent Johnson was that they would be landing in Washington.

Northwest...

He set aside the earbuds.

Something was wrong. Agent Johnson had no way of contacting the pilots that Joseph knew of, so they couldn't be acting on any new commands coming from him or his dad. Could they have gotten orders from some command center to land else-where? Were they in restricted airspace? Had they not logged a flight plan and some air traffic controller was wondering what they were doing there? Was NORAD about to blow them out of the sky? Joseph had no idea how any of that worked, and decided to go see if he could figure out what was happening.

He got up and walked toward the cockpit. As he came up on the closet, he noticed that Agent Johnson had left it open. He could see the remaining two parachutes sitting in the open case against the wall. He supposed they were for the pilots in the case of an emergency. Or, he feared, maybe they had always planned to double-cross them, and they were going to jump out of the plane themselves, leaving Joseph to crash and burn. But he was pretty sure the Russian guy wanted him alive. So could they be working for the Russian government or the CIA? Joseph really didn't understand what was going on despite his dad's best efforts to fill him in. Agent Johnson seemed to know them and trust them, so that theory didn't seem too plausible.

The two pilots were still talking to each other and not paying any attention to Joseph, so Joseph knelt, pretending to tie a shoe in case they looked back. He reached inside the closet and grabbed one of the chutes out of the case, whipping it around to his left where it couldn't be seen from the cockpit.

He got back to his feet and stepped forward, placing his hands on either side of the cockpit door and leaning his head in. He still couldn't hear what they were whispering about, but whatever it was, he could tell they weren't happy about it. Something about "new orders" and "who knows" and "not our concern" and "sell out" and again "not our problem" and "what choice do we have?" Even at fourteen, thanks to movies and his family's more recent history, he had no trouble filling in the gaps. These guys were following orders they didn't like, but felt they had no choice in the matter. He cleared his throat, and both pilots appeared to jump out of their skins.

"Hey, little man," one said, trying to recover.

"Need anything?" the other asked.

"No," Joseph said. "How long before we get to Washington?"

He saw the two pilots exchange an uncomfortable glance.

The one on the left answered, "Oh, about two and a half hours or so."

Joseph forced his best smile, making sure that it seemed like forced politeness, because after all he'd just been through, anything other than forced manners would seem suspicious. "It's still a little cold back there from the door being opened. Can I grab a blanket?"

"Yeah, there should be one in the closet right there," the pilot on the left said, nodding back behind him.

"Thanks." He turned and went to the cabin, grabbing a stack of folded blankets and taking them back into the cabin with him. He sat in the seat closest to the bathroom, and when he was sure the pilots weren't looking, he took the blankets into the bathroom.

He got to work quickly. He wanted to do this while they were still over Alaska and as far south as possible. It might get colder the farther north they went, and he knew that wouldn't be a good thing, either in the air or on the ground.

He pulled his pants down to his ankles and began wrapping his legs with two of the blankets. They weren't thick blankets like on his bed at home (he had no home, he realized, but pushed the thought away). These were thinner, smaller. He wrapped them around his calves and thighs as tight as possible so that he could still get his pants up over them. It was a tight fit, but he was able to get his pants back on. Then he took off his shirt and started to wrap two more blankets over his shoulders, making an X out of them before wrapping them around his chest and tucking them into themselves. He pulled his shirt and sweatshirt back on over top.

He walked back to his seat, concealing his bulky movement beneath one of the remaining blankets, which he'd draped around his shoulders. He grabbed his backpack and made his way to the seat nearest the cabin door. He took Hugh out and discreetly used it to cut a slit into one of the blankets. Then he slipped his backpack on backwards so that it was resting against his chest. He looked out the window. There was still land down there, but up ahead was only blue water. It was now or never.

He had left the bathroom door closed so that if the pilots looked back and didn't see him, they would assume he was still in there. He pivoted out of the seat and went to the cabin door. Reaching down for the parachute he'd positioned there, he dropped the remaining blankets, pulling the pack onto his back and quickly adjusting the straps so that they were tight. He wanted to make sure he wouldn't slip out of the pack.

He then picked up the blanket he'd cut and wrapped it around his head and face so that the slit aligned with his eyes. He used to do this with long-sleeve T-shirts when pretending to be a ninja, tying the sleeves into a knot at the back of his head. The blanket didn't have sleeves, though, so he twisted the back into a rope, wrapped the tail around his neck and tucked the end down his shirt. He figured it was better than nothing.

He had paid special attention to everything Agent Johnson and his dad did. He had watched how they opened the door, had watched them fall through the sky, even counting the seconds until seeing their chutes deploy. He'd taken in all the instructions Johnson had given his dad about opening the chute, what to do when hitting the water, etc. Though Joseph didn't plan on landing in the water. Not if he could help it. Which was why he needed to go now. Even if he survived a water landing, he had no wetsuit or snowsuit or winter jacket or gloves. He'd probably freeze to death before he could even get to shore, but even if he did manage to drag himself onto dry land, he knew he'd be a human Popsicle within minutes.

He opened the door and launched himself into the freezing atmosphere before the pilots even knew what was happening.

71

STACEY ROCKED THE CHAIR from left to right, trying to get it to tip over. If she could just get the chair's front legs off the ground a little, then maybe she could slip the straps around her ankles beneath them. She tried again. The chair was heavy, and she felt weak. It barely moved. She tried again and again, each time throwing her body to the side, leaning with her head. The left legs came off the floor for half a second. She tried again, all the many reflections seeming to laugh at her efforts. But then she got the chair up onto its right legs, and the heavy thing seemed to just teeter there. Somehow, she'd managed to find the perfect balance. Like a stunt driver getting a car up on its side, riding on two wheels, she found herself hovering at a forty-five-degree angle, suspended between going all the way over and retu rning back to where she started. She leaned her head as far to the right as she could, and it was just enough to force the issue, tipping the scales and allowing gravity to do its thing.

The chair went over, and the impact sent a jolt through her entire body, the restraints on her ankles and wrists digging into her skin. She located the doorway that Fedyenka had retreated through in one of the mirrors and saw that it was empty. She tried to move her feet, to work the strap down and over the wooden legs, but it was too tight. She kept trying, but the bonds only bit her back.

Noise came from outside the room. Footsteps. Not running, but not walking either. She slid her ass as far forward as she could and tried one last time to stretch her feet past the chair legs, but it was no use.

Then, duplicated in the mirrors, she saw two of Fedyenka's stooges enter the room. At least she thought there were two. There could be eight of them, but if so, half of them were in some perfectly timed choreography, their every move perfectly mimicked by each other. Four pistols coming up in the same hand at the same time and at the same exact angle. Four other pistols simultaneously followed a different pattern.

What was happening? she wondered. Had the SVR found them, and now Fedyenka thought it best just to have her out of the way? One less problem to worry about? She was about to open her mouth, to say something—though she had no idea what—when the two men and all their duplicates (multiplying even more when their reflections passed through the splintered glass) were suddenly off their feet and flying forward through the air, their chests puffed out and their arms back behind them as if they'd been struck in the back with Nordic sledgehammers.

They landed on their faces and didn't move, their hands turned out, fingers curled into the air. They were either unconscious or dead.

Stacey strained her neck, trying to get a clear view of the doorway for herself. Finding one, she watched as a silhouette slowly began to take shape in it. Finally, a clear image emerged, albeit sideways and almost upside down from her position on the floor. Entering the room was a man with a silenced MP5 held tight against his shoulder, and for a second she thought that it might be Jack, as impossible as that would be. But then the light from the room fell on the person's face, and she saw that it was actually the man from the plane. The man who had slipped the poisoned ring into her body. Who had given her the blanket.

He stepped over the dead bodies and knelt beside the chair. Withdrawing a knife from an ankle sheath, he quickly snapped her restraints. She rolled out of the chair and onto her stomach before crawling to her knees.

The man whipped a backpack off his shoulders and pulled something black and shiny out of it. "Here," he said, handing it to her. "It's all I could find. Fedyenka's got a thing for leather, I guess."

She took it from him.

"Hurry," he said.

There was no use being shy in front of him. He'd already seen her naked on the plane and had practically become a second gynecologist to her. So without a word—there was no time for them—she stood and worked to get the leather Trinity outfit on. She saw that he was staring at her body as she wiggled into the thing, but she knew he wasn't looking at her tits. Rather he was taking note of all the recent injuries that mapped the canvas of her body. The red scrapes painted against purple and yellow bruising.

"Sorry, I couldn't git here sooner," he said.

She zipped the one-piece all the way up. It was snug in all the right places, and she wondered if Fedyenka had picked it out just for her or if all the women in the painting fit a specific body type. It was one of a thousand thoughts flying through her head that were not important right now.

"What about this?" she said, pointing at the bomb collar around her neck. "He said I can't get too far from the transmitter—"

He cut her off. "He ain't goin' nowhere without you."

She shook her head. "He doesn't need me. He knows I don't know where my son is." She watched his eyes as he considered it.

"We'll figure it out," he said. "But we gotta move now." He grabbed the pistol from one of the dead men and handed it to her. While she checked it, he took the pistol from the second man and tucked it into the back of his pants. Then he took both submachine guns from their backs, slinging one over his shoulder and handing the other to her.

"No shoes?" she said, looking down at her bare feet.

He shook his head. "Sorry."

She looked at the two men sprawled before her and took note of their shoes. She knew they were too big. She'd be running around like Ronald McDonald in them.

"Take one of their radios," the man said. He already had one on his hip.

Stacey bent over the nearest body and snatched the walkie-talkie. The leather suit had no pockets, so she unzipped it down to the swell of her chest and slipped the radio beneath it, clipping it over the zipper. Then she quickly took the shoelace from one of the guys' boots and used it to tie her hair into a high ponytail.

"Ready?" the man asked.

She nodded and followed him out of the room, trying to avoid stepping in broken glass.

STACEY MOVED QUICKLY THROUGH an area of the compound that she hadn't yet seen, following the man from the plane down one concrete corridor after another, passing closed doors on their right and left. She wondered how he knew where he was going, how he knew where to find her, but she didn't dare ask him now. As long as she had a bomb around her neck, she had no choice but to trust him.

A man in winter fatigues rounded the corner fifteen feet ahead, coming face-to-face with them. But he was obviously not expecting to run into an adversary because he was carrying his rifle across his body, the barrel pointing at the wall beside him rather than aimed at any possible threat ahead. While he struggled to bring the gun around, the man from the plane put two suppressed bullets into his chest. Then he put another into his head as they walked past him and to the end of the corridor.

Just before going around the corner where the Osprey agent had come from, the man stopped and turned toward her. "There ain't much cover out there. Be ready. Shoot anythin' that moves."

She nodded and raised the MAC-11, her leather arms squeaking as she did so.

He led them out and into the next room, Stacey right on his back shoulder. But it wasn't a room that they found themselves in, rather they were on a balcony that wrapped around some sort of atrium. There was another wraparound balcony above, connected by a set of stairs across from them. But it wasn't the main lobby that was beneath them, as one would suppose. There were none of the huge windows overlooking the water here. There were no windows at all as far as she could tell.

She walked out to the railing, her eyes up on the level above, expecting a gun to appear over the side at any moment. When none materialized, she leaned over the railing and looked down. There were more dimly lit balconies below, each connected by a short set of steps. She frowned. Stairs descended from the lowest balcony, spiraling down and disappearing into a dark void. "What the hell is this?" she asked the man. But she knew, didn't she? The balconies were just an attempt to disguise it.

But before he could give her an answer, a gun did appear over the railing above them.

Stacey swore and jumped back from the railing as the deafening *crack-crack-crack* of an AK-47 rebounded back and forth through the cylindrical space. She ran back for the corridor as bullets chewed into the concrete balcony and ricocheted off the metal banister. The man from the plane returned fire, spraying the balcony above with fire from the MP5. At least one of his shots must've found their target because a body suddenly toppled over the banister. It fell past them, striking another banister two levels below and rebounding off into the center of the shaft. It continued to fall until swallowed by darkness. A couple of seconds later, they heard a sickening smack echo back to them.

"Let's go," the man shouted. He followed the balcony around to the other side and to the stairs that connected the other levels.

Stacey ran after him. "Where are we going?"

He glanced back at her, and though he didn't say anything, his eyes answered her question. He wasn't exactly sure.

Great, she thought. But he had a better idea than she did. He had known where she was and how to get there. And if he was the one who had planted the explosives she'd heard, then he had to at least have a basic understanding of the layout of this place. She again wondered who he could be. Was he FBI? CIA? Had to be someone on the inside. And if so, then surely he would have already sent word about what Fedyenka was doing here, what the Russian madman had built inside this Alaskan hillside.

But if he had, then why hadn't it already been dealt with? Once more, she forced all the questions out of her head and focused her attention on following the man down the stairs, the whole time certain that the necklace was tightening.

72

JOSEPH COUNTED OFF THE seconds in his head, though it took every ounce of concentration he had to do so. The thrill of the jump was almost overwhelming, the adrenaline rush unlike anything he'd ever felt before. It was like the best part of a roller coaster only it wasn't ending. And the view... The snowcapped mountains and winding rivers below filled him with a sense of awe he wasn't prepared for. It was an existential experience. In a way he couldn't describe, the majesty of it filled him with a warm sort of peace that made him forget his numb fingers and ignore his frozen tears. And he thought that if his chute didn't open at all, that would be just fine. Such an experience would be worth the ultimate price of admission.

The scenery below seemed to remain fixed, not getting any closer at all despite how fast he was falling. And he had no words to describe what that felt like. But then, very quickly, that changed, and those snow-covered peaks began to grow, and the autumn carpet crystallized into individual trees. Now the ground was coming fast, and he felt like Johnny Utah in *Point Break* during his first jump. *Would "euphoria" be the right word?* And then more scenes came to mind. *Eraser, Reign of Fire, Get Smart, Mission: Impossible — Fallout,* and plenty of WWII movies where paratroopers ended up dangling from tree branches.

But despite all of that, the clock in his head was able to coordinate with his dad's own deployment. As he pulled the chute, he could only hope that the plane's altitude had been in the same ballpark as when his dad and Agent Johnson jumped from it. Because if it had been much higher or lower... Then what? He could hardly bring himself to care.

The parachute unwound above him, the harness tightening around his chest and shoulders as the wind filled the canopy. And suddenly, he was no longer flying through the air on his stomach, arms and legs spread-eagle. Now he was dangling feet-first and on his way down an invisible escalator. He tried to spot a clearing below that he could aim for. Lights out at the end of an extreme adrenaline rush was one thing; getting caught in trees and having your dangling feet nibbled on by grizzlies was something completely different.

He spotted a snow-covered area free of trees and rocks and hoped it wasn't a lake. Crashing through ice and drowning, his body never to be found, was also not one of his preferred ways to go.

He swooped down over the clearing and briefly wondered what the impact would be like. He'd seen videos of people landing in a sort of casual walk—like just stepping off that invisible escalator—but he'd also seen people crash so hard that they broke bones.

And then, before he knew it, his feet were in the snow, jogging along at a leisurely pace. *Nailed it*, he thought, proud of himself and wishing his dad (or Priscilla) could have seen it.

The blue and red chute was drifting across the ground ahead of him, and he slowed to a stop and sat down to keep it from pulling him over. There was a slight breeze that was filling the canopy, but it wasn't strong enough to drag him. He freed himself from the pack and then slipped out of his school bag. Only then did he notice that the blanket around his head was gone. He touched his ears and couldn't feel them at all. He figured that probably wasn't good, though there was nothing he hated more than cold ears and fingers. If they had to be this cold, then he was glad he couldn't feel them.

The parachute pack began to move away from him, carried by the wind. He wondered if he should go after it, if he would need it. Could he use it as a blanket? Or as a tent maybe? He figured it was better to have it and not need it than to need it and not have it, so he got to his feet, slung his backpack onto his back, and ran down the gliding pack. He felt like a giant marshmallow running after it with the blankets packed down his pants.

He picked up the pack and waddled over to the canopy, looking up at the sky as he did so, wondering if the pilots had circled back to look for him. But he didn't see any signs of the plane. In fact, as he took in his more immediate surroundings, he didn't see any signs of anything.

And then he felt the cold through his shoes. In his face. His nose and cheeks. His fingers. He realized he could already have frostbite. He needed to get a fire going ASAP, wouldn't survive the night without one. He wrapped the parachute cord around his elbow and then bunched the canopy into a giant ball. He tied part of the cord around it and tried stuffing it back into the pack. He managed to get half of it in, the other half sticking out the top.

Then he found the tree line and started walking.

I've done this before, he told himself.

Yeah, that was West Virginia in the summer, he shot back at himself. *This is the Alaskan wilderness in November!*

The snow crunched under his feet, the sun glaring off its surface and hurting his eyes. He hoped that jumping from the plane had been the right thing to do, but there was no use thinking about it now. He put one foot in front of the other, each step bulky and awkward.

He kept his eyes on the tree line, praying—yes, actually praying to Jesus—that there were no wolves watching him with hungry eyes.

73

JACK STARED THROUGH THE veil of steam clouds escaping his mouth and scanned the shore ahead. Johnson was seated behind him and paddling the raft, navigating away from the building's line of sight. The huge building gleamed in the afternoon sun, sitting atop a bluff at the end of an inlet. Approaching it straight on in an open sea would have probably brought their mission to an abrupt end, so they were circumnavigating to the left side of the inlet, where Jack could see nothing but rocks and tall trees awaiting them. They could only hope that Osprey watchmen weren't posted outside the inlet, and that once ashore, they would be able to make it through the woods and to the top of the bluff undetected. It wasn't a great plan. Hell, it was probably a terrible plan, but it was all they had. Jack tried not to think about how it was a miracle they were even here at all and how many more miracles they'd need to pull this off.

"See anything?" Johnson asked over the sound of the paddle dipping into the water.

Jack didn't see any sentries along the shoreline or posted in the trees, and the fact that neither of their heads had been blown off already suggested that there weren't any. "No," he called back through chattering teeth.

When they got within ten feet of the shoreline, Johnson stopped paddling and hopped out of the raft, the icy water reaching his knees. Jack jumped out too, and the two of them pulled the boat to shore.

"Let's hide it in the woods," Johnson said, nodding ahead.

They pulled it until the stones gave way to grass and they were in the shade of towering evergreens.

"Should we cover it?" Jack asked.

"No time." Johnson pulled his gloves off and pulled the army bag out of the raft, unzipping it. He pulled out Jack's MP7A2 and handed it to him. Then he pulled out the M&P 15T that Stacey had used at the farm, and rezipped the bag. He lifted it out of the raft and slung it over his shoulder. And then he was on the move, pulling his gloves back on and heading for the steep incline that led up through the trees and to Stacey.

Jack followed after him, his heart pounding. It was uncomfortable hiking in the wetsuit, and the soaked snowsuit on top of it only added to the awkwardness of it. He felt like a medieval knight weighed down by a hundred pounds of soggy armor.

He worked his way up the steep incline, trying to keep up with Johnson, his teeth chattering so hard, he thought they might crack and tumble out of his mouth like Chiclets.

74

JOSEPH FOUND IT INTERESTING, the different and seemingly random roads his mind had him traveling. Sometimes he was focused on the task at hand, a four-lane highway heading for some major city of revelation pertinent to his predicament, and then suddenly he was on an offramp to some town he'd never heard of before. There seemed to be no rhyme or reason as to which way he was turning. But before long, paved roads marked by big signs had led to gravel roads, gravel roads to dirt roads, and dirt roads finally to a labyrinth of nameless footpaths and switchbacks in some remote wilderness of misfit thoughts, no idea how he'd gotten there and no chance in hell of retracing his steps.

Currently, he was thinking about the smell of hot dogs, and for the life of him couldn't fathom why. When he realized it, he shook that ridiculous idea from his head and began searching for a route back to relevance.

He found one that at least made sense given his immediate surroundings, though it proved to be uneasy company: bears. But more specifically, the scene in *Michael Strogoff* where Michael fights off the bear. Joseph didn't think he'd be able to fight off a bear. Not with his bare hands. Not even with Hugh. He needed to find something that he could use as a weapon if he was to stand any chance of surviving a run-in with an Alaskan predator. Something long that would keep an animal at least an arm's length away.

He abandoned the demolition derby of random thoughts and instead focused on searching the ground for branches that he could make into a spear. Like the one he'd made before. Like the one he'd stabbed that man in the woods with.

He turned in the direction of the sun and tried once more to get a bearing on which direction he was heading. He didn't want to be heading west. Or northwest. The Bering Strait was that way. And Russia. He wanted to be heading east or south. But then, at the same time, he couldn't really risk running into anyone who might have caught the national news in the last few days. After deciding on a heading, he continued on, cupping his hands and blowing warm air into them. A hundred yards later, and about twenty yards into the woods, he found his stick.

He picked it up and swung it against a nearby tree, testing to see if it was rotten or not. The sound of the impact echoed around him, and the hollowness of it, the way it seemed to stretch on forever through the forest, filled him with a sudden sense of loneliness. He shivered. He was truly alone out here. But loneliness was good if it meant the absence of people trying to kill him.

The stick didn't shatter against the tree, but bounced heartily off it. He crouched down and used Hugh to whittle the tip of the branch into a point. As he did so, leaning against the tree for support, his mind once more started traveling down highways of intersecting thoughts. But he was traveling in a bumper car that kept colliding with another one over and over again.

The bumper car he was in was about *Michael Strogoff* and why the Russian guy would have wanted him to read it. Had it been some kind of threat? Or was it meant to foster some kind of imperial pride, making a hero out of someone who had been loyal to the tsar? But why should that matter to the guy, whether he felt any such way about any particular politic? Regardless of whatever motivation had put the book in his locker, he would draw inspiration from it now.

Casting aside any political aspirations or government allegiance, he would simply revisit as best he could how Michael had survived crossing Siberia. He would try to recall everything he'd ever read about survival and bushcraft, had ever seen in a movie, and he would find a way to make it through yet another wilderness alone.

The other bumper car that kept crashing into these thoughts was being driven by the man he had stabbed with his spear back in the Appalachian Mountains. Had the wound he'd inflicted been a mortal one? Had he actually taken a human life? He didn't know, and a big part of him didn't want to know.

He worked the razor-sharp edge of the knife against the wood, watching as long strands curled up over the blade, trying not to see it puncturing a man's flesh, muscle, and bowels.

75

JACK ARMY-CRAWLED UP BESIDE Johnson. They had made it up through the woods undetected and were now lying at the edge of a clearing, careful to stay just inside the tree line. Ahead of them was a large clearing, and the building stood right in the middle of it.

"I don't see any guards," Johnson said, his eyes scanning the scene.

Jack didn't either. "Could we be in the wrong place?"

Johnson pulled out the tablet and brought up the display. The dot that was Stacey was glowing just a few hundred yards from them. "No, this is the place," he said. He put the device away, replacing it with a monocular from the pocket of his snowsuit. He looked through it, searching for any sign of activity. "That's interesting," he muttered.

"What?"

"Missiles on the roof." He swung the monocular to the left. "Helipad." He went quiet for a while, the scope drifting back toward the right. "There," he said. "Northwest corner."

Jack's mind spun as he tried to figure out where northwest was. It took him a few seconds to flip everything around in his mind, the water to the west, them looking south. Johnson handed him the monocular, and he looked through it for himself, spotting the single sentry standing at the corner of the concrete building. The guy was in a black suit and holding a submachine gun in his hands. Jack thought he looked nervous in the magnified lens. And then movement to his left drew Jack's eye, and he saw another guard positioned closer to them, walking from out of the trees and heading toward the building. He was in black fatigues and moving with a quick sense of urgency. "There," Jack said to Johnson, pointing out the walking sentry.

Johnson didn't need the monocular to see the guy. He jumped to his feet, pulled a knife from inside his boot, and took off running.

Jack raised the MP7, ready to lay down some cover fire if needed. But whatever had the guy heading back to the base so quickly must have been the only thing on his mind, because he never even looked behind him. Never heard Johnson, the snow-suit *swish-swish-swishing*, racing up behind. At least not until it was too late to do anything about it.

Standing over the corpse, Johnson waved Jack over to him, signaling for him to leave the trees and to cross the field. For now, they seemed out of the other guard's periphery, but if he decided to shift his location...

Jack didn't hesitate and sprinted awkwardly across the open grass. He looked up at the building looming over them three hundred yards away; its blackout windows seemed to be staring directly at him, making him feel naked and exposed. He slid to a stop alongside Johnson, who was kneeling over the dead guard and working him out of his uniform. Jack saw blood all over the ground, but the guy's uniform looked unscathed. "You're doing this here?" Jack asked.

"I heard an explosion. Something's happening in there," Johnson responded.

Jack looked up to the building, but it just stood there dumb and silent.

"Go get the guard." Johnson nodded toward the building. "Take his suit. Be quick about it. They may have called for backup."

Jack hesitated.

"C'mon," Johnson hissed, "Now is our only chance. Whatever is happening has them focused inward. And it's probably Stacey that's happening. She needs our help, Jack!"

Jack snapped out of his stupor, shaking off the absurdity of what they were doing and that they were doing it right out in the open for anyone who looked their way to see. Johnson was right. This was their only window of opportunity and perhaps miracle number two. He went for the building, angling for its east side, hoping to stay out of the guard's line of sight.

But, of course, the guy turned. Probably to see what was taking his partner so long or, if they had radios (Jack hadn't noticed), why he wasn't responding.

Jack was fifty yards away when the sentry spotted Johnson in the middle of the field and pulling the clothes off the other guard. He left his post at the corner of the building and started running, gun raised.

The Osprey guard was so focused on Johnson that he ran straight past Jack. So with no choice, Jack raised the MP7 and shot the guy in the back. The report of the blast rebounded off the tree line and echoed like the world's loudest firecracker. Jack froze, waiting for machine guns to open fire all around him.

But nothing happened.

Johnson finished pulling on the guard's jacket and ran in his new attire to the man Jack had just shot. Satisfied that he was dead, he grabbed him by the ankles and began dragging him back to the side of the building. Once there, he began undressing him too.

Jack joined him and offered cover, even though his first thought was that it seemed rather ridiculous to be taking the time to change clothes. Yeah, they did it in the movies all the time, but most of those movies cut out the actual process of having to take off your clothes, undress a corpse, and then re-dress, the impression left with the viewer that it only took a few seconds to complete the wardrobe change. But Johnson was right. If they could pass as Osprey guards responding to what was happening inside, then the chaos would cover them and offer what might possibly be their one and only chance of getting out of there with Stacey.

Stripped down to his wetsuit, Jack took the contractor's jacket from Johnson and slipped it on. As he did so, he heard faint popping sounds coming from inside the building. There was a firefight going on.

While Johnson worked the man's pants down over his ankles, Jack ripped the tie from his neck.

JACK LOOKED DOWN AT himself in the suit. He thought he looked ridiculous. Like a Secret Service agent or a bouncer. But at least it fit him okay. The training regimen that Stacey had put him through over the last couple of years had transformed his body from that of respectable dad bod to ninja, so he had little trouble slipping into the fit man's clothes. Even the shoes were a good match. If only the wetsuit still beneath it weren't so uncomfortable.

He looked at his watch. It had taken him three minutes to change.

"Ready?" Johnson asked, waiting for him.

In his new threads, Johnson looked just like the sentry he'd traded places with. They should have no problem moving about unchallenged in the confusion. If anything, the clothes would provide them with an element of surprise, and they'd have a small edge before anyone who identified them as impostors could do anything about it. "Yeah, I'm ready," Jack said.

Johnson had taken the radios from both corpses and handed one of them to Jack. Then he turned and led him around the front, or the back—Jack wasn't sure which—of the building. The edge of the cliff was just fifty feet away, the sea beyond it. Jack quickly looked out at the water and tried to imagine where they had landed. He wasn't sure how anyone looking could have missed them. If he was correct in where he thought they'd splashed down, they would have been in clear sight for a while before clearing the cove. He figured no one had been looking because they were all too busy with whatever was going on inside. Yet another miracle.

They walked to the front doors, trying to match the same sense of urgency the guard from the woods had exhibited, pretending that they'd just been recalled from their posts to assist with the issue inside. *If you believe it, they'll believe it,* Jack told himself. But there was no one guarding the doors.

Johnson tried them, but they were locked. He stepped back and saw the card reader. "Access cards," he said, thrusting his hands into the pockets of his new clothes. Jack did the same. And they both had a credit-card-sized piece of plastic in their fingers when they removed their hands.

Johnson held his to the pad, and the doors slid apart.

They went in.

No one.

The lobby, or whatever the large empty room was supposed to be, appeared to have been completely abandoned. If there had been anyone there to begin with.

"Which way?" Jack asked.

"The stairs," Johnson said, and moved through the room and past an elevator. They ran down a hallway, a door standing at its end. Johnson rammed his side into the panic bar and went through it, Jack following right on his heels.

They found themselves in a concrete stairwell. Johnson took out the tablet again and glanced at it. Then he was racing up the stairs, taking them two at a time.

Jack followed, his heart racing, until the sound of muffled gunshots reached their ears. He stopped, and Johnson did too. They stood there halfway between floors and listened.

After a few more seconds of gunshots, Johnson continued moving. "C'mon," he said. And he went to the next door they came to and pushed through it, his rifle tight against his shoulder and ready to fire.

They were in another hallway and facing the atrium. It was about a hundred feet away.

The gunshots were growing louder, closer, coming from that direction. They chased after the noise, approaching a balcony that wrapped around the atrium and able to see other levels looping around the cylindrical space above.

Two men in Osprey garb suddenly appeared in front of them, coming up the steps on the other side of the atrium. But they were shooting upward at someone on the next balcony. Then both of them were punched backward and sent sprawling to the floor. Blood splattered against the wall.

"That was two weapons," Johnson said, looking up at the ceiling.

"Stacey!" Jack cried, his voice echoing up and down the atrium. He was leaning over the railing and craning his neck to look up. At first all he could see was a towering shaft lined with balconies.

And then a head appeared, popping out from the level above and looking down at him.

Their eyes met.

"Jack?" the woman's voice called down.

"Stacey!" Jack's voice echoed up and down the building's hollow center.

"Stay there," she said, and her face disappeared.

Jack slowly backed away from the railing, trying to process what he'd just seen and heard. Stacey. They had found her.

Johnson grabbed his arm, snapping him to attention. "We're not out of this yet, amigo." He pointed to a set of stairs that connected their balcony to the ones above and below them. The steps were facing away from them, so they couldn't see whom the footsteps belonged to. They aimed their weapons.

But it was Stacey who appeared at the bottom of the steps, turning toward them, a man on her heels.

Jack's breath caught in his throat, and time seemed to stop. He forced his feet to move, and the next thing he knew (just like when he'd hit that ball in Little League), he had his arms around her.

They held each other for a few seconds, squeezing as tight as they could, as if testing out whether or not this could all be a dream.

Jack finally let go of her and stepped back, looking her over. "You look like Trinity," he said, taking in the leather outfit.

"And you look like John Wick," she answered, observing the suit and tie, his long black hair, his short beard.

"Jack Wick," he said, smiling. Though Neo would probably be preferable right now. But then his eyes found the collar around her neck, and his smile faded. Before he could say anything though, Stacey was looking past him and waving to Johnson.

"Hello, Stacey," Johnson said.

"You guys're lucky we didn't shoot ya, lookin' like Osprey the way ya do," said the man who had come down the stairs with Stacey.

Jack squinted, finding something familiar about the guy, but not knowing what it could be. And then his eyes popped, and he stood ramrod straight, the rifle swinging upward in his arms. "What the hell?"

The man didn't attempt to raise his gun in response but instead held up both of his hands in surrender. "It's okay, Jack."

"Like hell it is," Jack shot back.

Stacey looked back and forth between them, confused. "Jack," she said, "this guy saved my life."

Without taking his eyes off the man, Jack nodded. "Maybe, but he's also the man who kidnapped your son and left your husband for dead."

Stacey blinked and looked at the man from the plane, seeing him in a sudden new light.

"It's true," the guy said, looking at her. Then he looked back at Jack. "But I'm also the man who let 'im go."

76

JOHNSON STEPPED BETWEEN THEM, clearly thrown himself by how this man from their past had somehow ended up here. But he knew this wasn't the time or place to get to the bottom of it. "Can we discuss this later?" he asked. He went to Stacey and took a careful look at the collar around her neck. "What the hell is that?"

She shot a furtive glance at Jack as she answered, "Bomb collar."

Jack's eyes snapped away from the man from Appalachia, his wife's words redirecting them to her neck. "How do we get it off?" he asked as he leaned close to see the thing for himself.

Stacey shrugged in the leather body suit. "He said it's a combination lock. That the wrong combination would set it off. Also said if I strayed too far from a certain frequency, it would detonate."

He said. Jack's mind grappled with the words. Fedyenka. So she had talked to him. He tried not to think about what else might have happened during that encounter, instead forcing his attention to the four buttons that were lined up on the back of the device. Four buttons. How many possible combinations did that make? There was no way to know without first knowing how many digits made up the combination. Three? Four? Seven?

A gunshot exploded behind them, and they all spun to see the man from the mountains aiming his smoking rifle at one of Fedyenka's men now sprawled at the bottom of the stairs. "We can't stay here," the man said.

"Can we leave?" Jack asked, referencing the collar.

The man shook his head. "I think we need Fedyenka to get that thing off. Anything else'll be a gamble."

Stacey looked at Johnson. "Do you know what this place is? I mean, what it *really* is?"

Johnson frowned. "What do you mean?"

"You didn't see the silo?" she asked.

"Silo?" His frown deepened.

Stacey pointed in the direction she and the man from the plane had come from. "I'm pretty sure there's a missile silo. I don't know what he's planning on using it for, but we have to alert the Agency."

Johnson shook his head. "If that's true, then there's no guarantee that they don't already know about it. Or worse."

"Then we need to destroy the place now," Stacey said.

He nodded. "Okay." Then he shifted his attention to the man who was covering the stairs. "James," he said, getting his attention.

Stacey's head whipped around at hearing the man's name for the first time. "James?" She looked at Jack, her eyes asking: *The man you said Joseph stabbed with a stick?*

Jack nodded, his eyes responding: *Yes, that James.*

Johnson said, "The explosions we heard..."

"That was me," James answered.

"Anything bigger around?"

"There's a munitions wing on the north end of the buildin'. Might be somethin' there."

"Okay, then," Johnson said. "Let's split up. Jack and Stacey, you go after Fed. James and I are going to start a fire."

James held up a radio, noticing the ones that Jack and Johnson had taken from the Osprey guards. He gave them a frequency and said, "I got no idea what Fedyenka's thinkin' right now, but if he's thinkin' of takin' off, then probably he's headin' to the garage. Which is ground floor on the west side of the buildin'."

Stacey nodded and tugged on Jack's arm, prompting him to move. His mind was reeling. Just how in the hell had James gotten to Alaska? The seeming juxtaposition had him so disoriented, he thought he might be dreaming. But then an answer as to why he might be here came to him, and suddenly his presence wasn't such a mystery. But Stacey crossing his path at exactly the right moment and his willingness to save her? The probability of that seemed insane, and the miracles seemed to be piling up. Maybe God was answering his prayers after all, sending His angels to nudge things in his favor.

Jack ran after Stacey as they passed the stairs and continued on down the hallway, heading for the door standing at its end. Jack wondered if it might lead to the same stairwell he and Johnson had taken earlier. "You look pretty hot," he called out to her back.

"You too," she answered over her shoulder. "But why don't you stop staring at my ass and watch for—"

"Ass-ass-ins?" he asked, cutting her off.

She just shook her head, her high ponytail wagging back and forth. It brushed the back of her neck, sweeping over the bomb collar.

Any lightheartedness or even thankfulness that Jack had been feeling for even getting this far took a sharp left turn into a sudden burning rage that seemed to have appeared full form in the pit of his stomach. That Russian son of a bitch had locked a bomb around his wife's neck. And perhaps that wasn't even the worst of what he'd done.

Jack covered the hall behind them as Stacey opened the door and secured the stairwell. "It's clear," she said. But before moving on, she asked about Joseph. "Where is he? Is he okay?"

There was no time to explain everything that had happened since they'd parted ways, so Jack just assured her that he was alright.

She nodded, the answer enough to postpone all the rest of her questions. "We need to end this, Jack. He can't get away."

"I know."

Stacey thought of telling him how badly Fedyenka wanted their son. That he must have big plans for him. But she didn't want to reintroduce all the questions that she was sure had already been like a thousand mosquitos feasting on his brain. She knew that even now his mind was probably working to crack the code in the background, like a computer program running nonstop, the status bar slowly moving to the right. Would it reach 100%? Would he figure it out? She couldn't figure it out herself, yet a faint voice within said that was a lie. In any event, she needed Jack to be in the present moment and not distracted by something that might or might not have happened fifteen years ago. She leaned forward and planted a quick kiss on his lips. Then she led him into the stairwell and to the ground floor.

A minute later they were back in the empty atrium that Jack and Johnson had first encountered when entering the building. "Where now?" he asked.

And then an accented voice boomed from above them. "Well, look who has come to pay us a visit."

Jack spun, his eyes going up to the second-floor balcony, and for the first time in his life laid eyes on the man who, for years, had been trying to destroy his life. Fedyenka stood there like Al Pacino in *Scarface*, suit, machine gun, and all.

"Hello, Jack," the Russian bellowed. He raised the machine gun up over the banister and fired.

IF IT WEREN'T FOR the explosion that shook the building right as Fedyenka pulled the trigger, Jack was sure he'd be looking at his own body from the floor on the other side of the room—seeing his headless corpse first teeter and then fall. Either the explosion had startled Fedyenka, or the blast had moved the ground beneath his feet just enough to alter his aim. The first bullet coming from the storm of automatic fire grazed Jack's left bicep, tearing the suit and carving a cylindrical groove into his skin. The rest of the bullets strayed to the right, chipping at the floor behind him.

Stacey fired back, forcing an end to Fedyenka's barrage, making him seek cover beneath the banister.

Before Jack could fully recover from almost being mowed in half (he didn't even know what the miracle count was now),

Stacey was already halfway up the steps, running like a bat out of hell. Jack swore and laid down some more cover fire, trying to keep Fed pinned down. He could see in his mind's eye the Russian aiming his machine gun at the top of the stairs and waiting for Stacey's head to appear so he could blow it apart like a swollen watermelon. But Stacey must have imagined that too, because she raised the submachine gun above her head and began firing at the balcony before she got there.

Jack then went for the stairs himself, wondering along the way what would happen if they killed Fedyenka before they could get the combination to Stacey's necklace.

By the time he reached the second-floor balcony, Stacey and Fedyenka were gone, the only evidence of anyone having been there the spent casings littering the ground. He called out for her, and his answer came in the form of more gunshots echoing up the immediate hall to his right. He aimed down the corridor. Three doors stood ahead of him. Left, right, and one at the end of the hallway. Again he heard gunshots. It wasn't the full-auto that Fedyenka was carrying, though that quickly sounded in response to them. Jack ran down the hallway and tried the door on the left.

Another long hallway.

Crap.

He sprinted to the end of it, passing doors along the way, and whipped his head around the corner just in time to catch the ceiling lights dancing off Stacey's leather outfit before she turned down another hallway. "Stacey! Stop!" he called out.

He ran after her.

More gunfire.

There was a dead soldier lying in the next hallway, and another at a stairwell entrance at its end. Jack felt dizzy as he tried to conjure up the layout of the building. It felt like they were just running in circles. He'd lost his bearings a while ago and figured there was no way he was going to get them back now. He reached the end of the hall, stepped over the body, and leaned into the stairwell, listening. He heard a door open below and leaned over the railing. He caught a flash of a leather arm and then the sound of someone slamming into a panic bar.

Jack took a handful of stairs and then vaulted over the railing, landing on the next platform below. He repeated the move two more times before finding himself at another door. The stairs kept descending, but he was certain this was where Stacey had gotten off. He went through the door and into another hallway.

It was quiet. He could hear himself panting, his heart pounding in his head.

The walls were not the concrete blocks they'd seen in other sections of the building. This looked like drywall and paint. A door stood open on his left. He began moving toward it.

And then an entire section of the wall to the right of the doorway exploded into the hall, a person's head and shoulders blowing it apart and sending plumes of dust and chunks of sheetrock showering across the corridor. In the midst of the exposed metal studs, now bent and twisted outward, was Stacey's face. A bundle of electrical wires running horizontally through the studs had caught her, preventing the rest of her body from landing in the hallway at his feet. Suddenly, large hands appeared, reaching through the debris and grabbing Stacey's shoulders. Then she was pulled backward and out of the wall, disappearing just as quickly as she had appeared.

Jack ran through the doorway and into an office-sized room. It was empty, and an open door in the back right corner led to another identical room. When he entered it, he saw Fedyenka standing right in the middle of it, facing away from him and towering over Stacey. She was lying on her back, her face, hair, and shoulders white with drywall dust. Both their guns were on the floor ten feet away from them, but Fedyenka had a knife in his hand and was stepping on her chest.

"I do not think you will get to watch Joseph grow up after all," he growled, leaning forward and putting more pressure onto his foot.

Stacey gripped his ankle and tried to twist it, but it wouldn't budge.

Jack raised the MP7 and fired.

Fedyenka pitched forward and stumbled past Stacey.

Swinging her legs up into the air and over her head, Stacey rolled backward and onto her knees, facing Jack. Before she could say anything, however, machine-gun fire sounded from the next room, and holes began lining the wall by where Jack was standing.

Jack threw himself forward, getting below the line of holes and shooting back through the wall himself. The wall blew apart, sending clouds of dust into the air.

The MP7 clicked empty, and Jack tossed it aside, pulling out the pistol. Then he waited for whoever was in the other room to step through the doorway. Behind him, he could hear Stacey and Fedyenka going at it again, knuckles striking flesh, grunts and groans. But the knife... He wouldn't be able to hear that, so he risked one quick glance over his shoulder to see if Fedyenka still had it. Stacey was on his back and delivering blows to the sides of his head while he was slamming her into the walls, cracking the drywall.

Jack returned his attention to what was left of the wall just in time to see the barrel of an assault rifle poke into the doorway. Calculating where the person holding the rifle was standing in relation to the door frame, he fired three quick shots at the wall. The person collapsed sideways and fell on his knees and into the doorway. Jack put another round into his head. Then Jack spun on his knees and watched Fedyenka, Stacey still on him, launch himself backward and straight through a wall and out of the room.

The huge Russian landed full on top of her, his feet up in the air, her body taking every bit of his weight. Jack would be completely shocked if she hadn't at least cracked a couple of ribs, if not broken her back. He was certain that she at least got the wind knocked out of her and was afraid that she would be defenseless for the next few moments.

Fed got to his feet and pulled off his jacket, tossing it aside. A dark spot on the back shoulder of his shirt surrounded the hole that Jack's bullet had made.

Jack ran forward, throwing himself through the wrecked wall even as Fedyenka reached down for Stacey's head. Jack felt a drywall screw catch his arm just above where the bullet had grazed him, but his momentum carried him all the way through, and he slammed into Fedyenka's side. The impact sent them both tumbling sideways, and they collapsed to the floor.

An explosion sounded from somewhere in the building, and the lights in the ceiling flickered.

As Jack stumbled to his feet, he registered a radio squawking. He reached to his hip where he'd clipped it, but it wasn't there. He looked back toward the sound and saw it wedged in the wall, caught on a stud. He could hear Johnson's voice coming from the speaker but had no idea what he was saying.

He took one step toward it when he was suddenly on his back and something was striking him in the face. Blinding, white flashes popped in his vision, and he felt hot blood pouring down the back of his throat. Jack reached out and grabbed Fedyenka's neck with both hands, but it was like trying to squeeze a column of concrete. He caught Stacey moving behind them in his periphery. She had Fedyenka's knife in her hand.

But the recognition in his eyes betrayed them, and Fedyenka turned his head just as Stacey flashed the knife, aiming for his face. Fedyenka went to block the attack with his left hand, but Jack reached out and grabbed the cuff of his sleeve, trying to prevent the block. But Fedyenka was strong and only pulled Jack's hand up with his.

Jack cried out as Stacey's blow caught his forearm, slicing through the jacket and ripping flesh. He let go of the Russian's arm and slid out from under him while Stacey brought the knife around for another blow.

Again, Fedyenka blocked it. He caught her wrist and twisted it, sending the knife clattering to the floor. But even as he continued to twist her arm, pulling her down, Stacey swung her other hand up and smacked him open-handed on the side of the head.

Fedyenka barely seemed to notice the blow. He let go of her wrist and grabbed two fistfuls of her leather top. Lifting her off the floor, he threw her to the side. She flew through the air like a rag doll, completing one and a half airborne cartwheels before coming to a stop against a wall ten feet away. The wall buckled from floor to ceiling as she rebounded off it and landed on her side.

Jack went for the knife, which was back on the floor, and lifted it just as the huge Russian came at him. He stabbed it at his neck, but Fedyenka blocked it with an open hand. The blade went straight through his palm but stopped just short of piercing his neck. Jack took a step back, his hands now empty, and almost slipped. He'd stepped on his pistol. Quickly, he kicked it toward Stacey. It skittered across the floor and came to a stop against her thigh. She grabbed it, but Fedyenka, seeing her raising it at him, turned and ran straight through the broken wall, squeezing between the metal studs and stumbling into the hallway beyond.

Stacey fired at him, but if any of the remaining bullets had found their mark, they didn't stop him. Not immediately, at least.

He disappeared.

"Are you okay?" she asked Jack, getting to her feet.

He held up his forearm. "You stabbed me."

Another explosion shook the walls. They smelled smoke.

"We need to get out of here," Jack said.

"I'm not leaving until he's dead," Stacey answered.

The radio sounded again, and this time Johnson's words drifted clearly through the room.

"The building is burning; explosives are set in the silo."

"I don't know where my radio went," Stacey said, looking around.

Jack went to the wall and grabbed his. He brought it to his mouth and hit the transmit button. "How long?"

"Thirty minutes."

Jack said, "We're in pursuit of Fedyenka."

"Forget about him. Get out," Johnson responded.

"And what about Stacey?" Jack asked.

"We'll find another way," he said.

Stacey was already at the doorway, MAC-11 in hand. She'd taken the magazines from the dead guards. "Well? Are you coming or what?" she asked Jack.

For the briefest of moments, the rabbit from the rabbit hole peeked its head out and whispered that this was all Stacey's mess and that someone should be there to reunite with Joseph, so why shouldn't it be him? Cut and run.

The corner of Stacey's mouth turned into a playful grin, and he couldn't help himself. He whack-a-moled the rabbit and followed her out of the room, ignoring Johnson's pleas to get out.

THE FIRE WAS SPREADING fast, and alarm bells were ringing everywhere. Jack had no idea where the bombs had gone off, whether the fire was racing through the entire structure already, or if they just happened to be in close proximity to the blasts. Water was spraying from the sprinkler system, raining down on them in a feeble attempt to put out the flames. Stacey's ponytail must have come out while fighting with Fedyenka because now her hair was soaked and hanging in long strands over her face. Backlit by firelight, the tight leather accenting her features, the determination and confidence on her face… Jack thought she looked incredibly hot.

She looked at him. "What?"

"Nothing."

But he knew she could tell from his eyes what he was thinking, even if it was an odd time to be thinking it. She stepped to him, gripped the back of his head, and pulled him to her, kissing him hard, her tongue filling his mouth with feverish urgency. When she released him, she stared straight into his eyes.

"Let's finish this," she said.

He nodded and then realized that he was scared. Scared that there was no *way* to end this. Scared that at any moment, the bomb collar around Stacey's neck would sever her head from her shoulders. Scared that he would never see Joseph again. Scared that even if they did get out of this, they would just be hunted down by their own government tomorrow. And maybe that was what she'd seen on his face, not his attraction to her, but all of his fear. Or maybe the two were somehow the same.

Another explosion sounded, and a section of the ceiling collapsed nearby. They circumnavigated the debris and ran to a section of floor-to-ceiling windows that overlooked the grounds east of the building.

"Look," Stacey yelled over the blaring alarms, pointing out to the grass.

Two Nissan Frontiers were pulling up to a rear entrance, men with guns packed into their beds and hopping out before the pickups slid to a stop.

"How much ammo do you have?" Stacey asked.

"Two more mags and whatever's left in this one."

Stacey took the radio from Jack's belt. "Do you know what channel it was on before?"

"Four."

Stacey changed the channel from the one they were using to communicate with Johnson and set it back to the one the Osprey contractors had been using.

Nothing.

"Either they switched channels, or it's radio silence," she said.

Jack watched the men enter the building. "Osprey?"

"I don't know." She changed the channel on the radio and tried to get Johnson on the other end.

No response.

She pulled Jack away from the windows. "C'mon, we can't wait."

77

THEY SEARCHED FOR ANOTHER way out, navigating the flames that were spreading along the ceiling and creeping over the walls.

"There," Jack shouted, pointing to a set of open double doors across from them.

Stacey ran through them and into a large, mostly empty room. She stopped dead in her tracks, though, a wall of heat striking her in the face. The room was ablaze and felt like an oven. Jack stood beside her.

"There's no way through," Stacey said, peering into the hellfire. She looked up and saw a camera's domed sphere in the ceiling. Could someone be watching them and directing reinforcements their way? She raised the MAC-11 and destroyed it just in case. Then she backed out of the room and went to a window. They were still too high to jump.

She was about to turn and say something to Jack when two utility task vehicles suddenly appeared racing away from the building and speeding for the woods. They looked like dune buggies. Four-seaters with a flat bed and an exposed cabin enclosed by a roll cage. One of the men in the UTVs was wearing a gray shirt with a dark spot on the back shoulder. "It's him," she said to Jack, who was peering past her and out the window himself.

She spoke into the radio even as the fire from the nearby room began to spread its orange fingers toward them. "Johnson, Fed just took off in a UTV. He's heading west for the woods."

This time he did respond. *"Where are you?"* he came back.

"We're looking for a way out. The fire is spreading like crazy."

"We're on the south side and coming to an exit now. We'll circle around and take out whoever is left around the trucks. Can you get there?"

"Don't wait for us," she said. "Take a truck and go after him. We'll catch up."

"Copy."

"C'mon," Stacey said to Jack. "We have to go back."

Jack shook his head. "Why would he leave? We're still alive, and he doesn't know where Joseph is."

Stacey wondered about her open-handed slap to Fedyenka's head and the ring's poisoned needle piercing his skin. After using it, she had tossed it, not wanting to risk poking herself or Jack now that the cover was gone and the pin sat exposed. The poison had obviously not worked right away, either because of where she'd struck him or because whatever was on the needle was not a fast-acting agent. But maybe he was feeling the effects of whatever it was now. But that wasn't the explanation she offered Jack. "Maybe because the whole building is about to come down."

Jack frowned. "You think—"

She knew what was going through his head. The smoke from the fire would draw attention, and Osprey would be scrutinized as a result. It would get national attention unless Fedyenka had internal help that would help suppress the whole thing—which seemed likely. But he would still be feeling the pressure of needing to avoid unwanted attention, nonetheless. Whoever he had helping him on the inside would want to make sure that nothing could be traced back to them. Which was why what Jack was thinking made perfect sense.

They heard men on the stairs nearby.

"What do you want to do?" Stacey asked, her eyes darting from the stairs to the room on fire and back again. They could either try going through hell, or they could shoot it out with a dozen heavily armed ex-special forces with the little ammunition they had left.

Jack considered even as the footfalls grew louder. This was no place for a shootout. Sure, they had the high ground, and they could keep the enemy pinned in the stairwell, but all it would take was for someone to toss a grenade up at them. Or for their ammo to run out.

Stacey read the answer in his eyes and nodded. "Into the garbage chute, flyboy!" she said, quoting Princess Leia.

They ran into the fire.

THE HEAT WAS INCREDIBLE. Jack could feel it searing his skin even as he buried his face in the crook of his arm. He held his breath, the air burning his lungs. His eyes stung, and tears streaked across his cheeks.

They ran for the door that stood on the other side of the room, dodging pieces of the collapsing ceiling, sparks exploding around them like fireworks.

Jack prayed that the door wasn't locked. If it was, they'd have to find a way to break it down. Or go back through the furnace and into waiting guns. Jack could feel the hair on his face singeing, and his mind flashed to the stories of the Christian martyrs his grandmother used to tell him about. And of the witch trials centuries later. He'd always thought drowning would be the worse way to go, but as the sleeve of his stolen suit burst into flame, he thought he might prefer being a human buoy to a human candle.

He could barely make Stacey out through the shimmering air. His eyes seemed to be melting. "Where's the door?" he yelled, suddenly unable to see. Everything was red and moving. The fire on his arm raced up to his shoulder.

"Here!"

He heard her voice, but still couldn't see her.

A loud crack sounded from behind, and a tsunami of extraordinary heat whipped past him, tossing his long hair forward and around his face. He looked back and saw that a huge wooden beam had splintered in half and fallen through the ceiling.

The fire on his arm and shoulder crawled around his back and lit his other arm. Everything was so bright, so hot. The flames on the jacket were licking his neck now. He could feel the skin blister. His lungs ached for air. Hornets were stinging his eyeballs.

"Stacey!" he shouted, spinning around. He'd lost his bearings. Spinning in circles, all he could see was fire. Fire everywhere. Fire *on* him. Consuming his clothes, melting his flesh. And just when he was sure that this was it, that he would literally go out in a blaze of glory, two hands grabbed his belt and began hurling him through the room and toward what appeared to be a wall of living colors. Tongues of red and orange licked the air, gliding like waves of lava from the floor all the way up to the ceiling before rolling back on themselves. It seemed impenetrable, that just getting close to it would mean annihilation. It raced toward him, and he put his arms up, hoping that he hadn't already died and that this wasn't the opening credits to his ever after.

But then, somehow, he was on the other side of it.

"You're on fire," he heard Stacey's voice say. It sounded a hundred miles away.

He tried to help her get his jacket off, but the left sleeve got stuck around his wrist, caught on his watch. He started to panic, knowing that if his pants were to catch fire, things would get a whole lot more interesting.

Stacey got the sleeve over the watch, tearing fabric, his injured arm screaming in protest. The flaming jacket now hung off his right wrist, rolled up on itself and tight. He stepped on the other sleeve, pinning the jacket to the ground, and ripped his hand up toward the ceiling, yanking it free.

Stacey kicked the flaming bundle aside. "Are you okay?"

He patted his legs, making sure no tongues of fire had managed to sneak into his pants. The hair on his arms was singed, and he could tell he had some burns on the back of his neck that would need some attention if they did manage to make it out of here, but other than that, he thought he was okay. He nodded while rubbing his eyes and trying to catch his breath. He looked back to the inferno and saw hands of fire gripping the doorway, trying to pull the rest of its blazing body into the room after them. Smoke was snaking against the ceiling and getting close to their heads. Then he looked at her. "Your feet," he said.

She looked down at her bare feet. They were soot stained but miraculously, after everything, there didn't appear to be any blood. "I'm fine." And she pulled him across the room to an adjoining hall. At the end of the hall, two Osprey soldiers stood facing a descending flight of stairs, their backs toward them. Stacey shot them both. They pitched forward and tumbled down the steps.

They followed the bodies down, stopping only to take the radios from them and exchange their nearly empty weapons for a pair of fully loaded MAC-11s. At the bottom of the stairs, they found themselves on the ground floor and facing big glass windows that looked out to the vehicles that had recently arrived.

Stacey raised the rifle and fired at the glass, but the bullets just ricocheted off it. They'd have to use the door. She took off to the left, searching for one. "Can you see how many are out there?" she called out behind her.

"Four, maybe five," Jack said, counting the dark figures by the Nissans as he chased after her.

A door ahead. The same door the men from the pickup trucks had used to get in. Stacey's mind played through a couple of scenarios. Maybe they could take them by surprise, bust through the door shooting. Or maybe they'd get mowed in half before even crossing the threshold. She swore and pulled the radio from Jack's belt. "We have to find another door and circle around them," she said to Johnson.

"Go out there. We'll cover you," Johnson's voice chirped back.

"You're outside?" Stacey asked.

"We have the trucks in our crosshairs. We'll light them up on your signal."

Jack nodded.

"Okay," she said into the radio. "Do it."

Suddenly, the men standing by the two pickups were now scurrying back and forth, seeking cover while simultaneously trying to detect the source of the attack.

Jack went out the door shoulder to shoulder with Stacey, feeling too much like Butch Cassidy and the Sundance Kid for his liking. They immediately took out one man who was standing in the bed of a truck and another who was still sitting in the passenger seat. Two others were thrown down by Johnson's suppressing fire.

Jack moved on the trucks, not knowing where Johnson was positioned but trusting him to clear their way. He knew there was at least one more operative positioned at the rear truck, hiding on the other side.

He saw Stacey heading for the other pickup in his periphery and turned toward her in time to see her dive onto her stomach in front of the truck's front wheel. She rolled to her side, clearing the wheel and aiming beneath the truck. But before she could get off a shot, she was rolling back behind the wheel, the grass she had just been lying on suddenly chewed into flying clumps of sod. Jack came up on his own Nissan and threw his back against its side. He took one more glimpse at Stacey, who had just gotten to her feet and jumped up onto the hood of the truck, sliding across it and shooting down over its side. The move had been quick, fluid, and seemingly choreographed straight from an action movie. *Trinity, indeed,* he thought, and then swung around with his right shoulder against the tailgate.

Nothing.

He swung around the other side, aiming up toward the driver's side door—which was standing open like a shield, a man standing behind it and aiming a rifle through the open window at him.

He tensed, and then the guy's head whipped to the side, and his body collapsed to the ground below the door. It was all clear, silent.

Jack looked up at the building, wondering where Johnson and James were. Then he went to Stacey, who had just finished pulling a dead body out of the lead truck. She slipped behind the wheel and said, "Get in."

Jack ran around the front of the Nissan and climbed up into the passenger seat. Stacey fired up the engine, and just as she was about to floor it, they saw Johnson and James running toward them from around the building. She started toward them.

"We'll follow in the other one," Johnson called out as she rolled down the window.

Stacey nodded and was about to hit the gas when Johnson ran up to the door.

"What?" she said impatiently. Fedyenka was getting away.

"I just heard from the pilot," he said through the open window.

The look in his eyes indicated that something had happened.

"What?" Jack asked, leaning forward past Stacey.

"They got orders to redirect."

"From who?"

"Homeland."

"To where?"

"They were turning west…"

"And?" Stacey said, growing impatient.

"And so Joseph jumped out of the plane."

"What?" Jack said, blinking.

Stacey just sat frozen.

"A chute was missing," Johnson said.

"Did they see him?" Jack asked.

Johnson shook his head.

Jack stared out the windshield, his brain running a hundred miles an hour. He glanced at Stacey, knowing that she didn't have enough information to gauge what any of this might mean. "Did they give you the location?" he asked Johnson.

This time Johnson nodded. "If Homeland knew he was on the plane, then there's a chance Fedyenka may have known too."

"And did the pilots report back to Homeland what happened?"

"Yeah."

"So Fedyenka might know that, too."

And then Stacey screamed, striking her palm against the dashboard. "Who cares if he knows?" she yelled. "You're telling me my son jumped out of a plane?"

"Stacey," Jack said, putting a hand on her shoulder while watching her chest stretch the shiny black leather as it heaved with each breath, "Joseph had just watched Johnson explain the whole procedure to me. I'm sure he deployed the chute."

She turned her gaze toward him, her eyes red. He knew she believed what he'd said, but he also knew that she knew what he hadn't said—that deploying the chute at the right time might be moot if he happened to land at the top of a mountain or in the thick of a forest or in the middle of a lake.

"We'll find him," Jack said. "Before Fedyenka does."

She nodded. "Fedyenka won't find him." She put the truck in gear. "Because he'll be dead."

And just then, the faint sound of a helicopter met their ears, drifting over the water and past the burning building.

They all turned, looking past the building and to the watery horizon, where a small shape seemed to hover in the sunlight.

It grew larger, like a gnat transforming into a fly. Then a fly into a dragonfly.

"Search and Rescue?" Jack asked.

"Probably," James said from behind Johnson. "But not for us."

The helicopter was another Black Hawk. It cleared the water and flew straight through the towering column of smoke, continuing on past the burning building and heading for the trees.

"They're going after Fed," Stacey said.

"And then after Joseph," Jack added.

"Just get in," Stacey said to Johnson and James.

They abandoned the other pickup and hopped into the empty bed just as Stacey hit the gas and propelled them after Fedyenka.

As she drove, the Frontier bouncing over the uneven terrain, Jack looked back over his shoulder and watched the building begin to shrink. He wondered if the collar around Stacey's neck was shrinking too. She had said there was a signal being transmitted. Was that signal in the building they were getting farther away from, or did Fedyenka have it on his person and they were actually getting closer to it? Jack prayed that his wife's head wouldn't explode as he sat there beside her.

STACEY NAVIGATED THE TRUCK through the woods, following the tread marks left by the two UTVs. They could all hear the helicopter, but couldn't yet see it through the thick canopy. "Keep an eye out for one of them circling back," Stacey said.

"There," Jack shouted.

Stacey's eyes went to the trees, looking for signs of another UTV, until she realized Jack was looking up through the tree-tops.

"Did you see it?" he asked.

She had. Just a glimpse, but it was enough. The helicopter was about a hundred yards ahead and to their right. And descending.

Stacey closed the distance quickly, the helicopter growing louder and louder, the sound of the rotors rebounding off the mountains like a jackhammer. Then the trees ahead of them vanished and they were rocketing through a clearing. Stacey wrestled with the wheel as the pickup skidded across tall grass.

The Black Hawk was ten feet off the ground and staring at them with its insectile cockpit eyes. There was a single UTV parked beneath it, right in the middle of wind-flattened grass. Three people were standing on the bed and reaching up for the landing skids when either Johnson or James opened fire at them from over the Nissan's roof.

The three figures abandoned their attempt to board the aircraft and climbed into the roll cage, ducking behind the seats.

"Someone got on," Jack said.

Stacey caught a glimpse of someone sitting in the cabin as the helicopter rose in an evasive maneuver. Was it Fedyenka? The door slid closed before she could get a better look. "Jack," she said. She was thinking what it would mean if it was Fedyenka and if the helicopter were to get away.

"I know," Jack responded, and leaned out the window as Stacey gunned the gas. He raised the rifle and started firing, his bullets bouncing harmlessly off the chopper's metal belly. But then the helicopter pitched forward, bringing the canopy into view as the pilots prepared to fly past them. The last two rounds in the magazine punched through the glass, and the pilot lurched forward, collapsing into the collective and sending the nose of the helicopter straight down.

The rotors hit the ground and sent dirt whipping into a rainbow ark around it.

It seemed to hover in suspended animation for a second, hanging there at that ninety-degree angle, nose pointing at the ground, rear stabilizer aimed at the sky, and the rotors carving the earth like a circular saw. Until, finally, the rotors snapped and went spinning end over end like giant lawnmower blades into the woods, severing trees until running out of steam.

Stacey slammed on the brakes with her bare foot, and Jack, still leaning out the window, was almost launched from the truck.

What was left of the chopper's blades grabbed the ground and flipped the helicopter onto its side. Then, like a spiked wheel, the broken rotors propelled the vehicle forward across the ground, sliding it on its side through the grass until one of the blades found a rock, and the entire chopper did a cartwheel, flipping into the air and crashing down onto its other side.

The rotors stopped moving, and everything became still.

"Holy shit," Stacey whispered.

Jack sat back in the passenger seat and turned toward her, a look of unbelief on his singed face.

Stacey had been hoping to somehow commandeer the helicopter and use it to get to Joseph. But whether Jack meant for the chopper to crash or not, what choice had he had? If Fedyenka got away, they would never have found him again. And if he got to Joseph before they did...

Two men in the UTV were now exchanging fire with Johnson and James. The third man must've been struck by one of the rotor blades because he was lying beside the vehicle in three pieces.

"Hold on!" Stacey yelled, hoping that Johnson could hear her. She hit the gas and turned the wheel, bringing the UTV directly in front of them. The pickup sped past the broken helicopter, bounced over the ruts and divots caused by the blades, and bore down on the men shooting at them. Bullets bounced harmlessly off the windshield as the UTV grew larger and larger.

"What are you doing?" Jack asked, gripping the handle on the door and pushing himself back against the seat.

Then all but the frame of the UTV's roll cage disappeared beneath the dashboard, and there was a giant impact and a loud crash. The vehicle flew to the left, spinning in a couple of complete circles, one of the men thrown ten feet into the air and landing on his head some twenty yards away.

Stacey turned the wheel hard to the left while slamming on the brakes, spinning the truck around and facing back the way they'd come. The last guy had climbed out of the mangled UTV and was now on his hands and knees and trying to crawl across the field. She revved the engine, and his head shot up out of the grass like a spooked deer. The man was a trained killer, and as Stacey propelled the Nissan toward him, she saw only hatred and icy defiance in his eyes. The weight of the truck crushed his vertebrae like packing bubbles.

Stacey swung the pickup around and drove back to the helicopter. She and Jack threw open their doors simultaneously, jumping out into the field. Johnson and James, still standing in the truck bed, covered them.

Jack got to the helicopter, which was still on its side, and climbed up onto the wheel. From there, he pulled himself up onto the helicopter and walked to the cabin door. Crouching, he reached down and tried to pull it open, but the metal was dented, and the door wouldn't slide on its track. He pulled harder and managed to get the door open just enough to see down inside. He could see a person beneath him, resting twisted against the opposite door. His head was bent at an unnatural angle, his arm up behind him.

But it was not Fedyenka.

"He's not here," Jack called down to Stacey.

Stacey relayed the information to Johnson.

"Look for radios," Johnson yelled to Jack before he could jump down off the helicopter.

Jack walked to the cockpit door and lifted it open, swinging it up and away from him. He looked over the lifeless pilots, searching for whatever they'd been using to communicate with Fedyenka. He found a radio on the co-pilot and leaned across the first pilot to get it. Then he hopped down and tossed it to Stacey.

A voice came through just as she caught it. It was in Russian.

"Get in the truck," Stacey yelled, suddenly running for it herself. She could tell she was losing feeling in her feet, but she wasn't about to let that stop her.

"What?" Jack asked as he raced after her.

James and Johnson had just gotten out of the truck and were now climbing back into the bed.

"They doubled back. They're heading to the shoreline," she said.

"Boat," Jack guessed as he slid into the passenger seat again.

Stacey moved the Nissan back toward the woods and left the field behind.

A knock against the back window made Jack turn around. Johnson was holding the tablet up to the glass so that he could see the red dot against the satellite image of the area. Jack reached out the passenger window and took it from him.

Stacey glanced over and saw their current location displayed on the screen. She turned the wheel to course-correct, squeezing between two trees and scraping the paint off the right side of the truck.

The red dot began heading toward the water.

78

JOSEPH WALKED THROUGH THE trees with his new walking spear in hand. He shielded his eyes from the sun and tried to guess how much daylight he had left. His hands were numb, and he kept alternating which hand he had in his pocket and which held the stick. His ears were freezing too. He lowered his gaze from the sun and again looked around. Nothing. Or, rather, *everything.*

He realized that if he could disassociate his personal circumstances from the environment, he would actually find his surroundings to be quite awesome. He was Michael Strogoff trekking Siberia. And though this wasn't Siberia, it was close enough. Literally. But no matter how beautiful it might be, Joseph knew that the temperatures would soon be unbearable if he didn't manage to get a fire going.

Unbearable. His brain tripped over the word. *Un-BEAR-able. Bear.*

He gripped the spear tighter as the hair on the back of his neck stood tall and then seemed to freeze there. He had no desire to meet another bear. Not out here, and not like this. He tried to recall his books. Would a fire keep a grizzly away like it would wolves? If the books had mentioned it, he didn't remember.

Dying of exposure while asleep did sound better than being chewed to death by a Kodiak bear though. But he thought about that. Kodiak bears were the world's largest bears, weighing twice as much as grizzlies, but he was pretty sure they were isolated to Kodiak Island, which he knew he was not on right now. Still, wouldn't that be the premise for a good creature feature? Kodiak bear somehow ends up making it onto the mainland and causing all hell to break loose, feasting on the locals? Actually, he thought the plot didn't seem half bad. Maybe he'd write it himself, someday. Maybe during his breaks as a park ranger. *Smokey the Bear meets Jason Voorhees*, he thought. Though he knew the idea had been done before. He'd seen a few of them on Netflix. He'd have to find a way to make his story unique. Had a Kodiak bear ever gotten off Kodiak Island? That would be the first thing he'd have to investigate.

And then he thought about polar bears. He'd read that polar bears were the most dangerous bears in the world, that if you were to hear their roar, it would most likely be the last sound you ever heard (other than, perhaps, your own screams). He wondered if there could be polar bears out here. He wasn't exactly sure where the polar bear population was in Alaska. He knew definitely north and a little south during the winter. But how south and how close to the winter? He thought he was south enough to not have to worry about it, but he couldn't be sure.

He tried to stop thinking about bears, because now he couldn't stop searching trees for them. But then he remembered being in the diner with his dad on the way to their camping trip and how he'd shown him that YouTube video of the old Russian Bear commercial. The memory made him smile, and the hairs standing frozen on his neck defrosted and lay back down.

He trudged along, and as he covered the next fifty feet, his mind got off the bear highway and pulled into the school parking lot. He'd been thinking of his friends a lot, but it was mostly in the back of his mind with all the excitement and terror of falling out of helicopters, running from men with guns, and worrying about his mom, but now, suddenly, in this perfect stillness, he had no trouble seeing all their faces. In fact, they were so clear that he had trouble convincing himself they weren't there with him. What if they'd died in the explosion and were keeping him company as ghosts? If they were ghosts, were they here to help get him through this, or were they here to haunt him? To blame him and his family for their deaths?

Tommy. Moses. Zane. Priscilla...

What were they thinking about him right now? He was sure they'd seen the news, overheard their parents talking. More than anything, Joseph wanted to tell them that it wasn't true. None of it. *Well, most of it, anyway.* He missed them and couldn't help wondering what he would be doing with them right now if all this hadn't happened. What day even was it? He had no idea. If it was Saturday, he might be going over to Tommy's tonight to watch a movie and play *Sniper Elite 4.* Or maybe it was already tonight in North Carolina. He wondered what Priscilla would be doing in this alternate timeline. Would she be making TikTok videos with Julia and Haley? Or going out to dinner with her family (as he knew they often did on the weekends)?

Maybe, after Tommy helped him gather up some courage while killing a few hundred Nazis, he would've finally written her a message. A handwritten message, old-school style like his parents did back in the day. Like kids did in all the classic high school movies. He'd give it to her in school on Monday. At the end of the day, of course. He was way too chicken to give it to her in the morning. It would be torture going through the entire day not knowing what she was thinking. Or worse... Maybe she would tell him exactly what she was thinking. And in front of everyone.

But that was an alternate time line that would never happen. He would never see those people again. Never get to explain himself. For the rest of their lives they would think of him as "that kid with the terrorist parents."

Did it really matter, though? Seeing that he was most likely going to die soon? And then wasn't *that* a fun thought? It wasn't that he feared death. In fact, he could convince himself that it would be cool to see his sister again. To be in a place where there was no more sadness or pain. To be with God, like the youth pastor had talked about. It was just that there were so many things he still wanted to do in this life.

I'm not ready to die, he told himself. And then he laughed out loud, thinking, *So says everyone ever.* And then his brain started playing a song he'd heard somewhere. He couldn't remember where, just that it had made him think at the time. Something about everyone wanting to go to heaven but nobody wanting to die. He hummed the tune, trying to get the right words to fall into place, and the sound of his voice carried through the stillness. He found it a bit unnerving.

I'm going to die... He stopped singing. He digested the thought, and with its bitter comprehension—that everything in this life was coming to an end—his gut wrenched in protest. It was similar to the feeling he'd gotten when waking up from a dream where he'd stolen his neighbor's car, blew a stop sign, and ran over a pregnant woman and her two young children who'd been crossing the intersection. Why he'd stolen the car and where he was going in such a hurry were details the dream didn't offer. But he'd sat bolt upright with his heart beating out of his chest and an overwhelming sense of dread that burned like an inferno in his stomach. For thirty seconds, *This can't be happening*, was the only thought that went through his head before he realized that it wasn't. But this was no dream. This *was* happening.

"Get a grip, Joe," he said aloud, ignoring how creepy the isolation felt contrasted against his voice. He took a deep breath, stood as straight as his freezing body allowed, and added, "Gird up thy loins, dude." And the fire in his belly started to go out, quenched by the willpower to press on.

Something up ahead caught his attention. He couldn't say why or what. Maybe he'd detected some movement in his periphery, or maybe the sun had glinted off a rock. Regardless, he marked it as his destination and pressed ahead. He counted the steps out loud, his teeth chattering. But even as he counted, his mind twisted and pulled at the predicament he found himself in.

Would the pilots report his escape? Of course they would. But to whom? The Russian guy who wanted him so badly or the US government? How long would it take them to start searching for him? Was there a way Agent Johnson and his dad would find out that he'd parachuted from the plane, or would they not know anything was wrong until there was no one to meet them at the rendezvous? He figured it was most likely the latter, which meant that the only people who would be looking for him out here would be the very people he needed to avoid. He would have to find his way back to civilization on his own.

And then what?

Yeah, and then what? He couldn't think of anything, but he knew he was too cold and tired to really trust his own thoughts. He could feel himself beginning to grow delirious, his mind starting to break free of its moorings and drift toward an icy sea. He'd build a fire, rest, and then think it through again once he wasn't so exhausted.

He continued counting out his steps.

79

BY THE TIME THEY returned to the building, the entire thing was ablaze. Flames could be seen dancing brightly behind the floor-to-ceiling windows, and where some of the windows had exploded, tongues of fire were stretching into the day and licking at the sky.

An empty UTV was parked on the other side of the building, near the edge of the cliff. It hadn't been there before.

"How much time do we have before Johnson's bombs go off?" Stacey asked.

Jack looked at his watch. "Ten minutes, maybe."

Her eyes searched the building for signs of a trap. "We'd better make this quick, then."

As if on cue, James jumped out of the truck bed and sprinted toward the UTV. Before Stacey had the Nissan in park, Jack was out of the passenger seat and taking off after him. Stacey and Johnson covered them. Even as far away as he was from the building, Jack could feel the heat of it redden his face.

James passed the UTV and went straight for the edge of the cliff. From Jack's vantage point, it looked like James had simply run straight off its side, there one second and gone the next. But as Jack got closer, he saw that there were stairs. He also saw that there was a boat sitting in the water halfway to the horizon. A smaller boat had just left it and was racing toward the beach, its white wake dividing the calm sea in two. And then it disappeared beneath his vantage point, blocked by the remaining hilltop.

When he reached the stairs, he saw that James was already near the bottom of them. Jack started down, the wind off the water seeming to swirl around him, forcing him to take hold of the handrail. After a dozen more steps, though, he was able to let go of the railing and pick up his pace. His footsteps against the metal echoed after him.

James was off the steps, past a body that was lying facedown on the ground—one of the two men from the UTV, Jack supposed—and running across the stony beach. Then he disappeared around a rock outcropping that jutted out from the cliff face.

A shot rang out.

Jack ducked beneath the railing.

Another shot.

It echoed off the rock wall and out over the water. Jack looked around, trying to find the source of the shooting, but didn't see anything. Except for the motorboat suddenly turning away from the shore, drawing a huge hook in the water as it arced wide and headed back for the larger boat it had launched from. Was someone shooting at the boat?

"Where'd he go?" Stacey's voice called out behind him.

He looked back and saw Stacey and Johnson coming down the stairs. He took note of Stacey's bare feet on the metal and wondered how she could be coming down the stairs as fast as she was. "James is on the beach," he called up. "I think someone is shooting at the boat." He pointed out to the motorboat. It had stopped halfway between the shore and the yacht.

"I think that's the boat they brought me in," Stacey said.

Jack thought that if she was right, then they must have been coming to pick up Fedyenka, and that whoever was shooting had scared them off. But if she was wrong, then it could be the SVR coming to kill him, and it was probably Fedyenka who was shooting at them.

There was only one way to find out. He continued down the stairs and to the shore below.

STACEY'S FEET WERE ALMOST completely numb by the time she stepped off the stairs and onto the stony shore. She cursed herself for not at least taking a pair of socks off someone. As she moved as quickly as she could across the uneven terrain, her eyes more focused downward on avoiding sharp rocks than up and scanning for enemies, she marveled at how much things had changed since being brought ashore here just hours before. From a naked and freezing prisoner to an armed predator on the hunt, Fedyenka's castle burning to the ground above her.

"Jack?" she called out, sweeping the MAC-11 back and forth and stepping past an Osprey agent with a hole in his back (the other man from the UTV, she assumed). The water lapped gently over the shore, the sound of it eerie in the otherwise silent space. She hobbled forward and could hear Johnson right behind her, his boots crunching across the stones.

"Get on my back," he said.

"I'm fine," she answered.

"You're not. You're going too slow."

She knew he was right, so she nodded.

He came alongside her and bent over. She jumped up onto his back, wrapping her legs around his waist, her arms around his shoulders and chest.

"Hold on," he said. And he started jogging toward the outcropping she'd seen from the boat on her way in. It stood forty yards ahead of them and ran like the tail fin of some huge spaceship, stretching out of the cliff face and slanting down past the beach and disappearing into the water five yards from the shore.

As Johnson got close, Stacey began searching the rock for handholds they could use to climb up and over. She didn't see any. "We have to go around," she said into his ear. She thought she heard him swear under his breath.

When they reached the slanted divider, Johnson followed it into the surf, walking until his feet were submerged, and then until the water was at his shins.

"Listen," he said, stopping.

Stacey could hear muffled voices over the water, coming from the other side.

"Can you pull yourself up?" he asked.

She handed him the MAC-11 and reached both hands up onto the wall. She climbed up Johnson's back until she was standing on his shoulders and looking over the top. And then she was off his shoulders and swinging herself over the rock and dropping down into the water on the other side.

"Dammit, Stacey!" she heard Johnson yell.

The water was freezing and up to her knees. She began making her way to the shore, her hands moving against the rock as she tried to keep her footing on the cove's stony bottom.

Another twin outcropping stood thirty yards down the beach, isolating this particular section between two natural walls, as if a god from some long-lost mythology had used a giant ice-cream scoop to carve out a portion of the hillside.

She saw three people standing right in the middle of it.

A splash behind her made her turn her head, and she saw Johnson hurrying toward her through the lapping tide.

"Here." He handed her the MAC-11.

She took it, and then she let him wrap his arm around her waist and carry her the remaining fifteen feet to shore.

They moved toward Jack and James. They were standing ten feet away from Fedyenka, both their guns trained on his face. Fedyenka's head was bleeding, and a long trail of blood was running from his hairline to his chin. His hands were empty. It was clear that something was not right with him. His skin looked pale, and Stacey could tell he was sweating profusely. Whatever had been on the needle was going to town now.

"What's going on?" she whispered to Jack as they came up beside him. But her mind was already unwrapping the scene. Had James known that the poison would take this long to work? Or was there something about Fedyenka's physiology that had managed to delay it? Or where she had stuck him? If it was a slow-acting poison, then using it the way James must have assumed she would could've gotten her killed. Judging from the cold look in his eye, James didn't really care about rescuing her as much as he cared about killing Fedyenka. She'd seen that look before. Had *had* that look before. And there was no doubt in her mind that James was about to put a bullet between Fedyenka's eyes.

Fedyenka turned his attention to Stacey. "If you kill me, you will never get that thing off your neck." He seemed to wobble on his feet.

"You're dead already," James hissed.

Fedyenka looked at him. "I do not know who you are, but I am going to kill everyone you have ever cared about."

James took a step closer. "You already have, you son of a bitch."

Fedyenka blinked. A bead of sweat fell from his eyelash.

"You hired us to take their son," James explained, pointing at Jack and Stacey. "Then you told the Baker gang to kill us." He took another step forward. "You killed my brother."

Realization crept into the Russian's eyes. "You are one of the hillbillies from—"

James cut him off. "Yeah, and then you hired me into Osprey, you dumb piece of shit."

Fedyenka moved his eyes from James to Stacey, and a surge of anger flushed some of the color back into his face. "You were working with *her*? From the inside?"

James shrugged, content to let him believe this theory. "But, like I said," he continued, "it's you that's already dead. What yer feelin'... The chills, the sweatin', the dizziness... You've been poisoned."

Fedyenka's hand instinctively went to the side of his head where there must've been some sort of irritation marking where the needle had punctured his skin.

James continued, "I gave Stacey a poisoned ring. I guess at some point durin' your tusslin' she managed to slap you with it. It works a little like the Novichok you assholes like to use."

Fedyenka's eyes went wide.

"Yeah, there's an antidote. I got it right here in my pocket. Just in case Stacey pricked herself by accident." He looked over at her. "You didn't, did you?"

Stacey shook her head.

James shrugged. "Then I guess I don't need it no more." He took a small vial out of his pocket and dropped it on the ground. Then he lifted his foot and set his shoe on it.

"No!" Fedyenka cried.

Jack stepped forward too, quickly blurting out to Fedyenka, "The antidote for the code!"

James paused, considering it. "Well," he said, "how 'bout it, asshole?"

Stacey could see the surrender in Fedyenka's eyes. The outburst of anger had left him exhausted, and he knew he was dying.

"How much time do I have?" Fedyenka asked.

James said, "If yer thinkin' of gettin' help without this"—he tapped the glass with his shoe—"then probably not enough. You'll need this just to get ya to a hospital."

Fedyenka wiped sweat from his eyes. "What the hell is it?"

"A little concoction an associate of mine brought back from the Middle East."

Fedyenka sighed heavily. "Vial first."

"Like hell."

"Then she dies too."

James shrugged. "I'm willin' to take that risk."

Jack started to protest, but Stacey grabbed his hand, stopping him.

She said to Fedyenka, "You didn't actually give me a live bomb at the senator's party. I think you're bluffing now, too."

Fedyenka smiled. "It is not a bluff."

"As much trouble as you've gone through to get Joseph, I doubt you'd risk blowing my head off before getting his location out of me." She shook her head. "Bluff."

Fedyenka eyed the vial under James's boot, knowing that if Stacey truly believed he was bluffing about the collar, then he had no hand to play. He was out of options if he wanted to live. "Fine. But just in case you plan on killing me once the necklace is off, I will tell you that I have given Joseph's last known coordinates to my men. They are on their way to get him now. Their orders, in the event that I am killed, are to eliminate him on sight." He swayed on his feet, meeting each of their eyes. Then, "Seven-three-nine-two-eight."

Stacey heard Johnson on the stones behind her. Then she felt a little pressure at the base of her neck as he started hitting the buttons. For a moment, she second-guessed the situation. What if the bomb was enough to take out all four of them? The blast would knock James backward, his foot coming off the vial rather than down on top of it. Fedyenka could then recover the antidote and continue after Joseph. She opened her mouth to stop Johnson from hitting the last button when a sudden *click* sounded, and the collar fell off her neck. Reflexively, she reached out and caught it before it could hit the ground. She thought about putting it on Fedyenka's neck, but she was sure it wouldn't fit. Instead, she turned and threw it into the water.

Jack said to James, "Give it to him."

James bent over and picked up the vial. He looked at Stacey as if contemplating whether to give it over or to just shoot the bastard in the head.

Stacey nodded, her eyes begging him to give over the antidote.

He tossed it to him.

Fedyenka caught it with shaking hands and managed to pop the top off, greedily draining the contents into his mouth. "Now what?" he stammered.

Now we're wasting time, Stacey thought. If Fedyenka's men managed to grab Joseph before they could, then they would be right back in this same scenario, only it would be them who wouldn't have a hand to play. It would be game over. *Shit.* It seemed as if Fedyenka had won. Unless... She looked at Johnson. "Do you have the location?" she whispered, referring to Joseph's last known coordinates.

Johnson looked down at the phone he'd been discreetly using and nodded.

Stacey's mind raced. They needed to get out of here now. Every second counted. But they had no helicopter, no plane, no—

She turned and looked out into the water. "Is that Osprey?" she asked Fedyenka, pointing at the motorboat and the yacht beyond it.

He shook his head. "If those were my men, you would already be dead."

"So who are they? You came here for a ride, didn't you?" Jack asked.

Fedyenka turned his attention to him. "Jack," he said, as if really seeing him for the first time. There was a biting contempt in his tone. "Deep down you must know, right?"

Stacey's heart skipped a beat as she contemplated all the possible things that might come out of Fedyenka's mouth next.

"How the hell would I know who they are?" Jack asked, thinking that Fedyenka's question was about the boat.

Stacey needed to divert the conversation before it went any further. Not because she was sure that Fedyenka was right in his line of thinking. But because she wasn't. Stacey grabbed Jack's hand and squeezed it, her thumbnail digging into the ball of muscle behind his thumb. "He's trying to stall," she whispered. "If Osprey gets to Joseph first, we have nothing."

But before Jack could respond and right as Fedyenka began saying something else, Joseph's name rolling off his tongue, a loud and sudden *thud* sounded, and Fedyenka's body spun away from them, clockwise and in a cloud of red. Even as he was falling, the *crack* of a rifle struck their ears, the noise traveling late over the water and rebounding off the cliff.

Stacey jumped, and Fedyenka landed hard on his side. They all turned and looked out over the water behind them.

The boat that had been floating between the shore and the yacht was now speeding toward the yacht.

"They're leaving," Johnson said.

"Look," Stacey said, pointing up at the sky above the boat.

Two dark smudges blotted the distant sunlit sky.

"Helicopters," James said. "Think they're friendly?"

"I'm not sure there is such a thing as 'friendly' anymore," Johnson answered. "Let's—"

Another shot sounded out, but this one was closer and louder than the last.

Stacey dropped to her knees, twisting at the waist and swinging the MAC-11 around toward the blast.

Fedyenka was lying on his side and aiming a small pistol at James.

James looked down at himself. He seemed content that no bullet had struck him.

Fedyenka must have had it concealed in an ankle holster or tucked into the back of his pants. But his hand was shaking wildly, and the barrel swayed as if the gun weighed a hundred pounds. Sweat was running down his face and stinging his eyes, causing him to keep blinking. He fired again, but again he missed. Then, exhausted, he dropped his arm to the ground and closed his eyes.

Johnson ran over and kicked the pistol away from him. It skittered across the stones.

Stacey lowered the rifle and stepped gingerly toward Jack. "You okay?"

"Yeah," he said. "You?"

She nodded.

Jack turned and looked back out to the water, and Stacey did the same. The dark spots were growing bigger, getting closer. Pretty soon they'd be able to hear the *thump-thump-thump* of their rotors. And, like Johnson said, whoever was coming was probably not coming to help them. They needed to get out of there fast. But to where?

"What do we do with him now?" James asked, pointing his own gun at Fedyenka.

"Bring him with us," Stacey answered. "In case he was telling the truth."

Johnson seemed doubtful. "He's a big boy, and those were a lot of steps."

"Yeah," Jack said. "So we shouldn't waste any more time talking about it." He walked over to Fedyenka, who appeared to have lapsed into unconsciousness, and rolled him onto his back. The big Russian's arms flopped outward and his ankles crossed like some cruciform parody. Jack bent over and grabbed him under the arms. "Grab his legs," he said to Johnson.

Johnson took a large leg under each of his arms, and together they moved him across the beach and to the water.

Stacey could see Jack's biceps bulging in the suit, and knew that, if not for his training over the last couple of years, he wouldn't have been strong enough to carry the sack of shit ten feet let alone all the way back up the cliff. She followed behind them as they walked awkwardly into the water and around the rock outcropping, floating the unconscious body between them when the water was deep enough, and then dragging him back up the other side and heading for the stairs.

The sound of the helicopters finally reached their ears, rebounding like hammer blows off the rock wall ahead of them.

Stacey looked back for the yacht, but it was gone.

They began climbing the steps, James in the lead, Stacey taking up the rear, Jack and Johnson wrestling with Fedyenka's dead weight, blood getting onto their hands and arms.

The choppers would be there within seconds, and Stacey could only hope that the pilots would be too distracted by the burning fortress to notice the five of them scaling the side of the cliff.

JACK TURNED HIS ATTENTION upward as the pair of choppers streaked overhead, disappearing beyond the cliff. Either the pilots didn't care about them, or the smoke from the fire had shielded their ascent. *Or they're dropping off a kill squad that'll be waiting for us at the top of the stairs*, he thought. He heard Stacey identify them as Seahawks.

"Come on," Johnson said from Fedyenka's feet. "Almost there."

Despite the cold, Jack wiped sweat from his brow, streaking his forehead with blood in the process. Whether it was his or Fedyenka's, he didn't know. Only one section of stairs remained. Two dozen steps. His lower back was stiff from bending over, his quads and biceps on fire. He wanted to trade places with Johnson just so that he could stand up straighter, but there was no room within the railings to make such a maneuver. They'd have to lay the Russian down and walk over him, and Jack could just imagine Fedyenka waking up and grabbing his feet, pitching him down the stairs. Twenty-four steps. He could do it. He backed up one more step.

Twenty-three.

Twenty-two.

Twenty-one.

One of the Seahawks suddenly swung back over the cliff, maneuvering above them, and Jack braced himself for the bullets that would finally end this nonsensical dream. But the chopper banked and circled back toward the fire, its rotors scattering the pillar of smoke into swirls of cursive ink. Then it was out of view again.

"Do you hear that?" Stacey asked, looking down from ten steps ahead. "They're setting down."

And, indeed, Jack could tell that the sound of the rotors had changed. They weren't as deafeningly loud and seemed to have settled into a more idle humming. But who were they? CIA, SVR, FBI, or Osprey? If only one chopper had arrived, then Jack might assume some ranger service was responding to the smoke and coming over to check it out. But not two military-looking helicopters. No, this had more of a spec-ops vibe than a *Cliffhanger* one. These Seahawks were like the choppers the FBI's HRT had used in the mountains to rescue him and Joseph.

By the time he finally reached the top of the stairs, it seemed as if his heart was trying to leap out of his chest. Johnson let go of Fedyenka's legs and motioned for Jack to stop. Jack set the Russian down, careful not to let his mangled head slam on the last metal step. He tried to catch his breath.

"Let Stacey and James check it out first," Johnson said.

"How much time do we have?" he asked.

Johnson looked at his watch. "It's gonna be real close."

Jack looked up and over the railing to find Stacey, but she was already halfway to the building, the bottoms of her soot-stained feet flashing beneath her leather legs. Then James was coming up behind Johnson, hopping up on the railing and tightroping past the FBI man, Fedyenka, and then Jack. He hopped off and sprinted to the abandoned UTV that was still sitting there. He hopped behind the wheel, brought the engine to life, and got the tires turning so fast that they shot clumps of dirt over the cliff as he peeled out and went after Stacey.

James drove up alongside Stacey, who was training her weapon on the building's northwest corner for any sign of Osprey. Jack heard James yell something, and then Stacey turned and hopped into the seat beside James. Then they flew around the building and out of sight.

Jack looked down at Fedyenka. The man's eyes were still closed, and his face seemed ashen. His shirt was soaked with sweat and blood.

Jack stretched his back, feeling the muscles loosen a little. Blood began to circulate in his arms and legs. "What are they doing?" he asked Johnson.

"We need one of those choppers. It's our only chance."

"How many men—"

But Jack's words were cut off by the sudden appearance of a pickup truck speeding past the flames and heading straight toward them. He thought it was the same Nissan Frontier they'd commandeered before, and as it got closer, he could see James behind the wheel.

"They're back with the truck," Jack said, bending over and grabbing Fedyenka under the armpits again. He willed his muscles to work, and the two of them carried Fedyenka off the stairs and to the waiting truck. Stacey had the tailgate down and was watching the building as if expecting it to either explode or for an army to come out of it.

Jack and Johnson tossed the big man into the truck bed and climbed up after him. Stacey hopped over the side and slid back into the passenger seat. James had the truck moving back toward the building before she could even close the door.

As they passed the building, Jack saw the remaining Nissan and the UTV where James and Stacey had abandoned it. Then Jack saw the two helicopters resting on the helipad, their rotors still turning, ready to fly. James floored the gas, and the truck bounced over the uneven ground, nearly tossing Jack over the side of the truck.

"Where are the men?" Jack asked, not seeing the squads of men in tactical gear exiting the choppers and running toward the building.

"One of the choppers must've covered the other while they fast-roped down to the building," Johnson explained.

Jack figured they were about to find out. If there were platoons still sitting in the choppers, yet to deploy, they would no doubt perceive the charging Nissan as a threat and open fire on them. But if only the pilots occupied them, waiting for further instructions or for their passengers to return, then Jack didn't know what they'd be able to do other than lift off before they got to them. James had the truck heading straight at their rear, so maybe the pilots wouldn't even see them coming.

Then, twenty yards away from the helicopters, James hit the brakes and yelled for them all to get out.

Unsure what James was thinking—and if they had the time to do it—they all obeyed, Stacey jumping out the passenger door, Jack and Johnson rolling Fedyenka off the back of the truck and hopping out after him.

Then James hit the gas again.

Jack and Johnson lifted Fedyenka to his feet so that they were carrying him upright between them, their arms around his bloody torso, his limp arms around the back of their necks. Stacey walked to them, all three of them watching the pickup get nearer and nearer to the closest helicopter.

The truck smashed into the tail section, and the whole helicopter spun on its wheels. When it stopped spinning, Jack could see that the rear stabilizer was nearly snapped off, hanging like a lizard's broken tail. James was out of the truck and running for the cockpit.

Jack turned to look at Stacey, but neither she nor Johnson was beside him. He blinked and then noticed that Fedyenka was now lying on the ground at his feet. He must've spaced out for a moment and dropped him when Johnson took off—Johnson and Stacey already pulling the pilot out of the other helicopter.

James was now out of the broken chopper and running toward Jack, motioning for him to help get Fedyenka into the other helicopter. "Hurry," he yelled.

Jack could see that Stacey was already behind the controls and hitting switches above her head. He glanced at the building, wondering how many seconds they had left and if he'd actually register the explosion before it killed him.

James pulled on Fedyenka's arm, yanking him up to a sitting position. Jack bent over and grabbed his other arm, and the two of them dragged him on his ass across the grass and to the helicopter. Johnson was standing in the open cabin, looking back toward the fire and watching for signs of the chopper's former occupants.

But when they reached the chopper, Johnson set his rifle on the cabin floor and bent over, grabbing Fedyenka by the collar and helping lift him up and onto the floor of the cabin. Jack and James climbed in, and the three of them heaved Fedyenka up into a seat.

"Hold on," Stacey said from the cockpit.

Johnson looked at his watch again. "Hurry."

The wheels left the ground.

As Jack buckled Fedyenka into the seat, Stacey worked the collective, swinging the chopper around and away from the burning Osprey base. She took them up over the trees and headed inland just as the sky behind them disappeared in a flash of white.

The silo exploded like an erupting volcano, whatever munitions had been stored near the bombs contributing to the blast and disintegrating half the building in the blink of an eye. The mushroom cloud rose high into the sky, red and orange fire shooting upward before rolling back on itself with living fury. The explosion blew the cliff wall into the sea, and then the whole hillside began to collapse. Whatever remained of the burning fortress went over in the landslide and crashed onto the beach below.

"Holy crap," Jack whispered. Had they been one minute later getting the helicopter off the ground, they'd all be dead. Another miracle.

"Are we clear?" Stacey asked back over her shoulder.

James leaned out of the cabin, searching the skies. "Yeah."

"Where am I going?" Stacey asked next.

Johnson leaned forward and relayed the coordinates he'd gotten from the pilots. She punched them into the GPS and then banked left.

James and Johnson closed the cabin doors against the cold.

"Do we know who these guys were?" Jack asked, even as his eyes swept the interior of the cabin, looking for words.

"They were American," Johnson said.

Jack spotted some words in English over the cabin doors. "So probably not SVR."

Johnson shook his head. "If the boat left because the helicopters were coming in…"

"And the boat was trying to kill Fedyenka…" Jack added.

"That would make the pilots CIA," Johnson concluded.

"Osprey wouldn't have tried taking out Fedyenka on the beach, so the boat must've been SVR."

"If this is the Agency's chopper, then they'll be tracking it," Johnson said.

"You think he had a boat coming to pick him up?"

"Probably. Maybe got spooked when they saw the yacht out there," Johnson explained.

Fedyenka's eyes opened a little, and James stared directly into them. Jack had little trouble reading the thoughts of this man his son had skewered in the woods. They were the same thoughts he was having himself, though perhaps to a slightly lesser degree. Jack had no idea how close James had been to his brother, and even though Jack had an overwhelming urge to put a bullet in Fedyenka's head for the threat that he posed to his family, Jack hadn't actually lost Stacey or Joseph. If Jack or Stacey were to end this bastard's life, it would be out of a sort of self-defense and not the revenge James was aching for.

Fedyenka's lips started to move. He was mumbling something. "Your son deserves to know, Jack."

"What?" Jack asked, leaning closer.

"Know his…heritage. His destiny…"

"What the hell is he saying?" Jack asked James, who seemed to be trying to read his lips.

James shook his head.

"Were you trying to destabilize the Kremlin?" Jack asked.

Fedyenka's head was starting to loll, like he was high or drunk. "Ukraine," he mumbled. Drool fell from his lips, and his eyes closed.

"The poison tends to loosen lips," James said to Jack, explaining Fedyenka's behavior.

"Like a truth serum?"

"Not really. It clouds the mind. It won't force him to tell the truth, it'll just make him not care about hidin' it."

Johnson snapped his fingers in Fedyenka's face. "Hey," he said. "What about Ukraine?"

Fedyenka smiled. "Won't allow NATO in…"

"Russia won't? No shit," Johnson said.

"If a NATO missile flies into Russian airspace…it will be…World War Three."

"Which is what you've always wanted. What the CIA has always wanted," Jack said.

Fedyenka's eyes rolled, and it seemed as if he was going to pass out again.

"Put pressure on his wound," Johnson said to James.

James reached forward and pressed his hand against the dark spot on his shoulder.

"How much longer?" Jack called up to Stacey. He knew that Stacey couldn't hear any of their conversation, and part of him was glad. He was hoping to get some other answers out of this prick before he died. Answers he wasn't so sure Stacey wanted him to have.

Stacey turned and yelled back over her shoulder, "Twenty-five minutes!"

James lightly smacked Fedyenka on the side of his face. "Hey, no sleepy sleepy yet."

The Russian's eyes opened. "Putin is a pussy," he hissed. "He does not have the balls to do what needs to be done. So I will do it…"

"How?" Johnson asked.

But Jack interjected with another question before Fedyenka could answer. "What does Joseph have to do with all of this?"

Fedyenka blinked in slow motion, moved his eyes in his direction. "You do not know?" Fedyenka smiled. "After all of this time, Jack...you must...know."

Again, Jack's stomach clenched into a fist. "What does he have to do with this tsar shit?"

Fedyenka leaned his head back and licked his lips. "Vadim Sidorov..." His deep voice rose a few octaves, as if he were speaking in some singsong drug-crazed revelation. "I never understood...why she chose him." He seemed to go contemplative then. "Maybe it was my paintings. I think that bothered her." He turned his attention back to Jack, his head flopping down as if his huge neck had turned into a pillar of noodles. "You know that I handed him over to the CIA? And then...when he became a double agent, I reported him to the FSB?" He was slurring his words. "Anna's mother, Viktoriya, was...reactivated with orders to...kill her son-in-law." He smiled again. "But there was you..."

Jack was fascinated by all of this, but he knew that he was running out of time with him. He needed answers to bigger questions. "What was with the poster you sent Stacey? The *Anastasia* one? And the *Michael Strogoff* book in Joseph's locker?"

"Michael Strogoffffffff... Russian hero. Loyal to the tsar..."

But Fedyenka's mind seemed to have gone elsewhere.

"Hey," Jack yelled.

Stacey looked back at them.

"How long...before the antidote begins to...work," Fedyenka whispered.

James narrowed his eyes. "What antidote?"

Fedyenka's eyes opened wide, as if he'd been hit with a shot of adrenaline. Jack and Johnson looked at James too.

"You gave me the antidote," Fedyenka said, his brain fog clearing for a moment.

"There ain't no antidote," James said.

Fedyenka blinked.

"That's right, you piece of KGB shit. You're dyin', and ain't nothin' in this world can save you."

Fedyenka sat forward a little, but it was as if he were operating in his sleep. His lips moved, but no words were heard.

"Now comes the paralysis," James explained. "Motor function'll start to shut down. Your ability to communicate'll evaporate. But your mind…" He tapped the side of his own head. "The fog'll go away, and you'll be sharp as a tack."

"What was in the vial, then?" Johnson wanted to know, confused.

"Always be prepared to manipulate an asshole," he said. "It was a simple thing to carry around a vial of water just supposin' I might need some kind of leverage."

Jack got the impression that this wasn't the first time James had used such tactics. "So how long does he have?" he asked, upset at James's deception, yet realizing how insane that was since it had gotten the bomb collar off Stacey's neck.

James looked back into the Russian's cold shark eyes that just hours ago had been full of conspiracy, perversion, and grand schemes of power. Now they contained nothing but fear. "I'd say six to seven hours of discomfort before he's just rotting meat."

Jack looked up past Stacey and out the canopy. He could see nothing but water to the left and trees to the right. A terrible thought struck him. *What if Joseph didn't survive the landing?* He threw the thought away. It did absolutely no good to worry about that.

Instead, he turned toward Fedyenka again, about to press him on the poster and the book and why he wanted Joseph so bad. What it had to do with Vadim. But there could only be one answer to that, couldn't there? But it was impossible. "Hey," he said.

But Fedyenka's eyes were closed, his chin resting on his chest again. He was unconscious.

80

IT TURNED OUT TO be a frozen pond that had caught his attention. The sunlight had caught a fraction of the surface at just the right angle and sent a flash of light across his eyes. Joseph stood beside it now, shivering. Most of it was covered with snow, but the wind had blown a trail across what he thought was its center. Not that he could be sure that the ice path actually split the mostly concealed lake into two equal halves. He looked left and right. No trees for hundreds of yards in either direction. The lake could stretch the entire length of his vision. Or maybe it wasn't a lake at all. Maybe it was a frozen puddle in a field.

He blinked. He was so tired. He looked behind to see how far away the tree line was and was shocked to see his tracks going on for what seemed like forever. The trees were the size of his thumb when holding it up to his eye. He didn't remember walking all that way. Had he been sleepwalking? He looked down at his feet.

Wait, he thought.

If it was a frozen lake that he was chasing after, then he might already be on it. His heart thumped in his chest as he recalled a few movies of people trekking across a snow-white field only to find out the hard way that it was no field at all.

He got down on his knees and swept the snow away.

Ice.

It seemed solid enough, but if he were to come across a weak spot, he knew there would be no surviving it. Even if he did manage to pull himself out, he'd have to walk or crawl all the way to the woods and then somehow start a fire. Even Michael Strogoff wouldn't have been able to pull that off.

He got back to his feet, swayed for a second, his eyes so heavy, and turned around. It wasn't worth the risk. He'd go back the way he'd come and try to start a fire just inside the tree line. Then he'd sleep. He wanted nothing else. Warmth and sleep. He'd trade his playlist for it. He'd trade almost anything for it.

He started walking, concentrating on placing one foot into one backward footprint at a time.

WHEN HE FINALLY REACHED the trees again, he immediately began looking for sticks. He had about five good ones in a pile when he thought he heard something. He stood straight, his staff in hand, his ear cocked. The image that came to mind was the old box fan his dad used to run in their New Jersey house when he was little. He remembered lying on the floor in front of it and letting the air and the noise lull him into long naps on hot summer days. But then a distinct sort of clicking began to accent the hum. Like a drum track fading onto an instrumental.

No, not the clicking of drumsticks on the rim of a snare, but the steady thumping of a base pedal.

He looked up into the sky, through the patchwork of slightly swaying branches, and allowed his mind to dismantle the box fan and assemble a new picture from its parts.

He turned back to the lake.

Crap.

His single set of footprints stretched forth through the untouched snow like a signal beacon.

The sound was louder now, coming at him from the woods, and there was no mistaking what it was.

A helicopter.

Joseph began to panic. He didn't know what to do. They would see his tracks on the lake, set down, and then come after him. He didn't think he had the energy to evade them for long. He was too tired and too cold. Too weak to fight. Hiding was his only option, but he'd need to find a spot void of snow, where they wouldn't be able to follow his tracks. He looked around, but saw no rocks, only frozen dirt where the canopy had been too thick to allow snowfall. He began walking in that direction. He didn't know what else he could do.

The sound of the chopper continued to grow until a skittering, broken shadow passed over him, the sound suddenly beginning to fade as the vehicle cleared the woods and flew over the lake.

Joseph watched it bank to the left and come back around. It wasn't a military-looking helicopter like he'd almost fallen out of before. It was a red and white helicopter with a cross on its door. Some kind of search and rescue, he guessed. But what department would be looking for him? How would they *know* to look for him? Had some hunter seen him land and reported it over a radio or satellite phone?

He didn't trust it. He took one last look at the helicopter now hovering about ten feet over his footprints, its two bulbous insect eyes seeming to stare right at him, and then continued making his way out of the snow.

And then he heard a voice shout something, and he stopped dead in his tracks.

"Joseph!"

His name echoed across the flat terrain.

It was his father's voice.

He turned back, wondering if he could be hallucinating.

"Joseph!" his father called again over what could only be some sort of PA system on the helicopter. *"Joseph Green!"*

It was his dad's voice alright.

"Joseph..."

This time it was his mom's voice that had called out to him. *Mom!* His dad and Agent Johnson had found and rescued her! He turned, his heart suddenly light and his chest full of hope, and ran toward the lake. He no longer felt tired or cold. He felt nothing but excitement and joy. "I'm here!" he tried to yell, but he couldn't hear his own words. He tried again, stumbling toward the tree line. "I'm here!" This time he did hear himself.

He kept calling out, using the stick to steady his stiff legs. He burst out of the trees and waved his arms.

The helicopter set down, its skids landing on the ice. Joseph hoped they knew that they were landing on a lake. He was about a hundred yards away from them now, and tears of relief began to slide down his cheeks.

Figures emerged from the sides of the helicopter, jumping down onto the ice and jogging toward him.

His dad. His mom. Agent Johnson. And... He didn't know who the other two people could be. "Mom! Dad!" he cried out.

There was a loud crunch, and suddenly his stomach was flipped completely upside down.

He was falling through the ice!

Even as his legs plunged into the icy water, he managed to turn the stick sideways and hug it against his chest and beneath his arms so that it spanned the width of the hole and stopped him from going completely under. He held onto the stick, the lower half of his body submerged and already numb. He looked up to the people running toward him. It would be okay, he thought. As long as the ice held beneath the stick, he would be okay. His parents would pull him out and get him onto the chopper. They'd take him somewhere warm where he could sleep.

But as the figures approached and their faces came into view, he knew that something was wrong.

None of them were his parents or Agent Johnson.

81

JACK STUDIED THE WILD terrain below. Every minute that passed ratcheted his nerves tighter. He thought his very being would soon rip in half from the stress of it. They had spotted nothing that would indicate someone having parachuted down there. Though, as if to emphasize the danger Joseph faced, they had spotted a grizzly bear leading its cubs over some rocks.

Jack tried to get a read on Stacey's own feelings, but he couldn't see her face from his position. He thought of climbing up over the center console and sliding into the empty chair beside her, but he didn't want to risk accidentally sitting on a switch that could put them in a tailspin or something.

Besides, he wanted to be within earshot of Fedyenka in case he woke up and started talking again. Though, from the looks of him, Jack would be surprised if the man ever spoke another word. He was definitely on his way out. And, Jack thought, shouldn't that fact alone come as such a satisfying conclusion to this whole mad story? Yet Jack felt none of the elation or relief he'd expected to feel. Because Joseph was not with them, and because of that, this victory over Fedyenka, years and years in the making, seemed totally anticlimactic.

Indeed, if Joseph were with them, or he at least knew he was somewhere safe and waiting for them, he would be doing everything he could to wrestle more answers from the dying sack of shit. Answers to questions about Viktoriya and her husband, Vadim and the cruise ship, the whole Senator Newell business (which he was sure he still didn't know the full scope of), what Joseph had to do with this whole imperial delusion...

Jack stared at the Russian, imagining the answers to so many questions just sitting there behind that scarred skull but with no way of getting to them. Even in death, he realized, the Russian could still win. Because any outcome that didn't include a reunion with Joseph would he a catastrophic defeat and render all their efforts over the last few years entirely moot. Their mission had always been Joseph. Anything short of that was unacceptable.

"Look," James said. He was still sitting across from Fedyenka, but he'd grown bored of the man's pain and had instead begun to help look for Joseph. "Tracks," he said, pointing.

Jack and Johnson shifted in their seats and craned their necks, trying to get a glimpse of what James was seeing.

"Human?" Johnson asked.

"Yeah," James answered.

Jack saw the line of prints through the snow and wondered how James could tell they were human. The guy was from the mountains, so he'd give him the benefit of the doubt. He leaned forward and got Stacey's attention, pointing at what the rest of them were looking at.

Stacey nodded and adjusted their heading.

The helicopter banked and came in line with the footprints. They led straight into a wooded forest a mile ahead.

The tension in Jack's gut loosened a few notches. He looked behind them, trying to spot the track's origins. A spent parachute blowing in the wind would have been an amazing sight to see, but he knew that was hoping for too much. And, indeed, the tracks vanished in the other direction beneath some dense thickets.

They flew to the treeline and then over it, trees now filling their view as far as they could see. The canopy was so thick that Joseph could be waving to them, and they wouldn't know.

"I'm going to take us higher," Stacey called back. "To see how far these trees go."

Jack nodded, even though he knew she couldn't see him doing it. The trees started to fall away, and his stomach, just as much as his eyes, informed him of their sudden ascent.

Johnson climbed up into the cockpit to help.

As they rose into the late afternoon sky, the green carpet grew longer and longer until, finally, it stopped at a sharp white line. Stacey continued forward, trying to see if the tracks exited the forest.

"What the hell is that?" Stacey asked, leaning forward and peering out the canopy.

Jack shifted his gaze from the treetops to the sea of white beyond. There was something there, sitting against the snowy backdrop. It was too far away to tell what it was, but it had to be something large to see it from this distance. "A bear?" Jack asked.

"I don't think so," James responded, leaning up beside Jack and looking over his shoulder. He had a toothpick in his mouth.

Johnson lifted his binoculars to his eyes. "It's a helicopter."

Stacey swore and pushed the collective forward. The front of the helicopter pitched forward at a downward angle, the remainder of the trees flashing by in a blur.

As the spot on the snow grew closer, it began to take shape, as if it were a pixelated image that was slowly rendering.

It was red and white and clearly a helicopter.

"Looks like a Type Two Bell that a fire department would use," Stacey said.

"There's men on the ground," Johnson said, still looking through the binoculars.

"What are they doing?" Jack asked, leaning into the cockpit.

"Oh my god," Johnson muttered.

"What?"

"They're on ice!" He passed the binoculars back to Jack. "Someone fell through."

Jack took them from him, but by the time he got them to his eyes, they'd gotten close enough so that he could make out the person sticking out of the ice without them. They were holding onto a stick or a pole that spanned the hole. Through the lenses, the person's face came into view. "It's Joseph!" he yelled.

And that was when the sound of their own helicopter must've finally reached the people on the ground, because all five people, all in black and standing out like ants on whipped cream, suddenly stopped and turned to look at the sky behind them.

"Let's swing around and drop us in front of them," Johnson said over to Stacey.

Stacey nodded. "Do you think they're Search and Rescue?" she called back.

"No," Johnson answered.

Jack opened the cabin door, filling the cabin with freezing air. He could only imagine how cold Joseph must be. "Hold on…hold on…hold on…" he whispered over and over again.

Fedyenka stirred beside him.

Stacey and Johnson passed the red and white helicopter and then swung around, putting themselves just behind Joseph. The nearest person was about ten feet away from him, and if Johnson was right about them not being Search and Rescue, then they could just as easily shoot Joseph in the head as pull him out of the water. Though if they wanted to kill him, certainly they could have done so already.

"Turn sideways!" James yelled.

Stacey turned her head and saw James pointing forward out the door. She rotated the helicopter so that the open cabin faced the men on the ground.

"Get lower," James hollered next. "So they can see his face!"

Stacey understood. James thought they were Osprey and wanted to show them that they had Fedyenka on board. She lowered the chopper to just a few feet off the ice.

Jack saw that the men all had rifles, and though they were aiming them, none had pulled a trigger yet. He could also see Joseph holding onto the stick for dear life. He had no idea how long he'd been holding on like that or how much strength he had left in him. He wanted to jump out, to go to him, and certainly would have already if he wasn't afraid that his landing on the ice would collapse the entire section of the lake and send everyone into the water. Though, depending on how things went in the next few moments, it could be his only option.

The rotors pulled snow off the ground and sent it in long wispy fingers curling up and around them. But they were all close enough to see each other's faces. James turned Fedyenka so that he was facing out the side door and held a pistol to his head. "Tell 'em to get back," James told Jack.

Jack waved at them, telling them to back away.

At first the men just stood there staring, unsure of what to do. Jack hoped that they recognized Fedyenka. If they didn't, if they'd never actually seen their boss before...

But they must have, because the closest guy took a step back. Then another. And soon they were all backing up.

"The rope," James said, turning to Jack.

Jack looked around the cabin, remembering that Johnson had said one of the teams must've fast-roped down to the burning building while the other covered them. Since there was no rope dangling loose from their chopper, he'd figured it had been the other one that James had crashed into. But then he spotted it. It was coiled around a hook on the other side of the cabin.

He grabbed it off the hook and threw it out of the cabin. It landed straight across the hole, passing by Joseph's right shoulder. "Grab the rope!" he yelled to his back. He could see Joseph turn his head, but he didn't make a move for the rope. "Just grab the rope!" he yelled again. But either Joseph couldn't hear him over the helicopter, or he couldn't move his arms without slipping beneath the ice.

"Screw it," Jack said. And without a second thought, he jumped out.

It was only a four-foot drop, but when his feet went through the thin layer of snow and hit the ice, they flew straight out from under him. He landed hard on his back and heard a crack. For a second he thought he'd broken the ice, but then realized it was just the rifle still in his hands that had smacked its surface. He rolled onto his stomach and scrambled to his feet. "Joe, it's Dad! I'm coming."

Joseph said something in response, but Jack couldn't make it out over the sound of the two helicopters. As he got closer, he heard what Joseph was saying.

"I'mmmmm...s-s-s-s-s-l-l-l-l-i-p-p-ing..."

Jack was ten feet away from him but was afraid that one inch closer might send them both under. "Do you think you can grab the rope?"

"C-c-c-an't m-m-m-ove m-m-y armsssss..."

Jack looked past Joseph and the Seahawk and to the other helicopter, to the men now climbing back into it. Apparently, they did the easy math and deducted it was time for new employment. He could see Stacey's face through the cockpit window and read the helpless expression in her eyes, the fear that they had only arrived in time to watch Joseph die.

There was no more time.

He quickly made a series of hand motions to her and then picked up the rope and tied it around his chest.

Joseph started to slip.

Before a gust of wind could rock the helicopter and pull Jack away from his son, he dove for the hole. He flew through the air, belly-flopping onto the ice just two feet away, hands outstretched, hoping to grab him before he went under.

When he landed, the ice shattered like glass beneath him, and he plunged through the surface.

IT WAS LIKE FALLING into a pool of needles, and the shock of it paralyzed him. For a moment, he thought that he'd just sink to the lake floor and drown before he could regain any motor function. But then his foot kicked. His arm moved.

He realized that his arms were wrapped tightly around something.

Joseph.

His momentum must have carried him to the hole and into Joseph as the ice collapsed beneath him.

But they were both under water now, and Joseph didn't seem to be moving.

Jack opened his eyes and looked up, seeing the daylight shimmering through the fragmented ice above them. He tried to kick his legs harder, but it was like they were in glue. They weren't moving any closer to the air they needed.

God, please! He cried out in his head.

Something gripped his chest so suddenly and so tightly that for a split second he thought that he'd just been cut in half. And then they were crashing through the underside of the lake's icy surface and flying sideways across the top of the lake, their legs dragging through snow. Jack looked up and saw the helicopter at the other end of the rope, dragging them.

He wished he could tell Stacey to keep going, to drag them all the way to the woods and just set the chopper down, but she would never be able to hear him, and he was sure he wouldn't be able to hold on to Joseph that long. He could barely feel his own arms and knew he was about to lose his grip any second. But then he twirled on the rope so that he was actually sitting on the ice and being dragged backwards across it, Joseph now sitting in his lap.

He held Joseph tighter, putting his face against his and hoping for any sign of life. If he needed to perform CPR, then they needed to start right now. He saw the other helicopter leaving, and then lowered his gaze to the road of ice they were leaving in their wake.

And then the frosted surface changed, and a green stripe began to grow in its place.

The tension that was pulling them disappeared, and they both fell onto their backs.

Jack rolled Joseph off him and struggled quickly to his knees. Which he couldn't feel at all. The rope was lying across the snow and dead-ended about fifteen feet away from them. Someone must've cut the rope when they noticed the ice had given way to grass. Jack ignored how tight the rope still was and bent over his son, ready to start chest compressions.

But Joseph's eyes were open, and there was a pale smile spread on his lips. His teeth chattered so hard, Jack was afraid they might break.

"Hey, p-p-pal," Jack said, surprised to hear his own teeth clacking together equally as hard.

"H-h-h-I, D-d-d-d-a-a-a-a-d."

The helicopter came to a rest fifty feet away, the downwash making a large green circle in the midst of the white dusting.

When Jack turned his head in its direction, he saw Stacey in the ridiculous leather outfit running for them. Her feet were still bare. Jack didn't know how she'd managed to work the pedals without something on her feet—feet he was sure she'd stopped feeling hours ago. And now here she was running through the snow...

Jack tried getting to his feet, but his legs weren't working. He couldn't tell if it was because his pants had frozen solid or if his entire lower half was numb.

Stacey slid to a stop beside them, her hands touching Joseph's face, running her fingers through his hair. Then Johnson was there and picking Joseph up, pulling him from Jack's arms. Jack watched as Johnson trotted back to the helicopter with his son.

"C'mon, Jack Wick," Stacey said. She grabbed his arms and tried to pull him up.

Jack shook his head. "I can't m-m-m-ove." Then he looked down at her feet. They were purple. "Your f-f-f-eet."

"Stopped feeling them a long time ago," she said.

"I f-f-f-f-igured," he said. "N-n-n-ot good."

"Probably not," she agreed. "So let's get the hell out of here, and maybe I won't lose them."

A shadow fell across his face, and Jack looked up to find James standing there, bending over and reaching for him.

"Let's go, Jack-o," the Appalachian man said, and in one quick motion, he pulled Jack straight up and over his shoulder. James then started moving, Stacey following them back to the helicopter.

82

JOSEPH OPENED HIS EYES. He could feel deep vibrations running through his body and could hear a loud, dull thumping. But when he tried to place his surroundings, it was like he was looking through a fishbowl. He couldn't seem to bring anything into focus. He could see shapes and blurs of color, but that was it.

He was out of the ice. Wasn't sure where he was now or what was happening, but he knew he wasn't in the ice. That had been way too close a call. Michael Strogoff would not have been proud of him.

"Hey you," he heard a voice say. It was his dad's voice. Or at least he *thought* it had been his dad's voice. He'd thought it was his dad's voice that had come from the loudspeaker, too. And had he actually seen the person who pulled him out of the lake? He couldn't remember. But even if he had seen his dad's face, could he really be sure it wasn't some kind of *Mission: Impossible* thing where the guy was just wearing a mask of his dad's face and a chip on his neck that mimicked his voice?

He blinked and tried as hard as he could to focus on the face sitting across from him. The fishbowl drained, and he was able to see a little more clearly through the empty glass, though he thought for sure there must be some distortion going on because what he was seeing was impossible. He blinked again, but the person's face didn't change. In fact, he was pretty sure that he was seeing just fine. Which meant that he was either dreaming...or dead.

Because sitting across from him was the same man who had been in his dreams for the last couple of years.

It was the man from the mountains. The man he had stabbed with his makeshift spear.

The man was looking at him. He took a toothpick out of his mouth and grinned. "Hey there, Joseph. Remember me?"

And at that moment, Joseph was sure the guy was going to reach up, grab his chin, and pull his face off, revealing that he was actually Ethan Hunt. Then everyone else would pull their faces off too. There would be Ving Rhames and Simon Pegg and Jeremy Renner and Sawyer from *LOST*.

Joseph realized they were in a helicopter. Though whether they had been from the beginning of this scene or if the dream just uploaded that detail as he realized it, he wasn't sure. He was lying on his back and looking up at the ceiling.

He moved his eyes around, and in addition to the guy from the mountains, who obviously couldn't really be there—either because he had died from being stabbed or because it just made no sense for him to be—he saw his dad lying on the floor with him. He didn't see his mom or Agent Johnson, but if they were here, he figured they were the ones flying the chopper.

And then he saw another guy that he'd never seen before. He was sitting by the cabin door next to the mountain man. He looked like a zombie, and he wondered if this could be some kind of purgatory thing. Zane had told him about the Catholic concept of purgatory and that guy John Tetzel and his indulgences (played by Doctor Octopus in the Joseph Fiennes movie he had yet to see but had planned on talking Tommy into watching with him).

"It's me, kid," the mountain man said.

And then Joseph was no longer seeing the man from the woods, but the guy in *Last Crusade* who had given young Indy his hat at the beginning of the movie. But then the tomb raider from the 1989 film lifted his shirt and revealed a nasty scar right where Joseph had stuck him. Joseph's head spun, and for the first time since opening his eyes, began to feel the cold. But before the man could introduce him to all of his dead friends and welcome him to hell, Joseph's eyes closed again, and all the faces, whether real or masks, faded away.

83

THEY WERE FLYING OVER the water and heading north up the coast. Johnson was next to Stacey in the cockpit, studying the tablet, using the GPS to try to find a spot they could set down on that was within walking distance to a town.

As soon as they'd gotten back into the helicopter, Johnson had taken Fedyenka's shoes and socks off and handed them to Stacey. She looked ridiculous in her skintight leather and a pair of men's dress shoes, but she didn't care. All anyone cared about was how freaking cold they were. None of them were dressed for the outdoors, and they had been exposed for hours. But it was Jack and Joseph who were the worst off, having fallen through the ice. They needed to set down and get a fire going as soon as possible.

Jack's body shuddered against Joseph. They were lying on the metal floor of the cabin, trying to share body heat. He was so cold that his brain seemed to be stuck in idle. He was having trouble keeping his eyes open and processing basic ideas. He moved his gaze from Fedyenka's bare feet and up to James.

Fedyenka had betrayed the man, and the betrayal had resulted in his brother's death. Next, Jack shifted his gaze to Johnson's back. Fedyenka was, in one way or another, responsible for the death of everyone on his team. Maybe it was the CIA who had taken them out, maybe the SVR, but it was Fedyenka's pursuit of Joseph, his Osprey agenda, and his trying to trigger WWIII before that, that had made it all possible. The man had been a pain in a lot of asses.

And who knew what the hell he'd done to Stacey, his "Little Anastasia," the pet name he'd apparently given her in their past.

If anything *had* happened, then he knew Stacey would never tell him all of it, just like he was sure she hadn't told him everything there was to know about the senator business, her ex-husband, and who knew how many so-called "targets" over the years. He said he didn't want to know, yet the not knowing kept gnawing the locks off the rabbit hole and tormenting his imagination.

Fedyenka's eyes opened, and he looked down at Jack, meeting his gaze. At first, Jack wasn't sure that he was seeing things clearly, that maybe he was shivering so bad that it was distorting his vision. Because it looked like Fedyenka's eyes were suddenly clear and sharp. And then his lips stretched into a grin.

Jack blinked. Had the poison worn off? Was he recovering? It looked like he wanted to say something to him. Maybe whatever it was that he had been trying to say on the beach. Something about Joseph's destiny. Jack thought that any chance at cracking that riddle had evaporated with Fedyenka's unconscious state, but perhaps he had one more chance. One more chance to find out why this Russian asshole who had tried to start a war between Russia and the US, had turned Stacey's ex over to the CIA, had delusions of leading some sort of third-party tsar campaign against the Kremlin, wanted his son so badly. *Needed* him, it seemed.

"Anna," his voice boomed, calling up to Stacey.

His voice sounded strong, and Jack looked at James, wondering if they needed to worry. They hadn't tied him up or anything, and he was free to move if he could. But James had a pistol on his lap that was ready to go if needed.

Stacey turned away from the controls and looked back over her shoulder.

"Why is it, do you think, that I kept Vadim around like I did? Always putting up with his shit." His voice rose over the engine. "Even when you fell for him, I could have ended his life so easily. God knows I wanted to. How it killed me to see the two of you together."

Stacey returned her attention to the view ahead of them.

"Ukraine would have only been the beginning, the West pushing and pushing and pushing until finally the people would have demanded a response. A response I would have provided. And while the missiles were in the air, Osprey would have led the coup d'etat." And just like that, his energy was gone again, and he was back to dying. He closed his eyes.

But Jack still didn't understand what Joseph had to do with any of it. He was about to ask, when Fedyenka's eyes flicked back open.

"There really is no cure?" he asked James.

James shook his head.

"And it will only get more painful?"

James nodded. "Oh yeah."

Fedyenka sighed and turned his head, looking out the window and to the land below. Then after a moment, he looked down at Joseph. He stared at the boy for a long time with eyes impossible to interpret. They seemed sad, like all his dreams were dying, but that wasn't all. There was something that specifically had to do with who Joseph was. The Russian's expression seemed to revere him, as if he were looking at some child of promise. But then he blinked, and those icy shark eyes were back, if only for one last moment of defiance.

He quickly leaned forward out of the seat, practically falling on top of Jack and Joseph. He didn't have a weapon in his hands, and he didn't make any sort of move to harm them. Only put his lips to Jack's ear and whispered.

Jack was so startled that he almost didn't realize what the Russian was doing. He heard three words before the sudden sound of air rushing into the helicopter drowned out the rest of what he was saying. And then Fedyenka was flying backwards and away from him.

Jack forced himself to a sitting position, not sure what had happened, and saw James closing the cabin door.

Fedyenka was gone.

Stacey was turning in the seat and trying to see what was happening. "What the hell is going on?" she yelled.

"What—?" Jack blinked, unable to comprehend what he knew could be the only possible explanation.

James leaned forward and looked out the window.

Stacey tilted the chopper forty-five degrees sideways so that she could see across the cockpit and out the window to the ground below. The new pitch helped lift Jack forward and onto his knees. He grabbed the seat to his right and pulled himself to his numb feet. Then, without being able to feel his legs, he stumbled across the cabin and to the door, crashing into it. With his face pressed against the glass, he caught sight of Fedyenka's flailing body just before it struck the rocks along the shore. Even at one thousand feet, he could see the red halo appear around the bastard's head.

Jack couldn't believe it. Fedyenka was dead. After all this time, after all they'd been through, the man was dead. Gone.

They were free.

The helicopter leveled off, and for a few moments, no one spoke.

JOHNSON LOOKED UP FROM the tablet and pointed ahead. "That's good."

A wide stony beach lay sprawled before them.

They set the Seahawk down.

"How far away is the town?" she asked as they hit switches.

"About a mile and a half," Johnson said.

Stacey nodded. "We need to get a fire going ASAP, or we're all going to die of hypothermia."

Johnson opened the door and jumped out onto the stones, ducking beneath the rotating blades. He tucked the tablet into the back of his pants and went to the cabin door. He slid it open and helped James get Jack and Joseph out onto the ground.

After letting the Seahawk cool down a little, Stacey shut off the engine and joined them. "I'll stay with them," she said to Johnson. "Can you get the fire going?"

James interjected, "How 'bout I get the fire started, and you two get 'em into the woods."

"Fine," Stacey said.

James turned and ran for the trees.

"How do you want to do this?" Stacey asked Johnson.

Jack looked like he was fading in and out of consciousness, and Joseph was completely out. Both their faces were ghost's faces, their lips thin lines of blue.

Johnson looked to the tree line. It was about fifty yards away. "Stay here with Jack. I'll take Joseph to where James is setting up the fire. Then when you see me coming back, we trade spots. You go to Joseph, and I'll come get Jack."

Stacey didn't like the thought of leaving either Jack or Joseph alone for even a minute, but there was no way she could carry Joseph across the rocks in the oversized wingtips. She nodded.

Without hesitation, Johnson leaned down and scooped Joseph up into his arms. He turned and followed after James.

"Is he okay?" Jack's voice whispered up from his position on the ground, his back against the helicopter's wheel.

Stacey squatted next to him and threw her arms around his shoulders. She squeezed tight, trying to spread what little warmth she had to him. His clothes were still wet, and it made her leather top slippery. "I don't know," she said. "They're starting a fire."

Jack nodded, his eyes still closed. Then he said, "You do look pretty h-h-hot."

She kissed his cheek, feeling with her lips that his beard was frozen. She ran a hand through his long hair. "Johnson is coming to get you," she said. "Hang in there."

Johnson stepped out of the trees empty-handed. He waved her to him.

"Here he comes," she said. She let go of him and stood. Before she ran after Joseph, she looked back at her partially frozen husband. He was staring at her. "See you in a minute," she said, and turned and ran as best she could across the rocks.

As she and Johnson crossed paths, he called out over his shoulder, "You look ridiculous."

She made it to the trees and saw Joseph curled up in a ball beside a pile of twigs. James was kneeling and already blowing gently into it, trying to grow the small flicker that was there into a larger flame.

"Find me some branches," he said between breaths.

Stacey looked around, spotted some deadwood ten feet to her right, and went to collect it. When she brought it back to him, the pile of twigs and sticks was smoking. James stood and took the branches from her, snapping them over his knee one by one and standing them up like a teepee over top the kindling.

"More," he said.

She went, collected an armful, and dropped them on the ground beside him.

James nodded. "Now curl up next to him an' try rubbin' some heat into his arms."

Stacey did, but first she looked back to the beach and to Jack and Johnson. Johnson was half carrying, half dragging Jack toward them.

The flames jumped out of the kindling and began licking at the longer branches. James continued to feed it, and the fire continued to grow. Stacey could feel its heat already, and it felt wonderful. She rubbed Joseph's arms. They would have to get him out of these wet clothes soon, but not until the fire was hot enough to boil water.

"Hey," James said, looking over the fire to her. "Sorry 'bout before. On the plane. I didn't know what else to do."

She blushed.

"I coulda just switched it with the real one, but I didn't know how well that bastard knew ya. Didn't know if he woulda noticed it wasn't yer usual ring and taken it from ya."

"I'm glad you gave it to me," she said, hoping he didn't read anything into her meaning that wasn't there. "It slowed him down. Made him sloppy and vulnerable." She thought about it. "If I hadn't slapped him in the head with it, I don't know that I would've survived that fight."

James nodded, knowing it was true. "Still, I wish there'd been another way. I'm sorry."

She found Joseph's hands and held them in her own. They were so cold. "Don't worry about it."

"Don't worry about what?" Jack's voice suddenly asked.

They both looked up and saw Johnson helping Jack up and over a rock just a couple of feet from the tree line.

But just as Stacey always had, she lied. "About kidnapping Joseph and trying to kill you," she said. She knew that the last thing her husband needed right now was to picture James leaning forward with his hand between her spread legs. And hell, that would be like an innocent boy stealing a peck on the cheek beneath the mistletoe compared to whatever Fedyenka had done to her. James seemed to get the hint and dropped the subject, probably more than happy to not have to explain his actions to her husband.

Johnson got Jack near the fire and set him down.

"I'll get more wood," Johnson said, and went to find bigger branches.

The fire continued to grow, engulfing the teepee and flickering above it. Stacey began to undress Joseph while Jack inched his way closer to the flames.

James stepped away from the fire and walked over to Stacey, helping her get Joseph's pants off. He had stuffed blankets into the legs, and they were like blocks of ice. James began rubbing Joseph's legs, trying to get the circulation flowing while Stacey worked his top off.

"Y'all probably don't wanna hang around too long if ya don't wanna give up the game," James said.

Stacey looked out through the trees and to the Seahawk sitting there in the open. He was right. The Agency would be coming after it.

"I'll do it," he said.

Stacey looked at him, dumbfounded. "What do you mean?"

"You know we gotta get that thing as far away from you as possible. And I know yer thinkin' that you'll fly it far away and hope to somehow meet up with yer family again afterward."

That was exactly what she had been thinking.

"Take me up," he said. "Teach me what I need to know to put it on autopilot. Then you rappel back down."

"But what about you?" she asked, not really believing what this man was offering to do for her and her family.

He shrugged. "Alaska's a great big place. Lotta room to get lost in. To start over in. Hell, maybe I'll fly straight to Siberia and defect. Tell 'em I took care of their rogue agent for them."

"Why?" Jack asked, overhearing the conversation. "Why would you risk it?"

James positioned Joseph's legs closer to the fire and turned so he could see Jack. "Figure I still sorta owe ya. Call it payin' off a debt, call it tryin' to right a wrong, call it whatever ya want. I blamed Fedyenka for killing my brother, but truth is, it was me who got him killed. My momma made me promise I'd protect him, and I didn't." He paused for a second. "A lot of my life don't sit right with me no more."

"Well," Jack said, "if it all had to happen, I guess I'm glad it was you." Then he quickly added, "Not saying I'm glad your brother died—"

"I know what yer sayin'," James said. "I guess I'm glad it was me too."

"Shoot," Jack said. "If it weren't, then we would've never got out of the mountains."

"And I would've never got out of that building," Stacey added.

James smiled. "So yer sayin' we're even?"

"James," Stacey said, "I'm saying that I think God put you where you were for a reason, and that I can't thank you enough."

HAD JACK ACTUALLY HEARD that right? Did Stacey just credit God for helping save their family? He couldn't believe it. They had debated lightheartedly on the subject their entire marriage, her being an atheist and him an agnostic. Though since the cruise-ship incident, he'd drifted a lot closer to Grandmom's faith in design and purpose than toward Stacey's belief in random pointlessness. He did recognize a couple of cracks in her defenses over the last couple of years, but nothing so big as to warrant this new development.

Johnson came back with some larger pieces of wood and set them beside the fire. Then he sat beside it, holding his hands to its flame. They all inched as close as they could stand it, and the cold slowly left their bones.

Jack was feeling better already, the feeling in his ears coming back, his fingers working. Joseph still looked to be sleeping. Perhaps that was the best, he thought. Better to sleep through the discomfort and let the body do its thing than to be conscious through every agonizing moment of it. If only they had a bacta tank. And then scenes of people fighting hypothermia came parading through his mind. From *The Saint* to the *X-Files* movie to *Wind River*. He shooed them all away and let the dancing tongues of fire draw his gaze.

"Ten minutes?" James asked Stacey.

"Yeah," she answered.

And the next thing Jack knew, those ten minutes were gone, and Stacey and James were standing up, getting ready to leave.

James came over to Jack. He offered him his hand.

Jack took it, and they shook. "Good luck," Jack said.

"You too," James answered. Then he looked at Joseph. "Tell the kid I'm rootin' for him."

Then he walked out of the woods.

Stacey bent over Jack and kissed him on the head. "I'll be right back," she said. Then she left the woods, too.

Johnson came up beside him. "I'm gonna see him off." Then he left too.

Jack watched the three of them walk to the chopper, where Johnson and James seemed to get into a little conversation.

"Dad?"

Jack looked over and saw that Joseph's eyes were open. Jack quickly moved closer to him. "Hey there," he said. He couldn't keep the smile off his face. He felt a burst of relief fill his chest.

"Where's Mom? Did you get her?" Joseph asked.

Jack pointed out through the tree line and to the water. "Yeah. She's right out there. She'll be back in a little bit."

Now Joseph smiled. "You are like Mel Gibson."

Jack frowned, not understanding his meaning. And then he remembered. The conversation they'd had right before Joe was kidnapped. Something about Mel Gibson always being out for revenge or trying to get someone back. The memory was fuzzy, but he did remember thinking (and maybe he'd said it, too) that Mel Gibson had a bad habit of dying at the end of a lot of those movies. Evidently, the thought of him being a Mel Gibson character hadn't left Joseph's mind over the last couple of years. Not sure what to say to it, Jack just ran his hand over Joseph's hair.

"Where are we?" Joseph asked next.

"Still in Alaska," Jack said.

"Is Agent Johnson here?"

"Yeah, he's over there with Mom."

"Do you have my backpack?" Joseph asked.

Jack nodded. "It's right over there."

Joseph smiled and closed his eyes. "Good," he whispered.

Jack thought he'd fallen back asleep, but then, with his eyes still closed, he said, "Dad?"

"Yeah?"

"Christian Bale to Patrick Swayze."

STACEY SLID DOWN THE rope and landed on the stones beside Johnson. Then she waved up to James. He was sitting in the cockpit.

"Everything go okay?" Johnson asked over the beating rotors.

She shrugged. "I guess we're about to find out."

The Seahawk began nosing forward.

Neither of them had any idea what James was planning to do. Without a parachute, raft, wet suit, or warm clothes of any kind, his options were pretty scarce. Yet he insisted on doing this thing. He had flown in smaller helicopters before and had paid careful attention to how things worked, but nothing like this.

Stacey and Johnson had gone over the basics, how the pedals and collective worked. They hadn't gone into the instruments or even talked about landing. They all knew there would be no landing. He was going to put the thing at the bottom of the ocean so that everyone could assume it went down with all hands. Hopefully, with Fedyenka out of the picture, all parties involved would be happy to write them off and move on.

But that didn't explain how James was going to get back to land after ditching the aircraft. She wondered if, having exacted his revenge, he was content to call it a wrap. Fly off into the sunset, and that would be that. But the look in his eyes suggested that he still had a desire to live. To start over.

The helicopter moved away, still hovering low.

"He engaged the autopilot," Stacey said.

Johnson held his hand up over his eyes, blocking the sunlight. "You set it up?"

She nodded.

"Heading where?"

"Northwest."

As they watched the Seahawk fly toward the horizon, Johnson asked, "So are you going to tell him?"

Stacey met his gaze. "Tell who what?" But she knew.

He just stared at her.

She shook her head. "There's nothing to tell."

He looked down at his feet, then to the water. He nodded, acknowledging that it wasn't really any of his business. "I probably wouldn't either if I were you." He turned away from the water, the helicopter now the size of a bird on the horizon, and started walking back to the fire.

Stacey stood there and continued to watch James work the helicopter until she couldn't see it anymore. Part of her was expecting to see the Seahawk bank and climb, James knowing how to fly all along, but that didn't happen. She thought about what Johnson had just asked. What he said he'd do in her situation. She didn't see how she had a choice though. Especially when she didn't know for sure. It made sense, given all that had happened. But no matter how much sense it made, she still wouldn't believe it. Not without evidence. And she had no desire to look for evidence.

She went back to her husband and her son.

"He just woke up," Jack said when she walked near. "Asked where we were."

She felt a sense of relief wash over her. "How did he seem?"

"He seemed good. Just tired. He drifted off a minute later."

Then she heard her boy's voice. It was tired and weak, but it was there. "Hi, Mom," he said. His teeth weren't chattering anymore.

She went and sat beside him, and he leaned up enough to wrap his arms around her shoulders. She held him tight. "Hey, buddy," she whispered, kissing his ear.

"I had a weird dream," he said.

"Oh yeah?"

"Yeah. I dreamed that the guy from the mountains was with us. The one we told you about, that I stabbed."

She smiled. "That wasn't a dream, honey."

His eyes grew wide. "Are we dead?"

She laughed. "Not yet. But you just sleep now. We can swap stories tomorrow. I want to know all about your own little adventure."

"Mom?" he asked.

"Yeah?"

"If that wasn't a dream, then who was that other guy?"

"That was the person we've been looking for. The guy who was trying to steal you away from us."

"What happened to him?"

"He's gone now. We don't ever have to worry about him again."

The corner of his mouth turned into a half grin, and he let go of her, rolling onto his side and curling up in her lap. "Good."

Stacey looked over at Jack and saw that he, like her, had tears in his eyes.

IT WAS NIGHTTIME, AND they were sitting around the fire. So far, neither the CIA nor the FSB had arrived looking for them. Joseph was almost back to his normal self, and Stacey's feet weren't as bad off as they'd feared.

Jack watched Joseph. Currently, his eyes were fixated on the flames, and it was clear that his mind was a million miles away. Maybe with his friends. Maybe falling out of the helicopter, or jumping out of the plane. Maybe under the table in the diner with bodies dropping all around him. Maybe under the ice. Or maybe he was thinking of James, working through the story they'd told him about how the man he'd stabbed had shown up and helped saved the day, how he'd said to tell him that he was rooting for him. Or now that Fedyenka was dead, maybe he was trying to imagine what the rest of his life was going to look like. Where it would be lived.

"I'll head off in about ten minutes," Johnson said. He was going to walk through the woods to the nearest town and see what he could gather in the way of supplies. Food, clothes, maybe a vehicle.

"What are we going to do?" Jack asked. "I mean, without the passports and the money, how are we going to start over?"

Johnson shook his head. "I should never have left it on the plane," he said. "I'm sorry about that."

Stacey waved him off. "You didn't know they were going to get other orders. And if you'd taken it with you, left it with your other gear, we would've had to run back to get it before taking off after Joseph. And we wouldn't have reached him in time. Osprey would have him or worse."

Joseph blinked, and the fire's tractor beam seemed to release its hold on him. He looked at Johnson. "What are you talking about?"

Johnson explained, "The passports and money your mom had so that you guys could start over somewhere with new names and stuff was in one of the bags we took onto the plane. I thought we'd get it when we met you at the hangar. And if something happened to us and we didn't come get you, the pilots were supposed to make sure you got it."

Joseph smiled.

Jack and Stacey exchanged quizzical glances.

"What?" Johnson asked.

"Hand me my backpack," Joseph said.

Jack reached over and grabbed the bag. It was still a little damp. He stood and, still not understanding why Joseph wanted it, handed it to him.

Joseph took his bag and unzipped it. Then he reached inside and pulled out a ziplock bag.

Stacey and Johnson leaned forward.

"I took it out of the bag before I jumped," Joseph said, holding up the bag his mom had taken from the fireplace in the cabin. He looked at his dad. "I saw it in there while you guys were getting your stuff together. I didn't want to leave it behind."

Stacey's hand went to her mouth, and Jack blinked as he tried to reverse his entire line of thinking on a dime. They had hope again.

Johnson laughed. "That'll make getting stuff a lot easier."

"Should one of us come with you?" Jack asked.

He shook his head, and Jack could understand why. They wanted to draw the least amount of attention to themselves as possible, and a beautiful woman walking out of the woods dressed in some BDSM outfit would probably not go unnoticed.

Jack stared at Joseph, studying his face, his eyes. The boy had sure been through a lot, but he had survived it all. He was definitely his mother's son. And then the rabbit hole flew wide open, and he found himself looking for any signs of himself in the boy's features—physical or otherwise.

Joseph's eyes found his, and they held each other's gaze for a moment, the firelight flickering across their faces. Jack wondered if Joseph knew what he was thinking. He hoped not. It would kill him to know that Joseph knew he was questioning such things. And there was his answer. It was the only answer he would ever need again. The rabbit hole shut and then imploded on itself as if sucked into a black hole. And just like that, he was free. Not from the truth, but despite the truth.

Stacey sat down next to Joseph and leaned her head on his shoulder. Jack thought it was the first time he'd ever seen her do that, and it had a profound effect on him. He wasn't sure why, but it seemed to carry a truckload of meaning. Like she was acknowledging a milestone in both their lives, acknowledging that he was now a man, and that someday soon, they would be the ones relying on him for his support. A line from *Superman* came to mind—Marlon Brando saying, "The son becomes the father, and the father the son." Jack smiled at Joseph and then moved his eyes to his wife, setting this line of thinking aside for another day.

"How's your arm?" Stacey asked him.

"What happened to your arm?" Joseph asked, noting the bloody sleeve.

"First I got shot, and then your mom stabbed me," Jack said.

Stacey shrugged. "It was an accident."

"It's fine," Jack said. He was sure it could use a few stitches, but he'd survive.

After a moment of silence, Jack asked Johnson, "So you think we're off the hook?"

Johnson picked up a stick and poked the fire with it. "I think that as long as we're missing, they can frame this whole thing any way they like. They probably don't want to find us because that will lead to official investigations that they won't want. But if you're asking if we can just go back home and live a normal life..."

Jack saw Joseph's jaw clench, and then he looked away from them. He knew the answer that was coming wasn't the one he was hoping for.

Johnson said, "I told you before, this isn't a movie that's going to end with congressional hearings digging through illegal CIA programs. There's no happy ending where we're exonerated and the truth is printed on the front page of every legacy media outlet in the country. That's not how this works. If the truth ever does come out, it will be decades from now, long after people have stopped caring about it and those responsible are dead. And even then the story will just be a footnote."

"I know that," Jack said. "Whatever their agenda was, it'll just be morphed into something else with a different name. But the bombing at the school, the deep fake of me breaking in... I don't get it."

"You weren't supposed to survive the FBI raid," Johnson said. "The video was all they'd need to get the public to buy the whole thing. Case closed."

Jack frowned. "I survive, Stacey and Joseph get away, so instead they release the video to try to find us."

Johnson shrugged. "It doesn't matter. Osprey is over, the CIA will probably claim you died in the helicopter crash, and the Kremlin would probably be happy to believe that as well. I really think that if you're careful, you can start over somewhere."

Joseph looked back to the fire. "Again."

Stacey sat up, lifting her head off his shoulder, and looked him in the eye. "It will be the last time," she said. "It'll have to be."

"Where?" Joseph asked.

"Not in the United States."

Joseph swallowed. "So I'll never see my friends again. Or even find out if they're still alive."

"I'm so sorry, Joseph," Stacey said. "I'm so, so sorry. If there was any other way..."

"It sucks," Jack said. "It totally sucks. *But...* we should at least be grateful to be alive right now. We all should have died a dozen times, and here we are, still together and, hopefully, *finally*, free."

Joseph sighed. "So where are we going this time?"

"Costa Rica," Stacey said.

"You have all that set up already?" Jack asked.

"I do."

"Costa Rico," Joseph repeated. "Near the beach?"

"Near the beach," Stacey confirmed.

"Forever?"

Jack wondered if he was mentally waving goodbye to his park ranger career.

"Not forever. At least not for you," she said. "I don't see why you couldn't eventually come back if that's what you decided you want to do."

"Costa Rica," he whispered, staring into the fire as if watching his future unfold in it.

"What about you?" Jack asked Johnson.

Johnson bit the inside of his lip. "Not sure yet. I have to see how deep this stuff goes, if I need to run, or if I'm safe now."

"Your team is dead," Stacey said. "They can't just sweep that under the rug. They'll have to at least pretend at an investigation. They'll need to blame it on someone."

"You think they'll pin it all on me, somehow?" Johnson asked.

Jack held out his hands. "You're the one who said they can use AI to create any video evidence they need. Maybe they have you and me and Stacey sitting in a nightclub somewhere, exchanging agency secrets. Or maybe they have you in the back seat of some car with little boys."

Johnson seemed to think it over. "I still have to see. I owe it to them. To their families to at least try."

"What about Brown's family?" Stacey asked, recalling her promise that they would save them.

A cloud fell over his face. "I'm sure they're dead now, but I'll look." He stood. "But first, we gotta get you all out of here." He reached out his hand to Stacey. "Mind if I have some cash?"

She handed him a wad of bills. "We'll need the change."

"Yup." He stood as close to the fire as he could stand, as if his body could store its heat for later use. Then he turned and started walking. "I'll be back," he said, looking at Joe. Then, "Don't wait up."

Jack moved over to his family and sat down beside them. He put his arm around Stacey, wanting to ask her about Fedyenka, but knowing now was not the time. Or if there ever would be a time. He tried to stop thinking about the past and imagine the future.

STACEY OPENED HER EYES and blinked. She continued to blink until the scene around her came into focus. The first thing she noticed after registering the woods in the dim dawn light was the cold. It seemed to be in her bones. She saw that the fire had burnt out in the night, only a lazy wisp of smoke coming from the few pieces of charred wood that remained.

A sound.

She moved her eyes, reaching for her gun.

It came from the woods behind her. Something moving across the forest floor.

There it was again. Whatever it was, it wasn't trying to hide itself. Steady footfalls, snapping twigs. But she could tell it wasn't an animal. She rolled to her side, quickly noting Jack's and Joseph's sleeping forms huddled beside her. She looked through the trees and saw movement, her breath clouding in front of her face.

And then she saw him.

Johnson.

She relaxed, having to remind herself that Fedyenka was dead, his body riddled with poison and bullets and dashed on the rocks. She watched Johnson walk through the woods. He had a big duffel bag slung over his shoulder, and it was knocking branches and rustling through patches of high grass.

"Morning," he said when their eyes met.

She sat up and crossed her arms over her chest, huddling against the cold. "You been gone all night?" she asked. He looked exhausted.

He nodded and let the duffel slip from his shoulders. Then he bent over and unzipped it. Reaching inside, he withdrew a sweater, a long-sleeve turtle neck shirt, a green coat, a pair of wool socks, jeans, a pair of boots, gloves, and a winter hat. He tossed them all to her.

Jack started to stir.

Stacey held the heavy knitted sweater up to the morning sunlight. "Where the hell did you find all this?"

"Don't ask. Not sure about the sizes. Weren't too many choices."

"Damn, it's cold," Jack's voice announced as he sat up and rubbed his eyes.

Johnson threw him a brown parka and a pair of tan corduroy pants, gloves, and a hat.

Stacey got up and took the clothes farther into the woods. She was concerned about her feet, but right now they just seemed cold in Fedyenka's shoes and socks. The leather outfit was frozen, and she squeaked when she bent her arms and legs. She couldn't wait to get out of the stupid thing.

Once concealed by some undergrowth, she unzipped the leather one-piece and stepped out of it. For the second day in a row, the cold bit at her naked body. She hoped this would be the last time she would ever have to bare all to the elements. She pulled the long-sleeve shirt over her head. It was a little tight, but she wasn't complaining. The sweater was heavy and warm and fit just fine. The jeans were a size too big and a little short, but again, she wasn't complaining. She sat on a rock and pulled on the wool socks, happy to see that her feet were not black with rot. The boots fit fine. She stood, pulled on the coat, slipped on the hat, and stuck her hands in the gloves.

She left the leather outfit and the dress shoes in a pile behind her, wondering what someone would think if ever they came across them. They probably wouldn't assume that the shoes belonged to a rogue Russian agent who had been a breath away from starting WWIII.

By the time she got back to the others, Joseph was awake, and they too were all in their new threads. They all looked much warmer, and she couldn't be more grateful for Johnson's provision. Hell, if it weren't for him and James helping them out… And then she thought of all the others who hadn't made it due to their willingness to help them out. Like Donny and Johnson's whole team.

"Come on over," Johnson said as he dumped the bag's remaining contents on the ground. A small pile of granola bars, protein bars, peanuts, a jar of peanut butter, crackers, and half a dozen water bottles. "Breakfast is served."

Joseph picked up a granola bar and greedily worked the wrapper off. "Thanks," he said. "I didn't realize how hungry I was."

"Me neither," Jack added, selecting a protein bar for himself.

"How was it?" Stacey asked Johnson. She grabbed something out of the pile, too, even though she wasn't that hungry. But she knew she had to eat. Her body had been through a lot, and it needed nourishment.

"Cold," Johnson said.

"We should get a fire going again, let you take a nap," Jack said.

Johnson waved the suggestion away. "We need to get moving. There's an airport about fifty miles from here. We should be able to hire a pilot."

"To go where?" Stacey asked.

"I figure we start making our way toward Anchorage. Find a resort or hotel to lie low in, get tickets for a cruise that goes out from Whittier, take that to Vancouver, and from there…"

"Costa Rica," Joseph said, his mouth full of granola.

Stacey walked over to Jack and took his cold hand in hers.

"Fifty miles," Jack muttered. "And another cruise ship."

Johnson shrugged as he worked a wrapper off his own breakfast. "We can probably catch a ride in the town."

"Around the world in eighty days, it is, then," said Joseph.

Stacey could feel Jack's hand in hers. He was rubbing her skin with his thumb. And then he stopped. He looked down at her hand and frowned.

"Where's your engagement ring?" he asked.

She followed his eyes to her hand, spreading her fingers apart. "I had to replace it with the ring James gave me," she said, hoping Jack didn't inquire into how James had managed to get her the ring in the first place. "I swallowed it."

Jack blinked. "You *swallowed* it?"

She nodded. "Couldn't think of anything else in the moment."

Joseph overheard and asked, "That gonna be a problem later?"

Jack looked at him and nodded. "Yuck, right?"

"Major yuck," he said.

Stacey just shook her head.

Fifteen minutes later, the four of them began retracing Johnson's steps to the town, Stacey between Jack and Joseph, her hands in both of theirs. As they walked, she thought of her life. Of her parents. Of her time in Russia. Of meeting Fedyenka and Vadim and then marrying Vadim. Of being recruited by the CIA. Of Trenton and so many things like it, working for neocon goons and justifying it any way she could. Of meeting Jack. Birthing Joseph. Bethany. And everything since. It was insane.

But now everything was different. The trajectory of her life—whether launched by destiny or fate or God's will or random chance—had finally been disrupted. She was at an offramp and leaving the superhighway of deception that she'd been traveling most of her life.

Sure, the future was just as uncertain as it had ever been, but Fedyenka was dead and his plot along with it. At least as far as it concerned her and her family. She was sure the neocons in DC would never sleep until they got their war with Russia, but she, Joseph, and Jack would not be pieces on their game board any longer. No, she was looking at a brand-new life. And if God's angels could resist the psychopaths pushing the world to nuclear Armageddon just a little longer, then perhaps she could even enjoy the rest of her life on this spinning rock.

Maybe she would even start knocking on doors she'd always passed by. Metaphysical doors. Spiritual and philosophical doors. Doors that might actually lead to meaning and purpose and hope. She thought Jack would like that. And that Joseph needed that. That maybe everyone needed that.

But as for her past, she put it all in a mental closet and locked the door. It was done. Like baptism, she would emerge from these woods a new person living a new life. They were the Violas now. And she could only thank God that she'd had the foresight and means to create this escape plan. They had names supported by official records, a story they would learn to believe themselves, a destination already set up with believable back stories to explain their arrival, and the cash to pull it all off.

She squeezed the hands holding hers and let herself smile. After all, didn't she owe a life of purpose and meaning to those who had sacrificed their own lives to protect hers? She wasn't exactly sure what that meant or what it looked like, but she was determined to figure it out.

The sun continued to rise above them, and for the first time since she could remember, she found herself in awe of its beauty.

85

THE SUN WAS SETTING over the Pacific, and Jack stretched his feet out in the warm sand, interlocking his fingers behind his head as the breeze off the ocean played with his long hair. He scanned the waves, trying to spot the familiar orange stripe down the side of Joseph's board shorts.

His son was seventeen now and barely recognizable from the boy he'd taken camping years ago. He was tall and muscular and mature beyond his years. On one hand, it made Jack proud; on the other, it just made him feel old.

He found the flash of orange just in time to see Joseph positioning himself to catch the next wave. It looked like it would be a good one. He swam hard on the board, moving his arms at a calculated speed, instinctively predicting where and when the forming wave would be catchable. Joseph called those waves "green waves."

Jack didn't know the first thing about surfing and hadn't yet tried it himself, but Joseph had become quite the pro over the last couple of years. In fact, he had gotten so good that Jack was afraid one day he might pop up on someone's YouTube channel or be the subject of a trending TikTok. But Joseph had found a sort of freedom in the sport, and the way he said he felt out there riding the waves could have been a line straight from *Point Break*. Jack couldn't rob him of that. If surfing was how he coped with this crazy life, then good for him. And if he became the best surfer in the world and wanted to go to the Olympics... Well, they'd have to figure that out if and when the time came. For now, all seemed okay.

Jack, of course, spent a lot of time scanning the horizon for CIA helicopters and NSA spy boats, but so far, they hadn't noticed a single thing out of place since arriving in this island paradise two years ago. It really did seem like the world had moved on without them. And that was just fine with him.

Joseph was using long paddle strokes while looking back over his shoulder in an effort to match the speed of the wave. Jack watched him put his head low just as the wave started to lift him, putting weight over the nose of the board to keep it from sticking too far out of the water. The swell built behind him, and he rode it until, at just the right moment, he put his hands on the board, arched his back, and popped up.

It was a great catch, and Jack watched in awe as Joseph gracefully navigated the wave as it barreled. He moved the board from side to side in the water just like Jack used to do with his skateboard on concrete when he was a kid. Joseph streaked from left to right, entering beneath the curling wave and catching a rare tube ride. Jack lost sight of him until he came out the other end, where he turned and rode the rest of the wave toward shore.

"That was a good one," a voice behind him stated.

Jack turned and looked up to see Stacey standing there in a blue bikini. She had gone into town after dinner to get some things and to check up on the status of world affairs—or as much as they could discern for themselves from the globalist propaganda machine. In an effort to reduce their digital footprint, they had decided not to use cell phones or computers for the time being. Which meant they had to get their information the old-fashioned way—word of mouth and the legacy media. And then, like Jerry Fletcher, they went to town rearranging headlines, connecting dots, and reading between the lines. It passed the time on Friday nights.

"You going in?" Jack asked, noting the tan flesh that the small bathing suit failed to cover.

"Yeah," she said, pulling her hair back into a ponytail. "You?"

He shook his head, and his eyes went to the scar on her neck from the knife Seth Baker had dragged across it. It stood out against her deeply tanned skin more so than at any time before. Hell, all their scars did. She had more scars on her stomach from being stabbed. He had scars on his head and arms from being shot, slashed, burnt, and being beat up by a mountain. And of course, Joseph has scars of his own. It was a constant reminder to them all of how lucky they were to be alive.

"Any news to share?" he asked, his gaze heading south of the white line.

She sat down in the sand beside him. "Not really."

Jack turned away from Joseph, who was now paddling back out for more waves, and toward Stacey.

They hadn't heard from Johnson in months, but over the first year, he had been able to get a few messages to them since parting ways, his first updating Stacey on Brown's family. They were alive, released by Osprey operators when no further instructions came down from Fedyenka, staging the whole operation to look as if thugs had kidnapped them for drug money.

He'd told of the dismantling of Osprey, not due to its relationship with a CIA black op attempting regime change in Russia, but for some other, lesser (and no doubt fabricated) crime.

He had provided little details to the headlines they were seeing, headlines that painted a nuclear holocaust on the horizon. Like how long-range missiles had been shot into Russia using Western technology. How Russia retaliated by firing a new missile that no known defense system could counter (though without a payload). How there had been talks of providing Ukraine with nuclear weapons. And how the UK and France were considering sending in troops, which, given what Europeans were currently dealing with in their own countries, Jack was sure would go over like a lead brick, maybe even providing the spark that would set off an all-out revolt. And still Ukraine's foreign minister was urging NATO to grant them membership.

Jack wondered if Fedyenka would have already made his move by now, forcing everyone's hand by launching a missile from that silo, Osprey taking over the Kremlin in the chaos and then, out of the ashes, presenting the country with a biological heir from the Romanov line as their new leader. Jack looked back to Joseph, who was now straddling the surfboard and waiting for the next green wave.

A new administration back home seemed to be pumping the brakes on WWIII a bit, but with everything going on across the globe—from Ukraine, Romania, and Russia; to Israel, Palestine, and Iran; to Syria, the Congo, the spreading of radical Islam, and social unrest across Europe—the powder keg seemed to packed tight. "If the new administration is really sincere about transparency and rooting out corruption and exposing the Deep State... Do you think there's a chance we could ever go back?"

"And be exonerated of the bombing?"

He nodded.

"Maybe for the bombing," she said, but added nothing more.

Jack knew what she meant. Sure, an actual government for the people by the people might clear their names of the bombing, but what of all Stacey's prior acts as part of the very black ops programs they were trying to shut down? If people were going to be prosecuted for crimes against the Constitution, like in the case of JFK or 9/11 or the recent assassination attempts on the current commander in chief, then would they be taking a closer look at Trenton? If so, then Stacey could be facing prosecution for her role in it.

"It's okay," he said, smiling as he grabbed her hand. "The revolution will go on without me."

An awkward silence settled over them for a few moments. Then Joseph caught another wave.

"Wow, look at him," Stacey said.

"Yeah."

"Oh," Stacey said. "I ran into Kim at the store. They want us to come over for dinner on Tuesday."

Jack nodded. Kim and Steve were a couple of ex-pats they'd gotten to know recently, and they liked playing poker while sipping bourbon. "Look," he said, nodding to his left and toward the surf.

Stacey followed his gaze and caught sight of a group of five kids walking their way. They both watched as a few of them tried catching Joseph's attention, waving to him. Joseph noticed and waved back. Then he began paddling, lining up to take the next wave in.

Jack wasn't sure what he thought about Joseph's new friends. Some of them seemed pretty cool, but there was at least one he didn't like at all. But he was glad he had them.

After learning that the Agency had declared that he and Stacey had been killed while attempting to flee to Russia, their true country (that was the thanks Stacey got for her service, apparently), they'd also learned that Joseph was one of the two official casualties of the school bombing (the other being Mrs. Hatfield). That had been wonderful news for Joseph, knowing that all his friends were alive and well even if he'd never be able to see them again. And, as kids always do, he'd made new friends, and though he missed Tommy, Moses, and Priscilla, life, as they say, goes on. And it had. For all three of them. Johnson too, from what they could gather, though they weren't exactly sure what his current status was, only that he was still in the States. As for James, no one had heard from him since he'd disappeared over the horizon in the autopiloted Seahawk.

They watched Joseph—aka "Mark Viola"—ride the smaller wave into the shallow surf and hop off the board, snatching it up under his arm and jogging toward the group of kids waiting for him on the beach. After talking with them for a couple of minutes, Joseph stuck his board in the sand and headed their way.

"That was a nice one," Jack said.

Joseph smiled as he ran a hand through his long wet hair, hooking it behind an ear. "Thanks. Can I go to Santiago's with John, Cody, and Valentina?" He nodded toward the group.

"What are they going to be doing?" Stacey asked.

He shrugged. "No keg stands, beer ping-pong, or coke lines, if that's what you're thinking," he said. "Probably just a guitar around a fire."

"Okay," Stacey said. "Check in by noon though. And we're going to the church tomorrow night."

"Thanks," he said. "I gotta run back to the house to grab some clothes."

"Love you," she said.

Joseph turned and joined his friends, grabbing his board and walking with them down the beach.

"Looks like we're going to have some alone time, Mr. Viola," Stacey said, leaning into him.

"What are you suggesting?" he asked. He held her hand, feeling the engagement ring against his fingers (getting that back had been an ordeal).

She stood, pulling her hand free, and began walking toward the water, looking back at him over her shoulder. "It's Friday night; use your imagination," she said, and pulled on the sides of her bathing suit bottoms, making them into a thong.

Jack smiled. There was no one else looking, and he enjoyed the show. He watched her enter the water and start swimming. When she got far enough out so that she couldn't touch the bottom, she turned around and faced the beach. She waved for him to join her. Maybe he'd go for a swim after all.

The last two years had been the best years of their marriage so far. Not only had they become better lovers, but they had become friends again. With no phones or computers or jobs to distract them, they had rediscovered themselves and each other. And with Joseph pretty much an adult, they were able to spend most of their days in each other's company, just hanging out. It had been great. They were basically living their retired lives while still in their forties.

As for the rabbit hole and the elephants that lived in there... Against his better judgment, he'd asked her strategic questions, spread out over time and usually after she'd had a few drinks. The answers she gave, when added up, helped paint a picture. And though there were still parts of the story that didn't make sense to him, he had figured out enough of it to satisfy his curiosity.

Like what Fedyenka had wanted with Joseph. That was as clear as day to him now that he had a couple of the puzzle pieces figured out. Fedyenka had made a comment to Stacey, insinuating that there was a bigger reason he'd tolerated Vadim over the years. He believed he knew what that reason was, as crazy as that reason seemed. Fedyenka had believed (whether verified or not, Jack had no idea) that Vadim was descended from the royal Romanov bloodline. Jack figured that belief was probably what had led to Fedyenka targeting Vadim in the first place, Vadim himself not even aware of his own lineage.

Jack had no idea what Fedyenka's plan had been for Vadim, whether he'd planned on using him as the face of his tsar movement or if he had been waiting for the next generation of Vadims—which became a possibility when Vadim and Stacey married. And then came Joseph, just about nine months after Viktoriya had arranged a reunion between Vadim and Stacey.

Of course, Stacey had sworn to Jack that Joseph was, in fact, his, and that she'd even gotten a paternity test just to be sure. But Jack had never seen the test himself, and obviously Fedyenka had believed Joseph to be Vadim's son and the rightful heir to the throne in St. Petersburg. But did he have genetic proof? Wouldn't he need it? And then there were those three words that Fedyenka had whispered into his ear before being thrown out of the helicopter.

He. Is. Not—

He had no trouble imagining the rest of it, but he was still grateful that James had cut the words off when he did. None of it mattered to him anymore. Joseph was his son, whether biological or not. But then there was no proof that he knew of that said Joseph wasn't his biological son, so...

Of course, there was one other explanation that would explain Fedyenka's obsession over both Stacey—"Anna"—and Joseph. One that would add more meaning to the *Anastasia* movie poster he'd sent to the hospital and his pet name for her.

That it was *Stacey* who was the descendant of her namesake.

If that were true, then had Fedyenka known about her before she'd even traveled to Russia? And had he known about Viktoriya and Stacey's father long before that? Or, taking things to the next level, maybe the CIA had known about her lineage and that was why they had recruited her and sent her abroad. Maybe they had been orchestrating this whole Romanov thing for decades. And if that was so, there was no telling what their ultimate end game was going to be, how they had planned it to play out.

But if Stacey had ever tripped over that theory herself, she had never mentioned it to him. Jack often wondered, though short of a DNA test, they would never really know anything. And what would proving that Stacey and/or Joseph had Romanov blood accomplish at this point, anyway? Nothing but attention—which was the last thing they wanted.

And so here he was, finally content and at peace with his family, all of the elephants of the past having finally died off, the rabbit hole filled in and paved over. With the Agency out of their lives, he trusted his wife again.

He got to his feet and walked to the water, hoping that World War III would at least be postponed until tomorrow morning.

He swam out to her and took her in his arms, kissing as the sun touched the moving horizon behind them.

As he hugged her, he thanked God for this new life, no matter how long it lasted. He realized that there were more important things in life than nations and money and even physical freedom. He'd found that there was an even deeper liberation, a freedom of the soul. Apparently, Stacey had made a promise to God that had her searching for answers to questions she had never bothered to ask herself before. That alone was a miracle. He thought of his grandmom and knew that she'd be proud of him. Of all of them. "Hey," he said, kissing her neck. "What do you think about getting Joe a new dog?"

She smiled. "I was wondering when you were gonna ask." She wrapped her legs around his waist just as a big wave hit them. They both went under, tumbling about for a few seconds before coming up laughing.

Stacey wiped the hair out of her face and said, "Last one back has to do all the work!"

Jack grabbed her and tossed her into the next wave, giving himself a head start.

She laughed and followed him out of the water, where he let her catch up and take his hand.

Free book!

Visit www.jonhillwrites.com and join the mailing list to get my free novella *SEAGULL: A Novella of Avian Terror.*

Also by Jon Hill

Man In The Water
Man In The Woods
Man In The Fire
*Seagull**

About the author

Jon Hill lives in Pennsylvania with his wife, children, and dog (princess) Leia. He's been on three cruises, which inspired his story *Man In The Water*. He loves to read and write, preferably on stormy days, and spends too much time watching movies when he should be writing. He's working on the next story.

Visit www.jonhillwrites.com to link up on social media or to contact via email.